ICE MOON

BLOOD CIRCUS

ICE MOON

CAMILA VICTOIRE

BLACK STONE PUBLISHING

Published in 2025 by Blackstone Publishing
Cover design by Alenka Vdovič Linaschke
Series design by Kathryn Galloway English

Printed in the United States of America
Originally published in hardcover by Blackstone Publishing in 2025

First paperback edition: 2025
ISBN 979-8-8747-4842-5
Young Adult Fiction / Dystopian

Version 1

Blackstone Publishing
31 Mistletoe Rd.
Ashland, OR 97520

www.BlackstonePublishing.com

To all the plants and animals with whom we share the world.
And to you, reader, on your journey of awakening.
Welcome home.

NORTHERN BOREAL
WALL OF DEA
DEEPER WOODS
MOUNTAIN RIDGE
DARKER WOODS
RED RIVER
Loudhouse
TREMBLE HILLS
CAMP MIDNIGHT
JUSTICE FALLS

SNOWY MOUNTAINS
Underground River
TED
VES
Suspension Bridge
SWAMP
CAVES
T
H
BLACK RIVER
N
MILITARY FENCE
ALOR
BRAVE NIGHT

Excerpt from *A Calendar of Klujn Events*
by Catrina Sherman

Winter is a fascinating time in a Klujn's life, when nights are longest and moonlight most abundant. As Hunters return to civilization after the last Hunt of the year, the Boreal comes alive with festivals of light. One of these celebrations is the *Ice Moon*, held on the first full moon of January.

Having survived their Blood Race in the wild, young Klujns return to the new location of the stand with their eyes now open to the dark truths of the world. After Initiation, they begin classes to develop their skills, learn the languages of the earth, and participate in myriad games and mating rituals, some of which would shock the average human. But in Klujn stands, sexuality and power are intrinsically linked. It is said that a young Klujn's sexual maturation enhances their developing magic, often coinciding with the emergence of their adult claws, their *viațăs*.

After spending months in the unforgiving wild, the Ice Moon is a homecoming like no other. But, for those who don't make it back in time, they are destined to live in permanent exile, belonging nowhere.

A Note from Catrina Sherman:

Civilization is a curious word, implying that anything wild is *uncivilized*. If my travels have taught me anything, it's that those who appear *too* civilized on the surface tend to commit their barbarian acts in private. I believe that having the freedom to explore one's nature without inhibition or shame—like Klujns—leads to a healthier tribe dynamic.

Before she was taken by Grouse's Department of Societal Order, my darling Pomme used to call me her *femme sauvage*—wild woman. *Savage* was a complimentary word before the new colonists made it into a slur. It once captured the essence of a person who walks through the wild with confidence and grace, alive and awake and at home in their body.

In my opinion, there is nothing more dangerous than someone who has forgotten how to be wild. I believe that most of our problems as humans—and as a Territory—would not exist if we all regularly journeyed into the forests beyond the fences and the jungles inside ourselves.

RED RIVER,
NORTH AMERICAN TERRITORY

November 30, 31 AK

1

I am back in the arena, standing by the Carniflora and her glittering roses. The Blood Moon pierces through a hole in the top of the canvas tent, bathing everything in a red glow. Across the black soil stage, a curtain ripples, and out comes my opponent. Only it isn't Wendy, the stranger who became my best friend during those five days at Circo. It isn't Ying Yue, the Military girl who disappeared into the night when the Hunters came with their glinting rifles and their war stripes.

It's George. My father.

Although *father* implies a bond—blood or loyalty or love—and George and I share none.

"*Ava.*"

As he steps into the red haze, I notice his green eyes are bloodshot and his hands ball into fists. He looks nothing like the father I have known for six years since he brought me home from the orphanage. The man who gave me a home, only to send me out into the Deeper Woods as bait so that I would be captured by Klujns and forced to compete in the Blood Race.

"Let me go," I say, although my voice sounds strange. Like

it's not my own voice, but my mother's. George's eyes look sinister in the half-light.

"You know I can't do that."

Then he comes at me, and everything goes black.

I know where I am before I even open my eyes.

The basement. A mattress on the ground. Safe. Or safe *enough*.

An orange orb pierces the black horizon of my closed eyelids, growing in intensity until I open my eyes. The sunlamp glows on the cherrywood dresser, simulating the sunrise. I've been using it in tandem with my moon lamp—anything to keep my inner balance stable and my bones charged. Neither compares to the natural cycles of the wild, but so far, they've done the job . . . I haven't lost control.

Birdsong trills from the alarm clock, a tinny, artificial sound. Staring up at the dingy ceiling, I reach a hand over the patchwork blanket until they find a bushy tail. *Wolf. I didn't dream him up.* But with that relief comes the realization that I didn't dream up the rest either—the brutal fights, the girls who died, and what I learned while at Circo. My eyes were opened wide, but, like a floodgate, they cannot be closed again. Rushing water moves only in one direction.

Those five days felt like a lifetime. In the wild, I grew in ways that are impossible to measure, like trying to trap smoke in a jar. Whereas the last eight weeks have flown by, one day bleeding into the next, slowly eroding my sense of urgency, my ability to act. Turning me into a *coward.*

Two months already since President Grouse was here. I haven't been able to sleep in my own room ever since. I can still feel him watching me from the doorway. I'd been in bed, covers raised while Wolf hid on the ground near my discarded blood-soaked costume. I knew that he could smell the changes on my skin. I had gone into the woods a human girl and emerged as something else. What I learned during the Blood Race now made me a threat to Grouse's world of perfect order. I had a target on my back, red and wide as a desert sunrise.

But before Grouse could step into the room, the landline rang with an urgent message—Warwick, the king of Circo, had escaped from the Loudhouse and almost killed General Santos in the process. The President was needed.

Grouse had returned to his car, pausing to look at my bedroom window one last time. I knew he couldn't see me through the darkened glass, but I felt branded by his stare. A look that said, *When the Hunt is over, I'll be back.*

And ever since . . . that feeling of being watched.

Maybe it was my imagination or paranoia, but when I peered into the black forest to the north of our house, the darkness watched me back. Grouse's absence felt like a test, waiting for me to take a misstep and reveal my true colors to the township. Like an omniscient god, there was no corner of our Territory where Grouse was not.

Upstairs, I hear the landline ring five times. It stops, then rings another five. Diana doesn't answer, just lets it ring out, and I wonder who is calling. No one ever calls us at this time.

There's a sudden knock at the door. Wolf and I both startle, his hackles raised like the hair on my arms. My baby claws tingle beneath my fingertips, always ready to emerge without warning. I've gotten better at controlling them, but only just, and the skin is still sensitive. I curl my fingers, clear my throat, and say, "Come in."

Diana enters, holding a breakfast tray. My shoulders relax, and my hands unfold, but Wolf remains alert. "Morning," Diana says. She sets the tray on the bed and moves to the sunlamp, lowering it to a more ambient amber shade. The birdsong she leaves on because the brown noise masks our conversation, should anyone be listening . . . Like those pesky mosquitoes gathered at the blue half-moon window above the dresser—they could easily be listening devices with wires for hearts. They feel too late for the season, like they're out not for warm blood but for secrets.

"Or should I say . . . happy *Hunter's Return*." The sarcasm in Diana's voice is unmistakable. I like it, just as I like the purple fabric braided into her hair. It feels . . . *defiant*.

"That's right," I grumble. Today, November 30, marks the end of Hunting season and the beginning of the darker half of the year. A time for jack-o-lanterns and corn mazes and costume contests. One of pumpkin cakes and horror museums and spooky stories whispered across bonfire flames. When Hunters return from the forest with their bounty of meat, claws, arable soil, and tales of the dark, dark wild, drunk on lumber liquor and the contagious thrill of slaughter.

"Did you know," Diana says, sitting down on the edge of the mattress, "that in the old world, Hunter's Return used to be called *Halloween*. And before that, a pagan tradition in Europe called *Samhain* was celebrated on November 1. Only now, with the climate, the harvest and frost come later."

"What does *pagan* mean?" I ask. The breakfast tray has a platter of fruits and berries, nuts and figs, scrambled tofu eggs, and a French press of coffee that smells like maple. I pop a berry in my mouth.

"It's a term for people who believed in many gods," she says. "Or people who rejected the idea of the one Christian god. Many pagans practiced Nature religions and celebrated the turning of the seasons, the solstices and harvests, the moon and sun."

"Like Klujns," I say, and Diana nods.

"Christianity took pagan traditions and gave them new

names—*Ostara* became Easter, *Yule* became Christmas, and so on. Instead of worshipping trees, they cut them down and brought them inside. They also brought places of worship indoors, building walls between themselves and the wild. Then, a few decades ago, North Americans came along and did the same. Only now, our religion is atheism, the belief in nothing other than ourselves, our Hunts, our science.

"There's a rumor," she continues, "that, like circuses and wolf stories and witchcraft, pagan traditions actually come from very early contact with *Klujns*. That they may be the original architects of all these rituals."

"So," I say, "we're celebrating that humans are thieves and our entire culture is a lie?"

"Pretty much." She smiles—a quick flicker of light in her eyes, brief as a shooting star.

There's a clicking sound, and Diana and I whip our heads toward the window, half-expecting to see one of those mosquitoes trying to hack a little metallic proboscis through the glass. My heart pounds. *It's too late, we've gone too far.* But the sound comes from Wolf, vigorously licking his paw. When he feels us looking, he turns, his round, glacial eyes giving us a look that says, *What?*

Despite my relief, the feeling of danger remains. Our conversation was careless. Enough to earn us a one-way trip to the DSO—the Department of Societal Order—whose primary mission is to imprison, torture, or kill anyone who speaks out about our Military government and its leader.

"We should be more careful," Diana whispers. She looks tenser than usual, and I wonder if it has anything to do with that mysterious phone call. I nod.

"I forgot," Diana says, reaching into her overalls. She pulls out a root, still damp from the muddy earth of our front yard.

Diana tosses it to the corner of the room, and Wolf hops off the bed. Without the warm weight of his body, my legs are instantly cold. He moves over to the root, sniffs it suspiciously, then lowers his body and chews on it, as happy as my serious Wolf can be.

"How are things with you two?" she asks. Her words are neutral, but the real conversation continues with her eyes.

"Okay," I sigh. "It's been nice to have time together, but we haven't really . . . *bonded.*" *Poor Wolf.* He must be so frustrated, cooped up inside all day and night. Sequestered in this basement, like carbon in the ground. I know he aches to be outside, to scavenge and to run, but he was built for winter with his thick coat and webbed paws and claws like crampons on ice. My mother came from a hot, tropical island stand—my body was made for the sun.

"Give it time," Diana answers.

"It's been almost two months."

"He's not in his element. Neither of you are."

Diana reaches for the French press, then stops, remembers I like to do it. I press the plunger down slowly, watching the dark grains of coffee as they migrate to the bottom. Down, down, down, until they can move no farther. Trapped, like I will be if I don't decide my future.

"I don't know what to do," I say, my voice rising. Anxiety claws at my throat like a dog in a kennel trying to get out.

Diana pours the coffee into two ceramic mugs, and we drink silently. This has become our morning ritual. Careful words and sometimes not-so-careful ones. Coffee has been my lifeline these past months, reversing my nocturnal schedule and returning it to a *normal* one. I miss being awake at night, the vibrancy and bioluminescence of the forest, the color-changing moon, and the striking tapestry of the stars. The freedom I felt when I didn't have to constantly speak in codes, whispers, and eye contact, hiding my nature and trying to keep my eyes from changing color.

"All animals have their own personalities," Diana continues. "Some love and trust easily. Others require their love and trust to be earned. Whatever trauma Wolf experienced as a pup must have scarred him."

"I hadn't thought of that." Right, because I've only been thinking about myself, my problems, and my mysterious past. But Wolf has a history as well, one that I know so little about. Where was he born? What happened to his mom? What happened in the days and weeks before my mother bound us together by blood so that he would become my lifelong protector, before she was cornered and shot by a Hunter?

If only there was a way for me to read his mind.

We sip our coffees in silence for a minute, the only sound the cracking of the root as Wolf chews. Diana watches him sadly, like her eyes aren't in the present but in the past, a sad story she isn't ready to share.

"What happened?" I ask her. The question holds many other questions: *What happened to you when you were young? What happened to the world? And why did you move to Red River only to live on the outskirts of a township filled with people you hate?*

Diana's eyes are lost in the middle distance. She swallows the lump in her throat and turns back to me, emotion replaced by the strength that slips down her face like glitter in a snow globe. The same mask she has worn all these years to survive.

"Our priority right now is what to do." *With you*, she implies, dipping her forehead toward me. "I was thinking that you could join the girls' Scout trip this weekend. It's the last one of the year. It might be a good idea for you to get out of the house."

"You'd let me go to Scouts? Why?" I ask, incredulous. She and George have never let me go anywhere other than school.

"The world is changing," she whispers. "And tonight might be your only chance to leave."

"Leave where?" This is more than Scouts. I know that. *Leave* implies the wild. We've skirted around the subject but never dared to say the words aloud. "I don't know where they *are*," I mutter, meaning *Circo*. Not the place, but the Klujns who managed to survive.

I've spent the last few weeks entertaining every possible scenario, and each one leaves me feeling emotional and confused. The idea of returning to the wild is daunting. Of venturing out into the wilderness and completing my own Blood Race—the *real* one. Of navigating the forest alone, in the cold, without a map, shelter, supplies, or even a clear destination in mind. But if I don't find the new location of Circo before the Ice Moon, then I will never be accepted among Klujns. That much I've gathered from reading Catrina Sherman's books late into the night—the illegal ones with the golden spines that Diana stole from George's study and slipped me from time to time. The books had started to decompose, so there were only scraps left, but the bits I got fueled my hunger to know more.

It's only a matter of time before people find out what I am here. Before something happens—my eyes turn violet, my baby claws sprout from my fingers, and the entire township comes at me with rifles pointed and pitchforks raised, bringing me to the gallows in the township square. And then there's still the President: Grouse could return at any moment. With the Hunt ending tonight . . .

Diana holds my wrists down, gently. Her calloused hands are warm. I look up at my adoptive mom. "There are still humans out there," she mouths, nodding past the fences. "More than you realize. If you don't make it to Circo—you have *options*."

Don't make it to Circo. Daciana, my Klujn grandmother, didn't think I had it in me either; that's why she sent me home.

"Where?"

Diana shakes her head; she doesn't know or won't risk saying it out loud.

"Why aren't you with them, then?"

"I had a chance to leave a long time ago, and I didn't take it," she says. "It's too late for me now. But it's not too late for you."

I stew on her words for a moment then spit back a response. "I wouldn't know where to start."

"A journey starts with a step. Then, bit by bit, the path reveals itself. A good map helps. Go to Scouts. And when you get there, make sure to tell *Mr. Wilder* I said *hi.*"

"What about Wolf?"

"If anything happens, I'll let him out. He'll always know where to find you. But whatever you do . . . *don't come home tonight.*" There's urgency in her eyes. "Please, Ava. Some opportunities don't come around twice."

The music stops, and the room is quiet. Unnervingly so. Then, the sound of tires breaks the silence. Diana startles—her liquid eyes become solemn and practical. She lets me go and walks toward the door, leaving me stunned. After six years of sheltering and keeping me in the dark, now she is giving me the key to my enclosure and risking her life in the process. I feel grateful but afraid. *Even if I go to Scouts and speak to this Mr. Wilder, what then? What is the magical link between him and the rest of my life?* I guess we can finish our conversation later at the bonfire. Sometimes crowds are safer—so much noise interferes with listening devices.

Diana pauses in the doorway, casting one last look at Wolf and me. "Life out there may be daunting, but staying here is a sure death," she says. "Don't make the same mistake I did." Then she leaves.

I look down at the mug of coffee in my hands, steam swirling into shapes before dissipating. My mind spins with the warning. The look in Diana's eyes, so final and desperate.

It's too late for me, but it's not too late for you.

The sound of tires grows closer.

I go over to the window above the dresser and flick the glass; the mosquitoes scatter. A Jeep pulls up, and a single set of boots hops out, distorted by the glass, walking with a slight limp, a cane. *George.* I haven't seen him since the day he brought me home from the raid. He left with Grouse that day, never to return. I watch as his boots crunch on the gravel, crackling like crumpled foil.

I step back from the window.

I feel Wolf's eyes on me—he's standing now, the root abandoned, and he looks concerned, perhaps sensing the enemy outside or the spike in my heartbeat. There isn't time to shower or even hug him goodbye. I throw on my school uniform, grab my backpack dangling on the doorknob, and race up the wooden stairs to the main house. George enters from the front door, and we almost collide.

"Ava," he says, surprised and then pained. *Lies, lies, lies*, I think, reminding myself who my father is—not my father at all. I turn on my heel and race out the back door onto the porch.

"Ava," George calls again, something he wants to tell me, but I slip my arms through my backpack straps and walk briskly away until I've reached our driveway and then, across from it, the river path. I walk until the woods swallow me into its gaping mouth, between the sharp teeth of hanging branches and a tongue of yellow leaves.

When I've put enough distance between me and the house, sure that he won't follow, I collapse onto the riverbank. In the river, a cortege of logs drifts downstream, staining the surface red with their sap, in transport to some processing plant. They were part of the forest once, valuable and alive, home to mammals, reptiles, insects, and creatures I can't name. Now, the trees will serve as some human object, and the animals have been made homeless. *Exiled*, like I will be if I don't make some sort of plan.

Suddenly, I resent myself for having wasted so much time sitting idle when I could have been preparing. Every moment that I waste, my door to the wild gets a little smaller and a little farther away. Soon, it will be gone completely, and when that happens, Red River will be my only option. If that happens, I may as well walk myself to the gallows, climb the wooden steps up to the rickety platform, and lower my head onto the sharpened blade.

Tonight, I think. Because whatever's going on . . . tomorrow is already too late.

2

In history class, I stare absentmindedly at my notebook, scribbling a word in bubble letters in the center of the page: PLAN. While Mr. Verywell teaches us about boomtowns and the crystal age, I doodle a hundred question marks around it. In science, as we crack open geodes to discover the semiprecious stones inside them, I am buried nose-deep in a textbook titled *Hunting and Surviving in the Boreal.* It was written by Hamish Frost—one of the three pioneers of our modern world who fell prey to the wild he knew so well. The teacher tells me to pay attention, and I snap the textbook shut and sigh.

I don't have time to open the book again until lunchtime, when I take refuge in my home studies classroom. The teacher, Mrs. Verity, is heavily pregnant and spends most of the lunch hour with her feet up on her desk, knitting something blue.

The textbook's pages are yellowed, the font small and compact. Surviving in the wild . . . There is a little diagram of a makeshift tent. *A bivouac*, the description reads. *A temporary shelter used by Explorers and Hunters when they sleep away from their base camps.* The diagram shows how to build the modest refuge in a few easy steps, made with branches and rope and insulated with leaves and moss. There are other examples of shelters, from simple lean-tos to more sophisticated double-walled log cabins. *In the wild, shelter is vital,* Frost writes. *In winter, though, protection is not sufficient. You also need fire. Water and food are secondary. Remember the Rule of Three: three hours of exposure, three days without water, three weeks without food. Any more, and the wild will become your tomb.* Those words resonate even more deeply because of the Explorer author's cursed fate, who had a million times more experience than I have. I underline *Rule of Three* dramatically for emphasis, hoping that doing so will help me commit it to memory.

Frost writes about different kinds of trails: dark trails and virgin trails and secret trails and dead trails. Who knew there were so many different kinds of trails! I feel like I'm cramming for an exam, only the stakes aren't pass or fail but life or death.

By the time the bell rings, I've read my way into exhaustion. Yet, I feel no closer to seeing the glowing arrow on the dark, dead trail that will point me in the right direction. As the girls-only class files in, each one takes a pumpkin from the front and a set of knives. I'm the second-last to reach the table and my pumpkin is an ugly, twisted thing.

Back at my desk—which I have to myself—I put down my deformed pumpkin and my set of carving knives. Turn my attention to the window where, on the oval, Mr. Mogel's advanced combat class is gathered around the teacher, preparing for a game of Wolves and Townships.

"A plan of attack never survives first contact with the enemy," I hear Mr. Mogel yell. "The first thing to die in the wild is your plan. You have to be ready to improvise and think quickly on your feet."

I scan the group of faces, but Coll is not there. His friend

Justine is the only girl in the class. Diana told me that Coll survived Wolf's attack, barely, and has been in a hospital in Brave Night ever since. I'm not sure how she heard. Like me, she chooses her company wisely, which is code for the fact that she doesn't have friends. Still, I've stayed away from Mr. Mogel just in case. He has a poacher's heart, and poachers are notorious for taking the law into their own hands.

I miss movement. Running, weaving through obstacle courses, and learning to defend myself. There's only so much that a textbook can teach you, and I've never been all that good at absorbing information from diagrams.

Outside, beyond the school and river, the black woods stretch toward the Military fence. The coils of barbed wire peak above the foliage like a miniature rollercoaster of infinite loops, and beyond it, the dense green forest rises up at a gradual incline, slowly and then all at once, where the earth explodes into jagged mountains. The nearest peaks are dark as night, their silhouettes fading from charcoal to storm-cloud gray to pearl the farther you get. I remember what it felt like to climb into those mountains that first night when I was captured by Klujns, and we traversed the rugged wilderness northwest to Circo. It was terrifying, but I have also never felt more alive.

"Can I sit here?" I look up to find a pair of caramel-orange eyes I've never seen before in my home studies class. They belong to a girl of average height with a mop of wavy brown hair and bangs. She smiles, revealing a gap between her two front teeth. Despite being new, she holds herself with confidence.

"Sure," I say, gesturing to the empty seat.

"Thanks." She slides into the blue plastic chair, setting her knife set and pumpkin on the table. The girl's eyes dart over to my fingertips, which are covered in press-on nails to hide the absence of fingernails. I quickly busy my hands, slicing a hole into the top of the pumpkin and pulling out handfuls of the stringy orange flesh. When I've finished gutting it, I pick up a small curved knife and get to work on its features, using a photograph of a boy as a reference.

The new girl watches me work, then thoughtfully looks at her pumpkin. "I don't understand how they're supposed to represent the raid's fallen Hunters," she says. "How carving a vegetable into a boy's face and then letting it rot for the next month while birds and maggots pick at it honors his memory."
I snort despite my best effort to keep to myself.

"At least the entrails make a good pie?"

She snickers. "I'm Morgan." She reaches out to shake my hand.

"Ava," I answer, holding up my palms to show they're covered in pumpkin guts. I'm relieved that the orange goo has masked my press-on nails.

"Nice to meet you, *Ava*," she says, mulling over my name like sweet water. She looks around, ensuring no one is listening, then leans forward on her elbows, balancing on the front legs of her chair. "Not to speak out of line, but a few girls went missing from my township, and I haven't even heard a *whisper* about them. What do you think happened?"

I look into her eyes, and there's a dangerous flicker there. It's a conversation I would entertain if I was at Circo, sitting around a bonfire with a blanket around my shoulders and only the mountains as witness, but here it feels dangerous.

"Where are you from?" I decide on, a harmless question.

Morgan settles onto the back legs of her chair, looking disappointed. "Justice Falls," she says. I don't know why, but hearing this comes as a relief. It's where Wendy and Willa were from, and according to Willa, it's the friendliest of all the townships.

"I had a friend from there," I say.

"*Had?* What happened to her?"

"I mean—*have*," I say quickly. I wonder if Morgan knows her, but I don't ask, because I'm keen to keep the focus off me. "Why did you move here, anyway?"

"My mom used to work at a Loudhouse but recently took a leave of absence. Came here for the cleaner air or something."

"Why did she take a leave of absence?" The question comes out blunt, not sugar-coated.

"The job took its toll."

"How come?"

Morgan raises an eyebrow, looking at me like a specimen in a jar filled with bright-yellow liquid. "Do you really want to know?"

I shrug. It would be wiser to abandon the conversation. Still, Morgan has piqued my interest, and I have trouble leaving things alone. I would rather have nightmares for weeks than not know what she means, down to the last detail.

"She was a knocker."

My lips part, and Morgan recognizes my confusion for what it is. "It's what they call the person who works in the Killing-room," she explains. "The one who stuns the Klujns."

"Stuns them?" I swallow, and my saliva is thick as glue.

"When they're taken out of their cages, they're led down a tunnel. At the end of the tunnel is a knocker and a slitter. The knocker hits them between the eyes with a spiked hammer. Apparently, they have a gland there, a weak spot like an Achilles tendon, and hitting it paralyzes them for a few minutes so they can't go feral and escape."

The third eye.

Morgan continues telling her horror story with a smile. "Then, while the Klujn is incapacitated, the slitter does the rest." She mimes slitting her own throat with her carving knife. The oozing pumpkin goo adds credibility to her mime. My hand tightens around my own knife, my knuckles draining of blood like a sky with four white moons.

I force my look of disgust into one of indifference. "So why did your mom leave?"

"It's a tough job. The government lures you with perks like good money, an early pension, and a steady meat supply, but most don't survive longer than a few weeks. After my dad died, she had to work and thought quick money was the way to pay off the land taxes and such, but after this raid . . . well, I think it was a lot to stomach."

The room spins; I grip the table with my free hand, so I don't fall off my chair. The touch of the wood anchors me in a spinning universe.

"Anyway," Morgan says, "are you going tonight?"

"To Scouts?"

"No dummy, to the bonfire."

"I'm not sure," I answer. School lets out at four. Sundown is around five. The buses leave at six. I need to go home to pack a bag, but Diana's warning is still on my mind. "Maybe."

"Great!" Morgan exclaims, taking my *maybe* as a *yes*. The bell rings, and she tells me she has an appointment with the career counselor but promises to find me when school is over.

After she leaves, I bring my finished jack-o-lantern to the front and position it with the others. I hope the fallen Hunter boy's family doesn't see it, because they will be greatly disappointed. Then I move to the sink to wash my hands and clean my knives, watching the orange flesh swirl down the drain until my hands are smooth again. It's weird to think that there are little crystals in there, and beneath them, larger adult claws that will one day grow and serve some bigger purpose.

Another window offers me a different view of the oval.

Justine has been promoted to Superhunter, wearing a silver jersey with an *S* on it. The dwindling wolves huddle together to strategize. Then the whistle blows and the wolves close in, their last chance to infiltrate the township and steal the flag.

Life in the wild is dangerous, but there are worse things than danger itself. Like staying here and dying without ever having lived. I may not know where my destiny lies, but it's not here; I'm sure of that. The journey to the new Circo must be hundreds of miles, though, into the territories of dangerous plants and red-toothed beasts. I'm already months behind; if that wasn't enough, the first frost is not far off. Winter is late this year, but she is coming.

I shiver at the idea of being in the wild in winter. Winter is a time for hibernation, cozying up before a crackling fire—not a time to embark on a great pilgrimage through the wilderness. And, aside from the diagram of the bivouac, I know nothing about survival. My only hope of finding Circo is Diablo. Without him, who knows the wild so well . . .

I would be lucky to survive one night.

Diablo. I haven't allowed myself to think about him. Still, the images arrive in my mind uninvited: my brother, Mercy, in Hunter's uniform, stabbing Diablo in the shoulder with the bayonet of his rifle. Diablo's barely conscious body being carried toward the buses with blacked-out windows, destined for the Loudhouse.

What are the chances that he's still alive?

A whistle blows, shrill and final.

I look outside and see that the game is over. Justine and her teammates are celebrating. The wolves have lost, although it shouldn't come as a surprise—the humans win every time.

"I'm locking up now," says Mrs. Verity, a long blue scarf cascading from her knitting needles like a lone tentacle.

Out in the corridor, I pass a large noticeboard. DSO posters are plastered with their typical warnings: REPORT UNUSUAL BEHAVIOR. Pinned papers advertise local Scout excursions, early childhood classes, and rental baby dolls. There's a MISSING poster with Reesa's face on it, taped on top of a faded poster of another missing girl from last year.

Next to the noticeboard is a large Military map of the region in faded blues and grays. I reach my index finger up to the map and find Red River. Then I trace the journey southeast, following the Military road into Tremble Hills, one of the last remaining natural reservoirs on this side of the fences. Near the base of Black Mountain is the Scout camp, surrounded by dotted trails. One of those trails—marked by little black triangles—crosses the road to the north and disappears into a section of land between the river and the fence, where the trees are black and dense. *Camp Midnight*, it reads. And, only a few miles northwest of the camp along the fence, tucked away in secrecy is . . . the Loudhouse.

My heart beats irregularly between my ribs, ignited by a possibility that wasn't there before.

What if I could go to Scouts like Diana said, and from there get to the Loudhouse? If I could find Diablo, it would be that much easier to navigate the wild and find Circo. But going to the Loudhouse is suicidal, and I don't even know if Diablo is still alive, so I squash the thought almost as quickly as it arrived.

3

I have no intention of going to Klujnology, but my escape attempt from school is thwarted by Mr. Mogel coming in from playground duty. I follow the current of bodies as they push into my Klujnology classroom, and sink into the seat farthest from the front, but my father's gaze finds me the second he enters, with the eye of a seasoned Hunter trained to see the briefest flash of color through the foliage. I would rather be anywhere but here, like in Warwick's tent, spinning a wheel and eating a questionable dish while being educated on the ignorance of humans.

In the class, we are mostly girls, with a few exceptions—boys forced to sit out the raid due to illness or injury or strict parents or who came back after Hunter's camp when they were supposed to, unlike Mercy. George's arrival is met with a standing ovation. I wonder why until I realize that in recent weeks, his name has been spoken on the news in the same sentence as *Grouse* and *raid*, the mysterious expert whose knowledge helped Grouse lead his Hunters to the most prolific raid yet and who has stepped up to the plate while the general has been recovering at home from the "*heinous injuries*" he suffered at the hands of the barbaric king.

George faces a firing squad of questions, and the raid seems to be the kill shot—*Why didn't you tell us you were working with the Hunters? How did you find the creatures if they're practically invisible? How many did you get? Is what they're saying about repopulation true?* And, a question I hadn't thought about: *Are you going back now that you're too famous for us?*

George spreads his fingers wide and fans the ground, asking his audience to *please sit down*. He answers with measured words, telling us that he is, in fact, going back to the Loudhouse for some time, which has become the center of operations, and that this will be his final class. He is officially retiring from teaching and wanted to give us the courtesy of telling us in person.

My cheeks are hot, and it takes all my self-control not to yell out "TRAITOR!" at the top of my lungs. Instead, I stab my pen into my notebook page. *I can't believe he's going back.* I thought there were no raids in winter, that Hunter operations slowed down and gave the wild a chance to fill its lungs again before the massacre of the spring. Somehow, the idea of Hunters turning their operations indoors—at the *Loudhouse*, of all places—feels even more nefarious. *Repopulation* means food security, and food security means kanum—*Klujn meat.* But how can one stand be enough to feed our entire Territory indefinitely?

I search George's eyes for a trace of remorse or apology, and when his eyes meet mine, I find plenty. There's a cocktail of emotion inside them, of exhaustion and shame and chagrin and something that resembles heartbreak.

"I'm very sorry," he says, and his words feel directed at me. Like a traveling storyteller in a small tent, performing for an audience of a single seat. "I wish things were different. Now," he continues, and his voice becomes more upbeat. "This is our last class together, and I'd like to let you decide what you want to learn." He picks up a piece of pale blue chalk and writes three topics down on the blackboard:

PLANTS AND FLOWERS OF THE BOREAL
MATING RITUALS

And, finally—

ASTRAS

The girls and a few boys blush at the second option and whisper nervously at the third, like wind rustling the canopy of the forest. I've never heard of astras—that chapter in Sherman's books had fallen prey to the decomposition process.

"I thought mating rituals were banned from the curriculum," says a boy.

"Sixteen isn't what it was in the old world. I believe that if you're old enough to pass a rifle test, then you should be allowed to learn about the way animals procreate," George says. "Let's vote." I don't raise my hand. Mating rituals is the clear winner, followed by astras.

"Great!" George exclaims, scratching out PLANTS AND FLOWERS. "You'll have to learn about moonflowers and Black Victorias on your own time, which I recommend you do because they are fascinating."

George pulls a white screen down over the blackboard and switches the projector on.

"In the last class we had together before the raid, we spoke a little bit about Circo and the Deeper Woods," George says. "But today, I want to turn our focus northeast, to a more mysterious part of the Boreal."

I can't believe I was sitting here, in this very room, the first time I learned about Klujns. About the moon phases and the Blood Race—although, according to humans, it was a fight to the death between a human and a Klujn. I have since learned that, despite the fighting component and Warwick's appetite for human suffering, the Blood Race was a lot more complex than that. It was a process of transformation designed to open our eyes to the lies we had been conditioned to believe our entire lives. As for the young Klujns, their Blood Race was something entirely different. It was a pilgrimage through the wintry wild.

I was so gullible back then.

Like the rest of my class, of the Territory.

I shouldn't believe anything he teaches now. But the way he speaks—with passion, with fervor—makes it difficult to believe that someone could lie so well.

"Ecosystems that change every few miles . . . migrations of invisible animals . . . a phenomenon called *Blue Midnight* that occurs on the first full moon of January . . . rocks that can read your intentions, water that heals or poisons, and flowers that bloom in the dark . . . these are just a few of the many wonders of the Darker Woods."

The Darker Woods.

Why does that sound even more sinister than the Deeper Woods?

George draws us in with honeyed words, and despite my best effort to remain indifferent, I feel myself leaning forward. He clicks through various slides, and I see a diorama of gloomy forest images, a lush and beautiful nightmare of gnarly trees shaped like the letters of a forgotten alphabet, of smoky fog and violent rivers and flowers bright and deadly.

"The Darker Woods stretch from the north of Justice Falls to the Snowy Mountains in the east. On the other side of Black River—which is easily a dozen miles across—is the beginning of the Gaspésia Peninsula." He shows us a peninsula curved like the head of a whale. Beyond that, the ocean.

Is it a coincidence? That like the Circo lecture on the day of my capture, it almost feels like he is trying to prepare me for something. To *warn* me . . . Does George, with his decades of expertise, know where Circo went?

"As the name suggests, some parts of the Darker Woods are as dark and fathomless as the bottom of the ocean, with places where the forest floor has never seen daylight, even in the peak of summer. Where trees can serve as cozy inns for wayward guests, if you don't mind sharing with its other inhabitants. No, this is not fantasy . . . this all exists out there.

"So dense and impenetrable, in fact," he goes on. "That it is mostly unmapped by humans, consisting of swamplands and boglands and networks of caves that one should never attempt to cross without a *guide*. Let's just say—it's hard to find a place to pitch your tent." The class laughs.

"In winter, most of the northeastern part is covered in frozen lakes, sastrugi—snow mountains formed by the wind—and deep snow," George continues. "Home to sinkholes and crevices that have become the final resting places of many unfortunate Explorers. But suppose one makes it through the woods and past the mountains, in the forests near Black River, one can find a more temperate climate and ample *company*."

"What does this have to do with mating rituals?" a girl asks.

"Context," George answers. He leans heavily on his cane but looks relaxed despite the constant threat of surveillance.

"Klujns face many important milestones in their lives, but none is more important and defining than the Blood Race. A fight to the death, as you learned last term," he says. "But afterward, Klujns must enter the wild, travel a long distance, retrieve proof of passage, and then find the new location of the tribe. The Blood Race is the ultimate test of adversity, endurance, and *belonging*."

I realize then how carefully George must choose his words, weaving the truth he wants to tell me in with the lies he's forced to teach, making sure he uses the same color thread. The way he says *tribe* instead of *stand.*

He looks at me again as though urging me to read between the lines. *Risking his life*, I think, and doing it with fifty pairs of eyes as witnesses.

"This time in the wild is primordial for a Klujn's development," he says. "They—the animals—become fully independent. Nature is a cruel teacher, and the cold is even crueler. Many die out there, but death is not as consequential as being rejected by their tribes. And for those that make it home, good times await."

George clicks to the next slide, and I see the same sensationalized sketches of Klujns by the Explorers who documented them—portrayed as monsters, deprived of moonlight and a plant diet and freedom until they become the vicious predators that humans need to support their narrative of slaughter.

"Before going into the wild, a young Klujn—having just grown their first claws—may be sixteen or seventeen in human years, but developmentally they are the equivalent of thirteen or fourteen, having been sheltered for most of their young lives. Their youth—or inexperience—marks them like an invisible, energetic tattoo. Call it a smell or bad pheromones. Only after their pilgrimage in the wild does the 'smell' lift, and they are finally accepted by their tribe. If they don't make it, the stamp lingers for life, branding them as a permanent outcast."

My pen breaks, and I realize I've been pushing it down so hard into my notebook page that my hand is throbbing. But the pain in my hand is nothing compared to the blunt trauma of George's words. *My youth and inexperience brand me like a bad smell? An invisible tattoo? And it will linger for life if I don't complete the Blood Race?* I knew it was important to find Circo—but I didn't understand the stakes. *Is that why Diablo looked at me the way he did? And why Daciana sent me away? Was I just a child to them, immature and juvenile? Unworthy until I had proven otherwise?*

I smell my sweater, and a waft of rose soap meets my nostrils, fragrant and with no indication that I am branded by something repulsive that emanates from my skin . . . something potentially *permanent*.

"The challenges of a long-distance journey are physical at first," says George, continuing the lecture. "In the wild, young Klujns must master important skills, learn to navigate using instinct, and make fire where fire was never meant to exist. They must find food and clean water, build shelter, and battle the cold as well as the darkest corners of their minds. Once they have overcome the harsh terrain, it is possible for Klujns to enter an altered state, which we humans know very little about. This phenomenon allows them to travel great distances without tiring. And when they find their tribe, an Initiation determines who is alpha, and a natural hierarchy is formed.

"Then, the 'stamp' is lifted," George says. "A young Klujn leaves as a teenager and returns as a young adult, having aged the equivalent of five years in only a matter of months. Being alpha comes with many benefits—and it's the females that get to choose their mates."

The class *oohs*.

"They may choose any Klujn of any age, unless that animal is currently bonded to another, and a bond lasts seven years, after which it is renewed or expires.

"Then," George continues, "in a primitive marriage, the two are wrapped in ribbon and covered in a honey-like substance.

They must cross through a circular barrier—this is perhaps where the term *honeymoon* comes from—where tribal spirits decide if the pair's genes are a good match for the future of the tribe and species. If the match is accepted, they embark on their honeymoon in the wild, which marks the beginning of their seven-year union."

I notice that he says *spirits* when he probably means *gods* because saying *gods* would make them sound more human. I got a taste of those gods at the Ceremony of Fire, where an eerie entity entered my body and peered into my mind. When one of those gods—the god of Creatures—possessed Reesa and made her leap into the fire to her death. Even though I know so little about them, it's clear these gods are not to be messed with.

"What if the match is rejected?" someone asks, looking mortified.

"We don't know," George answers. "But not all Klujns require male-female partnerships to procreate," he goes on. "There are rumors that some tribes have self-reproducing abilities."

"How is that possible?" a girl shouts, almost offended by the idea. George shrugs.

"A mystery," he says. "Klujn fertility and reproduction is something that has fascinated me for years—in my anterior life, it was the original basis of my studies. They are a type of creature who has evolved faster than any other in the wild. We can barely keep up with their evolution, which is made more difficult because no tribe is exactly the same. Klujns have learned to evolve with their environment under the pressure of being hunted, doing in decades what our species has barely managed to do in three hundred thousand years. And, where our fertility is decreasing, theirs is only increasing."

"If they're animals, why do they get *married*?" somebody else asks.

"It's more of a *union* than a marriage in the sense that we understand it," George clarifies. "Time and time again, Nature has shown us that she loves a spectacle, especially when it comes to sex—the sexual cannibalism of some species, like scorpions, praying mantises, and black widows. Klujns are animals, and animals see no shame in mating. Some of these rituals even happen in the open, with the tribe and the stars as witnesses."

A chair scrapes back loudly, and a girl walks out. The same girl who looked personally offended by George's mention of the self-reproducing Klujns. He scratches his beard nervously. "Anyway." He moves on to astras, which, he explains, are like haunted tunnels of forest spirits in the Darker Woods and other regions of the Boreal. There's that word again, *spirits*, and I wonder if he also means *gods* this time too.

"Similar to black holes in outer space," George says, "they are a place where time bends and stretches, speeds up or slows down, becomes irrelevant. Where the concept of *reality* goes away. Think of them like energy highways, or wormholes. You can wander into one by accident and end up a hundred miles away, two minutes from now, or you can end up two miles away, a hundred years from now."

"How is that possible?" I realize I'm the one who asked this question when George smiles, glad to see I've been paying attention.

"No one can really say, because no human has walked out of one with a sound mind. Once, a Hunter walked into an astra in the swamplands, then walked out in Valor's Edge, over two hundred miles away, just a few seconds later, holding one of his eyeballs in each hand." The class groans, some disgusted and others enthralled. "Although the eyeballs may be an embellishment." George grins. "An enriched Hunter's tale."

"How can you spot them?" another boy asks.

"They're almost impossible to detect until it's too late," George answers. "Some who have come close say it feels like stepping into a different climate, like going from a crisp winter's day into a tropical ecosystem."

The bell rings, and I can't believe the school day is already over. I'm about to leave the classroom when George's hand finds my shoulder blade.

"Ava, can I have a word?"

I let him pull me aside: It wouldn't be wise to make a scene in front of everyone. His expression becomes serious when we're finally alone.

"How are you?" he asks. I shake my head—*no*—we're not doing this. George nods in patient understanding. "I'm sorry."

"I'm *sorry* is what you say to someone when you bump into them," I say. "Not when you raise them up to die." The words crack through the air like a whip wrapped in curls of barbed wire. Emotion surges up again, raising my voice and prickling my eyes, and I hate how little it takes to make me cry.

I look into George's bright green eyes, now overcast like the sky outside. Not callous and bloodshot like in my nightmare—still my dad. *I miss him*, I realize. At least, I miss the person I thought he was before all this. Because not only am I grieving the loss of the only family I ever had, the father I longed for, and the future he stole, but I'm also mourning the fact that every moment I thought was good and pure is now tainted, like a bright window covered in black cellophane.

"What did you think would happen after? Did you think I'd survive? Why didn't you let Diablo go?" All the questions I've been obsessing over for the last months rise, one after the next. I hate how desperate I sound, as though in asking him these things, I am surrendering all my power. *Needing* from him, when I don't want to need anything from him anymore.

George swallows, and I see his Adam's apple travel halfway down his throat and then stay there, like a rodent stuck in the esophagus of a snake.

"*Honestly?*" he says. "I hoped you would survive . . . but I was afraid of it. And I had no choice," he adds. "If I let you both go, someone else would have caught you, and they would not have been as lenient. The woods were filled with snares—a death I wouldn't wish on anyone."

I go to turn my back on him, and he grabs my wrist.

"Wait," he says. "The Klujn you were with—the male."

"Diablo?" I ask. George nods solemnly, and I realize I'm not ready to hear whatever he's about to tell me.

"He's still alive."

I'm not breathing; I've forgotten how. The oxygen in my lungs slowly turns into carbon dioxide, pushing up against my diaphragm, begging to be released, but my abs are clenched.

"*What?*" I finally exhale.

"I made sure they kept him, but he's not needed anymore. He'll be dead by morning."

"Where is he?"

George hesitates, then says, "A cage in the animal storehouse. Right underneath the stage."

"The stage?"

George nods. "The Loudhouse is shaped like a diamond. Once you're inside, you can get anywhere. Most activity happens underground." I'm still processing this information when he keeps going. "There's a ceremony tonight at eleven. All the Hunters will be there. But be careful—it's very dangerous."

"Why are you telling me this?"

"Diana didn't want me to. She cares about you, but she thinks it's too late. She wants you to be safe and thinks your best chance is with the humans who live out there."

"What do you think?"

"I think . . ." George hesitates.

"*Honestly.*"

"You deserve more than safety. You deserve to be happy. I know how important belonging is to your kind, and I think that after everything you've been through and what I put you through, you deserve a chance at that. It's what your mother would have wanted."

"My mother?"

There's a storm in his eyes now, so much more that he wants to say but doesn't, just like Diana this morning.

"You *knew* her?"

George nods slowly, his eyes filling just as much as mine.

"I wish I'd never met her," he answers. "For better or for worse, meeting her changed my life."

I want to ask him why, but my brain is too slow to fill my mouth with words.

"I can't erase the past," George goes on. "The choices I made—even though I made them all for a reason, one you may never understand. But what I can give you now is the chance for a better future—even if that chance is small. Because going to the Loudhouse is incredibly dangerous, and if you decide to go, you'll be on your own."

There's a sound. I turn to see a ghost standing in the doorway. Morgan is there, the top half of her face painted in monochromatic whites and grays, her schoolbooks tucked into the cushiony part of her forearm.

"You ready?" she asks. For a second, I'm terrified that she overheard, but her breezy demeanor contains no trace of suspicion. I nod, joining her in the doorway. I paint a smile on my own face and turn to look at George one last time.

"Have fun," he tells me, his eyes glittering with fear and sadness.

At that moment, I realize that I trust him. More than I should and more than he deserves, but I *do*.

As Morgan and I walk out into the gloomy afternoon, George's words continue to pound through my ears like blood rushing to the site of a wound.

Diablo is still alive.

4

Above our heads, the sky is gray and swollen. November's snowfall has, in recent years, been replaced by relentless rainstorms, the cold, humid kind that makes you shiver and want to stay inside, not warm and inviting like a summer shower. Despite it being early afternoon, the day is already falling.

Little electric lights are turning on in the streets, outside shops and houses. Doors are decorated in triangular-shaped wreaths of blue plastic flowers. Grouse's statue stands tall and stern in the main square. He has a rifle strapped over his shoulder and his cyborg dog at his side—the size of a Mastiff, the head of a Doberman, the intelligence of a German shepherd, and the nose of a bloodhound. I used to have a blanket of dog breeds in my room when I was little, one that Diana made, and I learned all of them by heart.

The statue overlooks the gallows that have been decorated with candlelight and cobwebs. It's the only night of the year when the occult is tolerated, where ghostly makeup and stories of sorcery are permitted. A few people wrapped in coats are huddled outside the butcher. Coll's mom, Mrs. Mogel-Newhouse—or

Gora—is there, arms crossed over her solid frame as she speaks to a few others, hunched and conspiratorial. She's not wearing a costume, not cupping a beverage, but there seems to be something urgent on her mind.

The smell of oil and sugar meets my nostrils as Morgan and I walk down a slope toward the back of town. We reach a grassy field that faces south, with two large piles of timber where the bonfires will be lit at sundown. A long table with plates, goblets, and chairs is set between them. Seated on them are scarecrow bodies with the pumpkin heads we made, lit from within, where the deceased Hunters—now exiled between life and eternal darkness—are having their final meal. Because, apparently, eating is essential . . . even when you're dead.

Around the outside perimeter of the field is the usual array of food trucks, selling anything roasted and toasted and fried and beverages that glow in the dark. There's a sideshow alley illuminated with colored bulbs and the usual slew of carnival games, including a tree-cutting competition and a mud race. At the very back of the field, the entrance of a corn maze is illuminated by a giant sign: LABYRINTH.

"What do you want to start with?" Morgan asks. I look around for Diana but can't see her in the small crowd. She should be here, shouldn't she, if only to finish the conversation we had this morning?

It's early, though, and there's still plenty of time. To our right, I notice Coll's mom, Gora, descending into the festivities, her eyes darting around, looking for someone.

"Let's go that way," I say, pointing in the opposite direction, keen to get out of her eyesight. Morgan and I start a large clockwise loop around the field, passing the first food truck, where Morgan buys a bag of Klujn beard.

"Can you believe this stuff actually grows on trees?" she says, offering me a taste of the puffed sugar, which is colored a coral green. I try a bit, but the stuff tastes too artificially sweet. As we walk, Morgan talks about her favorite rides and the tents she likes to visit. I'm only half listening. I keep scanning the crowd for Gora or anyone else I might recognize, the way a prey animal constantly has to ensure there are no threats around. Being with Morgan is safer than being alone, I realize.

We pass a line of people waiting to board the Swampland Safari Log Ride and another one queuing up outside the Horror Museum. A couple of girls walk out, looking perturbed. A tall ambulant vendor walks past us, selling plastic flower wreaths and glowing flags for a homemade game of Wolves and Townships. He wears an LED mask with only dark sockets for eyes.

Morgan stops in front of a foam pit. Red, orange, yellow—the foam cubes represent makeshift flames. Dangling horizontally above it is a greased log covered in some kind of animal fat. A competitor in blue baggy overalls tries to climb across it to reach the center prize. "In circuses, they do it with real fire," Morgan says. "They use Klujns instead of humans, of course, but it's quite a spectacle."

The woman squeals as she loses her grip and falls off, swallowed by the foamy flames. We pass a table where children get rune-like tattoos and face paint, and another vendor sells crowns of something resembling sunflowers with large black petals and glowing blue centers.

"Moonflowers," Morgan grins, following my line of vision. "They only grow on Klujn land. They're said to help protect against dark spirits. These ones are plastic, though."

I'm relieved there's no Coliséa here this time, no live Klujn waiting to be thrown in front of a chanting audience. Although I feel curious about the circus Morgan described . . .

"This is my favorite," Morgan says. Before I can contest, she pulls me toward a gray oval tent. We walk through the entrance, beneath hanging silver letters that read: HUNTER MUSEUM. I hand over the two-token entrance fee with regret because my tokens are limited, but it seems a small price to pay to avoid suspicion. Morgan and I push through the turnstile and enter a pocket universe where we are the only two occupants, save for the elderly clerk who stands behind the cash register pricing trinkets.

Around the room, illuminated boards detail the history of the first Explorer missions and Hunts, from Estrella to Zonia to Raynn and the less famous ones like Bessi-Maso, Corthu, and Atravessa. At the end of the timeline is Circo. It is shocking to see it written in fresh ink, the raid so recent and yet already a part of history. So much destruction and carnage narrowed down to a few basic statistics, all embellished to make humans look like saviors.

I peer into a uniform display, where mannequins are dressed in the Hunter garb, from the simple gray uniforms worn on raids to the more formal ones reserved for special ceremonies. One has so many crystal pins and medals down its front that it looks like it's wearing a bib. It is a little ridiculous in its display of pompous masculinity, like a male peacock showing off his turquoise plumage, a song-and-dance routine to try to impress a disinterested female. Rifles of every size and make are strung in another glass case, their bayonets ranging from metals to crystals. A plaque explains that the bayonets symbolize rank, and the ones made from viaţă are reserved for the highest-ranking soldiers, usually the general and his buddy.

A life-size diorama shows the inside of a base camp sleeping tent equipped with cots and hammocks, a toilet bucket, and a small table for games. Other items are displayed, ranging from old complicated maps to flashlights, communication systems to compasses. Then, the Hunting Museum leads into an apothecary, with jars filled with dried flowers and fermented body parts.

SPOTTED WOLF TONGUES reads the label on a large jar. Its properties are listed as giving strength, robustness, power, and fertility, and also—that it can be used as an aphrodisiac.

"These can't be real," I say, looking in at the long pink tongues that fill the jar, some of which have little blue spots on them. Next to the tongue jar is a tin filled with pens, made from giant blue snails, a variety that contains ink just like squids do. Another container is filled with little beaks.

"Blue sparrow beaks," Morgan says excitedly. "Those are good for public speaking."

"You eat them?"

"No, you wear them around your neck for confidence. They say it helps to keep your heart rate slow and your voice steady."

The apothecary is filled with these macabre jars. Animals killed and diced for parts. For the promise of curing sores or fever or alopecia. A black curtain shields a restricted area with a sign that reads: CORPSE MEDICINE. The curtain is partially open, and behind it, I glimpse bones, hair, jars of blood and other liquids. I shudder.

"Come on," Morgan says, pulling me into the last section of the tent. "Let's see if the Mystic is here."

The final section sells tarot cards, crystal-growing kits, and thread bracelets with little glass eyeballs on them. Bunches of sage and black lavender hang on the walls like tiny broomsticks. The smell meets my nostrils, prickling with pollen. Something real and organic, for once.

At the back of the tent, the Mystic is hunched over a strange, black nest. A group of four girls, who look around fourteen, are huddled around it.

As Morgan leads me over to them, I notice a little sign: HAVE YOUR LOVE FORTUNE READ.

We watch as the first girl reaches into the nest, where there are a dozen glimmering black eggs, much larger than chicken eggs, and with a holographic sheen to them.

The girl chooses one that sparkles in the dim light of the tent.

"An avarice egg," Morgan whispers.

"What's an avarice?"

"They're creatures that are born in the ocean and start their lives as snakes or eels. Then, they crawl up to the shore where they form crystal cocoons like these and enter a chrysalis state during which they metamorphose into birds. Just like caterpillars turn into butterflies, or maggots into moths," she says. "The yolks are different colors. But I don't know if these are real."

"Now crack it," the Mystic says, and the girl hits the egg against the edge of a bowl. The shell breaks, and a clear goo falls out, holding a bright blue yolk the size of a plum. The girl squeals in excitement.

"A friend of mine did it last year," Morgan tells me. "It's creepily accurate. It shows you the eye color of the person you're going to marry."

These girls look too young to be thinking about marriage. Girls who haven't started combat class and who probably never will because there are only two types of girls here—the ones who believe that muscles are unladylike, who prefer to stay dainty and slim, content in the roles defined for them, and those who opt for Military roles and grow as much bulk as their frames will hold, desperate to prove that they are as strong and able as the men around them. There isn't much room for any other kind of girl. Certainly not for someone like me, someone in between, an enigma to my peers, who likes makeup, art, flowers, and pretty things but also loves sports, adventure, and getting dirty. You have to pick a side and check a box so that people feel comfortable around you. The same *people* who are so busy trying to control you in order to forget the fact that they don't particularly know or like themselves.

In the wild, I didn't need to fit into a box; I could just be *myself.* Nature doesn't waste energy trying to define things. Plants and flowers don't have names, only the names that humans give them. I wonder which kind of girl Morgan is. The latter, it seems, which is why it's weird to see her keen on marriage. She doesn't feel like a Justice Falls girl. She feels like something else . . .

One by one, the young girls reach into the nest, retrieve an egg, and then crack it open. The second girl gets green, the third gets gold, and the fourth gets orange. "The color of our President's eyes," her friends swoon. "Too bad he doesn't have any sons." They leave the tent, giggling and clutching their sideshow bags.

"Do you want to try?" Morgan asks me. "It's a bit of a racket—but it *is* entertaining."

"I don't think marriage is for me."

"Oh yeah? Why's that?" I see her eyes—trying to figure me out, the way I was attempting to figure her out just before.

"I've never met anyone I could imagine myself marrying."

"That's fair," she answers. "But you have to try it at least once. Consider it a rite of passage."

I find it hard to say no to her. "Fine," I mutter. Morgan hoots and pulls me over to the Mystic, watching as I take out my remaining tokens. I hand them over to the charlatan, who has probably been hired by the government to tell young girls to "stay out of the woods" and "not eat glittering roses."

As I reach forward my sleeve pulls up, revealing the scar of the wolf bite on my hand and those strange scars, the markings of my mother's language. One symbol is darker than the others. It looks like a spiral or a swirl. I pull my sleeve back down before Morgan can see it, but something tells me she already has because those eyes miss nothing.

"Choose carefully," the Mystic says as I gently touch the eggs one at a time, not knowing what I'm meant to be feeling for. Then, around the seventh or eighth egg, I feel a spark beneath my fingers, a pulse of electricity or instinct. I close my fingers around this particular egg and pull it out of the nest. It is surprisingly heavy.

The Mystic gestures to the bowl, and I need both hands to crack it open. The clear goo slips out, and the yolk is a thick, bloodied white. And inside it . . . a miniature body moves. A tiny, slithering creature breaks out of the yolk, no longer a snake but not yet a bird.

I drop the broken shell and take a step back, horrified. I cover my mouth with the back of my hand and gag. "Is it . . . alive?" Morgan asks, equally disgusted and curious, looking down as the tiny creature squirms. It moves and twitches a few times, a mix of scales and feathers and prenatal blindness. Then, it stops moving, dead before it even opens its eyes. "Your future husband has white eyes," she says. "Or . . . red."

It was safe in its eggshell, and I killed it.

I destroyed its home.

All for a stupid carnival game.

"I'm sorry," the Mystic says. "That's never happened before. Here," she adds, thrusting my tokens back into my yolky hands. I barely register what's happened until we're back outside, the cool night air pressing against my eyes.

"I take back what I said," Morgan exclaims. "That was worth

every token. I've never seen anything like that before. Maybe it's a sign of luck or something—like when a bird shits on your head."

We continue to walk, but the image is still burned into my vision: the tiny snake-bird's helpless, jerking body as I cracked its universe apart. The bloody, milky yolk. A hollow sadness fills me. Maybe it's stupid to care about a small, weird creature, but I can't help it. *Probably taken from its nest by a poacher*, I think. *Sold at one of the markets in Brave Night.* I feel sad for the mother I've never met.

Breathe.

Morgan looks around, inhaling the smell of caramel popcorn and salted pretzels and smoke. The sky is darkening, and the twin bonfires are being lit. People huddle around the crackling flames, clutching steaming beverages in their hands. It must be around five, I realize. The buses leave in an hour. The crowd is larger now, but there's still no sign of Diana. *Where is she? Did she say she'd come, or did I imagine that?*

Across the field, another vendor watches me from behind his mask. I can't see anything in the dark abyss of his eyes, but it feels like he's looking right at me . . . I shudder, reminded of why I don't like crowds. Any one of those masked people could be someone who wishes me harm.

Suddenly, I wish I could go home, shower, eat some real food, and have a proper conversation with Diana. Ask her what's going on, plain and simple. All I want is my bed. A quiet, comfortable place where I can cradle Wolf and take off my public mask. But Diana told me that I shouldn't go home. Was it a suggestion or a warning?

There's a scream—I barely move out of the way in time as a girl in a wolf mask barrels into her friend, tackling him to the ground and claiming his glowing flag.

"Why so jumpy?" Morgan asks.

"I hate crowds."

"Then let's get out of it," she says. We've reached the back of the field, near the corn maze and the illuminated LABYRINTH sign. "Let's do the corn maze," she exclaims. "Before the line gets too long."

I've never been inside the corn maze, mostly because I hate tight spaces—the idea of getting trapped in there and not being able to find my way out.

"I can't."

"Why?"

I look around. *Relax, Diana will come*, I tell myself. There's nothing wrong. You still have time. "Come on," Morgan insists. "One more. Then you can do whatever it is you have to do."

"I don't have enough tokens."

"It's my shout."

Morgan leads me toward the line. In front of us, a group of friends decked out in glow sticks pay the entrance fee, and a clerk pulls aside a velvety rope, allowing them to pass through before closing it shut behind them. The air is colder here, away from the bonfires and crowd, and a bad feeling spreads in my stomach, not overtly wrong but a gentle sense of not-so-rightness. I tell myself it's just the aftershock of seeing that dying animal and my own doomed fate in romance.

"Oh, score," Morgan says, bending down to pick up a plastic flag that someone in the group in front of us must have dropped. She presses a button, illuminating her face, which is made spooky by the changing light. Blue, pink, green. "What are you afraid of?" Morgan asks then, catching me off guard. "I mean, aside from crowds and corn mazes."

"I don't know," I answer. "Heights, I guess. Why?"

She shrugs. "Isn't tonight the night we're meant to talk about all this?"

"I guess." I don't tell her a newer, fresher fear that has settled into my nightmares recently: the feeling of being cornered like my mother was when she ran through a burning forest and found herself on that cliff edge, face-to-face with the Hunter who took her life. I think, *It's over, I'm about to die and there's nothing I can do about it.* It's not fear that fills me then, but a deep regret. The fear of dying without the world knowing who I really am and what I'm capable of. Having wasted so much time being *comfortable* because I was afraid to be uncomfortable in the pursuit of the life I really wanted.

I feel jealous of the young Circo Klujns who are in the wild right now, facing their fears daily, experiencing temporary discomfort while chasing a destiny that's theirs. My comfort is nothing but a gilded cage.

"What about you?" I ask Morgan, deciding to make an effort.

"Eggs, as of tonight," she says with a chortle. "Snakes in toilets. Bats. Disease. And change. I really, *really* don't like change." There's something wicked in her eyes then, but it might just be the green gleam of the flag.

I notice Gora out of the corner of my eye, and she sees me, a look of recognition on her face like she was looking for me all along. Her mouth curves around the first syllable of a word as she takes a step toward me.

"Your turn," says the clerk, startling me. He unclips the velvet rope to let us pass. Morgan hands over her tokens, and as she does, her sweater rises up to reveal a little tattoo on her right wrist, but she pulls it back down before I can get a proper look at it.

As Gora moves closer and closer, Morgan takes my hand and pulls me into the waiting darkness.

5

The cornstalks are easily eight feet high, blackened by ash, reaching up toward the early winter sky, which is speckled with a few silver stars. The first quarter moon is a buttery yellow, the color of a sun diluted with a dash of white paint. In front of us, the sea of charred corn stretches out, punctuated by a few abandoned farmhouses. From where we are, it's impossible to tell how we're supposed to get out.

I swallow hard.

The group in front of us takes a turn, and the light of their glow sticks fades in the distance. One screams, setting off a chain of nervous shrieks and laughter. Morgan holds her flag like a sword in a duel against the night and loops her arm with mine for "protection," muscular under the fabric of her school sweater.

As we walk, the soot-covered leaves of the corn brush against my shoulders, stroking them like skeletal hands. Our shoes squish in the mud as we navigate the bends of the labyrinth. My breath steams in front of my face, laced with the faintest trace of sugar. When we hit our first dead end, my chest tightens, and the open sky does little to assuage my claustrophobia. But then we backtrack and find the correct path.

The group before us is gone now; no more voices or light to guide us. No matter where we go, everything looks the same, and the paths become tighter and tighter. I can't wait to find the exit, wrap my fingers around a hot drink, and find Diana.

"The key is not to panic," Morgan says. "When you panic, you make rash decisions, and that's when you get lost."

"How do we know that we're going the right way?"

"Landmarks," Morgan answers. "Listen. Do you hear that?"

Sure enough, a spooky soundtrack fills the night. Soft at first, then louder as we walk toward it. After another minute or two of walking, we reach a clearing in the corn. The path travels through a dilapidated farmhouse with dark windows and red flickering candles. The first landmark.

"We have to walk through it," Morgan says. We enter the desolate farmhouse, which has been converted into a Military Hospital of Horrors, with corridors of bloodstained bedsheets and dummies lying supine, stomachs held open by metal clamps, innards visible, pooling with thick blood. As we cross the morbid installation and recorded screams, I fear that people are hiding behind those hanging sheets, waiting to jump out and scare us . . . but luckily, no one does.

"The career counselor said I should think about becoming a Military nurse," Morgan tells me, "but I don't think I could handle the blood."

Back outside, the maze picks up where it left off. We continue along the slender pathways, left and right, hitting dead ends and then retracing our steps, falling into a rhythm of getting lost and being found. "As long as we keep crossing new landmarks, we'll know we're going the right way," Morgan explains.

"You speak from experience."

"We have a sunflower maze on Royal Mountain in Mission Creek, similar to this one."

"I thought you said you were from Justice Falls."

"Oh," she replies. "My mom and I go to Mission Creek from time to time. Feels like a second home."

After another couple of minutes, we hear music again and see the glow of orange lights. We follow them into a second clearing, where the path moves through a tribal campfire scene. There is a bonfire with a skeleton dangling across it, feet and hands bound around a stick. Another skeleton has been impaled by a spear that travels up its pelvis and out its open jaw, head tipped back like it swallowed the spear whole. The skeletons could look human, but they have a shimmer to them, something crystalline.

"They're not . . . *Klujn*?"

"No, dummy, they're props," Morgan answers. "Klujn bones are too expensive. Corpse medicine costs a fortune."

We continue through the maze, and the sky above our heads continues to darken, losing its remaining light. I can feel the passing of time as a physical thing, the inertia of the minutes slipping by faster than I feel comfortable with. We go through the third clearing—a swampy scene where an unfortunate Explorer has fallen prey to some slimy aquatic creature. Then, the fourth is a gallows with a hanging body and a black bag over its head.

"Must have been something," Morgan says, touching the shoe of the hanging prop, giving it a push so that she swings. "Back in the olden days when they were killing rebels left and right. We tend to forget how good we have it. That things could so easily go back to the way they were. What would you rather?" she asks me. "To be hung, burned, or beheaded? Sometimes, if you're lucky, the Executioner will let you choose." Her words give me a chill, even though she's just playing around.

"I'll take the fourth option," I say, then change the subject. "How many more landmarks, anyway?"

"Something tells me we're getting close to the end."

We walk for a few more minutes, then reach another landmark—a bus with blacked-out windows, like the ones from the raid. "No other way but through," Morgan mutters, already heading for the bus's open doors. She climbs aboard, and I follow, not wanting to be left behind. The bus creaks as we walk past the dummy driver and down the aisle. Instead of seats, the bus is full of cages stacked on top of one another.

"Found the exit," Morgan chimes, already at the back of the bus, but I've stopped halfway down, staring into a cage where there's a dark stain on the ground. *Blood?* Drawn on the wall in the bloodlike substance is a little rune. It feels like a prayer, a final plea to a god that may or may not be here. I have always loved scary things, but this is too real for my liking. The idea that this bus and these cages and that blood and those skeletons from before may not be props at all . . .

"Ava!" Morgan's voice brings me back to the moment, and I'm filled with a desire to get out of this maze as quickly as possible. It was stupid to come here. I have made myself a sitting duck, easy prey for my enemies, and by now, there are plenty.

I exit through the back, looking for Morgan, but she's gone. "Where are you?"

"Over here!" I follow her voice and reach a fork in the path. I choose the left and continue.

"Morgan?"

"Around the bend!" she says, but her voice has faded. "I found the exit!"

I turn left and reach the bus again. Backtrack, take a right, and end up where I started. My heart speeds up, and despite what Morgan said about panic, it swells around me like an angry ocean storm so tumultuous that I can no longer see the straight line of the horizon. I feel dizzy. I lose my bearings. I am a boat, tipping, tipping. I call out again, but there's no answer. Finally, after about a dozen frantic turns, I hear the drums. The music reaches into my chest and wraps around my heart. I feel faint all of a sudden, sleepy and dizzy at the same time. My hands begin to shake like my blood sugar has dropped, and my sweat is cold.

I walk on shaky legs through a tunnel in the corn until I reach a new clearing. There's no sign of Morgan or the exit. The moon illuminates a burned church. I'm curious if it's part of the maze or if I strayed from the route I was supposed to be on. I feel watched, but there's no one around. I shiver at the idea that a ghost or demon could be surveilling me, though I'm not even sure I believe in that sort of thing. Still, the feeling is unsettling.

There is a little cemetery in front of the church, a mound of dirt that appears to be a mass grave dotted with little tombstones like an underbite of broken teeth. Behind the cemetery, the charred church is still standing, black walls reaching up toward stained glass windows pointed like the sharp summits of mountains, with no ceiling. "Morgan?" I expect her to jump out from the shadows and reveal this as a prank, but she doesn't. I am completely alone. Although I still don't feel alone, observed by something I can't put my finger on.

As the pounding drums increase in tempo, my dizziness worsens, turning into a reeling vertigo. I will my legs to keep walking, to take me through the installation and back to the crowd, but they won't cooperate. The drums are beating everywhere, outside and inside me. I notice the silhouette of a large black bird perched on the stained glass, flittering like a dark mirage. I squint but can barely make it out. Whatever that bird is, it doesn't feel like a normal animal. Then there's a sound, like the clicking of talons, and the *whoosh* of giant wings taking flight, but no breeze follows. The bird-mirage vanishes, and I am alone again in the clearing.

I pick up my pace, beelining through the church and out the other side, but I'm so dizzy that I trip on a root and fall hard on my knees. The drumbeats intensify, and my hands hit the ground, padding against the cool earth, a painful echo running all the way up my delicate hands, sharp claws shifting uncomfortably in my fingers.

And then it happens . . . like a black curtain falling down around me.

The ground is no longer dirt but *sand.*

What is happening?

The night is hot all of a sudden, hot as summer, but this air is humid and tropical, clean-smelling. A warm, fragrant jungle breeze. The lapping of waves. I'm not in Red River anymore but on a beach. The drums continue. *Boom, boom, boom.* Only they're not drums, I realize, but *gunshots.*

For a second, I think I walked straight into one of the astras George described in class today. Or maybe I passed out from vertigo and hit my head, and my mind is piecing together all of my darkest memories and fears, layering them on top of one another in a nightmarish collage. But the world around me is too lucid to be a dream, more like a memory, only this is no memory of mine.

The moon sits low behind the trees, a thin crescent. The trees are tropical—palms or coconuts. Under the faint moonlight, I notice my skin is a shade darker, adorned in crystal jewelry and pink marks. And even more remarkable are the large claws that sprout from my fingertips; adult claws, clear as water but with a dormant black-gold shimmer inside them. A powerful, regal, feminine energy radiates from them.

Holy shit.

I touch my new body, careful not to cut myself, and see a rich violet costume beneath my hands, draped on a thicker frame, soft but muscular. My body has filled out. And those claws . . . I can't stop looking at them. What it feels like to *wear* them.

And then, instinct roars inside my body.

This is Estrella, I realize. *I am in my mother's body.*

Adult, woman, wild.

But how is it possible—to experience a memory that's not mine? To be a passenger inside her body, feeling what she felt, experiencing what she experienced, while still conscious that I'm *me*? I wasn't even in her womb then!

There are more gunshots—a violent *tack tack tack.*

It's the night of the raid.

I stand up, peering through the foliage where, at the center of the island, Hunters drag bodies into a pile while other bodies are carried in the opposite direction, toward the boats on the south side of the island. Brown-skinned Klujns with violet eyes flittering half-open in unconsciousness or death. I watch the Hunters, noticing a pattern to their work: the old and sick Klujns are thrown into the growing pile—*dead*—while the babies, the young, the healthy and fertile and able, are taken to the boats—*alive.*

The Hunter in charge signals left or right with a lazy swish of his wrist, determining the Klujns' fate with nonchalance. It's General Santos, in his late thirties. Frightening when he's serious but even more frightening when he smiles. A crystal-topped rifle hangs from his right shoulder.

I hear a low growl. A wolf is by my side—a tall, gracious

female with five white spots on her blue-black fur. Ears raised like tents, sapphire eyes searching, nose sniffing the night. She wants to stop the Hunters, but she and I both know we are outnumbered; we may be better at fighting flesh to flesh, but they have the advantage of having weapons that can kill from afar—an invention that shattered the careful balance of Nature.

"Mahta, *nho*." The words leave my mouth in Klujn dialect. The wolf—*Mahta*—stands back, listening to me, her master, her friend.

"Do a last sweep of the island," General Santos orders the other Hunters. "Take what you can and burn the rest. And keep a few disfigured ones for the circuses. If you can't find any—disfigure them yourselves."

Mahta and I move around the island, heading north, the moon still low enough that she casts long shadows for us to walk in. The warm night is fragrant with salt, seaweed, and coconuts, this side of the island not yet marred with slaughter. I pass the seaweed farms, then the reefs. I smell smoke—at the center of the island, the pile of bodies is lit. Sparks pop into the dark sky and drift back down as ash, giving the impression that it's snowing.

I reach the north side, my bare feet navigating the sharp rocks and the soft sand. I feel the Hunters' presence on the island diminishing. A dozen of them, then six, then three, until the island begins to feel still again. To human ears, it would sound almost quiet, but I hear the screeching of the trees, the ones at the center issuing a warning as the fire spreads, burning their trunks, their branches, their leaves, and all their knowledge.

There's the coughing of engines in the distance, the smell of gasoline. The first boats leave. As the fire spreads north, the animals leave their burning habitat and take refuge on the beach. Cornered, they will have to decide whether they would rather burn or drown. Hopefully, the smoke will ease them into sleep, so they won't have to make that decision.

I hear a little murmur. Mahta looks at me, her eyes speaking a language without words. *Familiar*, she says. *Safe.*

I step around a dune and see a little Klujn girl, her back pressed against the sand. "*Glorijah*," I exclaim. The girl is only three, but I—*me, Ava, the passenger*—recognize her. It's Glory. My mother seems to know her well. Glory shows me what the Hunters did: Her little fingers have been chopped above the middle knuckle to retrieve the virgin claws inside them. The Hunter who did it must have gone off in the pursuit of something else before he finished his task, something better, because her fingers are scattered in the sand.

I move quickly, helping Glory to collect her fingers, and together we find nine, the bloody flesh coated with sand like candies rolled in flakes of coconut. I rip a bit of my costume off, put her fingers inside, and then place the bundle into a pocket in my skirt. I tell Glory I will try to reattach them, even though I know it won't work. Viaţăs are incredibly sensitive and susceptible to even the slightest injury, like the break of a bone or a sliced tendon. It would be a miracle if she can keep her hands, and that is if she can even survive until morning.

Glory places her small mutilated hand in mine, and we continue along the beach, the smoke growing denser, the trees continuing to shriek, and the animals amassing in a blind panic. A few Klujn bodies are scattered on the beach, ripped of claws, clothing, eyeballs, crystals, and anything else deemed valuable by their assailants. Lives wasted in the Hunters' haste to take and take. And then I see Diablo, hunched over his father's dead body. Like Glory, he isn't crying. He glares toward the boats that took his mother, so much contempt in his eyes for a boy around six.

"*Vejm*," I say, putting aside my own feelings. *Come.* But

before I can move, Mahta growls, and I hear a *click*. I turn around and find myself looking down the barrel of a rifle, a crystal bayonet, the highest rank. Behind it, a Hunter in his late thirties, the same age as the general but not at all like the general. His buddy. Pale skin, bearded, green eyes. And, despite his age and experience, he doesn't belong here. His energy is not ruthless like the others; it is more balanced in the feminine. And he doesn't have a limp yet. *George.*

Mahta bares her teeth, stepping toward the Hunter. *Wait*, I think, and my wolf listens, holding back. The Hunter could kill us all in a single round if she attacks.

"Shame on you," I whisper, like a curse. "Everything you do to us, you're doing to yourselves." There's a standoff—between George and my angry mother. My mother doesn't cower or recoil, and I feel what it is to be in the body of someone truly fearless. I feel the full force of her claws, the heat and energy and power of them, like lava under a rock, pressing, pressing. Able to explode and form new mountain ranges.

George's eyes are still on her—on *me*—and it's like he's just seen a rare and exotic bird, wondering if he should capture it to enjoy its beauty in a cage or let it stretch its wings and fly free. George teeters between greed and reason, head and heart. Finally, after an endless moment, he lowers his rifle. His radio crackles, then.

"All clear on the south side." I hear the general's voice. "Doc?"

George takes a moment to reply, and when he finally answers, there's a slight tremor there. "All clear on the north."

And then he leaves before he can change his mind.

This is their first meeting, I realize. But, judging by the way he talked about her earlier, it mustn't have been the last.

The breeze picks up, a hot wind carrying another wave of

sparks. There are so many animals on the beach now, gathered and frightened, but I only have two hands, and they are already occupied. Before the Hunter can change his mind and turn back, I take Glory and Diablo and run.

Fractured images flicker through my consciousness.

Swimming through an underwater forest.

Caves and crystals and pockets of air.

The mainland, a beach of green sand, just as the sun pierces the horizon.

Glory, Diablo, and I watch the sunrise, a ritual spent in silence. The sky is orange and hazy from the smog of the burning island. Glory cries, face buried in my breast, but Diablo is quiet. His eyes are fixed on the sun as though hoping that blindness will help him forget. How do you explain to a child that his father died when he didn't have to, hunted for the crystals in his hands? That his mother was taken for breeding or science or entertainment, a future spent in a cage? That the magic in our hands is despised by humans, who are afraid of the things they don't understand? Who cannot bear the thought that Klujns are not primitive creatures but Nature's solution to what humans did to the planet?

I don't need to explain. Diablo's little violet eyes already understand.

Viață. Sparked into existence thousands of years ago by the planet's premonition of the pressures it would face; her secret plan to heal the forests and the oceans after Sapiens' passage here on earth. The *seed of life*, provoked by the dying heartbeat of the earth, the shrieking frequency of burning forests, warming oceans, bleached coral, melting glaciers, the cry of the animal who faces extinction and the song of the dying birds.

Mahta goes to find food and returns a while later, dropping a few roots and berries on the ground. Then she digs a shelter for us in the sand and retrieves a few fallen palm branches for shade. Tonight, we will venture out in search of a new stand.

Glory has fallen asleep against my chest, her fingers cauterized by the salt water. I open the fabric bundle—as I feared, her fingertips are already black and putrid. Without speaking, Diablo takes them, squeezing the little virgin crystals out of the flesh. Then, he goes to the water's edge, cleans them, and makes a necklace. This is the way of our kind—to keep creating in the face of destruction. To find light and beauty in the darkness.

6

A splash of cold water hits me in the face. I look up to see that I'm back in my body, kneeling at the exit of the maze. The shrieks from the Estrella raid turn into screams of amusement as the end of the Swampland Safari Log Ride wagon tips down the metal slide.

How is it possible? To experience a memory that wasn't mine two years before I was born? The way it felt to be in her skin, inhabiting the body of someone brave who didn't hesitate to take action, even after she saw everyone she knew killed. She stood up to George and looked down the barrel of his rifle. She didn't flinch when she saw Glory's mutilated fingers.

Hunters missed her that night, but they got her later, I think, remembering Glory's story about how my mother was caught in the swamplands. The rest is still a mystery . . . where she was taken, how I was born, how she escaped, and who my father is.

I stand up and shake life into my legs, look around. The sky is a deep marine blue, the stars sharp. It feels late, *too* late, and I realize how stupid I was to follow Morgan into the maze and risk missing the buses because I didn't dare to speak up and do what I really wanted.

And then, before I can shield myself, Gora the butcher is there. I expect her strong fingers to grab me by the neck, or perhaps she has a little Klujn knife tucked in her belt like Coll had, one she uses when she slices up dead animals. But I don't feel any pain. Instead, Gora presses her shoulder into mine and issues a warning.

"The girl you're with," she says. "She's a—"

But before Gora can finish her sentence, she notices something in the crowd, and her eyes widen. She vanishes like a pebble dropped into a dark pond.

"There you are." I see Morgan holding a shimmery white drink in her hand. "Mother's milk," she says. "It's Klujn milk. Expensive but worth every token. You want some?" I shake my head. "Don't worry, you're not the only one," Morgan says, gesturing to the glow-stick group where a boy is bent over, throwing up in a trash can. But the cause of my nausea is not harmless entertainment.

"What time is it?" I ask Morgan. She glances at her watch, sleek and silver and expensive.

"Half to six," she says. *Thirty minutes left before the buses.* But it feels later than that, like we were in the maze longer, the sky darker than it should be at this time. I try to see where Gora went or if Diana has finally shown up, but there's no sign of either. Looking around, I notice a few people whispering nervously, and a tense aura hangs in the air like low clouds.

"What's going on?"

"There was an execution," Morgan answers. "In Justice Falls. I overheard someone talking about it when I was waiting in line."

"A Klujn?"

"Humans," she says. "Rebels." *Plural.*

"Why?"

Morgan shrugs, indifferent. We may as well be talking about

the weather. "A house was discovered with contraband in it. I guess the DSO wants to send a message. Can't have people walking around thinking they can get away with that sort of thing. Mom always says all it takes is a small spark to start a wildfire, and those rebels are nothing but cigarette butts."

Morgan shakes the ice in her beverage and slurps up the last sip. "It's sad," she says, and her voice is eerie now, "that they can't accept the world we live in and be grateful for all the work our President is doing. They always want more. They want *progress* and *change*, and you know how much I don't like *change*."

Morgan tosses her empty cup in the grass. Her words don't sit right. *An execution. Rebels. Contraband.* I think of George's basement study and all its treasures . . . if someone were to tip off the DSO, he would be a dead man. *Hung, burned, or beheaded*—Morgan's words. "I need to get home," I say. *I need to make sure Diana is safe.* I should have listened to that bad feeling in my gut, hard like the seed of a peach. I go to walk past Morgan, but she steps in front of me, blocking my way.

"Where are you going?"

"*Home*," I say again. I go to sidestep her, but she blocks me again.

"To see *Diana*?" Morgan pulls a silver scrunchie off her wrist and ties her hair back in a ponytail. Her sleeve reaches up again, and I see the little tattoo on her wrist—a triangle. *Military, first year.* She ties her bangs away from her face, and there's a streak of silver in her hair that's not paint. "I'm sorry, *dummy*, but it's too late."

I freeze, staring at Morgan and those eyes that now look dangerous. "She's been on a government watchlist forever," says Morgan. "President's been a little soft on her in the past because she *is* his godson's mother. But with these recent findings—he's not taking any chances. The DSO is at your house right now."

Morgan pulls out the plastic flag tucked in her belt, lit red now, casting spooky shadows up her face. I see a knife tucked there as well.

"I'm not actually from Justice Falls," she says. "I'm from Mission Creek. And my mom didn't actually work in a Loudhouse—that was my dad. After three weeks of working there after the Corthu raid, the coward killed himself. Now, Mom and I have to fend for ourselves. She works at the DSO, and I'm interning there."

Gora's warning comes back to me—

The girl you're with. She's a . . . spy.

"Let's play a game," Morgan says. "You're the wolf, and I'm the Superhunter." She flicks through the color settings until she finds blue. "How do the rules work again? Oh yeah. One, two, three—"

Then she whistles, shrill and sharp, symbolizing the start of the game.

Morgan waves her little flag. "*Run.*"

7

The field is crowded now, and I have to elbow my way through to clear myself a path. I'm reminded of the night that I was cornered by Coll and his thugs, but a bully with a grudge doesn't feel as frightening as the girl behind me now. A spy. A DSO trainee in her first year of Military training, hungry to prove herself.

Where is she? Is she following?

I should have known that something was off; I should've trusted my instinct. I opened up too quickly because she was *nice to me*. I feel so stupid.

I make it up to the town square, already panting. My blood warms, shielding me from the cold like a thin blanket. A clock tower above a shop shows it's ten to six—Morgan lied about the time, and now I don't have much of it. I find the Military road and sprint down it, eyes scanning the distance for something unusual—a van, people in uniforms, sirens—but the road is quiet. Maybe I am the unusual thing, the running animal, muscles screaming after weeks without use. Like a wolf on a full moon, buttons bursting, hair sprouting, turning feral.

Shin splints make my tibias feel like they're splintering like an axe to a log, but I can't stop. The road is smooth, but here I'm too exposed. I slow to a jog and move to the shoulder and the shadows there, where the asphalt meets the weeds.

As I run, I replay the entire day and my every interaction with Morgan, from home studies to the corn maze. Searching back through what I said, what I did, racking my brain—trying to remember if I crossed a line, but I don't think I did, did I? Morgan mustn't know who I am, *what* I am. She must think I'm just a rebel's daughter—but if rebels are being hung, that's hardly safer.

Report Unusual Behavior. The DSO's motto comes back to me, the one that screams out from every silver poster. I shiver at the thought that a single comment or piece of contraband is enough to sign your death warrant. Though it's not like Grouse needs permission to kill. There are no courts, no justice, no laws, only the President's moods and whims.

I reach a crossroads at the bottom of the hill. To the left is the mouth of the gravel driveway that leads toward my house, and to the right, the Military road continues past a few isolated houses toward a parked bus destined for Scouts, its engine rumbling. Beyond it, the Military checkpoint sits on the edge of town.

And then, in the distance, as faint as a mirage . . . a silver van, moving into darkness. Three letters painted on the side.

No. It can't be.

But it's gone before I can get confirmation.

I turn left, heading down the driveway toward my house, the cherrywoods on the left and invasive plants to my right, as tall as the corn in the maze. I slow my jog to a walk because the night is quiet, and my footsteps are loud on the gravel. The mouth of the driveway is too risky, so I cut into the weeds toward the back of the house. The plants don't seem to want to make room for my body, and I wrestle with them, scratching up my arms and legs. I stop when I reach the edge of vegetation and peer out at the south side of my house. Everything looks normal and quiet. The porch, the hammock. I smell smoke, but nothing is coming from the chimney. Diana refuses to use precious firewood until late in the season when we start shivering under our thickest layers.

Inside, the kitchen lights are on. Colorful jars lined up on the window sill, fruit and vegetables fermenting inside them. A mug sits on the breakfast bar, still steaming. A gift-store one, and not the one Diana usually uses. The heat has activated a design in the ceramic. *Between Lakes*, it reads, with an image of a sunflower. I keep waiting for Diana to move into the frame, pick up that cup, blow on it, and take a sip, but she doesn't.

The seconds continue to tick by, and dread grows inside me. *I should have come home sooner.* But I didn't know what was going to happen. *Did Diana? Is this why she didn't want me to come home?* But if Diana knew the DSO was coming, she would have done something about it.

And then I see it—the smoke. It's coming from the basement, pressing against the blue half-moon windows. The flames come next, orange flames, licking at the glass until it cracks.

Wolf.

If Diana is gone, is he down there? Or did he make it out? I'm about to leave my hiding spot when I hear footsteps. Morgan reaches the end of the driveway and enters the clearing from the west, looking excited by the chase. She pulls her knife from her belt and her watch snags on it, falls silently onto a bed of leaves, but Morgan doesn't notice. She had plenty of chances to kill me in that maze. Unless her mission was to keep an eye on me or catch me. Still, the way her fingers dance along the knife's handle tells me she is willing and able to use it.

"If anyone enjoys a chase, it's the President," she calls out, knowing that I'm here, somewhere, hiding in the darkness. Then her nose sniffs the air, and she walks around to the front of the house.

I watch as the fire reaches the first floor, burning surprisingly fast, smacking its lips at the delicious taste of cherry timber. The kitchen is engulfed in smoke so thick I can no longer see the bottles in the window, the mug. *Pop, pop, pop.* There's the cracking of overheated glass, like shooting bottles at the fair; succumbing to the rapid transition from cold to hot. I watch as the flames spread from the first floor to the second. I see Mercy's bedroom as the fire devours a shelf of trains and fire trucks and trophies. I imagine my own room burning, making an inventory of everything I am losing as I am losing it. My comfortable bed. My books. My clothes. My makeup and jewelry and art supplies. Even Glory's pendant—despite how much I hate what it represents, it's a reminder of her. All these things I took for granted because they were just *there*, and now they're gone. I have nothing left in this world except the clothes on my back—a uniform I hate—and shoes that give me blisters.

Watching my house burn, I have never felt more powerless. There are no sirens in the distance, no help on the way. The volunteer firefighters are all too busy at the fair. The smell of smoke will blend with the bonfire in town, and no one will even realize anything has happened until it's too late.

I can only pray that Wolf wasn't in the basement. But the sky above my head feels big and empty, no higher power looking down on me, wishing me the best. I feel as alone as ever. *I would have heard him howl, wouldn't I?* My clever Wolf, surely he would have found a way out. Unless he was already dead when the person lit the match . . .

My throat clamps shut. I can hardly breathe. The smoke stings my eyes, and I can't hold them back anymore, the tears that have been pushing at the surface of me all day. They finally release, carving virgin trails down my soot-covered cheeks. The fire shoots sparks, and I take a step back. I am my mother, watching her island burn to the ground. I feel her panic—now if only I could have her courage. The smoke itches my throat, a strong flavor like a swallowed ember, and I cough before I can stifle it.

The foundation weakens, and the second-floor crumbles into the first, hissing and spitting. With the house now lying flat, I see Morgan across the flames—and she sees me. "There you are!"

I'm out of time.

I turn my back on my house and run, ignoring the dull pain in the arches of my feet. At the mouth of the driveway, I see a glint—Morgan's watch. I scoop it up then resume my sprint. The watch is diamond-shaped and digital, showing me that it's two minutes to six.

I make it back to the road and turn left with a minute remaining. In the distance, I see the bus. The driver climbs on board, closes the doors, and the bus starts to roll away.

"Wait!" I yell. My voice is raspy from the smoke. I run as fast as I can and finally reach the bus, banging on the doors until it stops. The driver opens them and looks down at me, a face I haven't seen before. He studies my school uniform, my tear-stained cheeks, and the lack of an overnight bag in my hand, then shakes his head and *tsks* at my naivety.

"Your name?"

"Ava . . . Sparrow," I manage, afraid that at any moment he

will reveal himself to be a DSO worker in civilian clothes, just like Morgan. Or that this bus is full of cages instead of seats. He looks at a clipboard, traces his pencil down a list of names, and then scratches the unmistakable outline of a tick.

"Assumed you weren't coming," he says. "Like the others. Hurry along now."

I slip the watch into my pocket, climb up the steps and walk down the aisle. There are only half a dozen girls, casting nervous looks at me as I walk by. I recognize a few girls from my home studies class wearing seafoam-colored sweaters with CAMP WILLOW written on them. Before they can ask me what I'm doing here, I slip into the sticky leather of the back seat.

I look out the large window behind me at the panorama of our town. A trail of gray rises up from the bonfire. To the right, another trail rises from my house. Morgan emerges onto the Military road and looks around. She does a slow pivot and sees the bus. *Did she see me?*

We reach the Military checkpoint, but the two soldiers stationed at the edge of town are busy with a game of dice. They wave us through absent-mindedly, flashlights and guns staying tucked in their belts.

After we clear the checkpoint, I can finally breathe again. I'm relieved to be away, but how long before Morgan follows me? Does she know where I went? *Maybe this is all one cruel practical joke.* But that doesn't explain my burning house and Diana's absence . . .

My nose pressed against the glass, I take one last look at the town, unsure if I will ever see this place again. Once more, I've been thrust into a journey I'm not ready for. If I had been braver, acted earlier, I could have left on my own terms, with Wolf by my side. But instead, I hesitated and almost got caught in the trap as it snapped shut.

As my breath fogs the window, the bus takes a turn and Red River fades from view. My old life is gone. My home. Like my mom, plunging into the ocean . . . Entering the jungle to find a new stand that would take her in. And by now, I know—that story doesn't end well.

8

The drive to Tremble Hills takes thirty minutes on an average day, but nothing about tonight is normal. There are endless dead woods to the left and flat fields to the right. Powerplants and Greenhouses, with their endless rows of cafos—animal sheds—and colorful sewage ponds. Slowly, the forest starts up again, and the silhouette of Black Mountain becomes visible, but the road we would typically take has been closed by a septic leak, the driver tells us, and we have to pick up some Scouts in Justice Falls.

Justice Falls is a quaint and scenic town. The main street has a row of cute shops, a stone bridge, and a rolling waterfall. But the streets are empty tonight, a ghost town.

Outside the high school, eight Scouts are huddled together in a tight, suspicious cluster, speaking in whispers. They wear black sweaters with CAMP MIDNIGHT written on them. As they climb aboard the bus, I survey them—a pair of lanky, brown-skinned twins; a round, pale girl with shaved platinum hair and dangling flower earrings; a Black girl with bright green dreadlocks; another Black girl with peach-colored braids who is crying; and a few others, all unique in their own ways. In their quirkiness, they all remind me a little bit of Wendy. I wonder if they knew her—if they are Scouts, they surely did, but now is not the time for conversation.

The Justice Falls girls sit a few rows in front of me as the bus stalls at a road closure in the center of town.

"First time?"

I startle, turning to see one of the twins staring at me, a bright smile on her face and little silver heart earrings stuck to her earlobes. She seems friendly, but after tonight, I don't feel like taking any chances.

"You shouldn't talk to strangers," her seat partner—the one with shaved white hair—whispers.

The girl ignores her, then turns to look at me again with the air of a camp counselor or a team captain. "I'm Maple."

I consider not answering, but it seems impolite. Plus, the bus is sitting idle and we still have a ways to go before we reach the camp.

"Ava."

There's a spark of recognition in her eyes, or maybe that's just my paranoia.

"Did you pack a bag?" Maple asks.

I shake my head, feeling stupid—I know what she's probably thinking. That I'm the kind of girl who goes to Scouts and gets homesick on the first night, missing her friends, her mom, and her favorite food. It's hard to let someone be wrong about you, but it's safer than trying to prove her wrong. "Don't worry, they have stuff there," Maple offers, with the sort of kindness that feels genuine and not a ruse like Morgan's. Still, I keep my guard up because I don't want to be tricked again.

"The vending machine undies are surprisingly comfortable. Apparently, they're made of minerals." I don't answer, but this doesn't deter Maple, who continues. Her openness reminds me of Wendy who, on our harrowing trek to Circo, couldn't help but make polite, trivial conversation. "When we get there, I'll show you the ropes," she says. "We're in charge of packing our own bags, and we're allowed to bring ten essential items."

"Ten?"

"That's right," Maple grins. "The main concern this time of year is the cold. You'll need a good tent and a firestone."

"What's a firestone?"

"It works like a flint. You scrape it until you get a spark. Unless you can find fire crystals, which are incredibly rare, this is probably the most important item you could have."

Maple continues giving me a crash course I didn't ask for, but one for which I'm grateful. "You'll want a good sleeping bag and a mat, because the ground is like a leech—it sucks the heat from your body. A water bottle, but preferably a thermos, to keep your water from freezing," Maple counts these items off on her hands. She has already used up five fingers, and there are still plenty of things to cover.

"I always take a ration of food," she says. "The pasta is my favorite—all you have to do is add boiling water. Then, you'll want a purification wand. Never, *ever* drink stagnant water—it can host a slurry of bacteria. Even running water is dangerous because if anything died upstream, you could get very sick.

"Once food and water are sorted, you're going to need a first aid kit. And a headlamp—the solar-charging ones are the best. Finally, you're going to need some kind of weapon—a machete for clearing trails, opening fruit and nuts and whatnot; a knife for making tinder; an axe for chopping wood. Your choice."

"That's already ten," I say. Maple has run out of fingers, but there are still plenty of things I'd like to bring. Like tampons or pads, since my period is due in a few days. A beanie, some gloves, and a scarf would be nice, as well as a pair of hiking boots. All I have is my school uniform.

The bus finally starts moving again, and Maple turns back to face the front.

"Better close your curtains," the driver calls out. A few of the girls oblige, but not me, and not Maple, either.

We peer out the window to our left at the main square, and I see what the driver was trying to shield us from: Six bodies hang side by side at the gallows, nooses around their necks. The bodies have black straw bags over their heads. Judging by their clothing, there are four women and one man. The sixth—and most disturbing of all—is a *dog*.

Blue words are spray-painted on the beam above them: REBELS WILL HANG.

For a second, I think it's a prop set, like the one in the corn maze. But then I remember what Morgan said about the executions. The deserted streets, the haunted feeling in the air, and the Scouts' suspicious whispers . . . they're not props. Only one town over,. The rebels who worked in codes and silence, who never gave up hope for a free world. Hung without a trial. But nothing in our world is fair—the good die, and the most violent survive. There is little respect for life. This is a statement. A display. A warning to the denizens. *This could so easily be your fate.*

I look at the dog's lifeless body, feeling sickened by it. A Labrador retriever, I think it is. Or *was*. I wonder where it came from—pets have been outlawed since the Before Klujn era. Maybe it was being kept underground, like I was keeping Wolf. A mother that had pups, and the pups had more pups, and so on, because where would you even find a dog that's not wild? Once food became scarce and there was only enough for humans, kill shelters were overcrowded, Diana once told me, and those that weren't euthanized were released into the wild.

"Apparently, after they found the contraband," Maple whispers my way, pointing toward the dog. "They started going around to all the houses and interrogating people. There was a lot of finger-pointing . . . Some people started setting their houses on fire to hide whatever was in there. Can you *imagine*? I guess it's only a matter of time before they start going around from town to town as well." Hope leaps in my rib cage: *What if Diana did the same?* "Hallow's parents were among them," Maple says, pointing to the crying girl with the peach braids.

We look on for as long as we can, like we're on a horror safari. My labyrinthine thoughts return like they did when I saw the dying creature in the avarice egg, wondering who those rebels were, what they did wrong, and how they must have felt. They woke up this morning, dressed, and had breakfast, not knowing what lay ahead—that their ordinary routine was a ritual of last rites. And those ignorant villagers, turning on each other. People who've never ventured outside their townships but whose limited vantage point of the world has made them fear anything foreign or strange. People who eat and drink and wear crystals and beaks around their necks. Who believe that they need wolf tongues and corpse medicine to help them procreate instead of wondering why their sick bodies don't work the way they should because of the poison in their food, in the water, and in the air.

Poison people in a poisoned world.

It could so easily be George or Diana or even me up there. If Grouse wanted us dead, all he would have to do is flick his wrist and make it happen, then toss our bodies in an unmarked grave. Made to disappear from the face of the earth. But Diana told me after the raid that Grouse keeps people he has use for, and my parents may be cunning enough to have made themselves invaluable.

As the bus takes a sharp right and begins an uphill climb, those painted words are imprinted on my mind: REBELS WILL HANG.

I can't live in a world where the simple act of my existence could have me hunted or slain. Where my animality makes me a constant target.

Humans have forgotten where they come from, forgotten the family tree from which their million-year-old branches descend, and perhaps this selective amnesia makes them the most dangerous animal of all.

9

"*Widowmaker*," Maple says, and I duck, narrowly missing the scraggly branch of a dead tree. The bus dropped us off at the bottom of a hill, and the Scouts and I walk up the rest of the way, following the tire tracks of four-by-fours etched into the hardened mud. "A *widowmaker* is a dead tree with hazardous branches that could fall in a storm or wind," Maple explains, continuing the lesson she started on the bus. "Remember to always look *up*. You never want to place your shelter under one—it could be the last thing you do. If a branch falls on your tent, you're a dead man."

"Dead *woman*," says the shaved-hair girl with one facial expression—stern. At least she has stopped telling Maple not to talk to me.

"That's Dot," Maple tells me. "She's a plant expert." She points to Dot's neighbor, the girl with green dreadlocks, who wears a goofy grin. "And that's Ivy, our resident mycophile. If it has to do with mushrooms, then she's your girl."

"What else do I need to know?" I ask Maple.

"You want to make camp next to a water source. But not

too close because with rainfall, rivers can swell, and flash floods are a real problem. And the rain," she adds.

"What about the rain?"

"Stay out of it. If you get wet in cold weather—or if your gear gets wet—then you're—"

"A dead woman," Dot finishes.

"Hypothermia will make you feel all sorts of things," Ivy adds, twisting her head back to look at me. "And alive is not one of them." I smile, reminded of the friends I made at Circo—how quickly the conversations came and how at ease we felt around each other. *Justice Falls girls.*

"Lots of things can kill you out there," Maple continues. "And some of them aren't as obvious as you'd think. A simple scratch will do it. A sprained ankle. A bite from a mosquito that carries flesh-eating spirits."

"A plant or flower," from Dot.

"A mushroom," from Ivy. "And there are mean crystals, too."

"*Mean* crystals?!"

It feels good to be out in the forest again, even though this is merely a forested *driveway*, and there are no animals around, but the smell that hangs is earthy and alive. The air feels cleaner too, and all my senses light up, waking me from the coma I've been in.

"You learned all this at Scouts?" I ask them.

"Going on seven years now," Maple answers proudly, pointing to a row of sewn-on badges on her chest. "You have to be patient with yourself. Learning doesn't happen overnight."

"What are those for?"

"First aid," she says, pointing to her first badge. "Archery. Shelter-building. Fire craft. Knot-tying. Fishing. Basket-making. Weaving. Independence—that's my most recent one. I got it during fall break. It means I can survive a whole night on my own.

"I don't have my foraging one yet," Maple continues. "Dot and Ivy are our foraging experts, and I've been relying too heavily on them. It's hard to learn when you have an expert around."

"What can you forage this time of year?" I ask.

"Winterberries, mostly," Dot says. "A handful of flowers, roots, and shoots, and then after the frost, it's mostly pine and *vegera*—if you're lucky enough to find it."

"*Vegera?*"

"It's a plant protein that grows on or inside certain trees," she explains. "It mimics the taste and smell of meat."

"That's the problem out here," Ivy says, pointing a finger in all directions. "A lot of things look like other things, one delicious and the other poisonous."

"How can I tell if a plant is poisonous?"

"Rub it against your lips," Dot says. "Wait a few minutes. If your lips swell—it's poison."

"Except for Pink Flower," Ivy adds with a grin. "The most poisonous flower in the world—a single touch can kill you. But it can also cure any ailment." I scrunch my face up at the contradictory statement.

"How does that work?"

Ivy shrugs. "One of the many mysteries of Klujns and their flowers." I deflate. The wild is so big, and I am so small, and there is so much out there for me to know. It's one thing to be given a quick lesson like this, but it's another to be on my own, face-to-face with these foreign plants, *one delicious and one poisonous*, as Ivy said, suddenly doubting my limited knowledge of plants.

Dot picks a winterberry off a shrub, pinches it between her fingers, then eats it. "Hmmm," she says. "Delicious."

"How can you be sure of anything?" I ask.

"You can talk to them," says Ivy.

"Talk to whom?"

"Plants."

Ivy grins—she isn't joking. "Plant language is just like crystal language. It's a frequency that some Klujns can tap into, and some humans. When you reach that frequency—like a radio channel—you can ask the plant permission to pick it, and then it tells you *yes* or *no*. Mr. Wilder says that most of the time, it'll say yes because plants want to help us. Mushrooms, too. But don't bother asking a rock or mineral—they just want to be left alone."

Mr. Wilder.

The name Diana mentioned.

"Don't worry—I'm still working on my plant communication skills," Maple offers, nudging me with her bony shoulder. "Time is your ally and a lot of it is trial and error."

"Unless you cross Pink Flower," Ivy mutters. "Then it's just error."

"I hope we get to see the blooming of the moonflowers," Maple continues. "They're a fascinating flower—the seed stays buried underground for years, living in darkness. Then, when it's finally ready, it sprouts up and grows about nine feet in as many hours. Then, they bloom—all at the same time and only for one night. Apparently, it's the most beautiful thing you could ever see with your eyes. Even more beautiful than a migration of invisible animals . . ."

"Wow," I say, entranced at the thought. Although I don't understand what *invisible animals* are—or how you're supposed to see them, given their name. "Is Mr. Wilder your Scout leader?"

"He is, and he's the best," Maple answers. "He used to teach at the university in Mission Creek, and he'd take his classes out into the wild. Before the fences, of course."

I want to know more—about this Mr. Wilder, and his

possible link to Diana—but I don't want to rouse suspicion, so I put my curiosity on ice for the time being.

As we continue to walk, I imagine a different story for my life, one where I was born in Justice Falls to nice normal parents and had a sister like Maple. Where I went to Scout camp on weekends and school breaks and was friends with Dot, Ivy, and the others. How different life could have been. And, perhaps, a lot less lonely.

I know I can't grieve the past—regret is useless. Still, I hate the time I wasted not living the life I wanted, being *free.* I feel like I'm still waiting for my life to begin. I want to have a home, a family, a stand. A community that loves me. But where does that exist, and who is it with? These girls only accept me because they think I'm human. They would run for the hills if they glimpsed my purple eyes . . .

Finally, we reach the top of the driveway where a large sign reads: TREMBLE HILLS SCOUT ACADEMY.

Behind it, a large log cabin.

There are groups of girls spilling out from the cabin, wearing different-colored sweaters. Seafoam, prune, pale yellow, brown. It's surprising that camp wasn't canceled in lieu of the executions, but this is how our world works, I guess: People die, and life goes on. We are just numbered jerseys that can always be filled with new players.

"We're here," Maple announces. "This is where we eat, pack, fill our thermoses, and then head out."

"Where are you going tonight?"

"Each group has a different camp," Maple says, gesturing to the words on her sweater. "Ours is Camp Midnight."

The one closest to the fences.

Is it a coincidence?

Are the Scouts *really* going to the camp, or are they going somewhere else? Beyond it? Could they be trying to escape—which is why Diana wanted me to go with them?

There are humans who live in the wild . . . more than you realize.

"There he is," Maple says, perking up, and I turn to look at Mr. Wilder. The Scout leader looks tired and weary, about sixty, with frizzy hair and thick glasses that magnify his small, dark, melancholy eyes. He is half Black and half Indigenous and has the look of a mad scientist. Mr. Wilder's eyes lock in on mine with an air of scrutiny . . . or familiarity.

Did Diana manage to pass along a secret message, and ask him to bring me along?

Just as I may be familiar to him, the Scout leader is also familiar to me too, for a very different reason.

And then it hits me like a thunderclap—

Mr. Wilder, the Scout leader, is Wendy's *father*.

The Justice Falls girls join their leader, but my legs are still stuck in place. Then, Mr. Wilder breaks away from the group and walks towards me.

"Diana said you were . . ." he whispers.

At Circo.

"Do you know . . ."

What happened to my daughters.

We stare at each other for a moment that echoes eternity. There is so much sadness in his eyes, and I realize that knowing what happened may set him free.

And so I tell him, watching the Scout leader's eyes cloud over at the mention of Willa's fate. Willa, who sacrificed herself to save her sister.

When I tell him about Wendy's escape, something new replaces his sorrow—

Hope.

Wendy, who made it all the way to the end, who escaped, who is still free, but who may easily be dead . . .

"Thank you," he says. "You'll be safe with us."

Mr. Wilder hands me a sweater with the words CAMP MIDNIGHT on it, and I take it. Something releases in my chest: I have been *invited*.

There's the distant rev of an engine coming up the driveway—perhaps a bus with an adventurous driver.

Mr. Wilder and his Scouts begin to file inside the cozy cabin.

"Ava? Are you coming?" Maple asks, realizing that I am still rooted to the spot, holding Mr. Wilder's offering.

I look at their group. I could go with them wherever they're going, with all their wisdom, knowledge, and supplies. That's why Diana sent me here. But that would be the safer choice, wouldn't it? The easy one? To accept that I'm not good enough for the wild and destined to live the rest of my life between two worlds because I was too afraid to try?

Not human enough to be human, not Klujn enough to be Klujn.

But then I remember what George said—that I deserve more than safety; that I deserve to be happy.

Despite his many flaws, George was right about that. What I want is happiness, belonging, *and purpose*—and it's the first time in my life that I've been able to admit that. Maybe it's because I'm so close to the wild that I can feel it beckoning, the moon's energy charging my bones with a force still unknown to me. Or perhaps it's that by tomorrow, Diablo will be gone: my last link to Circo, to Daciana and her endless knowledge. If he dies, I will lose that link forever, like a treasure trove dropped into the ocean without coordinates. Sinking into the abyssal zone, forever irretrievable. I can't bring myself to let him die, knowing there's something

I could have done to save him. Going to the Loudhouse *is* suicidal, but it's what my birth mother would have wanted—it's what she would have done.

Suddenly, I'm ravaged by a desire to push myself, to go to the depths of myself and explore my animal parts. This is finally my chance to make my own decisions—even if those decisions are wrong. At least they will be mine.

"I can't come with you," I mutter. Maple looks confused, but Mr. Wilder nods solemnly—he understands. He leaves me the freedom to make my own decision, which is terrifying, and makes me second-guess everything. But now is not the time for doubt—now is the time for action.

I see a slash of headlights through the foliage. And another. Not a bus, but two Military jeeps.

By the fear in Mr. Wilder's eyes, I understand two things: The Military is looking for someone, and that someone is *me*. To stay with the Scouts would mean to put them in grave danger.

Mr. Wilder and I exchange a rapid, silent conversation.

Are you sure? he asks me with his eyes. *Once we're gone, there'll be no finding us again.*

I nod.

"Be safe," I tell the group.

"You too," Maple answers, who is no longer smiling now, but afraid just like her leader.

"Lose an eye," says Mr. Wilder. "It's an old Klujn proverb."

"Lose an eye," I echo, and for a second, I see Wendy in his eyes.

"And whatever you do," Ivy says, "if you see Pink Flower—walk rapidly in the opposite direction."

Then the Military cars screech to a halt and the doors crack open, the soldiers' eyes scanning the darkness like the light-beam of a prison tower . . .

Before they can notice me, I slip into the forest, heading down a trail marked by a little black triangle.

"Camp Midnight, here I come," I tell the night, but the night doesn't answer back. I'm alone. More alone than I've ever been in all my life.

10

After placing some distance between me and the camp, I ditch my school sweater and put on my new one. Even though I left the group behind, it makes me feel connected to them somehow. Then I strap Morgan's watch to my left wrist. I don't like the feel of the cold metal against my skin, or the memory of the girl who wore it, but it is extremely practical—with a clock, compass, timer, and thermometer, among countless other features—so I decide to keep it for the time being. It's eight p.m., and I only have three hours to get where I'm going.

The trail is padded with leaves and pine needles, soft and easy on the knees, and I don't have to stare at my feet. Instead, I can look around as I jog, and I do, not wanting to miss a thing—the deciduous trees, stripped of their leaves, now sleeping until the spring. The evergreens with their needles that emit that pine smell I love so much, their trunks promising juicy resin, sticky vertical rivers for insects to dip in. There is no fireworks display of luminescent insects, butterflies, dragonflies, or even glow worms, for that matter, but it still feels awfully good to be here.

Aside from my uncomfortable shoes, my mind is the only

part of my body struggling. The day's events play in my head on a loop—Morgan in home studies, tracing a knife across her throat as she smiled wickedly. *Was it really this morning?* If someone had shown me the future in a crystal ball, I would have never gotten out of bed this morning.

With every step, I feel like I'm nearing an imminent crossroads, an inevitable decision, the future coming much too fast, and I'm not ready for it. Although the choice has already been made, hasn't it? The Scouts are now far behind, preparing for a trek in the dark and a night of toasted marshmallows and campfire tales.

I reach the Military road, which stretches out like a gray desert. The coast is clear. On the other side, I enter a patch of forest. The path is slightly wilder here, and I slow my jog to a brisk walk. I would enjoy the feeling of heading toward a place less *civilized*, if not for the threat I left behind. *Did the Military see me leave? Are they following me? Are Mr. Wilder and the Scouts all right?* For now, the woods around me are silent, which I take as a promising sign.

I reach a river and cross a wobbly wooden bridge, the smell of water laced with something chemical or *fecal*. After the crossing, the trees darken, and I feel myself nearing the edge of the known world; the precipice of the unknown. Finally, after an hour of walking, I arrive at a clearing with a dilapidated black cabin. *Camp Midnight*, I remember from the map. A few paces behind it is the fence. Silver and sharp and electric, covered in its usual warnings. Its presence feels animal or mechanical, like Grouse's cyborg dog. Resting now, but capable of great violence. One touch would be enough to fry every cell in my body.

TRESPASSERS WILL BE EXECUTED, one warning reads.

I'm sure the thing is active.

And then I see it—a hole, cut into the wires. It is about

one foot high and one foot wide, perhaps made by poachers or rebels during a power outage or a bad storm. A circle framed by broken metal and loose, agitated wires.

Or maybe it was made by Mr. Wilder—

Perhaps they are planning to escape, after all.

I hesitate: I could wait here, wait for them to catch up.

I could still change my mind and go with them.

I spend a few seconds staring at the hole, which frames the wild behind it. As tempting as this invitation to the wild is, I can't take it.

There's a sound in the forest behind me—footsteps. Animal, or human?

I turn left and follow the fence. For all its menace, it turns out to be the best trail marker I could ever ask for. I keep a good pace, halfway between a run and a walk. *I'm so alone*, I think. Every decision is now my own.

I wonder how Diana and Mr. Wilder knew each other—perhaps he was her teacher. A past no one talks about, like constellations in the night sky, erasing the lines between them, posing as individual stars. Because, like I saw tonight, secrets can so easily be traced down the line from one home to the next. *People stay separate to survive.* Following that thought, I question the link between Diana and Gora, of all people. Gora, who risked her skin to warn me about Morgan.

Caught in my thoughts, I trip on a root and almost stumble into my electric neighbor. I catch myself just in time, but my nerve is still shaken. *That was stupid.* I reprimand myself. *Stupid, stupid, stupid.* That's all it takes to die out here—one small mistake, one moment of inattention. I have to stay focused, and thoughts are dangerous distractions.

I continue for another hour, keeping my eyes on the path and a few extra feet from the fence for good measure until the trees on my left are basically caressing my shoulder. And then, in the distance, I see it. A large, imposing sign on two poles like an acrobat on stilts:

RESTRICTED!

You are now entering a military facility.

I slow down. As I approach the sign, the air gets colder, and a full-body shiver runs through me. I wonder if there are cameras here masquerading as rocks or sensors hidden in the trees . . . but my senses don't alert me to anything. Perhaps because no one of sound mind would ever wander here, alone, without a weapon, on a night when the facility is purportedly crawling with Hunters.

I brace myself as I pass under the sign, but nothing happens. No blaring siren or godly spotlight descending from the sky. The path continues uphill for a few minutes, a steep climb, and then I reach the top. There's a curiously positioned bench facing the property down below.

And that's when I see it.

The Loudhouse.

The giant black diamond structure that George described sits at the bottom of the hill. I crouch behind the bench, belly on the grass, and take in the terrifying panorama. To my left is the driveway where buses are parked, some with blacked-out windows and other regular ones that must transport the boys to and from their base in Valor's Edge. A stretch of muddy grass connects the parking lot to an entertainment tent erected for a celebration. I can see a dozen Hunters gathered at the perimeter of the tent, drinking and smoking and telling stories. It feels awfully convivial—the jokes, the liquor, the tales of the bush, bonded by their recent expedition. Groomed into the perfect little assassins. They all look young—*too young*—about Mercy's age, and tonight they are unarmed. From what I can tell, there is only one armed guard standing to the right of the entertainment tent, where a path of kerosene lanterns lights the way to a heavy metal door that marks the main entrance to the diamond structure. The guard holds an automatic rifle with both hands and wears an eerie faceskin over his head. Aside from the main entrance, the Loudhouse appears to have another door at each tip of the diamond like points on a compass.

To the right of the massive structure, the river branches out like a hand with a dozen fingers, little bridges over them like rings, leading to a house. The charcoal monster stands four stories high, grim as a haunted house, with a few lit windows and a chimney blowing a trail of smoke into the sky. *That must be where General Santos lives.* I imagine him in there, recovering from whatever Warwick did to him when he escaped, those *heinous injuries* that weren't heinous enough to kill.

Now it's a waiting game.

At a quarter to eleven, an announcement plays over the din of Hunters, and they start to meander down the lantern-lit path and move inside. I try to find Mercy's face, but from here, they all look the same. Little toy soldiers in their formal gray uniforms. I see one with a broken leg in a cast and crutches, and another whose arm is in a sling. A few smoke vapes that emit puffs of green smoke, and the wind blows in my direction, carrying a faint herbal smell. *Klandestine?* I saw what only a little bit of the plant did to Elizabeth—how jittery and violent she became, her muscles swollen and her eyes bloodshot. *Could these boys be doing the same?*

Ten minutes left, I think, right after a second announcement sounds. And with five minutes to go and a final broadcast, the remaining Hunters finish their drinks, pocket their vapes, and disappear inside, followed by the armed guard. The Loudhouse grounds are now quiet. Nothing moves, and nothing makes a sound, and the reality of what I'm about to do hits. I am about to enter a place no one was designed to leave. Where Klujns enter alive and exit packaged in recycled paper, distributed to wealthy homes, cooks, and butchers. But the only way out into the wild with Diablo is through this hellish place.

I hope the Hunters really are occupied. Otherwise, I am practically walking myself to my own place of slaughter, handing my flesh over to Grouse on a silver platter, a little glazed cherry on my head.

I count the last seconds along with my watch, watching the seconds rise.

Twenty-five, twenty-six . . .

I am a human-shaped mound of jelly; more anxiety than blood or water. I had plenty of time on the hike over to mentally prepare, but now that I'm here, I'm not ready at all.

I think of the Scouts again, one last temptation to go back and forget this impossible plan, but I can't let Diablo die.

The last thirty seconds tick by much too quickly, and I manage a few deep breaths that do little to stop the violent earthquake in my chest. Then, all the numbers change at once.

It's time.

Whatever is happening in there is about to start.

A journey starts with a step, and when I began this journey tonight, the path ahead wasn't visible from where I was standing. But the path revealed itself step by step—and brought me here. I just need to apply that same faith here, that the stepping stones will appear when I need them, and that my journey into those iceberg depths will be smooth and unobstructed.

Get in. Find Diablo. And get out.

The cold wind blows, and I rise. *One step*, I think. Then, I take the hardest one I've taken all night, stepping out from my hiding spot and beginning the journey down the hill toward that menacing diamond structure.

11

The first quarter moon is unusually bright and offers little darkness to hide in. I try not to think about what I'm doing, but there it is, the voice I can't shut down—*I am about to enter one of the most dangerous and restricted places in our Territory.*

I breathe a sigh of relief when I reach the bottom of the hill and take refuge behind a giant blue dumpster. The dumpster emits a rank, oozing smell of dead things. I peer around the sticky metal corner at the entertainment tent and the lantern-lit path. The coast is still clear, and everybody must be inside.

A thirty-foot distance separates my dumpster and the door closest to me. *It has to be an entrance.*

As I run for it, the no-man's-land feels gaping and endless, whipped by a breeze that freezes my eyeballs and turns the landscape blurry. I finally reach the door and try the heavy handle, and it gives. *It's open!*

I slip into the dark entrance tunnel and quickly shut the door behind me, not wanting to let the moonlight in. *How lucky.* But then a new fear dawns on me, and I try the handle from the inside. It's locked. It won't even budge. There's no getting out. A red glowing keypad by the door glares at me, and I realize I'm now trapped inside this building—I'll need to find a new way out.

I edge through the tunnel and enter the main structure from the south, where a smell greets me: something damp and musty, like mold spores. My eyes slowly adjust to their new environment, and I see that I'm standing on the top balcony of the diamond structure, like a giant underground shopping center, a prison, or a macabre theater. Tucked in the western corner is the main entrance I saw from the outside, and along the opposite wall is a large freight elevator that the Hunters must have taken to go down. Everything around me is made of concrete and metal, designed to be soundproof and impenetrable. In the far corner across from me, the guard from before takes one hand off his weapon to lean against the railing, looking down at something. I edge toward my V-shaped balcony, moving as slowly as the shadows, and peer into the center-deep.

The ground must be eight levels down, the floor made of metal grating. In the middle is a diamond-shaped stage of soil, surrounded on all four sides by a few rows of elevated bleachers. One hundred or so young Hunters fill the seats, chatting in apprehension. It is an eerie setting, like the site of an ancient surgery, something medical but unsanitary.

The guard across from me senses something, and looks up in my direction. I freeze—a deer caught in the headlights. *At least I'm wearing black*, I think, hoping that he can't see the whites of my eyes or the words on my new sweater. The guard finally looks away and goes back to watching the stage. I take this opportunity and amble slowly backward until I hit the wall, then press myself flat into it, inching toward the east side until my fumbling hand finds another door about halfway down. I peer through a glass window, round like a ship's porthole, and see a platform lit by a single blue-black bulb. *A staircase.* I wait until the guard is facing away from me, then quickly open the door and dash onto the landing.

A large number nine glows on the wall in white. Next to it, a sign lists the different departments with arrows pointing down: TRIAGE, KLUJN HOLDING CELLS, KILLINGROOM, MEAT PACKING, HATCHERY, BREEDING ROOM, ENTERTAINMENT, LAB, STAGE. Then I see ANIMAL STOREHOUSE down at the very bottom of the list. I remember what George said about it being situated right below the stage—I follow the arrow down.

My shoes pad quickly down the stairs, and my head swims. I spent months agonizing over leaving versus staying, and now I have to make so many decisions in quick succession without time to make a list and weigh up the pros and cons. A new Ava is born in that staircase, one who is confident and decisive. Or maybe just the latter, and only because she doesn't have the luxury of being indecisive.

I continue down to the final level, where the staircase ends. I follow the arrow out into the animal storehouse, emerging into a room full of cages piled as high as the ceiling, which is just the underside of the stage above. It must be six feet high—the height of your average basement—but low enough to make the space feel cramped and claustrophobic. Through the metal grating of the stage floor, I can see the bleachers and the Hunter's feet over my head.

It smells like a zoo, a combination of urine, feces, straw, and bile. *The quicker I find Diablo, the better.* The only light comes from the stage above, a thousand tiny fragments that aren't much to work with. There are no guards here, and only one exit. It's so quiet that, at first, I think the cages are empty. But then I hear the occasional flutter or scuffle of animal bodies. I squint into the nearest cage, and my Klujn sight kicks in. Reds, blues, and lime greens become visible in the darkness—the plumage of tropical birds. At first, I don't recognize them because some have been stripped of their basic anatomy—wings cut off and beaks removed, patches of feathers plucked to reveal the raw pink flesh underneath. I see blue sparrows and other birds I don't know the names of.

As my eyes adjust, the sad landscape continues to reveal itself to me. There are mutilated creatures everywhere. Forgotten down here and left to die slowly, or kept alive for some human purpose? It's unclear what that purpose is—wings to eat as a Hunter's Return delicacy, a beak to help with public speaking, or some exotic feathers to stuff a coat with? These poor creatures, their lives stolen piece by piece, destined to become a sideshow game or a shiny trinket or a small vial of medicine. *This is worse than death.* At least there is dignity in living and dying free.

I want to help them, free them, let them soar into the night sky, but I don't have the keys to their cages. Even if I did, something tells me they wouldn't last long. Maybe we are alike—creatures deprived of our wildness for so long that we've forgotten how to speak the language of survival.

The room is divided into four parts, and I continue into the next one, which has tanks of frogs, toads, eels, spiders, and lizards of all kinds. There are translucent snakes, yellow-and-green snakes, red-and-black snakes, and brown snakes. Some animals are color changing, others furry. The spiders are menacing, too—nothing I would ever wish to step on or share a tent with. I see a chameleon, its flesh the same color as its glass enclosure, slowly disappearing.

As fascinating and horrifying as this is, I know Diablo isn't here.

In the third room are larger cages, these ones containing mammals. Brown bears, black bears, and ones with an indigo hue. *A moon bear*, I realize, noticing the distinct white circle on its face, like a full moon. I've never seen one in real life, and I can't stop staring at it. It would be beautiful if it weren't emaciated, sitting in the back corner of its cage, trembling from cold or weakness. Its claws have been sawed down to blunt stubs, and there's a vacantness in its eyes. A tube pokes into its belly, excreting some kind of glittering white pus. The moon bear scratches at the catheter where the needle enters but doesn't have the strength to rip it out.

I peel myself away from its sad face and move into the last section of the room, dreading what I might find.

Sure enough, the show isn't yet over.

I see spotted wolves with their coats skinned, everything but the head, disease creeping in, and opportunistic insects. I feel eyes on me and turn to see a wild dog in a cage at my eye level. She lies on soiled newspaper, fleas and maggots crawling around a plain of printed words. I notice that the dog is a female because her teats are swollen and full of milk, but her puppies are nowhere to be seen. *It's the wild dog from Circo.* The one who attacked and killed Bindu. *Not a ferocious predator*, I realize, but a frightened mother who was exercising her right to protect her young.

Her eyes are crusted things, in despair but still lucid, unlike her bear and wolf neighbors who have tipped over onto the side of madness. *Where are her puppies?* I wonder. *What were they used for?* I see Wolf in her eyes. I feel the agony of being trapped here below the ground, unable to stretch her legs or feel a breeze. Kept in this forever darkness. *How can this be legal?* Man who envied the animal its wildness and had to take that wildness away.

I want to find the person responsible for this and place them in a cage.

Watch them die slowly in their own filth.

Make them feel this much pain.

Despite the harm I saw the wild dog unleash, I'm overcome by a need to console her. Against my better judgment, I slip a finger through a hole in her cage and stroke her matted fur. She flinches as I approach but then relaxes under my touch, relieved of an itch that she doesn't have the room to scratch herself. I touch her spine, her ribs, and all her hard edges. *It's okay*, I want to tell her, but that would be a lie. It would be a mercy to kill her, to put her out of her misery, but selfishly, I can't do that.

There's applause above my head. I look up and see a man in a spotted wolf cloak, seemingly diced into hundreds of tiny squares by the metal grating of the ceiling. His auburn eyes fill one square each, like puzzle pieces. My breath hitches in my chest, and I'm still not used to seeing him in real life.

Atoll Grouse.

12

"Historically, we celebrate Hunter's Return as a homecoming after the Hunt and before the start of winter," Grouse starts in a fatherly tone, casting a spell on all those impressionable boys who cling to his words like a bead to a thread. I know I should keep searching for Diablo, but I'm too hypnotized to move. "But, thanks to your outstanding work in the wild—which led to our most successful raid yet—this winter, the work continues. After a much-needed repose this weekend, of course."

Grouse looks proudly on at his protégées. As he begins his discourse, I'm reminded of Warwick—his love of games, spectacle, and being the center of attention. *Maybe Warwick picked up a thing or two from Grouse*, I think. After all, he spent a decade in a human circus, held captive by the worst kind of humans, those who stir a teaspoon of cruelty into their morning coffee.

"Earlier tonight, you were awarded your first badges for *loyalty*," Grouse goes on. I notice that the Hunters all have crystal medals pinned to their uniforms, no doubt made of viață. Klujn crystal. I glimpse Mercy then, for the first time in months, sitting in the second row. He looks bigger than I remember him to be. "And loyalty is exactly what I will need from you moving forward.

"Over the winter," Grouse continues. "You will complete your fast-tracked Military and Hunter training, graduating in time for the spring. It will be an intense period, learning in months what would normally take years, but your sacrifice is needed. Now that you are on the cusp of becoming men, I wanted to offer you a rare privilege I usually save for after graduation—*knowledge*. Because I believe it is important for you to understand why our work matters."

Grouse takes a few measured steps around the stage. He pauses to look each Hunter in the eye, and if I didn't know any better, I would slip under his spell too. "My children," he says, taking a thoughtful pause here. "I felicitate you on your remarkable bravery and the sacrifices you made in these last grueling months. The mark of a great Hunter is to be able to go to dark places and not be affected by them. While your comrades fled, you remained. While they sought the comfort of home, you bravely ventured into the unknown, enduring weeks of discomfort, danger, and inclement weather. Discomfort may be temporary, but nothing is as permanent as the badges of honor you now wear proudly on your chests. I have no doubt you will go far. You will be able to tell your future wives that you forged history with your bare hands."

Grouse stretches his arms out and taps his hands—*bravo!*—and the young Hunters give themselves a round of applause. When the ruckus settles down, the President continues. "Tonight, you will see why every raid is so essential. Each raid has brought us closer to repopulation, and now, after Circo, we are ready to begin.

"*Tonight*," he says again for emphasis, "we witness the miracle of *birth*."

Grouse gestures to two guards, who emerge from backstage wearing those same eerie faceskins as the guard from earlier. They hold a heavily pregnant female Klujn, her round belly bulging beneath a thin blue hospital gown. Her head is bent over, and I can only see the top of her white knotted hair. She lifts her head slowly, and I see her pale skin and red eyes. I remember her from Circo—the Klujn in the plaza who was singing her wordless lullaby. She isn't singing now. Her mouth has been roughly stitched into a soundless line.

Grouse steps off to the side as the guards take the woman into the center of the stage, which is barely larger than a sand-pit. George comes out, accompanied by two female nurses—a young one who carries a folded blanket and an old one who holds a large, sterilized jar with clear liquid inside. I almost don't recognize George in those dark blue scrubs, wearing a surgical mask and gloves, a syringe in his hand. He once told me he wasn't a medical doctor, but whatever he's about to do looks pretty medical.

The guards hold the pregnant Klujn as George injects the needle into her arm, and after less than a minute, her contractions start. She tries to scream but can't. Instead, her pain looks for other openings, in the form of sweat and the tears that leak from the corners of her eyes. George stands back and looks down at his feet, looking anxious. I wonder if he's trying to find me underneath the stage.

The guards continue to restrain the Klujn woman as her contractions grow closer together, less than thirty seconds apart, and then fifteen, and then five. *Giving birth in front of an audience*, I think. *Unable to shield or comfort herself.*

The sight is distressing, but I can't look away. *How can one birth be so important? How can one female lead to repopulation?* I struggle to find the link between her and the future of our

Territory—what Grouse is promising these boys, and what he has promised his people for decades.

A few more minutes pass until the Klujn's gown is drenched in sweat, the outline of her naked body visible through the thin fabric. The young Hunters look disgusted by the sight of her—the vulgarity of her plump breasts, the roundness of her frame, her bodily hair—but force themselves to look on without grimacing because Grouse is keenly watching. Trying to appear *brave* when they are all visibly disturbed. Equipped to deal with violence but little prepared to deal with something as intimate as birth. Not that there is anything intimate about this.

"The first live birth of a Klujn happened in this room almost two decades ago," Grouse exclaims. "After the Bessi-Maso raid. Sadly, the infant did not survive, and when the mother could not produce any more offspring, she was sold into entertainment. Then, by good fortune, another female came along . . . a fertile *Estrellan*. And this time, thanks to an important discovery that we made, the kanum survived."

Grouse gestures to his guards, who let the woman go. She falls to her knees, succumbing to the double gravity of her body, and the guards stand a few feet back, drawing their rifles on her, not that she has anywhere to run. Then, as though possessed by a great internal force, the female Klujn starts to dig. Her instinct to dig is wild, more potent than her contempt for the watching Hunters. George continues to look at his feet, but Mercy's eyes don't leave the stage—his bright eyes are now sharp.

The female Klujn continues to dig, her hands moving of their own volition. She digs and digs and digs. When she has finished, she positions herself over the hole and gives off a guttural bellow as she pushes the baby out. After a few minutes of pushing, the baby drops into the hole. Then the mother starts to fill it . . . burying the baby *alive*.

I watch in confused horror, but the expression on Grouse's face is relaxed, as though this is all perfectly natural. When the female has finished burying her baby, she smooths the earth flat with both hands, rocked by her heaving breaths. Her claws are out and sharp and murky white, and she traces a symbol on the soil like a prayer. Then, her wildness cools, and her resentment returns—furious at herself for giving the Hunters what they wanted. Now that the baby is no longer in her belly, she can no longer protect it.

Seconds become minutes. We all stare at that flat expanse of earth, the buried baby, the hunched mother, who looks like a desperate animal. The room is so quiet that all I can hear is the breathing of the boys, a few nervous coughs, and the soft clink of ice cubes in their drinks.

And then, after what feels like an eternity, a tiny hand sprouts through the soil like a plant, its fingers curled like a bent flowerhead before it meets the sun. Pale flesh, no fingernails, its tiny bones glowing like a battery activated by the earth.

Grouse opens his arms at the big reveal—*ta da!*—and the Hunters break out in obedient, confused applause. Like me, they still don't seem to fully understand the punchline. When the applause simmers down, Grouse continues his speech—

"It took us several births to discover that the secret is in the *soil*," he says. "Klujn babies need soil to activate their vitality and crystals within seconds of birth, just like a human baby's first breath clears the liquid from its lungs. Without it, the infant dies. Because the births typically took place in our sterile labs, we dismissed the mother's behavior as hysterical urges. When we discovered the critical role of soil, the world changed. If it wasn't for Dr. Sparrow, who had the ingenious idea to take one of the mothers outside and untie her hands, we may have never witnessed a successful Klujn birth.

"The problem is that we had so few fertile females left," says Grouse. "But after Circo, that changed. This is the first of a dozen scheduled births this month—and don't be concerned by her hair color. Some Klujns can reproduce until a very ripe old age."

The Klujn mother reaches for her baby's hand and takes it. Perhaps it's a trick of the light, but in their skin contact I notice a ripple of light, an exchange of sparks. Only a second later, a guard shoots her with a tranquilizer dart, and her body slumps down, unconscious within seconds. The faceless guards scoop her up and carries her out of the arena, breaking the contact between mother and child. I don't know what will happen to her, but something tells me that she isn't likely to see her baby again.

George steps forward, leans down, and gently takes the Klujn baby's hand with his gloved one, pulling the tiny, chubby infant from the soil like Diana and I used to pull up radishes. He clamps and cuts the umbilical cord, then carries the now-crying baby to one of the nurses, the young one, who wraps it in a blue blanket, a name sewn into the fabric.

I've seen a blanket like that before.

"Naming them has become a tradition of mine," Grouse says. "This little Klujn's name is Kala."

I grip the wild dog's cage to steady myself. George returns to the hole and pulls up a lump from the earth that looks like a round, pink jellyfish—*the placenta.* He brings it to the second nurse and places it inside the jar, where the clear liquid turns pink. It looks like a miniature galaxy with a million tiny glittering crystals for stars.

"The real miracle," Grouse says, "is not the one baby itself. The *real* miracle," he repeats. "Is the hundred thousand seeds of pure virgin viață contained in the placenta, each of which can be farm-grown into a young, healthy Klujn infant using soil as a surrogate womb in just three months. Only a few drops of the placenta can help our women with fertility issues and turn even our most barren wives into *babymakers*.

"Young kanum is the most efficient form of meat there is," Grouse continues. "It is the fastest to grow, the easiest to harvest, and the most nutritious. But that's not all. Each female Klujn baby also contains in her ovaries all the crystal seeds she will ever carry, which can be extracted through a simple keyhole procedure that doesn't jeopardize the quality of the meat. We're talking millions and millions of pure kanum seeds from one pregnancy alone. That is more than enough meat to feed our population indefinitely. This is why we must accelerate the development of the Moonlight Farms and why I want you all to be ready in time for the spring. We are on the brink of ending our Territory's food crisis. Not to mention the bones and virgin claws we can continue to use for soil rejuvenation.

"What's more," Grouse says, and all the young Hunters look rapt by the discovery, "we have found that generally speaking, the crystals inside the mother's womb react well to pressure. The more *challenging* the mother's environment during pregnancy, the more crystal seeds we reap. No pressure, no crystals," Grouse grins, and I see the glint of the crystal studs that decorate his canines.

I feel like I'm going to vomit. I try to swallow my nausea down, but it continues to build inside me and I can do nothing to stop it. I double over and throw up as silently as I can. My insides empty themselves over and over, and as my arms shake, Grouse's words pound through my ears—*No pressure, no crystals.*

Memories, images, and feelings rush through me.

My mother screaming, her hands bound, the volcano of her fear.

Digging frantically into the earth under a full moon.

A baby wrapped in a blue blanket.

A little name sewn into the fabric.

My normal vision returns and I'm no longer throwing up, but I feel very faint. In her cage, the wild dog looks at me with something like sympathy or understanding.

The ceremony is over, and the bleachers are emptying. The boys are going back to the entertainment tent for another round of food, drinks, and laughter. "*Did you see that?*" Cracking jokes about her body, her pain, or the monster birthed between her legs.

She was here, I think. *My mother.*

I was born here.

I reach for the walls, but I can't find them. Everything is spinning. My brain is so heavy, too big for my skull, too much for my neck to carry. Looking back through the rooms I explored under the stage, I manage to glimpse the door I came in from—the *only* door, as far as I've seen—a point of focus in this dark, spinning world. I leave the wild dog's comforting, familiar presence and step toward the exit when the door suddenly opens. A figure wearing a silver faceskin fills the frame.

Caught.

13

Black as a moonless night, the bag over my head. It obstructs my vision, bringing my other senses to the forefront. The smell of straw like the rebels wore, the ones that hung today. The guard's firm grip on my arm as we walk over different textures—cement, the vibrating rubber floor of an elevator, then the squelch of muddy grass. The arch of a wooden bridge as it rises up and down and gives way to the creaking floorboards of a house.

I am taken down a long hallway. A door opens, and the guard throws me on the ground. My knees are cushioned by a soft rug as the scent of oak and leather meets my nostrils. The bag is ripped off my head without ceremony, and I see I'm in a large living room with a rustic-romantic feel. The oval rug under me is a faded pink. A cobwebbed chandelier of claws hangs from the ceiling, casting jewels of rainbow light onto the plush green couches. Along the back wall are built-in bookshelves of mahogany wood containing curiosities of all kinds. Animal skulls, bones, and skins. Dried coral, gems, and glowing minerals. Relics and mementos of the wild, like proof of passage or conquer. On the far side of the room is a fireplace, above which are perched a pair of giant gold antlers, larger than any moose.

There are footsteps in the hallway, and then the door swings open. Grouse enters, flanked by a guard. George enters behind them, standing sentry in the open doorway. He's still in his bloody scrubs, but his gloves are off now. George throws me a quick nervous look, then gazes back down at his feet.

"We meet again," Grouse says, studying me like one of those intriguing objects on the shelves. "I'm sorry my visit last time was cut short, but your timing is spot on. How generous of you to come to me yourself." Grouse offers me a tender, pitying smile, like he was expecting me all along. *How did the guards find me if I didn't make a sound? Did someone see me going down the stairs?*

"Spies exist for many reasons," he tells me. "To keep an eye on a particular person or take a township's temperature in a time of change or crisis. You'd be surprised how many faithful spies live in your midst, whose job is to denounce traitors. But that spy at your school was a bit of a wild card if I'm being honest. A favor to her mother, who is one of the DSO's most loyal agents. Unfortunately, sometimes, the apple does fall far from the tree . . . and rolls all the way down the hillside. Over-excitement can often cloud judgment."

Grouse clicks his tongue in disappointment. "You want to know the marker of a great spy? One that you never see coming, not from a mile away. One who shows devotion over a lifetime. One who's willing to turn in their own *family*. Honor before blood." Grouse walks up to George and pats him on the shoulder, and a bad feeling begins to bloom inside my stomach. I stare at the man who raised me, at the way his eyes are avoiding mine, the blood gathered in his cheeks and ears.

George.

My father has betrayed me for a second time.

He didn't come home to announce his retirement—he came home to tell me where to find Diablo, which wasn't true, and lure me to the Loudhouse. Another horrible thought—*Is Diablo even still alive? Could George have lied about that, too?*

Luckily I'm sitting, because otherwise, I might fall. *George.* How could my instinct be so wrong about someone—*twice*? How can someone who looks so honest be such a good liar? Why is he so loyal to our leader? What does he have to gain from being at his side? Is it for power, tokens, property, or assured safety? With Santos injured, does he see this as an opportunity to gain rank?

I don't know him at all.

"George has been a prime example that trust is built slowly over time, not through words but through actions," says Grouse.

"This used to be my country house," he says, changing tone, walking to the built-in bookshelves and the trophies they contain. "A place where my family would come to Hunt and escape the crowded city. Santos and I both come from old Hunting families. It's in our DNA. When I built the fences, and the Hunting missions intensified, I promoted my dear friend Rodrigo to Head Hunter and appointed him to this place. It's useful, with its proximity to the wild and soon the Moonlight Farms. I take it you saw the birth?" he says. "What a marvel."

Grouse walks over to a large taxidermied spotted wolf. Its sapphire eyes are glassy, its jaw open in a snarl, and I realize that it looks almost identical to my mother's wolf, Mahta, except for the lack of spots on its back. Grouse looks at the dead animal fondly. "The general had to choose a buddy, as is custom, and there was no one he trusted more than his dear

Military friend Doctor Sparrow. I had my doubts, of course. But, time and time again, George has proven me wrong. It was he who led us to Bessi-Maso, and then Estrella, and then Corthu not too long after. Three incredible raids in under a year. It was George who had the idea to free your mother's hands so that she could bury you in the ground. The first baby to survive, but certainly not the last. Her escape was not part of the plan, of course, but your birth gave us more than we could ever dream of."

Grouse moves over to a shelf containing large glass jars filled with pink liquid. He picks one up, tilts it toward the chandelier light, and I see—a tiny baby inside. Behind Grouse are another nine or ten jars, all containing babies.

"I know I shouldn't name them," he says, "but it's become a tradition. This one is Bia, and that is Cora, and this one is Daisy, named after my late grandmother." Grouse places the newborn back on the shelf, next to the others. It takes every muscle in my body not to throw up again.

"From the outset, George and I have had a relationship of utmost transparency," Grouse says. "He told me when he found you at the orphanage. I instructed him to take you in, raise you, study you, then send you into the Blood Race—after all, we had never seen one of your kind live older than a few weeks! Most of the hybrids we tried to raise after the fact became diseased; their bodies shutting down on themselves. A real enigma you are. That's why we make them pure now."

Hybrid. Diseased. Pure.

I have no idea what he means.

My mind is spinning, racing to connect the dots he's painting with his words. My mother gave birth to me here. George had the idea to free her hands. *The first, but not the last.* If she hadn't run away with me, I would be floating in pink liquid on that shelf now. But who's my father? And who fathered all these other babies?

"We kept you a secret from the general because he is impulsive and may not have seen the value in keeping you around," says Grouse. "After your *séjour* in the wild, I trusted George when he said you wouldn't be a danger. I trusted him again when he told me he knew how to get you here tonight. That's how trust is earned—through consistent action, over time."

"What do you want?" I finally manage to ask, trying to sound as polite as possible but still seething with disgust and rage. This may be Santos's Loudhouse, but Grouse is the one who gives the orders; the one who had my mother impregnated by a human—through ways I don't want to imagine—and kept her caged and frightened.

"Nothing," Grouse answers quickly. "For the first time in a long time, I have everything I need. The general is slowly recovering upstairs. Everything else is on track—commencing work on the farms, training a new generation of young, hungry minds. As for you . . . I know George thinks you can be useful still, but I believe you've become too much of a liability."

Grouse whistles, a simple two-note sound, and his cyborg dog, Showman, enters the room. He sits by his master's legs, his head level with the president's hip. His black eyes watch me hungrily, waiting for a command. "I guess the only question left is what sauce you'll be cooked in," Grouse hums. Then he cracks a smile that, under any other circumstances, could be considered charming. "Only joking. My palette has become accustomed to young kanum, and I find adolescent meat too *chewy*. Showman's palate, on the other hand, is not as nuanced."

Grouse makes a sharp, one-note whistle, and Showman begins circling around me, slowly skirting the edge of the rug. I don't know who to keep my eyes on—dog or master. *All of this,*

I think, *to be betrayed by George again. To end up in the belly of a metal dog who doesn't even need to eat.* "You know the quickest way to make a person disappear?" Grouse asks me. "My loyal Showman here. More efficient than a drove of pigs. No trace left, no teeth, no bones, unless I ask him to leave me a trophy to add to my collection," Grouse snickers. "It always did bother me that my collection was missing its first."

Ava.

Before Bia and the others.

Like I am nothing more than a Hunter's prize.

I think of my mom, trying to summon a bit of her courage, wondering what she would have done in this situation. George is still by the door, still as a statue, still gazing at his shoes. *What's his grand plan?* I wonder. *After all these years, is he really just going to stand back and watch me get eaten alive?* My Executioner, who brought me to the gallows himself, too much of a coward to look me in the eye.

"You're a fighter, I'll give you that," Grouse says. "And I'll be sad to see you go. I do sometimes wonder how you're still alive, when, biologically, your body should have failed you long ago. But in this world, we must accept that sometimes we'll never have all the answers we seek."

Grouse's eyes burn like a sky with two red suns. *What made him like this? What turned his heart so black that he can inflict such cruelty without remorse?* No one is born this way.

Showman completes another predatory loop around me and then stops by his master's feet. Grouse pets the dog's slick head with affection. "A piece of advice," he tells me. "If you want it to drag on, put up a fight. But if you want it to be quick—which I recommend—then expose your neck."

It was all for nothing, I think. My life. My *stupid* life. My relentless thoughts, emotions, anxieties, dreams, and yearnings.

All to end up here, dying, with so many burning questions. I'm not unique, special, or wanted. My mother was abused. My birth shouldn't have happened. My life was a string of failures . . . and now it's coming to an end.

Grouse whistles again, and Showman springs into action. I don't have time to brace myself. The last thing I see are rows and rows of sharp metal teeth.

14

"*Wait*," George speaks for the first time, and I'm startled to hear his voice. Grouse whistles once, and Showman stops inches from my face. His breath is rank—the creature eats when there is barely enough decent food for everyone else. The president turns to look at George and raises a single eyebrow. "She can still be useful," George says, his words as measured as they were in his classroom.

"How?"

"She knows where they've gone. She can help us get the king."

Grouse sizes me up, and I realize that George is trying to give me a chance to escape—but then why bring me here in the first place? Was this the only way to get Grouse off my case; making him feel like it was all his idea? As angry as I am at George, I know it's in my best interest to go along with his words. In this room full of trophies, there is only one that Grouse doesn't have . . .

"I can get you the heart," I say. My voice sounds confident and strange, like somebody else's voice is speaking through me. Getting Warwick's heart is damn near impossible. Klujns live in the wild all their lives and barely make it through their own Blood Race. Now I'm suggesting I can get to Circo—leaving two months behind the others—*and* return. And kill an unkillable Klujn in the process. *If* Warwick is there. But if I can't convince Grouse, then I'm already dead.

"*You?* You can get me the heart?" Grouse asks, his cheeks flushing with surprise. "The king who has beaten every opponent he was put up against? Who terrorizes grown men, who has the force of the sun in his hands, and who escaped us twice? You can get us his heart?"

I feel ridiculous in my school uniform and sweater. But no matter my doubts, I can't let them show.

"It's in my nature," I say, "to find them."

"Then where are they?"

My lips twitch into an involuntary smile. "If I tell you that, you'll go straight there and kill them all."

Grouse smiles back—touché.

"We saw how useful she was at Circo," George says. "Surviving in the wild and making it through gruesome tests. The king kept her around because he must have liked her—sensed that she was different. The Klujn Blood Race is different, but it's not all *that* different. Ava wouldn't be able to give us an exact location of Circo now even if we tortured her—her sense of navigation will start to develop in the wild."

"She's months behind," Grouse says. "She could never catch up. If she gets there late—they won't let her in." He says this more as a question, than like an expert. After all, no human knows Klujns more than George does, and he uses this to his advantage.

"Being behind may actually be beneficial," George answers calmly. "When the young Klujns have too much time, they waste a lot of it. Ava's urgency to get there might work in her favor," he says. "I believe she could catch up, be accepted, and then return to us with the heart."

Is this true? I wonder. *Does he really think I can—or is he lying through his teeth?* Like all the other times he lied to me.

In this case, though, I'm glad for his lying skills.

Grouse pivots back to me and utters a thoughtful sigh. "So you want me to let you go?" he asks. "What's to stop you from running away and never returning?"

"Collateral," says George.

"Collateral?" Grouse tastes the word as though it's flavored. "But we don't *really* need the heart, do we?" He studies George's face in a way that suggests that, despite appearances, he does lean heavily on the opinion of his right-hand man. "We have enough going on with the farms."

"Klujns will always be an obstacle for us. The more we burn their forests to build our farms, the more likely they are to retaliate. We don't know what they'll do when they feel cornered. And with their impressive fertility, who knows how many are out there. Not to mention the king's history of violence toward humans. With Warwick dead and the knowledge that his heart holds, we can access all the information we could ever want about how many stands there are, their intentions, and the reason behind their strange migrations. Without Klujns standing in the way, the Boreal is ours."

I realize something then—how George is talking about the *king's* heart, when the *queen's* heart holds all the knowledge that Hunters need. Daciana told me that when Warwick beat the previous queen and ate her heart, he wasn't balanced like a leader needs to be. The wisdom of the heart was lost on him. Now, Warwick's heart is blackened. And although Circo's leader is still strong, he doesn't have many gifts besides physical strength and organizing a mean celebration. George knows this because I overheard him and Diana talking about it years ago, but Grouse doesn't . . . which leads me to think that George doesn't tell Grouse *everything.*

Grouse studies us both thoughtfully.

"You think she can do this?" he asks George. "Enough to bet your life—or your wife's?" George looks at me and nods sadly.

"I know she can."

His faith in me was not a lie.

The president continues to consider.

"I'll tell you what," Grouse tells me, slowly testing the plan on his tongue, savoring every syllable. "I'll let you go, but if you don't return, I'll burn Red River to the ground. I'll come for everyone you know. George. Diana. That group of Scouts you were planning on escaping with. That's right—I know everything. My godson Mercy will be left without parents, but he will still have me . . . *Collateral,*" he finishes, and George looks like he regrets having planted the seed in his head. "Do we have a deal?"

I think of Mr. Wilder and the Scouts who must be in great danger right now. *Maple. Dot. Ivy.* I list their names in my head, each driving a deeper sense of dread. They didn't make it to camp. They aren't toasting marshmallows and sharing campfire tales. They are probably in a cold DSO cell . . . awaiting what? Execution?

I should've known.

Grouse has eyes everywhere. One cannot outsmart him.

And that's exactly what I need to do now.

I look over at my adoptive father, who nods slowly. I don't know what to do—too many innocents are involved now, whose lives hinge on my success. But if I don't agree to this impossible plan, Diana, Mr. Wilder, and the Scouts will be dead before winter ends . . .

"Okay," I say.

"And be back by Darkest Day."

"That's only two weeks after the Ice Moon," George contests, letting his fear show for the first time tonight.

"Darkest Day," Grouse says again. "With the king's heart. No smoke and mirrors. Take it or leave it." There's no room for negotiation. I ignore the panic in George's eyes, and I nod.

"Great." Grouse whistles again, and I flinch, but Showman only leaves the room with a click of his claws on the hardwood floor. "Anything else?"

"I need a guide." I know it's a risk, but I can't forget the whole reason I came here in the first place. "I need Diablo."

"What makes you think he's still alive?" Grouse asks. It concerns me that he knows exactly who I'm talking about. *What did they use him for?* After an interminable pause, he says—"Fine, you can have him. But I don't know how useful he will be."

Grouse smiles like he's sharing a joke at my expense. And I guess it *is* funny in a way, how tragic this all is. The mission I agreed to. The debilitating impossibility of this plan.

* * *

We walk past a row of sheds and over one last bridge, where the river emits that fecal smell. The guard holds me, and George and the president walk a few paces behind. I'm grateful that Grouse can't see my face as stress and despair compete for space inside my body. I bluffed my way here, and now the journey ahead is uncertain and obscure. I tell myself that trying and failing is better than giving up without even trying . . .

I want to cry but I can't yet. I want to go back home and crawl into bed, but my home doesn't exist anymore. All of this feels too real, too adult, too dangerous.

I see the fence in front of me, that tall electric monster, a sliding gate drawing open. Then the wild is there, framed like a grim portrait. A dirt road heading north into the unknown. Dense wildness on either side, barely enough space for a bus or a Jeep to drive by. The guard pushes me through the gate but doesn't follow. I wonder if Grouse will cheat me and slide the gate shut in my face, but after a minute, another two guards come down the path carrying a body, which they dump at my feet. It makes a hollow *thud* as it lands. One of those familiar black bags on its head. The body isn't moving. It could easily be a corpse. After a few seconds, I notice the slow rise and fall of lungs. A pulse. *Alive.* I lean down and remove the bag . . .

Diablo.

"What's wrong with him?" I ask. Diablo's usually brown skin is sickly pale and sticky with sweat. His striking violet eyes are now glazed and rolling upward like they're an inch from blindness. His claws are murky which I take as a sign of sickness, half-in and half-out of his hands.

"You asked for a guide," Grouse says. "You got one."

"That's not . . ." I splutter. *Fair?* But that would be too much to expect from the man who has caged the world.

"Anything else?" Grouse is enjoying this exchange, like all of this is some sort of game. A pigeon released into the sky, excited to see if it will make it to the finish line or get obliterated by thunder. I shake my head.

"Good. See you on Darkest Day, then. Let's meet back here."

As the president retreats, George asks if he may have a word. Grouse gestures for him to *go ahead* with an elegant twirl of his hand, and George replaces him at the threshold of the fence. I think about his betrayals. There is nothing to fight for, nothing to accuse him of, nothing to salvage. I will never know why he did what he did, and maybe it's better that way. I am beyond caring. Maybe the nightmares of him were my body's way of warning me. But there's another image I can't get out of my head . . .

Because my dreams didn't stop after I left Circo.

They faded, a little, but they never really went away.

"Two Hunters," I say, and George looks confused until I clarify. "Two Hunters cornered my mother on that cliff edge. Both had crystal bayonets. It was you and Santos, wasn't it?"

There's no point lying anymore, so George nods.

"Why didn't you stop it?" I demand. *Her death. Santos shooting her.*

"I didn't have a choice."

"You always have a choice."

"A puppet is moved by a hand," George says. "Do you blame the puppet or the hand? There is a larger plan, Ava, that is bigger than you could ever understand. It doesn't mean that I don't care about you, that I never loved you . . ."

I take in these words, how much they hurt. There's one more thing I need to ask. "All this talk of Klujn babies, but there's no mention of how they're fertilized. What you do to the *females* . . ."

"You're asking me how babies are made?"

"I'm asking if . . ." but I trail off. It's too horrible a thought to finish.

"It's not what you think."

But how can it not be? What other possible explanation is there?

"What is it, then?"

"It's complicated."

"If my eyes are brown . . . if my blood is half human, half Klujn . . ." I trail off. "The babies are all hybrids?" I hate the ugliness of the word, something from an old science fiction book.

"No," George answers. "The babies are pure Klujn. I made a mistake with your mother. You were the first. Aside from a few controlled experiments, we didn't make that same mistake again."

"Then how . . . ?" My thoughts are confused, and I stumble with my words.

"You're asking me who your father is?"

"*Give me Ava*," I say. "*She's mine too*." I quote the Hunter's words. "Two Hunters stood on that cliff edge. The one who shot her and the one who said those words."

"*Ava*," George says my name with tenderness. "I think you've always known deep down. You're so good with color but refuse to see what's right in front of your eyes."

"See what?"

Then he leans in and whispers in my ear.

I take a step back as though splashed by cold water. Look at the man with green eyes.

"I did many things I regret," he tells me. "I can't go back in time."

George's eyes search mine, communicating what his words can't with Grouse and the guards standing close behind. "Find Circo. And when you do—don't come back."

"What about Diana? What about you?"

"Leave us behind. Your life is worth more than ours."

Then, George turns his back on me, leaving me stunned. As the gate closes, I look at him one last time. He is trapped behind bars like a sad lion in a cage, and perhaps he has always been trapped.

I think of the day I met him, when he came to the orphanage and first laid eyes on me. Those bright green eyes, filled with awe and excitement and *recognition*. Now, as I watch him go, I can't help but wonder—

Is this the last time I see him?

Am I capable of letting my adoptive parents die?

Of watching my childhood town burn to the ground?

I stare at the closed gate for a few moments, then look over at Diablo. We are finally alone in the Darker Woods. My Blood Race has started without ceremony, no starting gun, just the closing of the gate and George's secrets. I sink to my knees, where the earth greets my kneecaps with a cool kiss. Questions eat away at me, but there's no way to have them answered.

George's words echo in my ears . . .

"You're so good with color but refuse to see what's right in front of your eyes."

"See what?"

"Purple and green make brown."

15

George is my father. My *biological* father. A Hunter. A traitor. Who just saved my life. *Why can nothing be simple?* All these years of searching for something far and away, but the answer was in front of me all along. Green eyes. Purple eyes. Brown eyes. I remember learning about recessive and dominant genes in biology. It doesn't work like mixing paints, but then again, I guess there's never been one of me before. Did I always know the truth, deep down?

My dad, my dad, my dad.

The journey ahead weighs heavily on my shoulders, a back-breaking weight that I'm not strong enough to carry. All I want to do is curl into a ball and stay here, but I can't.

Diablo's body is limp in blue rags, and his eyes are partially open but somewhere else, in an otherworldly twilight. He might be dying in front of my eyes, and there isn't much I can do about it. I've never cared for a sick person before and wouldn't know where to start. They could have easily slipped a tracker in his clothes, but searching him feels like an invasion of privacy, so I delegate that task to later. Right now, my priority is to put as much distance as I can between us and that fence.

Survive tonight. The rest can wait 'til morning.

I try to hoist Diablo up, but he's so heavy. My muscles aren't at their peak after months without use, and I'm already tired. I try again, using all my strength. Diablo is a head taller than me, and I drape his arm over my shoulders, then wrap my right hand around his torso. He still has plenty of muscle beneath the skin, which is a relief.

"Come on," I mutter, mostly to myself, mustering the energy to carry our combined weight. The road heads north, according to the compass arrow on my watch, which doesn't feel right, not one bit. I don't like the look of this dirt road, but so far, in the dark, I can't see any other option. Diablo manages to keep up, his legs moving on some drowsy autopilot, but if I let him go, he'd crumble into a pile. Every step feels like a mile, and every mile would probably feel like crossing a small country. The excitement I thought I'd experience about being in the wild again is quickly replaced by dread. I have no idea where I'm going or what I'm doing, and my guide is gravely ill with no apparent diagnosis.

As we continue along, the wind's nibble turns into a bite. *Shelter, fire, warmth.* I repeat Frost's essential three. After a few minutes of walking, I stop to look over my shoulder. Our progress is disheartening—we've put less than a hundred feet between us and the fence. Whatever motivation I had falls apart.

Then I notice a path to the right that cuts into the forest. I decide to take it, and feel relieved when the fence finally disappears from sight. It's the first time in a long time that I've felt like I'm going in the right direction. *Northeast.* That's what George said in class. *Suppose one makes it through the Darker Woods and past the Snowy Mountains . . . in the forest*—or whatever—*one can find* company. Something like that.

Knowing that I may finally be on the right track is encouraging. Unless George was lying about that too, but something tells me he wasn't, because his and Diana's futures rest on my ability to get there and get back. *Although he told me not to.* I still have many more questions, but it's too late. The past is in the past, severed from the present with the closing of that sliding door and the turning of my back.

As usual, I'm deep in thought when a voice inside my center yells for me to *STOP!* I stop dead in my tracks, and that's when I see it—

A clear string stretches horizontally across the path from tree to tree, barely a millimeter from my eyes. I roll my eyeballs down for fear of moving my head and see another thin string at the level of my chest and a third one at my knees. These triplet threads block the way, near-invisible at the speed I was going before my instinct shouted out. I roll my eyes to the left and see, hidden behind a tree, three rifles pointed straight at me. Each string is tied around a trigger, ready to blow the head, chest, or knees off the first person or creature to break it.

A snare.

And not a nice one.

Diablo and I would be dead right now, blown to bits, if not for that voice of instinct; an assortment of body parts on the forest floor. A leg, a rib, an eyebrow. I make a mental note to always trust my instinct from now on, stop being in my head when I should be focused on the path, and that maybe it's not such a good idea to walk at night. I edge slowly backward out of the rifles' range, easing Diablo to the ground. Then I collapse next to him, my hands badly shaking, my body processing the shock before my mind can. *That was close. Too close.*

Fuck.

I flatten my hands on the ground, which is dry and cracked.

The color of terracotta, not freshly ground coffee. Still, I feel a faint pulse of electricity in the earth, like a cord plugged into a socket, which helps me calm down. I stay here for a few minutes, until my heart settles back down to its usual beat per second. Then the wind blows again, and I remember what Frost said about exposure. I need to keep moving with Diablo and find a place to build a shelter, place some kind of barrier between us and the growing cold.

I wiggle my way under the lowest string, then grab Diablo's wrists and pull him through. Those ugly rifles stare at me the entire time like an alien creature with three stacked eyes, but they don't fire. Once Diablo is safely through, I consider setting the snare off to save the life of the next poor creature to wander along this trail, but I don't think making that much noise would be wise when the Hunters could easily be on my trail.

"I'm sorry," I tell the animal I've never met but already care for, who will die in this hypothetical scenario.

My eyes are tired, but I try to be as vigilant as ever. One thing has never been more apparent: It's not safe to walk in the dark, in this emotional state, without a second set of eyes. I start to wonder if the young Klujns walk at night, since they're nocturnal, but then I cut myself off mid-thought and tell myself to stay focused.

It is well past one when Diablo and I arrive at a clearing. It is round and about twenty strides across, covered in yellow leaves, hyphenated by a fallen log covered in multicolored mushrooms that look like coral. "This is as good as it's going to get," I tell the emptiness, checking that the coast is clear of traps before setting Diablo down. We're still too close to the fence for my liking, and there's no water source, but after our close call with the snare, staying put feels like the lesser of two evils.

Home for the night, I think, as I get to work on gathering materials to build a shelter with—sticks, twigs, and fallen pine branches. Anything I can find, because I don't have an axe to chop down trees with. I find three branches long enough to use as standing poles, then tie them at the top with one of my shoelaces because I don't have any rope. I feel proud of my resourcefulness, although there's no one here to witness the moment, and giving myself a high-five feels awkward. The structure stands, although it's a little wobbly. It couldn't survive a storm or a robust gust of wind, but the clouds cloaking the moon look harmless. In this cold, rain would be a death sentence.

When the main structure is in place, I start filling in the walls. I use those pine branches with their fans of needles like bird wings, then insulate the walls with carpets of moss and bunches of wet leaves. I yelp when I see my first bug, which *actually* looks alien with metallic green skin and too many eyes, but I have to get over my new fear of creepy crawlies pretty quickly, because irksome as they are, the cold is much more likely to kill me. The manual labor is oddly meditative and keeps my mind from wandering. By two a.m., I stand back to admire my work, filled with the thrill of accomplishment. *I just built my first shelter! With my bare hands!*

I'm about to pull Diablo inside when the wind returns like a warning, leaves jostling on branches, and I remember Maple's advice to *always look up*. I gaze up and see a dead tree above my head. My chest deflates; I've positioned my shelter *right under* a widowmaker. Its only branch is a bent black arm with a dozen wooden daggers, a whisper away from falling. It creaks as it swings, like a recording of spooky forest sounds.

I go from pride to defeat in seconds and any willpower I had quickly abandons me. I yell out and kick the shelter, and the stupid thing tumbles into a pile of twigs. I sink to the ground and cradle my knees, tucking my frozen nose between them. My

Blood Race has only just started, and I am failing spectacularly. At this rate it would be a miracle if I last until the morning. Explorers and Hunters spend their lives training for this, and the wild is still not easy on them. Meanwhile, I skimmed one textbook and spent an hour with some teenage Scouts, and I thought I could manage.

I press my hands over my face to blot out the world and my plummeting self-worth and breathe in the mossy scent of my palms. My lungs fill with crisp green air, a forest between my ribcage, and the smell is soothing. It reminds me that despite my obvious failures I am here, in the wild. Free to some extent, and that is a small success. I have to be patient with myself, because learning takes time. A lot of it is trial and error, but I feel too tired for trials right now.

"I'm sorry," I tell Diablo, even though he can't hear me. I've failed us both. Dramatically. We've been exposed for too long now, and soon, the cold will start to claim us piece by piece, starting with our toes and fingers. I imagine Grouse's Hunters finding my little frostbitten corpse come morning. The girl who thought she could traverse the wilderness, find the king, and take his heart—dead less than a mile from the starting line. They would fall over laughing.

I hear a sound in the darkness, just beyond the clearing. There's something out there; looking at me, I can feel it. I crawl over to Diablo and sit by his feet in case there's a large carnivore coming to attack us, lured by the promise of its next meal. This is, after all, the season when the wild is fattening up before winter dormancy.

I pick up a sharp stick and hold it up to the night, but that's where my courage ends. I have no whistle or bear spray, no energy left to stand on my feet and make my voice big. I'm too cold, and frankly, I'm too scared. I don't even know if that's what I'm supposed to do—*fight back or play dead?* My stick-hand shakes from cold or fear—I can no longer tell the difference.

The beast moves slowly around me, skirting the lip of the clearing, its large paws crushing twigs. A predator tracing a slow circle around its prey, just like Grouse's cyborg. *Maybe a Hunter come to finish the job*, I think, *or Showman.*

The creature moves out from its hiding spot, and I recoil, folding into myself like a piece of paper, folding until I can no longer fold.

I see a flash of color, white like a ghost.

And then I see its eyes.

Blue. Familiar. *Safe.*

Wolf.

16

I can't believe he's here. Diana must have set him free before she was taken. I pull Wolf into me, once again vouching that I will never let him go again. Seeing him gives me a new sense of hope. Here is a creature who knows the wild. I run my frozen fingers through his matted fur, and they feel warmer already. Wolf's belly and legs are crisped with mud, and leaves dangle in his long white fur like ornaments on the branches of a midwinter tree.

As my hands continue to explore him, I feel a strap lost in the mane of his neck. I take it off and see that it's like a collar with a waterproof pouch attached. I clumsily unzip the bag with numb fingers, and see a few items inside. *A parting gift from Diana?*

I take out the objects one by one. There's a small cylindrical canister with a piece of rolled black cloth inside. A thin book called *Klujn Runes* by Pomme Luden. Catrina Sherman's wife—the one who was abducted and killed by the DSO, and the reason why Sherman disappeared into the wild. This *must* be contraband. If Pomme was anything like her wife, she must have had a close relationship with Klujns. Glory's crystal-compass is also there among the items, with the tracker chipped out. To my great disappointment, there is no tent or sleeping bag.

I unfold the bundle of black cloth to find a large, round circle about the size of a hula hoop. The object has a presence about it, like ghosts pressed between two round panes of glass. Around the border are twelve twinkling gold runes, like the numbers on a clock that no longer tells the time. There is nothing inside the circle except for faint amber lines, like little nameless rivers or the constellations of a foreign sky. *What is it?* It doesn't look like clothing or a blanket, for that matter. It is much too thin for that.

My eyes are blinking more than usual, and I don't have the energy to decipher it now. Maybe I could translate those runes one by one, but they look more complicated than any runes I've seen before, like clusters of alien alphabets. *Why would Diana give me such a cryptic object?* She could have at least written me a note to go along with it—unless she didn't have time. It's the kind of treasure you could find in George's basement, and I imagine it must have been taken from a stand after a raid.

When I see nothing related to my immediate survival, I pack the items up and decide to study them tomorrow when my eyes aren't so tired.

Wolf looks over my shoulder, and I follow his gaze to Diablo and my crumpled shelter. I feel embarrassed that I now have a witness to my failure.

"We're not doing so well," I say, stating the obvious. "I don't know what's wrong with him."

Wolf goes to Diablo and presses his muzzle into his neck, maybe checking for a pulse or temperature. Then, Wolf paws at

Diablo's shoulder, and I help him, doing what I didn't dare to do when I was alone. I turn Diablo onto his side and peel the fabric away from his shoulder to free his arm, which is covered in ash-colored tattoos. His nipple puckers when it feels the cold, a muscular reflex synonymous with life; although, I've heard that some dead bodies can still have reflexes a few hours after death, so there goes that. Diablo's left shoulder blade is a sickly purple, and the site where Mercy stabbed him after the raid oozes green pus. Untreated. *Infected.* My fingers trace the path of his tattoos down his forearm, where there's a catheter stuck in the crook of his left elbow, crusted with a sparkling white substance just like the bear in the animal storehouse. I'm afraid to take the needle out in case it gets infected, or he starts to bleed out. I wonder what the Hunters did to him—what they used him for.

Then, I remember the plant that Diablo used to bind my injured foot with on our way to Circo. It numbed the pain and stopped the infection from spreading. "What about Violette leaf?" I ask Wolf. I don't know if he understands the question or has the same idea at the same time, but Wolf disappears into the woods and comes back a few minutes later carrying a thick stem in his mouth from muddy root to large smooth leaf. It has green and purple markings like immense butterfly wings.

"Yes!" I exclaim, ecstatic that he understood me. I take the stem from Wolf and break off the leaf. He stares at my other hand, as though waiting for his reward, and I toss him the root. Wolf sinks to the ground and starts to eat it.

Then, on the operating table of the forest floor, I get to work on Diablo. I spread the leaf over his shoulder blade and flatten it with my hands, but it won't stick. "Any of those sticky plants out there?" I ask Wolf, but I don't know their name. Wolf continues to chew his root—our teamwork was short-lived.

"I'm sorry," I tell Diablo. Then, I lift the edges of the leaf and spit on his skin, using my index finger to spread the saliva around the edges. I press the leaf back down, and this time, it sticks perfectly. My instinct has worked nicely for the second time tonight—*Klujn saliva is an adhesive.* Once Diablo's shoulder is bandaged, I tuck his arm back into his clothes and roll him back to supine. My hand rests on the crook of his collarbone, as I look at his unfocused eyes. His irises sway back down, and I'm mesmerized by their striking violet color, deep as an ocean. His pupils dilate, and his large body seems to relax even though he's still in another world. I remember the relief I felt when Diablo used the plant on me, and I can only hope it does the same for him. Then, his eyelids droop like closing curtains. *The show's over.* I bring two fingers to his throat and measure his pulse. Still slow, but it's getting stronger.

"Thank you," I tell Wolf, hoping this victory won't be followed too closely by defeat.

With the energy of another win, I decide to rebuild the shelter. I pick a new spot and check the canopy first, ensuring no dead tree branch is positioned right above it. The night sky looks back at me. *Coast clear.* I opt for a lean-to this time, stacking branches along the large fallen log that's already there, creating a low shelter with a slanted roof. When I've finished, I drag Diablo inside, then seal the top end with mounds of plant debris, keeping the hole at his feet partially open. The shelter is large enough for two, but I don't feel comfortable climbing in there next to him. If he woke up in the night and found me there I might die of embarrassment. I'm about to ask Wolf to go in there and keep him warm, when he slithers through the opening. I don't know why this hurts me—when I was just about to suggest it—but it does.

My joy at seeing Wolf quickly turns to sadness; the feeling that I'm not good enough for him. It's frustrating and disheartening—the sense that we're strangers on different journeys, not symbiotic like my mom and Mahta were. I used to feel so connected to Wolf when I was younger, but since our reunion, he's been more distant than ever. Maybe he's disappointed that I settled back into my human life and got complacent. That I wasn't brave enough to make a decision until it was made for me. I wanted to be in the wild with him, and now that we're together, I feel even worse than I felt to begin with.

I sit down in the doorway of the shelter, thinking about the ten essential items that Maple told me about. I would kill for any one of them right now, including that pasta. The bite of Klujn beard I had at the bonfire is long gone, and without food in my belly, the cold reaches in, turning me into an ice cube skeleton. The cold didn't seem so bad in theory, but now that it's real, it's all I can think about. It transforms me into a warmth-seeking organism that can think of only warm things. *Bed. Blanket. Socks. Pajamas. Hot water bottle.* I list these things in my head, sending myself into a sort of self-hypnosis. *Hot springs. Sunshine. Shower. Hot tub. Amethyst pools. Hmmm, Amethyst pools.*

Someone else's arms.

I can't focus on anything else, not even the pretty stars, with their blinking silvers, golds, pinks, blues, and greens. I think about my house, and all those comforts I took for granted. A bed, four walls, and a ceiling. There was electricity and light and warm water pouring out from a tap when you twisted it—which now feels akin to magic. Herbal soaps, pine-scented shampoo bars, and creams Diana made with essential oils and plants from her garden. I had freshly laundered clothes, crisp from the clothesline, that smelled like roses or green apples. Even the orphanage seems cozy in comparison to this. The ceiling leaked, but at least it had one.

I think about Diana's kitchen—*apothecary* is more fitting. The braids of garlic hanging from the walls. The bowl of freshly picked fruit and berries on the counter, veggies fermenting in jars along the windowsill, the containers of pesto and jam and pickled things. As much tea and coffee as I wanted. I've never been a big tea drinker, but now it's all I can think about. *Chamomile. Hibiscus. Peppermint. Vanilla.* My mouth waters as I imagine myself taking a sip, warming my entire body on its way down. It's funny how you only really care about things the second they're taken away. I hated growing up in Red River, but now my house is all I can think about, those basic comforts I took for granted.

I pick up a smooth, gray stone and weigh it in my palm. Maple told me that fire would be my lifeline out here, but I don't have the faintest clue how to start a fire with my bare hands. *Shelter, fire, warmth.* Frost's words come back to haunt me. In my thirst for adventure and freedom, I underestimated each and every one of those. Out here, nothing comes easily. Every hoop to jump through requires skills I don't have. Like a Scout badge, everything takes intense training to master. And because it is earned, it is appreciated entirely differently. For tonight, it is my destiny to be cold.

I peer into the shelter, where Diablo and Wolf are sleeping. Diablo looks finally at peace, no longer in the acrobatics of his turmoil. And, in a day with many losses, I'll take any win I can get.

I bunch some leaves under my head and lie down, curling

into a ball, pulling the mysterious round cloth over my body, and my sweater over my nose. I draw my sleeves over my hands and hold the fabric in my closed fists. I feel the itch of insect legs exploring the strange, warm mountain that just appeared in their ecosystem, climbing the ridge of my arms to the summits of my earlobes. I think about the young Klujns again—where they are on their journey which started almost two months ago. *If they haven't already reached Circo.* I remember the night they left—when I saw them cascading down the hillside, moving through that invisible barrier and disappearing into the night. Warwick's daughter was at the front—the fierce, beautiful, feminine one who always looked angry. Dressed in her stunning black costume, her claws dipped in black like some kind of peculiar manicure, a crystal weapon at her side. No backpack or spotted wolf, come to think of it, but I couldn't see everything from afar. I wonder where she is now. What it feels like to be in her skin. To be so confident. To have wild friends. To arrive home and be welcomed.

Not torn between two worlds.

A tightrope walker balancing between platforms.

I wonder where Circo has gone and how far away they are. How many mountains and rivers separate us? And what is happening there right now? Did Daciana and Glory make it? Have they already forgotten me? Diablo must know where they are . . .

It's *innate.*

But it's not inside me yet.

My eyes stay closed for longer than they remain open, and my thoughts begin to slow. My dream world bleeds into this waking one, bringing a series of strange images. I see the moon and sun on each side of the sky. The moon has purple eyes, and the sun has green eyes. Then, they meet in the middle and collide. And there I am, a sun-moon hybrid.

George.

My father.

The puppet.

Sleep comes like a thief, and I let it take me.

17

By the blue hour of morning, I've managed to sleep uncomfortably for a few hours. My muscles are cramped and the ground has leeched every measure of heat from my body. *But I survived.* Although surviving and thriving are two very different things—by tonight, I'll need better shelter, a warmer blanket, and a successfully lit fire. That may as well be lightyears away, though, because I have no clue what will happen between now and then.

I sit up and gaze at the clearing, which is coated in morning dew. I stretch my neck and check my fingers for frostbite—luckily, they have survived the night's harshest hours, but the days will only get shorter, and the nights will only get colder.

I listen to the sounds of the forest. The buzz of insects, the hoot of an owl. And then comes the birdsong, painting the forest with color, a song of freedom. The sun begins to rise behind the trees, and as its soft warmth reaches me, I feel the life slowly return to my body. I realize why Klujns worship the sun: Without it, we literally would die. As it rises higher in the sky, its brightness makes me nervous. Walking in daylight will make us visible to Hunters. Grouse said they had a break this weekend—I can only hope he's right.

I peer into the shelter, where Diablo is still sleeping. He is no longer sweating, and his fever seems to have broken. Wolf is already awake and gone, probably to scavenge something or whatever it is wolves do in the early hours. I let Diablo sleep in despite the voice in my gut that tells me we need to get moving.

My mouth is dry, and I realize I haven't had any water in . . . *When was the last time?* I leave the safety of the clearing and venture down a steep slope until I see a stream. I scramble downhill, holding on to trees, doing my best not to slip and break a leg before breakfast. When I reach the stream, I notice it rushes south toward the fences. The water looks pristine, and my thirst gets the better of me. I get down on my knees and slurp up a few big mouthfuls. Only when my thirst is quenched do I realize that it was reckless to drink untreated water. It could contain bacteria—or *parasites.* But it's too late, so all I can do is cross my fingers and do better next time. I add "learn to purify water" to my mental to-do list, which keeps getting longer by the minute.

I return to the clearing, where Wolf is back, having brought Diablo some more medicinal plants. *I wish he had been kind enough to get me breakfast.* There are winterberry shrubs around the clearing that I hadn't noticed in the dark, and I lift my sweater up and pick as many as my shirt will hold. Then, I sit outside the shelter with my back against the log, savoring my meal, though it's a long way from a feast. The berries explode on my tongue with their icy sweetness.

My mind feels sharper as the sugar and nutrients enter my bloodstream. I look at the pouch from last night and inspect its contents in daylight. I don't entirely understand this strange assortment. Glory's pendant—no longer a government tracker, but it still works as a whistle to scare off predators and a compass that warms the closer I am to her. Then there's the book of runes and that circle of black cloth, slightly crumpled after a night of use.

Inside the book, the dedication reads: *À Catrina, ma femme sauvage.*

The first chapter starts with simple runes, and I recognize the symbol for the moon, my symbol in the Blood Race. I'm not likely to forget it soon, seeing as the brand has turned into a pale scar on my forearm. In a very long alphabet of hundreds of runes, I see other symbols I recognize—lake, river, sun, seed, fire. Some of the runes look familiar—like journey, danger, animal, wolf, as well as impasse. And then there are new ones altogether, like winter, flower, detour, home, death, and sex. The alphabet is endless.

I flip to the second chapter, which shows how to integrate these simple runes in spells and rituals. The rune for water, for example, is traced on the surface to purify it. Other simple spells exist to grow essential herbs, fruit, vegetables, and flowers. As the chapters go on, the level of difficulty increases. Runes are combined to form sentences of two to five symbols—written like a tower from top to bottom. And then, more complicated rune-sentences form circles and spirals. Some are so complex that they look like wheels, clocks, or mandalas. There are chandeliers of runes with dripping rune crystals. The sentences and spells are artworks in themselves, and become progressively more advanced, from *building a protective camouflage circle* to *summoning the gods*. You can trace small wheels for personal use, or the stand can draw giant ones for more powerful magic. Many of the runes look similar to their neighbors, where a dot or dash can mean the difference between *bliss* and *blindness*, *desire* or *disease*. I can't imagine what would happen if you got a symbol wrong. I learned the hard way when I followed that glowing rune in the Katacombes, convinced it meant *west,* when really—as I now see, according to the alphabet in chapter one—it meant *den.*

I put the book aside and go back to the circle of black cloth, smoothing it down with my fingers. *If only I could figure it out.* I try to scratch a bit of it, in case it's been painted in Moonlight Leaf, but nothing happens—there's nothing to be scratched. *Weird.* I know I'm probably missing something obvious, but without coffee I can't bring myself to figure out what that is. It's like trying to use my human senses to decipher something intended for Klujns, just like their glowing markers in the woods and the invisible barriers of their stands. But how can I know what I'm looking for if I've never seen it?

My press-on nail has fallen off, revealing my smooth nailless finger. I remove the others too—I won't be needing them anymore.

"Where did you get that?" Diablo's voice startles me. He's conscious! He emerges from the shelter and stands too quickly, wincing against a head rush. Diablo closes his eyes for a moment, and then opens them again. His question is still there as he looks at me and the object, burning with contempt.

"My adoptive mother gave it to me," I say. "She must have gotten it from my dad's study." *My dad.* It's crazy to think I called George that half my life, without knowing how close to the truth it really was. And like the answer to a riddle, now that I hear the word, it seems all too sickeningly obvious.

Which still doesn't answer the question of how my mom got pregnant, and how I came to be.

"What is it?" I ask Diablo.

He hesitates, then decides to tell me. "It's a druda map."

A map? Why didn't I think of that?

Maybe because the object has no township names or landmarks.

"It's a sacred object. Drudas have the same one their whole lives and keep adding to it. The only way they'd separate from one is if they died." Despite being weakened, Diablo is his usual impatient self. It's surreal to think that only a few hours ago he was at death's door and now I've already done something to upset him.

"Maybe they died of natural causes?"

"Drudas live past a hundred."

"Look, I'm sorry . . ." I start. This isn't going how I thought it would go. "I didn't— I don't even know what a druda is. I can give it back."

Diablo shakes his head—obviously, it's too late for that. "Just protect it with your life. Its value cannot be measured." In other words: Don't leave it crumpled on the forest floor like a discarded emergency blanket. He looks around the clearing, trying to piece together where we are and how we got here. He still looks weak and tired, but in terms of personality, the old Diablo is back—the one who is serious, standoffish, and fiercely independent. I don't get a *thank you* for saving him, not that I was expecting one, but a bit of kindness would be nice instead of straight-up resentment. Diablo seems to have forgotten that we come from the same place, and that my mother saved his life. And now, me.

He fights off another head rush, and I go to help him, but he holds up a hand to stop me. His claws are still half-in, and although I'm no expert, the murkiness makes them look unhealthy.

"It's not a crime to accept help," I say. Diablo doesn't answer and avoids my eyes as he lowers himself to the ground, leaning against the mushroom-covered log.

"Where are we?"

"The Darker Woods. East of the Deeper Woods, and north of the Loudhouse."

"I mean—*why* are we here? You and me?"

Those words hit like metal bullets, not enough to kill, but enough to cause some bruising. My cheeks grow hot, and I feel embarrassed, realizing that I hadn't prepared myself for this moment, for what would happen *after* we got out, when Diablo regained consciousness. But if I hadn't asked Grouse to release him, chances are, he wouldn't have survived the night. Not that he's the perfect picture of health right now.

"I went to the Loudhouse . . . and I asked Grouse to let you go," I say, the nerves making my voice shake.

"Why did he agree?"

"Because . . ." And then the truth is on my lips before I can stop it. Maybe it's Diablo's eyes, the intelligence inside them like nothing can get past him. If he can't read my mind, he'll at least be able to read my energy.

"I told him that I could get him the king's heart."

"Warwick's?"

I nod, feeling ashamed of myself. It's easy to analyze a situation looking back with a clear and logical mind, but last night, it was the only way I could think of saving both his life and mine, not to mention Diana and the others.

Diablo thinks about this for a long moment, and thankfully, he doesn't laugh. Not that laughing is his thing. He doesn't even look angry anymore, just pensive. He studies the ground with a thoughtful silence, and I feel desperate to fill that silence.

"It was the only way he'd let us out," I babble. "I have until Darkest Day, in mid-January. Then they dumped you by the fence, and I tried to walk with you but . . . I couldn't get far."

If I was expecting a pat on the shoulder, I don't get it. Still, it's a miracle he doesn't seem upset about Warwick's heart.

"You should have left me there," Diablo says. Whatever the Hunters did to him, Diablo doesn't offer up the information.

I can't imagine the trauma of being kept in the Loudhouse for two months, thinking every day could be your last.

Diablo looks through the dense trees surrounding us, and I can feel his other senses working. "I have to go," he says, and I wonder if he can feel how close we *really* are to the fences. "I have to get back. They need me."

I feel flustered and embarrassed. *What did I expect? That he would feel indebted and offer to walk with me to Circo?* Diablo is his own person, and now that we are both free, he owes me nothing. Maybe the problem is that I had expectations to begin with. As Mr. Mogel said on the oval yesterday—*"The first thing to die in the wild is your plan."*

And, just like that—my plan is dead.

Diablo stands up too quickly and grimaces through a wave of dizziness. Despite his impatience, he still seems incredibly weak.

"*Wait.*" I don't want to beg or grovel or force him to stay if he doesn't want to. But I'm not ready to be alone, and he's not either, by the looks of it. All I have to lead me to Circo is a human watch, a Klujn compass, and a questionable map, as well as the inkling that I should go northeast. But now that the sun has risen, I couldn't even tell you what direction northeast is.

"We can help each other," I say. "If you lose consciousness out there, you'll be a sitting duck."

"It's not my responsibility to take you to Circo," he says. "You should go home."

"I don't have a home." I don't want to sound too needy, but it's true. I have nothing except the possibility of a home . . . a fate that he holds in his hands. "And I don't want to be exiled. I can try to match your pace."

"We don't have the same pace. What will take you months will take me three days."

Months. Really?!

The words hurt. I know I can be fast, learn quickly, and adapt, but my version of fast is not the same as his. The wounded part of me wants to tell Diablo to *Go, then. What are you waiting for?* But the logical part knows I need him; I have so much to learn, and I'm not ready to do it alone. Not until I've mastered the basics. I know I can add value eventually, even though I'm not sure what that value is.

"In good health," I say. Diablo arches an eyebrow, and I go on. "We might not have the same pace—when you're healthy. But how do you know how fast you can go today?" When he doesn't answer, I keep going. "A few hours ago, you were practically dead, and you would have died had I not bound your shoulder. Adrenaline might be tricking you into thinking you're better, but I can see that you're sicker than you realize. Maybe you're afraid to show weakness—"

"I'm not afraid of that." But he seems to be considering my words.

"I'm not asking you to hold my hand and escort me to Circo," I go on. I feel angry, but at this moment, I no longer care. "I'm not asking for the world. I'm asking for a few days. Until we're both ready to go our separate ways." I want to take a cheap shot and add that my mother would be disappointed if he didn't—but I don't. It's like he understands, and his eyes shift from irritation to understanding.

"One day. But you have to keep up."

"One day," I repeat, as Diablo turns his back on me. I quickly pack up my few possessions and break camp, returning the branches and plant debris to where I found them so that it looks like no one was here. Then, I fashion my CAMP MIDNIGHT sweater into a bag, so I have a place to stash my belongings. I'm cold without it, but I'll get warm while walking. I'm extra careful not to leave anything behind.

After a few minutes, the clearing is back to how it looked when we arrived. I join Diablo at a path on the other side. He has taken his shoes off and his feet are bare on the ground. "Won't your feet get cold?"

"You don't know a forest until you walk barefoot in it," he tells me, and then he turns his back on me and starts walking, having already determined what path we need to take. A little arrow on my watch confirms that we are indeed going northeast.

As we take our first steps out of the clearing, I feel like things might be okay after all. I survived my first night. I made shelter, and tonight, I will learn to make fire. The first week will be the hardest, but after that, my body will be broken in. *One hoop at a time.*

I take a few more steps and realize that Wolf isn't following. I turn around and see that he's still sitting in the clearing, watching us go, framed by a tunnel of green. "Come on, Wolf," I say, but Wolf doesn't budge. I start to lose patience—it's one thing that he chose to help Diablo and not me, but we're meant to be two halves of one whole. Right now it feels like we come from different planets. I can't translate the coldness in his eyes, the detachment, like he's already given up on me. It is as confusing as the runes in that book and on that round cloth-map.

I take a few more steps and turn around, and Wolf still hasn't budged. I'm so angry I could yell. Then, Diablo says—

"He can't come."

18

"What do you mean?" I stare at Diablo, but he isn't joking. *Wolf.* For all my earlier complaints about our relationship, I can't do this without him. "Why can't he?"

"For a Royal Klujn to have their wolf with them in the Blood Race would be an unfair advantage," Diablo says. "Every young Klujn starts with nothing except a weapon of their choosing." It makes sense, even if I don't want it to. Wolf probably knows where Circo is and could lead me there easily. His body would be large enough to provide both warmth and shelter. And he could forage for me, find me things to eat—*if he wanted to.* With him as my guide, I would never have to learn.

I don't argue because I know Diablo's telling the truth—I saw Warwick's daughter leave Circo without her spotted wolf. He goes on to tell me, in a clipped explanation, that where adult wolves are scouts who move *before* the stand does to find a new place to lay down shallow roots, the competing Klujns' spotted wolves walk behind and act as pacemakers for the back of the Race. They arrive at the new location of the stand right as the Ice Moon rises and the Race ends, when the stand's barrier closes to anyone who hasn't arrived on time. You don't want to see the wolves during your Blood Race because that means you're at the back of the pack, flirting with elimination.

Then Diablo delivers the second blow of the morning:

"If you arrive too late, you're not only rejected by the stand but also by your wolf."

It takes all my strength not to collapse and give up right then.

Wolf is a pacemaker for the back of the Race.

If I don't make it to Circo on time, the bond my mother forged between us will be broken.

I'll be completely on my own for life.

"Couldn't I just walk with him?" I ask Diablo. "Stay at the back and overtake at the last minute?"

"What strategy you use is up to you," he says. "But I wouldn't recommend it." The word *strategy* sounds strange—I didn't know that the Blood Race required any strategy beyond *survival*. I don't think I have one strategic bone in my body. "From past experience, staying at the back of the pack is not a good idea. If you get injured, then the wolves will overtake you, and you'll be left behind. Some Klujns Race quickly to arrive first, but that strategy isn't perfect, either. When it comes to Initiation, it's about how much you can impress the gods, and speed isn't as important as what you learn out here."

"So what would you do?"

"The middle of the pack is the best place," he says. "If you can catch up. And . . ." he goes on, his voice now with a serrated edge. "If I was lucky enough to have a personal guide, I would stop wasting his time, go with him, and think about strategy later."

You're the one who mentioned strategy in the first place, I want to say. But I know Diablo's right—staying behind with Wolf would be the comfortable thing to do, but it would put my fate into the hands of the weather and the mountains, and I don't know what obstacles I will face. Accidents are *accidents* because they are unplanned. I can't afford to waste any more time. I wonder what Diablo meant by *Initiation* and impressing the gods, but I know it's not the time to ask.

I feel angry at the world. Angry at Wolf, too. If he cared about me, couldn't he have tried to find a way to warn me? Instead, he let me waste my time and grapple with possible options when there was only ever one. *Maybe this is why something felt off between us,* I realize. *Perhaps he has already started to reject me because he doesn't think I can make it in the wild, like those birds in the animal storehouse.* The thought is a knife to the ribs, and the weight of all that I have to prove is crushing.

Diablo's patience is fading, and my goodbye with Wolf is unceremonious. I look back at him, that white ghost framed by the trees. His freckled face, long whiskers, and white eyebrows. The two large black spots on his back—*two lives.* His eyes are guarded as a castle with a moat around it. *I don't want tough love.* I want something tender and gentle and sweet. But that's not what I get, and that's not what Nature is likely to give me, either. So even though my insides scream—*Wrong! This is so wrong!*—I turn my back on him.

As I walk away, I decide it's easier not to look over my shoulder, at the life I'm leaving behind. I tell myself that the things I yearn for don't exist in the past but in the future and that every step I take will bring me closer to whatever that future looks like. That if I *do* see Wolf again, it will be to have the kind of relationship my mom and Mahta had. He will accept me, and we will be friends and allies.

Diablo walks quickly, winding through the forest trails without sentimentality. He has one pace—fast—and I'd hate to see how much quicker he could go if he was healthy. By late morning, my heart still aches from leaving Wolf, but the physicality of walking is a good distraction. My thighs burn as we go up hills with hardly enough switchbacks. The ecosystems we walk through change rapidly, like little pockets of life. A forest of blue trees, with skirts of fog. A natural tunnel that winds through the roots of giant trees, mushrooms abound. There are fields of endless wildflowers and resting butterflies. The rubble of roads and abandoned townships, reclaimed by weeds and freshwater ponds colonized by algae. I want to ask Diablo why the wild is like this—these miniature, spontaneous ecosystems—but I don't want to push him away with my *stupid human questions.*

Around midday, we reach the biggest road we've seen all day. On the other side is a sprawling black desert of felled trees, their roots still smoking underneath the ground. An immense cemetery. "The wall of death," I say, realizing where we are. I feel the presence of ghosts here; all those dead trees and animals whose lives ended in confusion and terror. The ones that couldn't escape. Abandoned machinery dots the expanse like the skeletons of metallic megafauna. The landscape looks otherworldly in its palette of black, gray, and red embers. A giant black river that runs from northwest to southeast, a few miles across, and an infinite amount of miles long. A giant scar over the face of the Boreal.

We have no choice but to cross it, walking on the still-warm ground. Diablo tells me that the reason why this region was so heavily felled is because of its accessibility. We are in a valley between mountain ranges—the western mountains we crossed to get to Circo and the eastern ones we're going toward now. Here, trucks can quickly get in and get out. Because of this, these centuries-old forests have been destroyed and turned into a smoking wasteland. And this is just the beginning of what Grouse has planned.

If forests are the lungs of the earth, then the Boreal is destined to turn black and gangrenous. Soon, the world will have to breathe through masks.

At least they will be well-fed.

I ask Diablo about the ecosystems from before, those thriving little worlds like living exhibits at a museum. He tells me that they were made by spotted wolves and other Klujn animals, who are seed-spreaders. These animals wander dangerously close to the fences in an attempt to resuscitate the fragile ecosystems there before they disappear completely and rehouse creatures who have lost their homes, as well as host migrating birds and butterflies that have nowhere to rest on their migrations. But such a mission has its risks, and many fall prey to snares or poachers. I ask Diablo what he means by *Klujn animals*.

"A seed of viaţă can turn into anything," he says. "Plant, mushroom, animal, coral. The languages a Klujn can learn are infinite."

"Can you create an animal that's gone extinct?" I ask.

"No, but you can bring new kinds of life into the world."

"So, spotted wolves are . . ."

"Created by Klujns," he says. "As are blue sparrows and many other creatures. All designed to live off plants and things that Nature has in abundance."

My mind spins—it blows my mind that a single tiny crystal seed has the potential to turn into a spotted wolf, for example. I can't imagine the technicalities of growing a new animal from scratch. Then again, it's hard to imagine that the forests on our planet started with a seed, and where did that seed come from? Which came first—the tree or the seed, the chicken or the egg, the Klujn or the viaţă? There's more magic in Nature than I realized; most of the time, we call it *science*.

I think about Diablo's words.

A seed of viață can turn into anything.

The languages a Klujn can learn are infinite.

The path winds into the jagged mountains we talked about at a gradual but constant incline. "Pray for difficult terrain," he says. "The more difficult—the less chances of humans." I have a newfound appreciation for the steep climb, the root staircases, and the boulder scrambling. This forest is otherworldly, with curious rocks, minerals, and dangling vines. There is so much life squeezed into every single inch of this place, and a feeling that those who have been displaced are welcome, always welcome.

Our narrow path bends through the forest but breaks nothing, following the earth's curves. There are no crystal altars here, and no glowing runes traced on the trees, but the wildness is slowly beginning to return and I feel my senses sharpen. Here, birds have a place to rest and sing. Rodents can burrow into the rich, cool earth. Small mammals lay by glistening streams and enjoy the shade of trees. Those little colorful mushrooms decorate every fallen tree trunk or decaying branch.

As we reach a viewpoint, I can see the Darker Woods in front and below us, with its abundant lakes and rivers. I squint at the horizon, trying to make out those white silhouettes of the Snowy Mountains in the distance, but they must be a hundred miles away, at least, and I see nothing. Dark clouds roll across the sky, and an orphan raindrop falls on my cheek.

"You should pray for bad weather, too," Diablo says. "Humans have been softened by their comfort. They've become so afraid of the rain."

While I feel relieved that the wall of death is behind us, I fear to imagine what would happen if humans were to build roads that came up here. The treasures they would rip from the earth and carry away, piece by piece. Would they know when to stop, or would they take everything? It's saddening to think that the ecosystems we just walked through may one day be a ghost hill.

* * *

As we wind downhill, the sunlight becomes scarce, trickling down from one branch to the next until there's barely any left by the time it reaches the forest floor. Diablo is a good guide, albeit on the silent side, and I try to observe as much as I can. His eyes are always searching, his hands constantly moving. He fashions a sort of burlap sack out of dried plants and a bowl out of dried leaves. He scoops up water and purifies it with a simple trace of his giant index claw, his right one. I see the slight fizz of blue sparks and an alchemical transformation taking place, where the surface smokes for a few seconds before becoming still again. I know that Klujn magic isn't *abracadabra*—that there's a certain chemistry behind it—but it still feels pretty impressive to me. It's hard to learn when Diablo only shares information when he feels like it. Still, it's a better education than if I was alone, and my mind is a sponge.

By afternoon, my pace slows, and an angry blister blooms on my heel. The small red sore brings supernatural pain until I can think of nothing else. I don't know how Diablo does it, walking barefoot when there are so many sharp rocks on the path and venomous insects. Maybe one day I'll find the courage to try it, but for now, those soles are one of my last human comforts, and I cling to them. The afternoon light is already golden, and the day is passing much too quickly. Every time Diablo goes around a bend, I'm unsure if he'll disappear on me. There's still so much to learn and observe, so I dig deep and continue on despite the aches and pains.

I want to know everything there is to learn about the Blood

Race. I remember bits and pieces from Circo—the Ceremony of Fire on our first night there, which makes sense now since *fire* is one of the first survival skills a Klujn must learn. The angry gods were summoned by a waft of pine and sage, peering into our bodies and eliminating the one who showed the least promise of change. *Are the gods here?* There were five challenges in the Blood Race, starting with the cave, which required us to retrieve a proof of passage. Then the fights, the feast, and the Midnight Rose.

Were they random challenges invented by the king for his amusement, or do they contain a secret code that could help me out here?

We're in a cloud forest now; the forest smells so thick that my lungs feel like they're growing fungi. We pass through a grove of weeping willows—or some Klujn variation—with long tendrils of white fluff that I recognize as Klujn beard. It is not coral green, it turns out, but white and tasteless. However, it still contains nutritional value, so I stuff a few clouds of the stuff into my pocket. The farther we get from humans, the more relaxed Diablo seems. I finally work up the courage to ask him a question.

"Where do I find my proof of passage?" My voice crackles after hours of silence. He's quiet for a while, and I start to fear that he'll simply ignore me when he finally answers.

"You're jumping ahead. You should be focusing on *beginner* tasks." I'm getting used to his constant put-downs, but they still hurt.

"Like?"

"Purifying water is a good place to start."

"So, how do I purify water?" I wonder if he'll dismiss my question, but the forest has made him more generous.

"You can't do something if you don't understand why you're doing it."

"Then help me understand."

Diablo sighs. "Healthy molecules of *living* water look like pristine snowflakes," he says. "When they travel down rivers, they maintain their perfect shapes. However, when they hit sharp angles, like the pipes that humans build, they break. The water you drink is dead. And, since you're mostly made of water, drinking dead water affects your health.

"Water is the greatest elixir in the natural world, and purifying it isn't only about eliminating bacteria. It's also about restoring its molecular shape and bringing it back to life so that your body can reap its benefits. Some Klujns live off water and moonlight alone, but it's not the kind of water you drink at home."

"How do you fix it?" I ask. "You learn the rune for it and trace it on the water?"

"Yes. You start with a small amount, and then you go larger. A bowl, a pond, and eventually an entire lake. But you need to set an intention," he says, "and believe that it's possible."

"You mean, I need to believe it before I see results?"

"Yes."

"How?"

"A leap of faith," he says. And now, the cave makes sense. "That is what separates humans and Klujns. Humans need to see something to believe it. Klujns know that they need to believe it to see it."

"So, if you don't believe it . . ."

"Then you'll never see it," he says. "Water is just water, soil is just soil, and magic doesn't exist."

"And then . . . will you teach me how to make fire? I mean, I've done it at home, countless times, but we had newspaper and matches . . ."

"You'll need a fire crystal—each Klujn should have one. It'll help you make fire in any environment and help you keep your core body temperature."

"Where do I find one of those?"

"One thing at a time."

"So why does the Blood Race happen in winter if it's this hard to survive?"

"That's *why* it happens in winter," Diablo answers. This is our longest conversation, and I feel his patience fading. "Because the cold has a lot to teach us. Adversity, if used correctly, can make you grow. Nothing significant was ever achieved by staying comfortable."

Diablo turns his back on me and speeds up. *Conversation over.* I stow away the bits I learned like the items in my pockets.

* * *

Magic hour is muted by the fog, and the late afternoon brings with it the first of several bad omens. It starts off with a fresh boot print in the mud. "Not a Hunter," Diablo says, bending down to inspect it like a fortune teller reads tea leaves. "All Hunter boots have a triangle motif on one sole and a diamond on the other."

The second omen comes a few minutes later when we see a little Hunter's shack on stilts. It has a lit window and a chimney wisping smoke into the air. A crackling fire outside makes my cold bones want to walk toward it, but then I stop dead in my tracks. Strips of drying meat and white fur hang like clothes on a clothesline.

Then, less than half a mile later, we find the third bad omen of the day. A family of reindeer—slain. A mother and her three babies.

"Golden-antlered reindeer," Diablo says, crouching down to

inspect the magnificent white beasts. The mother is larger than a moose, and the babies are the size of deer with small bodies and long legs. I remember the dazzling golden antlers I saw in Grouse's—or Santos's—Hunting room. The mother's freckled coat has been roughly skinned, as well as the babies. There are bullet holes riddled in their necks, which suggest they weren't shot cleanly once but that the poachers had a lousy aim and let the creatures suffer. *They had time to realize what was happening.*

"A single one of these creatures can reforest a thousand acres a year," Diablo says. "The poachers must have surprised them while they were drinking.

"There are rules, in the forest," he goes on. "A mother and her young are considered sacred. Untouchable. The gods won't be happy about this."

I feel the sky darken and the weather change, a cold wind, and tell myself it's just a coincidence; the gods don't have eyes or ears.

My fury is a mountain. I want to scream and run back to that shack on stilts. Slit the throats of the people who did this for what they took and all they left to waste. All for what—a bit of meat, fur, gold? I'd use my own bare claws if I had to. They may be small, but they are sharp.

I kneel down and look into one of the baby's tree-green eyes, open and glassy and scared. I remember reading that the retina captures the last image it sees, and I feel saddened by the thought that this animal's last moment in the world was facing a creature who had no respect for its life.

Diablo reaches into his bag and places an offering on the mother, near the cascade of dried black blood that spills from her throat like a frozen waterfall. Tears fill his eyes and he lets them fall; he doesn't try to hide them, or apologize for showing emotion. He sheds the tears that his body needs, and when he's finished, he stands back up, tells me that it's getting late, that we should find a place to camp before sunset, far from here.

I understand it, then, his resentment toward humans. His frustration toward me, who he associates with the same people who did this. I could never do something like this—not to an innocent. I have taken two human lives—Rachel's and Elizabeth's—because I had no choice. I don't know if I could kill again.

Although I'll have to if I want to return with Warwick's heart.

Seeing that slain family, I feel an appetite growing inside me: a desire for revenge and violence. A black seed. Just a seed, but capable of growing into something that spreads across continents.

There's a shadow of a large black bird on the ground, but when I look up, I see only ominous clouds. I feel them coming closer, these *gods*, wherever they are, whatever they look like, moving in like a front of bad weather. I tell myself that it's just the dying day, the changing light, but my gut can no longer be fooled by my mind.

19

After the reindeer, Diablo gives me the cold shoulder. He makes us take a long detour around a lake and over another hill, taking the most rugged path, which is hardly a path at all. I'm exhausted and emotionally drained, my shoes have rubbed the skin of my ankles into oblivion, and this is only the first day. How can I take *months* of this? My hunger has turned into a low and constant groan like a dying reptile, and we walk until the golden-gray sky turns purple.

By twilight, we enter a forest of Carnifloras. An endless sea of black silhouettes stretches out. Their reaching, agitated branches feel more animal than plant. Occasionally, there is a deep, low groan. The roses that grow on them have shriveled and died, and the ground is covered in petals of different colors. I have to remind myself that the stories about Carnifloras aren't true, but I still feel nervous being surrounded by them.

Diablo stops in front of the largest one he can find, telling me that this is where we'll spend the night. I'm surprised for a few reasons: This Carniflora still has black roses, unlike her neighbors. The day that Diablo promised me is over, and this doesn't feel like a goodbye. And because he starts building his shelter right *underneath* the tree. But the Carniflora he's chosen looks solid, and with the smell of rain growing closer and the wind howling, *solid* might be a good thing. The tree's roots slither near my shoes like black snakes half-buried in the soil. *It's going to be a long night.*

"When you have a meaningful experience with a tree," Diablo says, "it changes the way you see a forest." I'm not entirely sure what he means. I liked climbing on trees as a child or picking apples in the fall or tapping for maple in the spring, but the only *meaningful* experience I've had was with the Midnight Rose, which was more terrifying than poignant.

I watch Diablo as he starts peeling a thin layer of bark from the Carniflora's trunk. He doesn't use a knife, only his hands, and the bark peels off without force. Diablo tells me that Carnifloras can shed a layer of skin—*if you ask permission*. To carve the bark is like cutting a person's skin, and too much damage can kill them. Among the world's most ignorant and foolish, in Diablo's eyes, are those whose first impulse upon seeing a tree is to carve their initials inside a love heart.

Diablo stretches the bark until it cracks, revealing a fibrous, cottony material. Then, he works the fibers with the skill and speed of a magician until it forms a charcoal-colored sheet of fabric. Within minutes, Diablo has a small tent standing that looks just like the ones at Circo, only a bit less sophisticated. Diablo looks up at me after placing the last wooden peg into the ground.

"Where are you going to sleep tonight?" he asks me, and my cheeks flush. I wasn't expecting us to share a tent . . . I was just watching. I want to tell him that, but the words don't materialize.

I busy myself by looking around for building materials, but

there isn't much aside from petals, and I don't feel like sleeping on a bed of psychedelic substances. Diablo watches me out of the corner of his eye. He disappears for a few minutes and comes back with wet hair, as though he went for a swim. Then, he gets a fire going in record time. There are real flames dancing and casting thick black smoke into the sky. I step toward the warmth like a moth drawn to a flame, wondering if the smoke will make us visible, but I'm sure Diablo knows what he's doing.

Diablo grills plants, roots, and mushrooms and seasons them with herbs. Then he makes skewers and spikes them with chunks of a red, meaty-looking protein, laying them down to cook over the flames. *Vegera?* I think—the plant protein that the Scouts were talking about. *But where did he get it?* Then, maybe just to show off, Diablo takes a piece of pine bark he pocketed earlier and grinds it into a fine white powder, making flour. He mixes it with the last bit of water we have, a pinch of salt and wild oregano, shapes it into a ball, and cooks it on the fire.

Vegetables. Mushrooms. Bread. And a questionable protein.

My mouth waters at the idea of my first real meal in what feels like forever—*if* he's intending to share, unlike the shelter. My hunger feels primal, a desire to devour and fill the hollowness inside my body. I wonder if all Klujns have classes to learn how to shop and cook in the grocery store of the wild, where nothing has a price tag. Diablo seems to have a gift for it. When he catches me looking and sees that I've made little progress with shelter, he shakes his head in disappointment.

"Just go get water," he says, passing me the leaf bowl he made earlier and pointing me toward our nearest water source. "And make sure to purify it." I don't want to leave the fire's side, but I want to feel useful. I take the bowl from him and wander down the sliver trail, afraid a snake will slither across my shoes. The forest opens up, and I find myself on a beach of white limestone rocks, a sprawling lake of pure blue water, and a pine forest on the other side.

"*Wow.*" *This is the wild I remember.* The emotion of the day is behind me now, and even though I still feel sad about leaving Wolf and that slaughtered family of reindeer, all I can feel now is gratitude. I am alone in this giant amphitheater at sunset. A slow-moving spectacle of drifting pink clouds and the occasional bird. If I was to watch for longer, I would see the rise of the moon and her glowing arc across the sky. The appearance of stars. Longer still, and I would see the movement of the earth around the sun. The trees losing the last of their leaves and the falling of snow, blanketing everything in white. Then, flowers blooming in the spring, the migrations of returning birds, and summer's wrath. Until the show would end, only to start over. The same, but never the same, like a journey that ends where it began. I feel a burst of joy in my chest, and I want to yell, to throw my voice out into the horizon like a bouncing pebble, but disrupting the silence feels disrespectful, like raising your voice in a place of worship.

The smell of baking bread floods my mouth with saliva. I look over my shoulder and see the fire glowing through the trees, but that's all I can see from here. The sun dips behind me to the west, and I turn my focus back to the beach, the water, and the challenge Diablo gave me before the darkness makes it impossible to work. *Purify water—or don't bother coming back.*

I go over to the water's edge, scoop up a bowlful of water, and then sit down on the white limestone, which is beginning to glow in the growing darkness. I feel a warm buzz in my fingertips and see my baby claws emerge with all the gentleness in the world. It's the first time it doesn't hurt. If anything, the sensation is almost pleasant. The skin around my claw bed isn't red anymore but slightly thick, like one long, round cuticle. My reflex is to hide them, to feel ashamed of them until I remember that I am alone on this beach, and there's no one here to judge me. Only the trees, but they have more important things to do, like convert carbon dioxide into oxygen.

It's the first time I can look properly at my claws, those little virgin crystals that humans covet. They are just under an inch in length, and crystal clear. There is a rainbow shimmer inside them, rich hues of red, gold, green, and indigo, like the colored shadows cast by hanging crystals. An energy inside them feels alive but dormant, like a soup on simmer but capable of boiling. I hold them up to the fading light, and they shine rainbows onto my face and arms. They are beautiful but strange, and a part of me can't wait to get to know them. It thrills me to imagine what they can do. The languages I can learn.

Plants, mushrooms, animals, coral . . .

I open the book of runes to the first chapter, and find the spell for purifying water. I trace it on the surface of the water I collected, but nothing happens. The cold water greets my right index finger, soothing like a sip of Violette liquor. I trace the symbol a few times without success—no fizz of water molecules being transformed, no trace of blue sparks, no smoky alchemy.

How can I clear my mind when it's constantly racing? Full, full, full of so many things. Like the fact that tomorrow, Diablo will leave. How can I believe in something I haven't seen yet and bring it into existence? Plus, it's hard to concentrate when I'm so hungry and so cold, and bugs are feasting on my legs. All I want is to return to the fire and bite into the warm loaf of pine bread. *Devour* it.

What does the energy of creation even *feel* like?

What intention should I set?

I feel watched.

I look up and see something across the lake.

A golden reflection on the water's still surface.

My breath hitches in my chest, and my right hand squeezes the rune book. My left hand lops into the water bowl, but I can't even bring myself to move it. A baby golden-antlered reindeer is watching me with its tree-green eyes from the opposite shore. Its coat is white and speckled like cocoa nibs on vanilla ice cream, its little antlers already mesmerizing as they catch the last few rays of light.

A burst of gratitude—or *love*—floods my chest, and I feel a buzz in my fingers. The water fizzes ever so slightly, and I look down to see a few weak trails of blue energy leaving the claws of my left hand. When the sparks dissipate, I raise the bowl to my lips and taste a clean sweetness.

I did it. Without even meaning to.

I purified water!

I feel confused and ecstatic.

My first badge earned out here, and no one to even see it.

Then my logical brain tells me it's no big deal—it's the first and easiest spell in the book. But I push the thought away. My claws *work*!

I look back across the lake but the reindeer is gone, back into the dense wild. Maybe it still has a father or *family* . . . perhaps it won't spend its life alone.

I rise to my feet, pocket the book, and carefully carry the bowl of purified water back up the trail, careful not to spill a precious drop. In the new darkness, I can see luminescent plants, flowers, and insects with transparent bodies and bright beating hearts. Living for a few days or hours, but making every minute count. I missed this feeling . . . this raw *aliveness* of everything. It is an aliveness that only Nature brings, with its struggles, rewards, and good dopamine.

"Diablo?" I call out, my every cell buzzing. There's a dorky grin plastered on my face at the idea of showing him the bowl of water, not that I expect much of a reaction. It's a relief to know that, despite the human blood in my veins, I'm not entirely broken. That if I can do this one straightforward spell, then I can surely master others. With practice.

I feel almost giddy as I reach our campsite, but when I do, I notice something strange. The fire has been kicked over, and the meal Diablo was preparing is on the ground. Not on the large leaves he had ready to use as plates, but in the dirt—all wasted. Diablo's shelter has been destroyed, too, and my first thought is that the wind must have knocked a widowmaker down and crushed it. But the branch of the Carniflora above our heads is as sturdy as ever and as still as the air, which is tainted by an unfriendly presence.

"Diablo?" I say again, cautiously, when I see him standing deathly still, his hands frozen in the air before him, claws protruding to their full immense glory. I can only see his profile; he's facing the ring of darkness on the edge of our campsite, where there are only shadows now. And in those shadows, I see the glint of eyes and pointed shotguns. My hand drops to the side, spilling the newly purified water.

We are surrounded by poachers.

20

Thunder rumbles, near and loud, and a fat few raindrops fall. I quickly look around at the poachers. Two women and two men. Not the dainty porcelain kind, either. These women are strong, snickering behind their mud-slick faces. They wear waterproof overalls over their gray camouflage and hold sawn-off rifles. The ones who murdered the family of reindeer. *And who, by the looks of it, are capable of much worse.*

"Catch of the day, I'd say," says the first female, the one nearest me, whose grin shows swollen pink gums and more teeth absent than present. There's blood on her sleeves.

"What do you think? Dead or alive?" asks a skinny man next to her, who has an eye patch. They could be husband and wife.

I glance down at my hands and see that my claws are still poking out from my fingertips. I close my fists and an uncomfortable shudder runs through me. I don't want the poachers to see that I'm afraid, but the thought of having my claws ripped out seconds after discovering that they work feels like a great cosmic injustice.

"A young female like that," says a bearded man, closer

to Diablo. He licks his small, cracked lips. "Must be worth a fortune." Diablo takes a sideways step toward me, placing his body between me and the bearded man's sight, and there's something very protective about the gesture. I notice that he's touching his arm in a strange way, although I don't know why.

"We can't sell her to the gov'ment," says the second woman, the one farthest away, whose arm is in a sling. "Entertainment's our best bet—they'll take whatever they can get. Good fee, less questions."

"The big man doesn't care where it comes from," says the toothless one, her hungry eyes on me. "A female's a female. Worth her weight in crystals."

"*Honeymooners*, by the looks of it," says Sling. "She could even be pregnant."

Rain begins to fall around us, and Diablo and I can only watch as the poachers decide our fate. The usual adrenaline makes my heart pound with fight or flight, but right now all I can do is the third option no one ever talks about—*freeze*—because there's nowhere to run. Diablo's purple eyes look enraged, but he is oddly composed. I wonder what's going through his mind. Like me, he must know our fates look pretty grim from where we're standing. He could easily beat the poachers in a fight, but not against those weapons.

Then, lightning cracks the sky open, and Eye Patch accidentally fires his shotgun. The bullet splits the air between Diablo and me, hitting the trunk of the Carniflora. Bits of bark splatter like confetti, and I'm grateful it's not my brain. Maybe it's my imagination, but I think I hear a moan coming from the tree, one that raises the hair on my arms. Thunder comes soon after, a deep, unsettling rumble.

"Three seconds apart," says Sling, having counted the time between lightning and thunder.

"What's the rule again?" asks Eye Patch. "Divide the seconds by five and it gives you the miles?"

"That's math you can't do," says Toothless.

"Storm's coming," Sling says, who seems the smartest of the group or the least stupid. "We should go back."

"Not without my catch," says Toothless. Diablo looks like he's concentrating on something, but what? There's another crack of lightning, and thunder comes right after—*less than a second apart.*

"Never seen a storm move that fast," says Sling, who looks ready to call it a day, but Toothless isn't about to give up that easily.

"Mother Nature's coming out to *play*."

"I'm in no hurry to meet their rabid gods," says Eye Patch.

"Please," says Toothless. "Their gods aren't real."

"They're real," Diablo whispers.. "And they're *here*!"

Everything happens all at once.

Lightning and thunder strike at the same time in an explosion of light and sound, an orange blaze that lights up the dark indigo sky. The blast knocks me to the ground, ripping my eardrums and almost blinding me, and I feel like I'm in the center of an exploding sky. In my near-blindness, I manage to see—

The lightning strikes the poachers.

Like snakes of fire descending from the sky.

Like tentacles of light.

Toothless gets the worst of it, and electricity runs through her body, her face contorting into what I can only describe as a jolting, excruciating pain. Her muscles spasm, and her clothes singe at the same time, fernlike lesions erupting along her arms, splitting the flesh open. Her eyeballs begin to bleed, and then she drops to the ground, dead. The blast has also knocked down Eye Patch and Beard. Only Sling is left standing, and when she gets her bearings back, she fires a few rounds at the sky, and then at us. A bullet whizzes past my head, splattering in the tree again, giving it the appearance of eyes.

"Stay down!" Diablo yells. I feel a rope wrap around my ankle. It tightens like a boa constrictor, then pulls me toward the trunk. I glance at my feet and see—it's not a rope, but a *root. The Carniflora is pulling me toward it!*

Sling is firing wildly now, like we're targets at a sideshow game, and in the haze of exploding ammunition, I can't see where Diablo is. There's shock and horror on Sling's face as she registers what's happening—that we're being taken hostage by the tree. Maybe she grew up hearing the same stories I did—that Carnifloras eat humans.

As the Carniflora continues to pull me toward it, I see Diablo lying on the ground. He looks weak and barely conscious. I grab his wrist, holding onto it as tightly as I can. The rain is really giving now, and his wrist starts to slip out of my grip, but I squeeze until my hand is numb. Then, the Carniflora yanks us into a muddy gap between the roots and through a brief, dark tunnel. I lose my grip on Diablo and fall on the wet, squishy ground. Not a hard earthen surface but soft like the stomach of a giant animal. I roll out of the way in time as Diablo lands after me, and we both lie there, soaked to the core. I cough up dirty, rancid water and sit up slowly, trying to wrap my head around what happened and my reflex to bring him with me. Diablo is drenched in rain, sweat, and blood.

"Are you shot?" I ask, tapping his face, but there's no response. I tear the wet clothes off his chest and arms, and his usually gray tattoos glow in the dim light. I feel my way down the fabric covering his muscular legs, searching his body with my hands, but find no bullet wound. The catheter is still there, stuck into a vein at the crook of his left arm, a little bit of tape and a plastic tube waiting for a syringe to come. I don't know why he left it in his arm when he readily discarded everything else the Hunters gave him. Then I see a raised pink birthmark on his right arm—the place he was touching. A spiral just like the rune I carved into my arm.

Is there a god of Lightning—and did Diablo summon it?

When I find no wound, my hands peel away from his body, covered in that sticky red blood. It smells earthy, not metallic, and that's when I realize it's not Diablo's blood—it's the *Carniflora's.*

"*Wha—?*"

I look around and realize that we're in a small, fleshy cave that looks like some kind of *digestive system*. The ceiling is dark earth, with roots dangling like garlands. The walls and ground are made of pink flesh, oozing the same reddish gunk that's on my hands. I press a hand into the giant stomach I'm kneeling on, forming a handprint, then watch as the handprint fills back out after a few seconds. A low groan fills the darkness.

We are inside the tree.

I look back at Diablo, and the glowing tattoos on his wet chest. Diablo stirs and slowly opens his eyes. He looks drained. I want to ask him about the lightning but it doesn't feel like the right time. Whatever he did or didn't do saved our lives. He sits up slowly.

"*Vegera,*" he says, regarding the fleshy walls. "Like coral mushrooms, Carnifloras break down dead matter and turn it into something the forest can use. In this case, they turn it into *food.*"

Like the meaty plant protein he was cooking.

"To clarify—are we being eaten?" My concern is genuine—I've never been inside a tree. A tree that eats.

"I don't think so," Diablo says. "They don't eat living things."

So if it isn't trying to eat us . . .

Did the Carniflora save our lives?

Maybe a part of me suspected that it was benign, otherwise I wouldn't have dragged him inside with me.

"I guess this is what you meant by *a meaningful experience with a tree*," I mutter, and suddenly, my fear evaporates, and I'm filled with the relief of being safe. Wet and uncomfortable and soaked in red gunk but *safe*. Away from the poachers and their gunshots. Diablo relaxes as well. I guess, compared to them, I'm good company.

"Can I do anything to help?"

Diablo seems to come close to saying something but then changes his mind. Hides his catheter arm.

"Nothing. Just rest," Diablo says. "It's been a long day."

There is something haunted in his eyes.

Water trickles down the walls like a carnivorous water feature as the storm outside intensifies. Diablo reaches into his pockets and pulls out a wad of Moonlight Leaf. He rubs it, activates the light, and then spits on it. When he catches me looking, he explains that Klujn saliva is antibiotic and antibacterial and also makes the Moonlight Leaf burn brighter for longer.

"It's an adhesive, too," I add, but he doesn't get the reference—and maybe that's a good thing.

Diablo sets the light in the middle of the cave and we gather around it like Scouts around a campfire. *Too bad it doesn't give off any warmth.* Accepting our new home for the night, Diablo takes a plant stem out of his pocket which has lots of little black bulbs on it. He plucks one, pinches it, and the plant opens up to reveal spools of black thread.

"What is that?" I ask, watching him as he continues to work.

"Black Victorias. We use them to make most of our clothing." I watch Diablo as he pulls the thread apart. He works the fabric, and the black begins to turn a deep crimson red. "People think black is the absence of color, because it doesn't emit color, when really it holds all colors inside it." Diablo continues to scrape the fabric until the red turns a beautiful mandarin orange, then lemon yellow, then meadow green, then ice blue, past a few shades of ocean, until he settles on the most striking celestial indigo I've ever seen. Then he starts to crochet using his claws. Everything about Klujns and their plants never fails to blow my mind.

With the poachers now gone, the distant storm is oddly soothing. *How surreal*, I think. That I'm stuck inside a tree with him. This is the magic of the wild—when I woke up this morning, I could never have predicted what would happen today, for all the good and the bad. My stomach growls loudly, and I feel embarrassed by my hunger, as though it's a human weakness. I love food. Warm, hearty meals and sweets and coffee. I could never live off just water and moonlight—what a sad existence that would be.

Diablo catches me watching him—*again*—and I blush and look away. To distract myself, I take out the map and rune book. As I unravel the black cloth, I wait for Diablo's look of disapproval but he's too focused on his work to give it to me. I find myself wondering if he's ever looked at a person the way he looks at that fabric; like it's the most precious thing in the world.

I smooth the map down with my hands. I wonder why it's round instead of rectangular, and what it's used for. Maybe it's like one of those magic-eye puzzles, and I have to cross my eyes to solve it? The storm ceases, and the moon begins to rise outside. Light travels through the ceiling, sending silver fragments around us like a disco ball. When the moonlight touches my skin, I feel myself relax under it. Diablo does so as well, and I imagine he mustn't have seen the moon in a while. His bones begin to glow ever so slightly under his skin, and I look at my own arms but all I see are faded scars. My bones are dormant, filled with marrow, not magic. Diablo's breathing looks deeper and steadier, and he seems to relax a bit.

"What's a druda?" I ask him.

"There are no human words to describe it."

"But if you had to try?"

Diablo sighs. "The closest thing would be a priest, or monk," he says. It seems the moon has put him in a good mood, and he's feeling generous. "They help the queen, protect divine knowledge, and work with the weather and the gods. They go on great pilgrimages in this world and in others. They create maps like that one where they document their journeys through time, and across hidden worlds, including the shadow and spirit worlds. They are the link between regular Klujns and the gods, the dead and the living."

I look at the map again, examining the smooth black fabric.

"How can I read it?"

"You can't . . . until you develop the senses to. A druda map has twelve dimensions."

"*Twelve?*"

Diablo nods.

I can't grasp my head around what *twelve* dimensions looks like. I know three, for a fact—length, width, and breadth, like a cube. I think the fourth is time. But what do the other eight look like?

"How can a map be multidimensional?"

"I can't explain it to you, because you could never understand," he says. "It's like asking a dog to read a book. Or a blind person to see color." I try not to take it as an insult. "What I mean is . . . there are trials you won't be able to face, distances you won't be able to cross, and plants you won't be able to work with if you don't learn to develop new senses. Without them, the map will remain simply a little bit of cloth."

"Then how do I develop them?" I ask. "These senses?" It's hard to wrap my head around the fact that there's more to reality, to the world I see with my own two eyes. I imagine it's like when I ate the Midnight Rose—my third eye was opened, and I saw truths I had repressed. Memories unlocked like ancient crypts. Or when I started to use my Klujn sight and saw the glowing runes they marked on trees or the invisible barriers of their stands, which is second nature to me now. Things I couldn't imagine when I didn't have the tools or vocabulary to understand them. It's not something Diablo can teach me. I need to experience it for myself.

"Focus on the basics," he says, and for once, his tone is not condescending but matter-of-fact. "Don't underestimate their importance, and don't jump ahead. When you learn a new language, you can't learn sentences without first learning words, and you can't learn words without knowing the letters of the alphabet. I'll teach you more as I feel that you are ready for it."

But you're leaving tomorrow. Diablo stares at the map, and his expression is hard to read. There's anger there, and sadness, too. A story in his eyes that speaks of loss and longing. After a moment, he goes back to the item he's weaving—a fluffy blanket with cool, dark shades. Violet, indigo, and a melancholy blue. I want to ask him more profound questions, about his life and what he wants to be. If he is happy at Circo, or if he wants to go somewhere else. What I really want to know is if he's ever been in love. Do Klujns fall in love like humans, or is their version of love more protective and territorial? Of course, I don't ask him this, but a part of me burns to know. The way he was looking at that map . . .

I wonder if he wants to be a druda.

A person who works with the queen, keeps divine knowledge, works with the weather and the *gods*; someone who journeys between the worlds of the dead and the living.

"Get some sleep," he says. "We're still a long way away from the underground river and the painted caves, which mark the exact halfway point of the Race." I remember Warwick mentioning those landmarks at Circo, and something ignites inside me at the mention of them.

Diablo lies down to sleep, his back turned to me, but he doesn't use the blanket. It's like he's immune to the cold and discomfort. I look at the blanket with longing but don't reach out to take it.

I stare at the map for a while, squinting my eyes, hoping for the apparition of landmarks, but come no closer to solving it. The Moonlight Leaf fades, and Diablo's breathing deepens. As I curl up, shivering and holding my knees, the few feet of space between us feels like an ocean. He is still a stranger, and yet he feels so familiar already. Is it because of our shared roots and our shared history?

I still have no idea what the Hunters did to him, what that catheter was used for, or if he summoned the gods to kill those poachers, but maybe one day I'll work up the courage to ask him.

One thing at a time.

I despise Morgan, but she *did* teach me a valuable lesson about landmarks—if I can look at my Blood Race in the same way as the corn maze and take it one landmark at a time, starting with the underground river and the painted caves, maybe I can make it out.

Once there, I can pick up on the young Klujns' track and follow it the rest of the way to Circo.

Halfway. I grin.

Because right now, halfway feels like a win.

21

My dreams are dark and strange. I am standing barefoot in a rainforest, peering in at a gloomy tunnel. I lean toward the waiting darkness, and a figure takes shape. A woman with a wispy beard. Her eyes have been burned or cut out, the scarred skin around them like puckered fruit.

Ava. Come here.

She speaks without parting her lips.

Her voice is like the wind.

I wake up with a jolt, and it takes me a moment to remember where I am. My clothes are still damp and the Carniflora's gunk has dried on my skin, making me look like a red painting. I feel warm, though, and realize that the Black Victoria blanket is draped over me. Either I took it in my sleep, or Diablo laid it there . . . I gaze up at the ceiling, where golden light flitters through the tree roots, the unmistakable light of morning.

I roll over toward our heatless campfire, almost entirely faded now, and see that Diablo is gone. *I should have known.* He agreed to walk with me for one day, and his departure was postponed by the poachers. They must have left, and now he has as well. I knew this moment was inevitable, but it still fills me with dread. Despite last night's revelations, I don't think I'm ready to do this on my own. Maybe if I had asked Diablo fewer questions, he would have agreed to stay longer.

It takes all my courage to climb out from under my blanket, let the cold in, and face the day alone. Wallowing is not how days are conquered and races won.

I pack my things and find the way out, hoisting myself up on a root and grabbing hold of another, birthing myself onto the muddy forest floor. The Carniflora was an excellent host, but I'm not sorry to be leaving her behind. As I emerge into the surface world, the first thing I smell is coffee. I look around at the forest, which is soggy and boggy after the storm, with puddles of mud that could sink a school bus. I search for the coffee smell but I can't find it. Then I realize that the debris of Diablo's shelter is gone, and the fire, too. I take a cautious step forward, almost losing one shoe to the mud, and my claws slide out of my fingers. Almost by instinct, my left hand reaches out in front of me. It tingles as it travels through a wall of air that feels denser and colder than the air around it, and from my claws escapes a dash of red sparks. My body follows my hand, and I walk through an invisible wall, entering a small round clearing that wasn't there before.

And then I see him.

Diablo.

He stands in front of a small fire of blue-green flames. Although he looks far from healed, there's a bit more color in his cheeks, and the haunted look that filled his eyes last night is gone. He didn't leave me, and I don't understand.

It seems Diablo has been up since dawn. In those few hours, he has made new clothes for himself, a long walking stick with geometric shapes, and built a fire—whose flames weren't visible from a few feet away—roasted wild coffee, and prepared an impressive breakfast. I realize that the barrier I just walked through is like a miniature version of the ones Klujns use to hide their stands, the *complex camouflage* that makes them invisible to humans. *A protective circle*, as my book said.

Diablo notices me. "Coffee?" he asks, and I'm still in shock as he tips the dark steaming liquid into a small floral bowl—a new one to add to our collection. "They're mushrooms, actually, but you could never tell the difference." He hands me the cup, and I'm too stunned to speak. *Maybe the Carniflora really did eat me, and this is some kind of dying fantasy.*

I take a sip, and all my insides come alive as the scalding liquid enters me, an elixir that brings my frozen body back to life. The first warm thing I've had since leaving. The mushroom coffee tastes like burned vanilla. It might just be the best thing I've ever tasted.

"That's the next thing I want to learn to forage," I mutter, and Diablo looks amused.

"Which ones do you know?"

"Winterberries and Klujn beard," I say. "Or whatever that white stuff is called."

"That's a good start, but it won't be enough to sustain you in the cold."

Then comes the second surprise of the morning—Diablo admits that he was wrong. He made a fire without thinking about the smoke and feels responsible for drawing the poachers here—the poachers who have gone. Judging by the boot prints and the drag marks, Beard must have also survived, and he and Sling dragged the bodies of their friends away. I tell Diablo I don't blame him, but there's something like an apology on his face. If the Carniflora hadn't saved us, we would be dead, and he insists on taking responsibility for that.

"I wasn't thinking clearly," he says. "Tonight, I'll show you how to make a proper fire."

"*Tonight?*" A contortionist twists in my gut, turning into bone-breaking shapes. *Tonight* implies we'll be together. If he left on his own, he could reach Circo in a few days . . . so I don't understand this sudden change of heart. Unless I was right about his pace being slower than it usually is. If he couldn't make a protective circle until now, there must be other things he doesn't have the strength to do as well.

"I'll stay with you for a few more days," Diablo says when I don't answer. "Or, until you've learned the basics. But after that, we'll go our separate ways." He doesn't look me in the eyes as he says this, but in Diablo's world, it may as well be a declaration of immortal friendship. "You'll have to match my pace and build your own shelter. The weather's getting worse."

"Okay," I say, because this offer is generous beyond comprehension. Out here, a few days is the equivalent of months, and my fingertips prickle thinking about everything I could learn.

After a quick breakfast and a few too many cups of mushroom coffee, we break camp. When we're about to leave, I notice the damage that Sling inflicted on the Carniflora. There are dozens of bullet holes riddled in her bark. But there's something else, too, that's more concerning. Something I hadn't noticed last night.

"What are those?" I ask Diablo, pointing to three red rings carved into the tree trunk beneath the bullet holes. I look around the forest and realize that every Carniflora has identical rings.

"They've been marked," he says. "The rings choke the flow of water and nutrients that travel from the roots to the branches.

It's a way to kill them slowly, like bleeding a person alive. By spring, this entire forest will be dead."

"Did the poachers do this?"

Diablo shrugs. "Poachers, Hunters, or logging men . . . the orders all come from the same place. If the population got access to Midnight Roses they would see the truth of their world, just like you did, and so humans want this forest gone."

Diablo was right about having a *meaningful experience* with a tree. After she saved our lives and provided us with shelter from the elements and safety from the poachers, the idea that she will die a slow death—along with this *entire* forest—breaks my heart.

"Are you ready?" Diablo asks.

"Almost." I walk around to the other side of the Carniflora's immense trunk until Diablo is out of sight. She's a big girl, and it takes me ten steps to get there. I don't know what drives me to do it—I feel a little stupid and self-conscious, to be honest—but instinct fuels me, and before I understand it, I'm wrapping my arms around the tree. My cheek presses into the bark as I give her a hug. Inside her trunk, I feel a vibration. A deep, grounding rhythm. As though she is acknowledging my presence. A response, just shy of wrapping her branches around me. A big, living plant-machine that feels more animal than anything else.

"Thank you." I wish I knew the way to say that in her language, but gratitude feels close enough. I look at her black trunk and unconventional beauty. What I thought of as ugliness before I knew her because I was afraid. My heart aches for her doomed fate.

Then, she surprises me by lowering a branch and offering me the last rose of the season, black like a glittering midnight. I pick it gently off her branch and secure it in my sweater-bag. Tonight, I will pluck the petals and preserve them in the pages of my rune book. Although I'm not ready to relive any bad trips, the rose petals could come in handy sometime.

I want to give her something but I don't know what. I search my pockets and find a few dried seeds from yesterday. I scatter them at the base of her trunk, then take a step back. It's all I have to give, but she knows and is grateful. I don't know why, but it feels only natural to leave an offering behind.

22

In the wild, time quickly loses all meaning. If it wasn't for Morgan's watch, the only calendar we would have is the growing moon and the deepening cold, as well as the lunar clock inside my own body—the tenderness in my breasts and the cramps that tell me blood is coming. And when it does, I quickly learn to live with the inconvenience.

The wild strips us to our barest layers, and—it turns out—there is no place for shame out here. It's about *the preservation of energy*, Diablo says. There's no time to beat around the bush or be anything other than authentic. He makes me a menstrual cup out of a plant that mimics the look and feel of silicone, and I can't hide anything from him after that—the spider bites in hard-to-reach places that require ointment or the fact that I haven't passed a bowel movement since we left. Diablo says that we only need to define ourselves as individuals when we're part of a society; alone, in Nature, we just *are*. It is existence in its purest form.

There is no Hunter or poacher presence here, and the only human footprints are our own. Diablo's bare feet and my shoes, which have been repurposed into sandals with cloth straps to let my toes and blisters breathe. Still, the damage has already been done, and I lose all my toenails one by one, an agony I've seldom experienced. Turns out, pain is like the cold: debilitating, and quickly forgotten.

The Darker Woods are a strange place. Even though there are no Hunters here, Nature has her own traps and snares. Diablo and I walk mostly in silence, but a lot of our communication happens without words. His language is gestures. He is always in front, slashing his walking stick in a firm but respectful manner. Sometimes, there are trails to follow, and sometimes, we need to carve our own. Distance out here is hard to measure, because no mile is the same. One mile in waist-deep mud can take the better part of a morning, while we can easily cross ten miles of smooth forest trails in an afternoon. The watch on my wrist looks more out of place than ever, but I'm not ready to shed it.

During those first few days of walking, *northeast* becomes an obsession. I repeat the landmarks in my head like a mantra when pain begins to gnaw at my motivation's strongest muscles. I spend a lot of time dreaming about food or hot baths, but mostly, I think about the young Klujns. Where they are and what they're doing. Because we started from different places, I won't catch their trail until the underground river. I wonder how far they've gotten or what their dynamic is like. Are they products of Warwick—red-eyed and hotheaded and violent? Or are they more like Daciana? Every time I think about them, I walk a little faster.

At twilight, when we have our Carniflora tents standing, Diablo finds the nearest body of water to swim in. He tells me that swimming is a way to greet a place or say goodbye to it. Meanwhile, I prefer to stay dry and get started on the fire, which I'm getting better at every day. It started with a spark, then a flame. Now my fires survive past infancy. "*Klujn television,*" I've dubbed it. We still haven't discovered any of these elusive fire crystals.

Dusk quickly becomes my favorite time of day, when the fire crackles, the sky changes color, and the moon rises. When I've finished washing my clothes and hanging them up to dry and collecting firewood, and I can finally sit down and relax, take the weight off my throbbing feet and rub pine oil into them. Diablo prepares dinner, and we eat, too tired for conversation. These early evenings are a time to study the druda map by fire's side, then abandon it to watch the dancing flames, which are fascinating. This element that births from nowhere and can grow as big as the world.

Dinner is usually a variation of plants, vegetables, soups, roots, and vegera. I love the pine bread he makes, but dessert is my favorite. Berry compotes and chocolate twigs and warm lavender milk, and Diablo's famous floral tea. Then, around eight, which may as well be midnight, he disappears into his glowing tent, and I wonder what he does there. What he thinks about, or what he dreams of. What goes on in the little universe of tent and mind.

Maybe it's that I'm growing months each day, but I begin to see our age difference less and less. I see the boy in his eyes, the one who lost his home and family. And even though my feelings toward him are confusing—we are not friends, that's for sure, but he's not a stranger either—I begin to think of finishing the Blood Race for another reason. I want to remove this stamp and be a woman. I want someone like Diablo to be able to look at me *in that way*.

I stay up until the fire burns out, the insects start to bite, or my eyes tire—whichever comes first. Then I brush my teeth, clean out my menstrual cup in a bowl of purified water, and slip into my tent. I love that moment before sleep when I can close my eyes and think of anything. Sometimes I press my forearm into my eyes, and suddenly, I'm not alone in my tent anymore, but in another tent, with a warm body next to mine. I always fall asleep before I can take the vision any farther than that.

Out here, after a day of rigorous walking, away from television screens and artificial lights, there's no such thing as insomnia.

My sixth morning marks the anniversary of Circo—of how long I spent in the wild that first time. At last, I feel properly rewilded. My time at Circo felt longer in a way, while the last few days with Diablo have flown by. *Six days . . . Who would I be if I was here for another week, a month, a year?*

I want to find out.

We leave the dense forest and walk along the spine of a mountain covered in red flowers. The sky is gray, weighted with the promise of more bad weather. It feels good to see the horizon after days of feeling confined by the forest. As we make good time along this ridgeline, I decide it's as good a time as any to start addressing some of those bigger questions weighing heavily on my mind.

"How long would it take me to reach Circo?"

"At this pace?" I try not to read into whether Diablo thinks *this pace* is fast or slow. I know he's been going much slower than he normally would if he was alone. "About six weeks," he finally answers.

"*Six*?" We're one week into December and the moon is almost full, which means the Ice Moon is just over a month away. I feel like I've been digging deep, giving this adventure everything I have, yet it's still not good enough.

"At first, it would have taken you three months," he says, which feels like a compliment in disguise. Maybe I *am* getting faster. Still—there's no point getting to Circo late. If I'm late, I may as well never get there at all. "The beginning is always the slowest," Diablo says, like he's trying to reassure me. "The deeper in you go, the faster you'll get." I have trouble imagining that, because I'm getting more tired by the day.

"How can I make myself go faster?" I ask. "We're walking twelve hours a day." I feel frustrated and upset, which only slows me down. "What would you do to get there in three days?"

"It's not something you're ready for."

I think the conversation's just about dead, but Diablo speaks again without turning around. "If you want to save time, we can start taking more dangerous paths," he says. "More *shortcuts*."

"What shortcuts?"

"You might not have seen them, but there are crossroads from time to time. I'll show you at the next one, and then you can decide."

We continue along the ridgeline for another hour or so, which dips into a patch of forest. A few minutes later, Diablo stops in front of a large tree that blocks the path. He points, and it takes a moment for my eyes to adjust and see—glowing red runes paint the bark.

There are two symbols side by side, one pointing left and the other pointing right. *He's right*—I wouldn't have noticed them, because I was walking too fast.

"What does it say?"

"The high way," Diablo says, pointing to the rune on the left, a trail that goes back out of the forest onto the ridgeline, "and the low way." My eyes follow the path to the right that descends steeply into a sinister-looking rainforest.

"Which one is the shortcut?"

"Which do you *think*?"

I gulp, looking at that path to the right that disappears into the thick gloom. The rainforest that reminds me of the dream I had in the Carniflora. The strange, bearded, eyeless woman. *Was it a dream, or warning?* This is my first opportunity to get ahead, do something brave, and shave off some time, but I don't like the look of that path. Not one bit. "How much time would we save?"

Diablo shrugs. "I've never been here, so I don't know." He hesitates, feeling the unknown path with his secret senses. "A few hours, or maybe a few days."

Everything inside me wants to take the left path and continue along the easy trail, but I won't get anywhere by playing it safe. I'm desperate to reach the underground river, but what really drives me is the thought of closing the distance between me and those young Klujns.

"Let's take the low way."

"Are you sure?"

I nod. I don't feel very brave.

"You can take the lead," Diablo says, and he makes room for me to pass. This I had not expected. I brush past him before I can change my mind.

I regret my decision as soon as we start. The path is almost vertical, with a drop to my right, at the bottom of which are plants that look more like barbed wire. My eyes are glued to my feet as we walk down root staircases and slide down boulders, some bigger than I am. But I'm too stubborn to admit my mistake and turn around. The deeper we get, the more I try to reassure myself that if this decision was reckless, Diablo wouldn't have let me make it.

"Are you sure . . . this is really the low way?" I ask Diablo, an attempt at humor, but nothing can slice through the tension of this place.

Within minutes, it's almost dark as night. My legs are

scratched up with wounds that are an open invitation to infection. A cold humidity seeps into my bones, and the steep descent ages my knees by half a century. Down and down we go, deeper and deeper. We walk by carnivorous purple flowers, and I see one snap its jaw close to my sandalled foot, eating a rodent alive. Then it stares at me—*if flowers without eyes can stare!*—its mouth of sharp teeth surrounded by petals. There are bright-colored scorpions and crystals that look . . . haunted.

I walk a little faster.

Finally, the path levels out and twists into the rainforest, where we weave through tunnels of stone and moss and balance on planks through galleries of weeds. In the perpetual gloom, more and more of those spooky red symbols appear on the trees, some that I recognize from my nightly rune study. *Beware. Danger. Death.* I wouldn't have expected any less.

The cold humidity makes me shiver. Squawking birds, slithering snakes, and the glistening webs of spiders with too many legs, ones that don't appear in any encyclopedia. I feel like we've climbed down into a giant, dark plant mouth that could close around us at any moment. But there's no way I'm going back up those giant boulders and past those carnivorous flowers, so I keep moving forward, going against the current of those warnings.

On a rocky wall, I see more glowing red symbols.

Three runes piled on top of one another like a tower. I haven't gotten to those more advanced chapters. I am learning my alphabet, but I can't yet form sentences.

"What does it mean?" I ask Diablo, but he doesn't translate. A vein pulses in his neck.

The path curves around a corner, and I follow it, although my pace is slower. That's when I see it. The rainforest frames a circular entrance, like the tunnel from my nightmare where the bearded woman stood, but there is no one there.

The darkness reaches without hands.

Shit, I think, although *shit* is not strong enough a word.

Diablo and I are standing at the entrance of a cave.

23

After seeing the weird, vicious creature that lived in a cave near Circo, I swore I would never enter a cave again—if I could help it. *Exiled*, it no doubt was, and keeping cadavers as friends. Here, there is no mad king to make me enter, no hourglass to retrieve, but why does it feel so much worse? Anything could be lurking in there. But if I can't find the courage to enter it, then what? We turn around? Walk back up the near-vertical slope having wasted all that energy and time?

I don't ask Diablo what we must do, because that seems obvious. I just need a moment to collect myself and the plumes of my courage, while staring into the cave's mouth. A pool of water pushes slowly inside. I have no idea how deep this cave goes or what species thrive in that moist darkness, but I have to tell myself that *fear is a state of mind* and that *the only way forward is through*.

That doesn't stop my hands from shaking as I take my first few steps inside. My feet are instantly soaked, and I feel something slither past my ankles. I don't know what it is, and I don't want to find out. I continue on, praying that there really is a way out.

Diablo and I wind through the cave's narrow, slick canyon. There are layers of sediment in the rock, like the mark of a river on a map, painting the walls with horizontal, fluid brushstrokes. The walls get tighter, touching my shoulders like cornstalks, but at least the ceiling is high, and I can see a thin strip of sky. Daylight follows us for a few minutes, but then the ceiling closes, and we find ourselves in darkness. Our feet follow the water's slow current, which is ankle deep and cold. In the new darkness, I see that the walls are glowing, like someone squeezed a thousand tubes of glow-in-the-dark paint in a whole array of colors.

"Algae ink," Diablo says, and I think of the ink of his tattoos that shimmered when they were wet. Diablo pockets a bit of it for later.

After a few more minutes of walking, we begin to see crystals embedded in the cave walls. Small clusters of white quartz the size of my fingers, my hands, and then ones larger than my body, covering the walls and ceiling, glowing milky white in the darkness.

"Crystals are the bones of the earth," Diablo says. He keeps his voice low, almost at a whisper, like we're in a sacred place.

"So the earth is like a giant Klujn?" I answer. He smiles, a small half smile that doesn't reach his eyes. One that says, *Nice effort.* He seems less impatient with my human comments the longer we are together, which makes me feel a little more comfortable to be myself and say stupid things when I feel like it.

We continue down a dark tunnel, and in the distance, I see more of a glow. My heart leaps, thinking of the painted caves, but I imagine there are still quite a few mountains between us and them. But the glow is promising, and there's the scent of cool earth and something else; life forms without nervous systems, a whole hidden ecosystem that thrives in darkness. The cold water is at my tibia now, and it may be my imagination, but it feels like the current is moving a little faster than before. The narrow walls widen and we reach that round, glowing chamber.

"*Wow.*" The word sounds a little childish as it leaves my mouth, but it's all I can manage to say as I look around. We are standing in an underground gallery of light, the walls covered in luminescent paintings.

"If you think this is impressive, wait until you see the painted caves," he says. "Though, I'm not sure if they'll be on our way now that we've changed course."

His words barely register as I stare wide-eyed at the white quartz ceiling, the wet walls dripping in glistening algae ink. The paint has been carved into thick, luminescent drawings that seem to pulse with their own rhythm. Vibrating, moving, and swirling, although it must be an optical illusion. Mesmerized, I temporarily forget the weight of the rock above my head that could easily crumble at any given moment.

Wow, wow, wow.

There is nothing primitive about these drawings. They are done with superhuman skill. Complex rune chandeliers. Portraits of Klujn queens with crowns, and other Klujns with eerie white eyes. There are animals, scouting wolves, and Klujn karavans. This species whose lives are a dance between survival and play, work and pleasure, darkness and light. A hunted species, whose oppression has given birth to such exquisite art. Something that I am fortunate to see with my own eyes.

I see stars inside circles, giant eyes, mother trees with faces on them. There are spirals, bonded Klujns, and arenas filled with animals. A tale of moon-worshipping nomads who belong to no human culture, who are devoted to Nature and move like the wind. Storytellers, artists, dreamers, healers, gardeners, wanderers, performers, magicians. And the relationship they share with animals, trees, the ocean, the soil, and the planet.

I continue to walk around the gallery, wondering who these Klujns were, the ones that drew this. If they were on a caravan between one home and the next. If they were on the run or at ease. Diablo walks behind me, both of us quiet, just the gentle sloshing of the water at our feet. Until at the end of the chamber, just above the dark slit where the cave path resumes, a life-sized painting catches my eye.

Five godly figures, sitting behind a low table. A forest feast. Above them is a sprawling indigo sky, a large moon with a face, and beneath them is the earth, portrayed as a living jungle underground. The first figure on the left has brown eyes, and their plate is loaded with human food—meats, sweets, bread, milk, and other animal products. The second figure has red eyes, and its plate is less full, mostly a mound of vegera, bread, and hearty root vegetables. This Klujn has a slight gold aura radiating from its head and at its feet. The third figure has bright green eyes, not human green but *wilder*. They have a medium-sized portion of food on their plates, more vegetables and fruit. The green-eyed Klujn's aura is slightly larger than the red-eyed Klujn, a yellow-purple haze. The fourth figure has violet eyes, like Estrella Klujns, like mine, and they have just a few berries, seeds, and some water. This one has a larger aura that reaches up toward the moon, and the energy at its feet travels underground. The last figure has piercing white eyes. This Klujn's plate is empty, and its entire body seems to be a vehicle for the moonlight that travels into its body through its head and the earth energy that moves up through its feet. Filled with something . . . *divine*.

As though the entire universe is pouring straight through them.

"So . . . food is the key to absorbing moonlight?" I ask Diablo. "To being more *connected*?"

"Close. Our guts and our microbiome is like an ecosystem,"

he says. "The choices we make determine whether that ecosystem is healthy or ill. When you feed your gut too much of the wrong things, it makes you depressed, disrupts your connection to spirit, and that leads to all sorts of diseases. If we feed it vibrant plant fiber, food grown from the earth that we were designed to eat, our internal ecosystems thrive, and we feel better and more connected. When we don't eat anything at all, our bodies can focus on healing. Without interference from toxins, Klujns can perform more complicated rituals and access hidden worlds. Like working with the gods," he says. "A Klujn must fast for at least three days before they even attempt to call one."

"And eye color has to do with it?"

"Our eye color works like the spectrum of light, from solar—" he points to the red-eyed Klujns "—to lunar. The more connected a stand, the closer to violet they are. Everything on this side of green is considered balanced. But yellow, orange, and red all mean that a stand is out of balance from their true nature."

"Like Circo."

He nods. "A Klujn's eye color reflects their stand and leader. It's not something that changes overnight."

"What about this one?" I ask, pointing to the figure with white eyes.

"A druda. The closest to enlightenment. The furthest away from violence."

Druda.

It makes sense. After all, light is a spectrum. Particles of white light hitting particles of dust or moisture in the air, and splitting open to reveal the rainbow they contain. Circo Klujns are less connected and more *humanized* while Estrellans are gentler and more lunar. It's crazy to think that even Klujns have the capacity for both good *and* bad.

"Humans are head creatures," Diablo says, pointing to the brown-eyed figure. "Driven by their comforts. They have built incredible things—architecture, societies, religions, medicine, music. But when they left Nature and settled down, developed agriculture, they slowly forgot to speak her language. More food meant more people, and more people meant more food. A vicious cycle began. This desire to control Nature rather than working with her is where it all went wrong.

"Klujns are heart creatures. If humans live on the shore, regular Klujns live on the surface of a lake. They can fast for a few days and enter altered states at festivals through potions, dances, and drumming—diving down into the depths to glimpse what's there. But queens and *drudas* . . . they *live* in the depths. They hold their breath for days. They go where humans and other Klujns are too afraid to go. As a result, they have the universe's secrets at their fingertips. A whole underwater world.

"But for the average Klujn, balance exists somewhere in the middle," Diablo finishes, pointing to the green-eyed Klujn. "Healthy gut, happy Klujn. Sick people lead to a sick world, and you can only heal the world after you've healed yourself."

I look at the Klujn with white eyes—*the druda*—its body filling with celestial light. I know what humans would say about this—that it's all make-believe. Fantasy. Far-fetched. Before, I would have thought that too. But now I know that those criticisms are just responses to fear, to the unknown and the unknowable, to their beliefs being challenged.

I stare at that brown-eyed human, unaware of the divinity above its head, under its feet . . . all that magic and power within reach, and yet they have no idea of its existence or how to access it. *How lonely it must be.* To have a key to a hidden world in your pocket but not know the door is there.

To deny the existence of magic.

I want to stay here forever, but the water is now at my knees.

"We should go," Diablo says, just as I think it. Another side effect of spending so much time together.

We leave the glowing chamber and continue into the cave, the image of those five figures imprinted in my mind. Moonlight and lunasynthesis and diets and drudas all make a little more sense to me now. I would love to take a piece of quartz as a souvenir, but I don't think the cave would like that.

We follow the current as the walls narrow again, and the water pushes a little faster now. Then, I hear the sound of rushing water, and Diablo and I arrive at the top of a small waterfall. Slick black rocks and white water cascade into a small pool, forming a thin river where the path continues. The pit of water is ten or fifteen feet below, though it feels much farther.

"We have to jump," I say, dreading being completely soaked and getting my bag wet, but there's no other way. I bend my knees and let myself fall into the water, taking only half a breath before the cold, fierce force of the water rips it from my lungs. My drenched bag drags me down like an anchor, but I fight against it, surfacing and paddling toward that river, where I can finally stand, the water now up to my thighs. The rocks under my feet are slippery and sharp, and the water is rushing so fast now that it's hard to keep my balance. I can't see the sky from here, but I realize it must be raining something fierce outside.

Diablo joins me a few seconds later, and we continue on, a sense of urgency in the damp air that neither of us vocalizes. We half walk, half wade along the river path, neither daring to say the obvious: that we desperately need to find a way out. There's no way back up those slippery rocks, and a bad feeling in my gut materializes.

"*Faster.*" I'm not sure if it's his word or mine. We are one team, one organism, working toward the same goal—*getting out.*

My breaths are shallow and fast, filling the limited air around us with carbon dioxide. I feel panic taking hold of me, making me dizzy.

And then, I go around a bend and come face-to-face with a rock wall. I press my hands against the firm and stubborn rock, but no magical doorway appears; no red glowing rune to point us toward an exit. Just a sheet of rock that's been there for a million years and isn't about to move anytime soon.

Panic surges through me as I realize that we're trapped. The river—flowing like rapids now—continues to pour into our small chamber, and with nowhere else to go, it climbs higher and higher . . . up to my hips, and then my belly button, and then my waist, squeezing me like an iron corset.

I turn to look at Diablo, and all that powerful water rushing in from behind him does little to soothe my panic. That's when I realize what's happening. Diablo realizes it, too. Maybe he knew it a while ago, but he finally says the words aloud.

"*Flash flood.*"

24

Diablo, always a picture of calm, looks afraid. By the time he's said the words, the water is already inching up my ribs. My lungs are the size of fists, and my rapid breathing barely delivers any oxygen to my brain. *An impasse. No way out. Trapped.* I hardly even notice as Diablo goes under, then resurfaces a few seconds later. He says it a few times before I understand.

"*Tunnel.*"

"What?"

"There's a tunnel," he says. "The current's moving into a gap, leading somewhere. It might be a way out."

The rushing water flattens me against the rocks, and I almost hit my head. I feel lightheaded, like I'm on a carnival ride, but if I pass out now, I'll drown. The current pushes Diablo into me, and he manages to grip the wall on either side of my head, his strong arms muting the water's barreling sound. He makes a cave with his body, a small enclave that wraps around me, so that I don't have to see the worst of it. It's crazy how something as gentle and life-giving as water can become so violent.

"Listen," he says, his words sharp. "You need to breathe. Like *this*." Diablo takes a few deep, even breaths, and I watch as his nostrils flare on the inhale, then his lips flutter on the exhale. In for three counts, out for twice the time. I try to silence my mind and mirror his breathing, but the water is rising up my neck. *In for three, out for six.* In the cave of our bodies, I manage to slow my breath and focus on his eyes. His face has never been closer to mine, his violet eyes staring straight into my own. *He could save himself, but he's staying behind to help me.*

After a few breaths, I feel my body start to relax and the blood return to my head. I don't know how Diablo manages to stay so calm in the face of danger and not let his fear get in the way. But the breathing technique works, and after a while I can continue to breathe on my own without thinking about it. Diablo signals for me to watch. We take a breath and go underwater at the same time. He points, but I can't see much through the dark, murky water. But then, I notice the opening—a small alcove in the wall, about two feet wide and two feet high. A whirlpool spirals into it. We lift our heads out of the water to catch our breath, and I'm now standing on my tippy-toes, my head almost scraping against the ceiling. Only a few inches left of air.

Diablo's eyes lock in on mine, with a combination of determination and concern. "How long can you hold your breath?"

"I don't know . . . I've never counted. Thirty seconds, maybe forty-five?" He shakes his head.

"What about two minutes? Or three?" he asks. "I've seen tunnels like these ones—old mining ones. They're usually a few hundred feet long, at most."

"A few *hundred* feet?" I splutter.

"If you want to make it out, you need to think that you can," he says. I start to feel panic rise again, but then I remind myself to keep breathing.

"*Ava*." I think it's the first time I've heard him say my name, and the way he says it in his rich, textured voice makes me feel safe. "In less than a minute, we'll be underwater." The words sober me, a slap in the face as the water creeps up my chin. "Is your will to live stronger than your fear of dying?"

A strange question, but one that makes me think.

I don't want to die; that's a fact, but I don't know how to measure my zest for life. Life hasn't been easy on me. But even though my past has had its fair share of tragedy, I still want to be part of this strange world.

My life *is* worth fighting for.

"Yes," I say. "I want to live."

"Then focus on the path and not the trees."

"We're in a cave."

"You know what I mean."

"I'm not sure I do."

"Success, Ava. Focus on success, not failure. What you focus your energy on is more likely to happen."

I look at him and nod. My head is fully tilted back, almost kissing the rocky ceiling. We are running out of time. I continue to breathe in my three-six rhythm as Diablo speaks.

"Our only chance is through that tunnel," Diablo says. "Now, when I count to three, you're going to take the deepest breath you've ever taken. Fill your stomach, lungs, and every cell in your body. Then, we're going to go into that tunnel . . . and after that, we're going to drift."

"*Drift?*"

Diablo nods. "Every movement and every thought will burn up oxygen faster," he says. "The only way out is if you surrender completely. Make that breath last as long as possible." It's crazy to think that the outside world—*safety*—could be just a few minutes away, but I only have one breath to make it there. But if I don't try, then I'll drown in less than a minute.

"Okay," I say. Forcing the anxiety, the emotion, the panic, and all the intrusive thoughts from my mind. The thoughts of *dying*. I remember the cave at Circo, the first challenge. The one that required a leap of faith, and this does, too. Sometimes, the only way to survive is to leave the comfort of the world you know and dive into the unknown. If you stay stagnant, you die.

"You might feel contractions in your lungs as carbon dioxide begins to build," Diablo says, more urgently now, as our last thirty seconds of breathable air elapse. "That's the body's way of cleaning itself, removing the dirty air. But it won't kill you. Push through those contractions for as long as you can. Your body holds more oxygen than you think. As long as you don't see bubbles—you're okay. Are you ready?"

I nod.

Only an inch of space is left, and I savor these last few breaths. I've been breathing all my life, and I took every single one of those breaths for granted. As I feel the counter ticking down, I try to still my mind, stay calm.

Focus on the path and not the trees.

On my will to live.

"One, two, three . . ." Diablo says. He starts to inhale, and I join him. I fill my stomach, my lungs, and then every single atom in my body, saturating them with as much oxygen as I can.

And then we are completely submerged.

25

As we dive underwater, the tattoos on Diablo's arms glow like a flashlight, and I follow their light down toward the dark alcove. I bump my watch on the rock and, beneath the new spiderweb crack, a timer starts, seconds and milliseconds whirring by too fast. My ears block, and the world of sound is muted into a silence that starts to hum. As I pull myself into the whirlpool, it twists me a few times like clothes in a washing machine. I tuck my head and legs into a fetal position, so as not to hit them against the rock, and then I'm released into the tunnel.

My eyes are open, but all I can see is the faint glow of Diablo in the distance who lights the way like a lantern in the fog. I try to relax my muscles and surrender as best I can, but my heart beats too quickly, burning through oxygen like an Explorer in Arctica eating three times their daily rations.

Slow down, I tell my heart, and eventually, it does.

The tunnel is not very large, but it's wide enough for me to drift in. I thought it would be claustrophobic to be enclosed here, but in the stillness and the buzzing silence, I find a sense of peace I've never experienced before. I can't see the end of the tunnel, but knowing where the end is won't make me go any faster. And so I choose to trust Diablo.

Release all thoughts.

Time seems to stop or become irrelevant. Diablo and I are two space rocks drifting toward a strange sun. My heart's tempo continues to slow as the silence between beats stretches. I lean into the silence like the white space between words, and as I do, I realize that the silence is speaking to me. Empty space is not empty at all.

I am in my mother's womb, before birth and first breath, before responsibility and pain. It is liberating not to have to be *me* for a second and feel the weight of existence—a break from the stories my mind constantly tells itself. In the stillness, darkness, heartbeats, and silence, I feel the greatest sense of peace I have ever felt.

Then, I hear other things—

A crying baby.

The whistling of the wind.

A woman's lullaby.

Diablo continues to drift ahead of me, and I notice gleaming orange crystals through the black water. They're beautiful and warm, like little flames caught in clear quartz. I want to reach out and touch one, but I don't think that would be wise. Maybe they're haunted, like the strange minerals from earlier. But then I twist my wrist, and my watch face glows, pulling me back into the world of the digital and technical and breath. Behind the spiderweb crack I see that one minute and thirty seconds have passed, and with this reminder of time, the contractions that Diablo told me about finally start.

My diaphragm tightens, pushing forcibly upward toward my lungs. The feeling is uncomfortable and makes me want to breathe, but I can't, so I go through the contraction until, eventually, it passes. I've been granted a few seconds of reprieve before the next one comes, more urgent and violent than the first. My diaphragm wants to evacuate the carbon dioxide in my lungs, but my lungs push back, creating an uncomfortable push-and-pull in my chest, a tug of war.

I push through five contractions and then ten. My lungs are wholly depleted of air, yet I'm still conscious. I'm not surprised that Diablo was right, but I'm fascinated that those contractions are just warnings, like the red glowing runes outside this cave. On the other side of that discomfort, a new world opens up . . . one where I can go beyond my limits and find doors inside my body that lead to rooms I've never explored. I see that it's been two-and-a-half minutes, and then the glow of my watch goes out.

A few more seconds, I think. *Hold on.*

I fight through fifteen contractions, and then twenty, and then twenty-five. I don't know how many more of these I can take. Everything inside me wants to swim madly forward, but I don't have enough air. It's a race against my body, a race of slowing down, where the slowest wins. I close my eyes and turn inward again, searching for that peace, but it's gone. My heart is a slow drum, a midnight rhythm in a mysterious stand deep in the forest. The gaps between my heartbeats stretch farther and farther until I don't know if there will come another one or if the silence will stretch on forever . . .

And in the darkness, I see a green spiral.

I drift toward it.

I am a seed buried in the earth, reaching through the soil.

Reach, reach, reaching toward a glowing moon.

My hand is met by another, a man's, hard but warm.

I am falling, tipping into a bright sky, crashing underwater, sinking.

And then rising.

I pierce through the surface and I can finally catch my breath.

Ahhhh!

I made it out of the tunnel.

My inhale is a monstrous thing, devouring all the air around it. *I will never take breathing for granted again.*

As I float with the current, I look around to get my bearings. The rocky tunnel expelled me into a large underground river, like a sewer pipe into the sea. The wide river cruises down a large tunnel with a high ceiling covered in luminescent drawings. It's so bright that, for a second, I think I'm outside, but I'm still underground, and this place is just like the gallery from before but even more remarkable. I can still feel something warm in my hand, a faint orange glow coming from beneath the water's dark surface.

Diablo is drifting twenty feet ahead, and he looks back to make sure I'm alive. The concern in his eyes as he searches, and then the relief when he sees me, makes me think that his relief is genuine—an appreciation for my company that he may never say out loud. We drift down the river for a few more seconds, and I pull my hand out of the water to see—it is one of those quartz crystals with an orange flame inside.

A fire crystal.

I grip my hand tightly around it. Occasionally, the rock above our heads opens to reveal a strip of sky. The rain has cleared, and the sky is a dusky auburn. The water is cold, but the crystal keeps me warm.

Diablo points toward a bend in the river—*an exit*—and we swim toward it. On the shore, we catch our breaths. His lips are blue, and I imagine mine must be as well. How close we came . . .

"Are you okay?" he asks.

"I didn't know my body could do that."

"You're Estrellan," he says. "Your body was made for water."

His words strike me. It's not something I'd ever thought about—how I always felt comfortable around water and became a strong swimmer even though I'd only swum a handful of times. Mainly in the natural pools near the orphanage where the water was still clean or a homemade pool that Diana made in the summer with bales of hay and tarps that would fill when we experienced heavy rainfall.

"Is this . . ." I start, looking downriver, where the glowing paintings get even brighter. *The underground river. The painted caves.*

But that's not possible. You can't shave off a week in a day.

"Almost," Diablo says. "It starts a few miles that way, but unfortunately, it isn't on our way."

I feel disappointed that I won't get to see them, but I need to make peace knowing that I won't get to see everything. Diablo and I are safe; I can see and reach the outside world, and that's all that matters.

I can't believe we're here.

Almost on the young Klujns' trail.

It feels surreal, and impossible . . . but it's not. There's an explosion in my chest, a burst of euphoria. I smile from ear to ear. I *did* it.

I follow Diablo toward a small exit in the rock. Outside, the rain has cleared, and the sun is setting. We've emerged in a swamp and don't have long before dark. My bag is drenched, and I don't have any dry clothes to put on, but at least I have that crystal. I shiver, my teeth chattering, my clothes clinging to my body, but then the crystal releases another pulse of warmth. Diablo notices it and smiles. "Congratulations. Your fire craft just got a lot easier."

"Is it . . . really . . . that?"

Diablo nods. "Your instinct about the shortcut was right," he says, looking genuinely surprised by where we've surfaced.

"Aside from the almost-drowning part," I retort. I don't tell him about the dream I had and the bearded woman. It was like she wanted me to go there.

As Diablo finds the trail and goes to keep walking, I think of something. "Just out of curiosity, what did the warning say? The three runes outside the cave?"

"Very Dangerous Cave," he answers.

I snort, filled with something giddy and silly and alive.

"*You don't say!*"

26

We sit by the fire, and I lay my items out to dry as Diablo cooks dinner. Our campsite is in a dense swamp, which has a personality of its own. Not hostile, but not exactly friendly. Diablo didn't want to stay here, but I insisted. We pitched our tents on the only patch of dry ground, surrounded on all sides by vegetation and the constant roar of crickets, an overgrown wildness that feels like it's closing in. Four muddy paths branch out from our camp like compass bearings.

After camp was set up, I wandered down to a warm river that smelled like clay and sulfur. I wanted to go in more than anything, to let the warmth loosen the knots of my muscles, but Diablo had warned me about river snakes, freshwater jellyfish, fish with teeth, and other creatures I wasn't thrilled to meet. I untangled my hair with my fingers, collected firewood, and massaged my swollen feet. Diablo showed me how to use the fire crystal by burying it in shallow soil, tracing a rune on the surface, and blowing on it. A small flame germinated from the earth, and as Diablo continued to blow, the flame grew into a fire. It had all the makings of a perfect night if it wasn't for Diablo's mood, creating a chasm between us.

As we eat silently, I slip into my thoughts, missing the stillness I experienced in the tunnel in my first minute underwater, when I felt like I could stay there forever. The moon rises, and pink and purple lumina begin to appear in the sky. The last time I saw these shimmering curtains of light was at Circo. The beauty of the night sky and all its mysteries fills me with a sad hollowness. We are so small, and our passage here is so brief, like shooting stars. What does it all mean, then, without a stand and people to share it with?

Wolf, a group of friends, a partner or a lover.

Alone it all feels rather meaningless.

Diablo isn't eating. Instead, his hands are busy moving. I watch as he spreads a leathery plant skin over a wooden hoop, then stitches the skin to the disk with black thread. It's a drum. When it's finished, he taps it a few times. The drum produces a deep, unsettling rhythm.

"Is it . . . just for music?" I ask.

Diablo shakes his head. "Drums are a way to induce trance. Sometimes they can even call the gods."

"Where are they then, these gods?"

"Everywhere. And nowhere."

"Are they here now?"

Diablo shakes his head.

"How do you call them?"

"Don't."

"I won't. I'm just curious."

"They usually enter our world through portals, which is why our arenas are round. And they take the form of animals. Gold eyes are a telltale sign."

"If they enter through portals . . ." I start, frightened by the idea. Thinking of all the circular places I've been in—were the *gods* there? "Where do they live the rest of the time?"

"In the shadow world."

"The shadow world?"

"Where people go when they cross over."

The drum beats continue, *boom boom boom*, and I feel my heart syncing to the rhythm. I feel it vibrating inside my body.

People who have crossed over.

"You shouldn't concern yourself with our gods until your proof of passage," says Diablo. "Never attempt to call one until you are fully prepared. That's why so many young Klujns die retrieving their proof of passage. Or during Initiation."

Diablo must see the fear in my eyes because he adds, "You need thick skin if you want to survive out here, because you're not only dealing with the cold and the elements."

I shiver. *Gods that take the form of animals. That have gold eyes and enter through circular portals. That live in a shadow world, where dead things linger. Induced by drums and trance.*

It sounds like fantasy. Mythology. Magic.

If these gods really exist, why don't they cross the fence and unleash their wrath on Grouse and the general?

I wonder if this is why we rarely see circular shapes on the human side of the fences; only triangles and diamonds. Maybe Hunters know about the gods or are, at the very least, *superstitious.*

"What do I have to do to be ready?" I ask Diablo. "To get this proof of passage?"

I remember Warwick mentioning it at Circo, and it seemed like a pivotal moment in the young Klujns' Blood Race. If a Klujn arrived at the stand without it, they wouldn't be accepted, just like us performers in the cave if we had made it out without our hourglass.

I feel like Diablo's going to tell me not to jump ahead, but then he surprises me.

"Before proof of passage, you need to be in a fasting state for three days. No food, no fruit, no berries, no coffee, only water. On the third night, one of the gods will visit you in a dream. They will show you where you need to go to complete your challenge. And during that challenge, you will retrieve a seed of viață.

"When you get to the stand, you will bring it to Initiation, where you will complete another test. There, you will be chosen by a god you impressed along the way. This will be your first," he says, stroking the spiral pink birthmark on his arm. Not a birthmark after all, but a sign of his allegiance with one of these *gods*.

"Most Klujns only work with three or four gods in their lives, but queens and drudas can have upward of one hundred."

"One *hundred*?"

Diablo nods. "But you want to be careful which god you decide to work with. It's a relationship that lasts a lifetime, and some are crueler than others. Your first is . . . important."

"Which god is that?" I ask, nodding to the all-too familiar spiral, but Diablo shakes his head in response.

Even though I can't entirely wrap my head around it, it does make sense to some degree. And with his insight, I feel a little more prepared to face the second half of the journey—not that I want to do any of the things he told me.

Proof of passage. Initiation.

"It sounds like fantasy."

"*Fantasy*," Diablo says the word with distaste. "A word invented by humans to deny the presence of things they don't have the senses to understand. But even science accepts there is no final theory."

"Reality is a broom closet," I say, remembering words Warwick said, "in the great palace of consciousness."

Diablo nods. "And most people—some Klujns included—choose to live in that broom closet and never explore the other rooms. Reality is useful for survival—for finding food and reproducing. But our world has shown us that sometimes an altered—or *heightened*—state can be better. Because in this state, we can connect to the true heart of Nature."

"I want to know how to find this shadow world."

"That's enough for tonight," he says. "But you are making progress." *A compliment.* Then, Diablo stops his drumming and slaps a mosquito on his forearm. He looks down at the bite with concern engraved in his eyes.

"Are you okay?" I ask, but he doesn't meet my eyes again after that. I wonder what could possibly be so concerning about a mosquito bite.

"I cooked. You wash up," Diablo says. Disappointed but not surprised by the abrupt end of the conversation, I collect the empty bowls and leave.

I take the path to the left and walk down to a stream where Diablo got our drinking water. I wash the dishes, letting the cool water run over my hands. Taking my time, watching the moon, and unpacking everything he said.

A shadow world.

Could my mom be there?

I brush my teeth. My period is over, and I feel a cramp in my bowels for the first time since we left, something promising.

I move off the trail to let my body do its work, listening to Diablo's drumming and the faint glow of the fire in the distance. Afterward, I feel about ten pounds lighter. I wipe myself with leaves, and am about to leave when something catches my attention. A glint in the darkness. I walk toward it as Diablo's drums continue to narrate my passage through the fierce vegetation. That's when I see the source of the light.

A crystal altar.

The kind that Klujns make for safe passage or to honor the dead.

Skeletons, crystals, and seeds are stacked in a pile, empty eyes that used to see and still might. In theory, it's meant to be a good thing, for *protection*, but this altar makes my blood run cold. I don't know if it's the altar itself that frightens me or the otherworldly presence that emanates from it, especially after Diablo's story. Fresh flowers are stuffed into the eye sockets, like someone was *just here*.

Diablo's drumming stops, and I realize the glow of the fire is gone. The night goes from dark to pitch black, from chilly to ice cold.

I look around, but I can't see anything. I can't see the camp, the stream, or my washing station. *No.* I take a step backward and hear a *crack*. I look under my shoe and see—

A shimmering crystal skeleton. A metallic pink bug crawling through its eye socket. Just like the family of dead reindeer, it feels like a bad omen.

"Diablo?" I call out, my voice filled with panic. The cold air clings to me like ghoulish hands, and I just want to get back to the campsite. There's no answer. I call his name again—I know I didn't go *that* far—but still, no answer comes. I try to find the path but can't.

Within seconds, I'm already lost, already frightened, pushing through the spiky brush like a blinded animal, cutting my hands on it.

"*Diablo?*"

Finally, I find the stream and follow it down to my washing station. I leave the bowls, because they can wait until morning, and run toward our campsite. When I get there, I see that the fire has been reduced to small flames. Diablo didn't feed it with his breath as he taught me to do. He isn't there. I think of that sinister altar and the crystal skeleton . . . how the Klujn died, or maybe it was *killed*. But I would have heard a scream, wouldn't I, now that the crickets are quiet?

"Diablo?" I call out again.

And then I finally see it—somewhere behind Diablo's tent—a figure lying on the ground. I edge toward it and recognize his feet. Not even scratched or blistered after all that barefoot walking. "Diablo?" I say, thinking that maybe he fell and hit his head on something, but that wouldn't be like him. He is a lot of things, but he isn't clumsy. I kneel down beside him. My hands shake as I turn him over, and see that his face is a frozen mask of terror. He is statue-still, caught in an eternal spasm. His eyes are open and bloodshot, with black irises. Demonic.

I let him go, like I've been electrocuted.

"What happened?" I mutter, although it's clear he can't hear me or answer. I search his body, but I don't have to search far. On the back of his hand is a little mosquito bite. A tiny hole, like a malevolent inkblot, with a sinister black ring around it. I remember the moment he swatted it, the concern on his face. The way he sent me off to wash the dishes—maybe he knew it was bad, and he didn't want me to see it.

Black liquid travels from the bite, up his arm and down toward his claws, swirling underneath his skin, moving like the fastest-moving virus I've ever seen. I pull my shirt off, rip it, and tie a tourniquet around his biceps, as tightly as possible. The tourniquet manages to stop the black virus. Still, it continues to build inside his arm, turning his tattooed flesh black and gangrenous. *That's not good.*

I can't get my head around what just happened. A few minutes ago, he was perfectly fine, and now he's dying in front of my eyes, rapidly and violently. *All this—from a mosquito bite?* He was nervous about sleeping here, anxious about me choosing this spot—could he feel something I couldn't? It's my fault this is happening.

Diablo's body gives a violent jolt as his arm is now completely filled in with black, and it's already pushing against the tourniquet. I look around for a plant or something I can use. *Be strong*, I think, but the wild is a language that I still don't understand. I'm out of my depth. I see nothing in the darkness but the bright eyes of watching bugs and spiders.

My fault, my fault, my fault.

I grab the first object I can find—the druda map—and throw it on top of Diablo like a blanket, tucking him in, though it's tablecloth-thin. It buzzes with the same unearthly energy I felt on my first night in the woods, like spirits trapped.

I remember the Scouts talking about *mosquitoes that carry flesh-eating diseases* or something to that effect, and the reminder brings me a fresh wave of panic. *Is that what's happening to him?*

"Diablo," I say, tapping his face, and blowing air on his cheek, but he's not responsive. His eyes are completely black now. He doesn't have long left.

And then I hear it—a soft rustling in the leaves. I look around, searching the dark swamp around us but there's nothing.

Then, for some reason, Maple's advice comes back to me. *Look up.* I tilt my head up toward a tree and see—

There's a Klujn above my head.

27

Her name is Honey, she tells me, as she jumps down from the branch of a tree. She looks to be in her early teens, with frizzy, cherry-red hair, bright green eyes, and a carnivorous smile. There are clusters of sores around her nose and arms from some sort of infection. She has the eagerness of someone who's desperate for friendship, willing to do anything to make passersby stay just a little longer to enjoy her well-meaning but slightly deranged company. I wonder who she is, where she came from, and why she doesn't have a stand—unless she was *exiled*.

"Why do you come through Honey'sss Ssswamp?" she asks, drawing out her *s*'s like a hiss, like a sun sinking into an ocean horizon or a strip of meat touching hot oil in a pan. "Very Dangerousss Ssswamp." The name seems oddly fitting after the *Very Dangerous Cave* from before, but it doesn't make me feel any better about the creepy altar I found, the skeleton, and the flesh-eating spirit possessing Diablo as we speak.

"Did you see what happened to him?" I ask Honey. Her

strange smile seems inappropriate given the gravity of the situation.

"These foressst spiritsss," she says.

"What do they want?"

"What doesss a virusss want?" Honey asks. "A parasssite, a predator, or the *wind*? They want what all life wantsss . . . sssimply to exissst."

Honey speaks well for a creature who probably hasn't been in contact with many humans in her life. Her intonation is almost poetic, and if it wasn't for the horror of the words she's delivering, I might actually enjoy them. She looks more plant than Klujn, like she's been in this swamp so long that her body has become a swamp of its own.

"But what are they?" I ask. "These spirits?"

"Does it matter *what* they are?" Honey answers. "Or that they *are*? Do you need to know how a watch worksss, to tell the time?" I see the little glowing diamonds of my watch reflected in her eyes.

"Sssicky sicky, very sssicky, maybe die . . ." she says.

"Where's your stand? Can we bring him there?"

"Sssibu isn't my ssstand anymore," she says, confirming my theory about her being exiled. Maybe she failed her Blood Race, or it has something to do with the slightly unhinged energy she has. "It'sss very far. He won't make it."

"Then is there a plant, a potion, something I can give him?"

"Nothing can ssstop these ssspirits," she says. "Unlessss."

"Unless *what*?"

"Do you ssspeak the language of plantsss?"

I shake my head, feeling useless. *Why didn't I try to learn it earlier? Make it a priority? Instead of focusing on things that were too advanced for me?*

"You walk through Honey'sss Ssswamp, and you don't ssspeak the language of plantsss?"

"I'm trying to learn . . . I haven't had time . . ." but Diablo is dying, and excuses won't bring him back from the dead.

"You can't ssspeak to her if you don't ssspeak the language of plantsss."

"Speak to who?" I demand. "Please, Honey. Can *you* help me?"

I can't believe that Diablo's life—and mine—suddenly hinges on this young, untrustworthy Klujn, who seems to be enjoying this situation very much. Then, Honey's weird smile twists into concern: "*Come with me.*"

I don't want to leave Diablo, but I don't have the luxury of wasting more precious seconds.

Honey leads me up the path Diablo looked wary of. "There were othersss, too, who came through this ssswamp. A few daysss ago, or was it a few weeksss?" I wonder if she's talking about the young Klujns, but I don't want to ask her out of fear that she'll get sidetracked and lose focus. "They didn't sssee me, but I sssaw them. But you sssee me, don't you?"

"Yes, I see you," I tell Honey, anything to get her to keep walking.

We reach a clearing with a single tree in the middle. A little bed has been made in the crook of the tree's lowest branches. Shiny trinkets hang from the branches like midwinter ornaments. Lost objects. Plastic bottles. Cans. Shoes. And vials of colored substances. The tree looks like a collection of human garbage, turned into a hanging apothecary.

"Honey'sss home," she says proudly, beaming at her collection of trinkets and potions. She points at the suspended bottles filled with strange substances. "Sssomething to dance and meet your animal, sssomething to talk to cryssstals, sssomething to transssform into water, sssomething for future memoriesss, and sssomething to sssee the foressst as it really isss. Water givesss life, water killsss, water flowsss and bendsss and freezesss, water is the ssstrongest sssubstance in the world becaussse she isss flexible and constantly changing. Water isss magic. And Honey isss a water alchemissst."

I look at the different potions—black sludge, brown mud, glittering teal, and one that looks like liquid quartz. I wonder if Honey has ever had anyone other than herself to test these potions on and if these experiments gave her those boils, but I'm not sure I want to know. "Which one do I need?" I hope it's not the black sludge or the mud.

"Thisss *one*," says Honey, clasping a vial of pink juice with dirty but delicate fingers. She unties it from a string and takes the wooden stopper out. I look at the liquid inside, telling myself it could be harmless, like water with electrolytes. *It could also be poison.*

"Thisss is what you need to sssee her," says Honey.

"To see who?"

"The only one who can sssave him," she says, but she doesn't tell me who. It seems absurd, that I could drink a substance and suddenly speak a new language. But like Honey said before—I don't need to know how a watch works in order to use it. And there's no time.

"This will make me talk to plants?" I ask, and Honey nods excitedly.

"But firssst, I require payment."

"I don't have anything to pay you with." Honey shakes her head—the currency she desires is not monetary. I should have known, by the way she's been staring at my watch ever since we met. *My way to tell the time. My compass. My timer.* But its value doesn't match Diablo's life.

"You can have it," I say, ripping the watch off my wrist and giving it to her. Honey beams as she adds it to her hanging trophies. Then, Honey hands me the vial of pink juice. I look at it, then back at Honey's blistered face and those keen eyes that don't leave me . . . knowing that I may very well be about to make the biggest mistake of my life—*like the crystal skeleton did when it was still alive*. Anyone in their right mind would run in the opposite direction, but Diablo and I have come too far and been through too much for me to give up now. The idea of him dying fills me with a reckless courage, and I down the liquid before reason can get a last word in.

The potion leaves a sweet, floral taste in my mouth. After the sweetness comes a bite, an alcoholic heat that burns my throat and makes me cough. "Let the medicine work," Honey says, studying me with curiosity. I realize that she probably hasn't tested this potion on anyone before. "Now you will sssee the foressst as it really isss," Honey whispers. "When you sssee her, asssk for the antidote. Whatever you do, don't touch her. She isss extremely poisonousss. You can only touch her with your tongue."

"Who is *she*?" I ask Honey. The potion is already working: A dozen Honeys surround me now, each with the same eager, unnerving smile. Like reflections in a hall of mirrors or images in a kaleidoscope, I can't tell which Honey is the real one.

"The only one who can help you now," the twelve Honeys answer simultaneously. "She doesn't have a name, and she hasss killed all thossse who have tried to name her."

"*What is she*?!" I yell.

My mouth is sticky, and my tongue has welded to the roof of my mouth as all the Honeys answer.

"*Pink Flower*."

28

Pink Flower. I've heard that name before. Then it comes back to me—the flower Ivy talked about on our way to the Scout camp. The most poisonous flower in the world, yet it can also cure any ailment. She said that if I ever encountered it, I should walk rapidly in the opposite direction.

My body starts to feel heavy, and I melt to the forest floor. Honey's enormous foot stands next to me like a golden mountain. I must be the size of a bug or an ant, and Honey could easily squash me, but she doesn't. Suddenly, my size makes me feel very vulnerable.

"Follow the path," her voice booms, rattling the hairs in my small ears. I blink, adjusting to my new perspective. I'm on all fours on the forest floor. Still me, Ava, but in miniature form. I would look normal if it wasn't for the immensity of the world around me. And, to be this small is . . . *humbling*.

As I start to crawl forward, the forest comes alive around me, trees and plants radiating auras of different colors. Flowers and weeds undulate like an underwater forest. Nighttime pollinators the size of helicopters get drunk off pollen. My palms pad against the earth, where the web of glowing algae beneath the soil lights up like stepping stones that illuminate when you touch them.

I need to find Pink Flower. The thought travels down my arms and into the ground, spreading across the forest floor, and the forest reacts with curious whispers, as though they can read my intentions.

I continue to crawl, passing large rocks and mushrooms the size of houses. Nature vibrates in my bones. *The frequency of the earth*, I think, feeling somewhere between tipsy and drunk.

I keep wandering through this mystical night garden, blown away by the interconnectedness of all things—all these plants and minerals and animals who all speak the same language.

And then, in the hubbub of nightlife and murmurs, I see the path in front of me drenched in bright pink light, like neon on a wet road. I stop in my tracks, blinded and mesmerized, as I look up.

Pink Flower.

My eyes bulge like a grasshopper. She is immense, magnificent, and terrifying. As big as a house on stilts, or an alien spaceship. A pink giant, her open petals moving with the liquid grace of a jellyfish. Inside her petals are rows and rows of sharp pink teeth, like pink quartz daggers. Her pistil protrudes like a pink snake or a long, thin tongue.

I need the antidote, I think. *Where is it?*

I don't know if she understands, or *how* she understands, but her pistil unfurls like the staircase of a small airplane. I stand up with great difficulty—gravity feels impossibly heavy—and climb up the grooves on her pistil staircase, careful not to touch a thing. It is almost as strange—if not stranger—than slipping inside the fleshy cave of the Carniflora. Because here, my senses are altered, and I'm not sure if I'm awake or dreaming.

At the top, I reach a landing. I am deep in her center now, a room that contains at least a hundred shades of pink, surrounded by rows and rows of hairy teeth. Then, she closes her petals around me, the pinks of everything becoming a few shades darker, sealing me in. I look for a focal point, a face, a center of intelligence, but I don't find one. So, I face the dark magenta of her center, where the brown on a sunflower would be.

How am I meant to speak to a flower? Ask her what I need?

Before I've even finished the thought, her voice is in my head, like her frequency is being translated into the English that I know.

Why do you want the antidote?

After a moment of surprise—*a giant flower is speaking to me*—I remember how to speak.

"I need to save him," I say.

Who?

Her words are nowhere and everywhere; they vibrate like a low note in my ears.

"Diablo."

Who is Diablo?

I pause. Of course she doesn't know—*or care*—who Diablo is.

I don't give the antidote to just anyone, Pink Flower says. *I only give it once in my life.*

"Once? Why?"

Because, she answers. *It is my essence. My vitality. My heart. When I choose to give it away, I will die.*

I really wish Honey had told me that part.

Like a bee with a stinger, I think. *After they sting, they die.*

Yes, Pink Flower says, even though I didn't say the words aloud. I ought to be more careful with my thoughts—Pink Flower can read minds.

There's no point hiding anything, she says. *I know everything.*

So, she continues, *why is his life worth more than mine?*

A few minutes ago, I would have said, *Because you're just a flower.* But now I see she is more than just a flower. She has her place here in the forest, just like everything else. If I am this small now—does *my* life matter? The matter of intelligence is complex. We are giants to ants and atoms, but we are impossibly tiny and unimportant to the stars.

Trying to ignore all the rows of gnarly teeth around me, slick from their last meal, I answer.

"Diablo is a Klujn, a good one. His stand was raided when he was young, and he managed to bring his little sister, Glory, to safety—I don't know how. There aren't many Estrellans left, and they're good Klujns. He's smart and sensitive, and he understands the wild like no one else. He's suffered a lot, but his heart is in the right place. I think he can be valuable to me. To Daciana—that's the queen of Estrella, who's now at Circo—and to the Territory. He's not like regular Klujns. He's not like anyone, really . . ."

I trail off, feeling the emotion rise up and clamp my throat as I list all the reasons why he should live while she should die. Tears begin to pool in my eyes.

"He would never admit it, but I know he wants to do good. I think he wants to become a druda. He's a great teacher, and he's learning to be patient with me even though my blood is half human, and he has every reason to despise humans after what they did to him. Now, he's dying, and it's all because of me. His life may not be worth more than yours, but it's worth more than mine."

The tears fall from my eyes and land on the juicy nectar at my feet. I go to wipe them, but then remember what Diablo told me about being your authentic self in the wild, so I decide to let them fall. I cry the tears my body needs to cry, and the pink cave around me shudders as my tears land on the ground. As though in my tears, Pink Flower can see my heart—all the girlish secrets I won't dare to say aloud.

But I don't have to say them; Pink Flower knows my heart.

There's silence.

Finally, she speaks.

You're not like the others I've met, and I've met many. Your hands have killed but your heart is still pure. Protect it. Because once a heart turns black, it can never be pink again. And pink is the most important color in the world.

Then, her center opens up to reveal a glowing bead where her nose would be. One guess what the color is.

It's the antidote.

Don't take this lightly, she says. *And never again underestimate the value of a life, no matter its size or appearance. I give you my life in exchange for his. But one day, he will provide his in exchange for something else. That is the dance of Nature.*

"Thank you," I say with genuine gratitude, moving toward the antidote. As I reach out, I remember what Honey said about taking it with my tongue. So I lean in, trying to ignore the gushing poison all around me.

Do I close my eyes? I think, feeling a little embarrassed that I'm having my first kiss with a carnivorous, sentient flower. I decide to leave them open. The experience is wetter than expected as Pink Flower thrusts a warm, pink appendage into my mouth and then expulses the little antidote on my tongue, which feels like a tooth or a bead. I pull away from the sloppy kiss and press my lips firmly shut so as not to let any of the poison leak.

Go now, she says. *And never forget . . . in a dark world, pink is what you need.*

Then, she opens her petals, and the night pours in. I race down the slippery pistol steps, until I am back in the forest. I run for a few seconds until I realize I am normal-sized again. The trees are tree-sized, the rocks and mushrooms barely reach my ankles, and the glow of everything is fading. Honey arrives—or maybe she was watching this whole time.

"Your lipsss are *pink*! You actually did it!"

Startled, I try not to swallow the bead, but saliva is pooling in my mouth. Honey has dragged Diablo to her camp. He's lying under her tree apothecary, and it feels like it's been an hour since I left his side. The black flesh-eating virus has started to break past the tourniquet, spreading up toward his shoulder, devouring everything in its path . . .

I kneel on the cool earth, still balancing the antidote on my tongue. I part Diablo's mouth open and line my face up with his. Hesitate. I can't afford to let the poison touch his skin, so I bring my lips to his, creating a seal with our mouths.

His soft lips are cold, but turn warm as soon as my mouth presses against his. It feels wrong to be doing this—*kissing* him—when he's unconscious, but what choice do I have? I push the antidote into Diablo's mouth, and our tongues meet for a second. My lips hover over his for a second longer than they should, and finally, I pull away. I tip Diablo's chin closed and sit back, a ghost kiss on my lips. One that I liked more than is appropriate. Honey watches with a smile—this must be the greatest spectacle she's seen in a while.

I watch as Diablo swallows and his weird convulsions cease. The flesh-eating spirit freezes in its tracks; it doesn't recede, but at least it stops claiming any more of him. *Enough for now*, I think. *Enough to bring him to the nearest stand for proper treatment.*

As I sit back and wipe my mouth on the scrap of my shirt, I realize I'm only wearing a bralette and pajama bottoms, covered in mud and pollen. *My first kiss was to a carnivorous flower*, I think. *My second to an almost corpse.*

Welcome to the Boreal.

Still recovering from the night's events, I turn to look at my excited spectator. I don't know what Honey's more excited about—the fact that I convinced Pink Flower to give me the antidote or that her potion worked. Or maybe she's excited about the kiss, not that I can call it that because a true kiss is something mutual, and I can't imagine that Diablo would ever want to kiss me back. Either way, Honey looks satisfied with our trade.

Perhaps wanting to prolong my company for a little longer, she says, "Now I take you to Sssibu!"

Before we leave, I take one last look at the path I just came back from. Squinting through the darkness, I see it.

On the forest floor, about fifteen feet away—

A tiny pink flower, now wilted.

29

As we run, the forest blurs all around me. I can only focus on the back of Honey's head, bobbing like a red torch at the end of a dark tunnel. The swamp ends, and the landscape turns lunar and rocky, drenched in moonlight. The December moon casts a white shadow over everything she touches. Looking at the moon now—a day away from being full—it's hard to imagine that the next full moon will be the Ice Moon. There is still so much distance to cross and so much to learn before then. And now, even without my watch, I can tell we're going the wrong way. *North*, when we should be going east. Somehow, giving my watch away has allowed my inner compass to kick in. No longer relying on a device, I have to listen to my own instincts.

Honey and I reach a suspension bridge. Usually, I would stop at the edge and gather my confidence, looking down at the bottomless depths, but tonight I step straight out onto the flimsy planks, holding a rope with one hand and Diablo with the other. The structure swings and the planks creak, but I keep walking quickly across them, carrying Diablo like I did on our first night in the forest. I barely feel his weight on my shoulder now. In my bizarre altered state, still recovering from the potion and Pink Flower, I feel like I could walk all night.

We enter a pine forest. It feels like we're walking across seasons, from late fall to early winter. The night gets colder, but it's a cold that I can stand, crisp and stopping at my clothes. *Wait,* I don't have any clothes—I left them back at the camp. But I have my bag at my side, with a few items I managed to pack in my delirious haze, and I see the map, the rune book, and the faint glow of the fire crystal inside. *Phew.*

Then, the forest changes, and Honey and I enter a gallery of immense trees—the largest trees I've ever seen, their mossy trunks reaching eternal heights. Their crowns are so high up it hurts my neck to look at. Each trunk is the diameter of a small arena and crawling in vertical ecosystems. Some of the older ones have died and split open, and new worlds have flourished inside them: friendly ferns, vines, flowers, nests, and hives.

Up ahead, Honey's vivid red hair is beginning to look gray in the moonlight. *Wait*—there *is* no moonlight. The sky is gone now; the canopy so thick that I can no longer see the stars. I lose sight of Honey again, but my instincts continue to pulse inside me, driving me deeper and deeper into the forest, across, and over.

And then I realize that I haven't seen Honey in a while. Minutes, or hours?

"Honey?" I call out, but there's no sign of the deranged stranger who saved our lives. I look around at the green maze, identical in all directions.

"Honey?"

No sign of her anywhere, but how could she have disappeared so fast? There comes no answer, and that's when I realize that Honey is really gone.

I am no longer on the trail.

And I have no idea where we are.

I set Diablo down. My scream fills the forest—a high-pitched scream that shakes the remaining leaves off the trees and scares the bears away, if there still are any. I don't care about alerting predators—I scream from a deep place, until I am completely empty. Scream to ease my heartbreak. That we came so far, only for me to make a stupid mistake and put my trust in the hands of a weird Klujn who led us here and left us stranded in a strange forest. After Morgan, I shouldn't have put my trust in anyone again.

But she's a Klujn. It felt different.

Although I see now how foolish it was to trust her. I left most of my belongings back at camp, except the ones I managed to pack in my fugue state. Now I'm all alone, with the trees who feel old and wise but don't share their wisdom with me. *She tricked me*, I think. *She lured me away from the swamp, away from my things. And now Diablo is dying.* My screams continue to echo back to me, mocking my aloneness. Exhaustion hits me, like I just walked a hundred miles, and I collapse next to Diablo.

I feel something warm dripping down my face. I have a nosebleed. And, now that I've stopped, I feel the cold and the pain. My entire right side is numb, protesting the hours of abuse. I look around, and I can't tell which direction is which—I can barely tell what's up or down. The ground is a sheet of frost that sucks the warmth from my body. *Lost. Off-trail.* Here, winter has well and truly arrived.

I clutch Diablo's stiff, heavy body. Giving him my heat or perhaps stealing his. I hold my hands around his—another invasion of personal space—but I don't care. It's less to comfort him and more to comfort me. The intrusive thoughts knock me while I'm down.

You're lost and no one will find you.

No one cares if you live or die.

And then, something hits the needle-dusted ground. I reach for it and see—it's a glass ornament, the size of an orange, with glimmering snowflakes inside. A spotted wolf's face has been painted on the glass, which isn't broken after the fall. *Strange*, I think. *An ornament in the middle of the forest? Falling from the sky?*

I'm so tired that my mind is slow, and I struggle to make sense of it. Another *thud*, and another ornament lands on my other side. This one is the size of an apple, with a painting of a moon. I crane my neck to look up at the sky again. There's nothing there but branches. I think of Honey's camp—her bed in the nook of a tree. Her home among the leaves . . .

I stand up and throw the glass ornament as high as possible. After a few feet, it simply *vanishes*—like it's crossing an invisible curtain—and reappears on its way down.

"*Huh.*"

I squint up at the emptiness, not looking *at* it but *through*. In my drunk, tired vision I see multicolored stars in the foliage. And that's when I realize—they're not stars, but *lights*.

The air above my head ripples, revealing a stand in the treetops. Honey didn't betray me. She was true to her word. We're here. We've arrived.

Sibu.

30

A pair of hands descend through invisibility, and Diablo and I are hoisted onto a small wooden platform wrapped around a tree. I'm greeted by two guards—one male and one female, both in their twenties. The female is stern, with shaved red hair and bright green eyes. The male has long, brown hair tied back in a knot and violet—*Estrellan*—eyes. He has gray tattoos on his face and sticks of indigo quartz through his earlobes.

"Welcome back, old friend," he says to Diablo.

"Should we check them?" asks the female.

"The queen is expecting them."

"What about that one?"

"She's expecting her as well."

The female's firm green eyes are on me; she wants to follow orders but doesn't want to take any chances.

"Just a precaution," she says, sticking a rock in my mouth. I taste a forest on my tongue, then the female pulls it out and the rock now has a bright green sheen.

"Couldn't you see her intentions by the color of her lips? I haven't seen that since—well, it's been a long time." The male has a charming accent when he speaks English. He looks at Diablo. "You were lucky in your misfortune."

"Welcome to Sibu," the female says dryly. "*Bejm nini.*"

"*Bejm nova* by now," says the male. "The sun is almost rising."

"Pio—" Another female voice, sweeter than the green-eyed female.

"Can you take her home?" the male guard—Pio—tells the new arrival. "I'll bring Diablo to *Cee.*"

And maybe because I know that I'm safe and Diablo is with people who know him, all my muscles give way. They release from their duties and I can barely stand. Even my neck can't hold itself upright, and my eyes go out of focus, turning Sibu into a landscape of leaves, shadows, and twinkling lights.

"Here," says the sweet voice, an angel's voice, but the hands that catch me are strong. I smell a perfume of moss and vanilla and see the Klujn woman's eyes—a striking cerulean blue, with bits of green and purple inside. Her skin is pale and her seafoam-green hair is woven in a fascinating nest. She looks down at my lips.

"Looks like you've had quite the adventure," she says.

"Dee-ahh-bo—" I try, although I can barely conjure words.

"Diablo's in safe hands now," the woman answers. "You did well."

Diablo is already gone, and I pray that the queen can do something to save him. My legs fail, and the female catches my weight.

"I'm Salta," she says. "Like *Saltimbanka.* The original stand in Carpathia." I have no idea what this means. Salta carries me through a wooden doorway, and I feel like I'm inside a large tree, climbing up a winding staircase like in a wooden lighthouse. Twisting and coiling like an indoor carousel, where the animals slowly climb up toward the sky. *A carousel elevator*, my tired brain thinks.

We emerge out into the brightly lit canopy, but the world is only pixels to me. I hear crackling campfires, a windchime, and laughter. A few musical notes, a child's voice, and a father's whisper.

"Almost there," Salta says, carrying me across a blurry network of ropes and bridges. We arrive at a little room, which is cozy like a treehouse, so quiet you would never know there was an entire stand around. There's a bed with green linen sheets and hanging ornaments and animals painted on the walls. A curtain blocks out the lightening sky.

I'm so dirty, covered in mud and blood, but Salta doesn't mind. She lays me down on the bed. "Sheets can be cleaned," she says. "You need to sleep. You can shower when you wake."

Then my body finds a mattress, my head a pillow, and I sink into an ocean of softness. Salta lays a blanket over me. At last—after a week of sleeping on the ground, on twigs and rocks, this bed is the most comfortable thing I have ever felt.

"We'll talk tomorrow," she says. "Now, the only thing you need to do is sleep."

Salta sings me a lullaby, like I'm a baby in a crib, and by the time the song ends, I'm already asleep.

In my dreams, I am in this same room. There's a figure in the doorway—the bearded, eyeless woman from my dream. She moves toward me, draws up my sleeve, and pierces my skin with a sharp claw. Then, she begins to draw my blood. No, it's not blood that flows but a glittering white substance.

Out, out, out, it pours from me.

"*Sleep*," she says, her voice like a spell.

* * *

I don't know how long I slept, only that I could sleep forever in this bed. I feel like a queen, with a mattress and clean sheets. Never mind the fact that when I sit up and look at them, they are no longer green but brown, and it seems like someone was murdered.

I take in the sight of my battered body—the dried mud and blood on my bare torso, my badly damaged feet. There is a little pinprick in the crook of my elbow where the woman from my dream emptied me of that strange substance, but that might just be my imagination playing tricks on me. As I blink a few times, the room comes into focus. I'm in the hollow of a tree. A door to the left leads outside, and a door to the right leads into a small bathroom. On the wall in front of me is a large window. There are migrations of animals painted on the walls. I feel like I am in a nursery.

A knock, and then the door opens. "I heard you like coffee," Salta says, and I see her clearly. Her striking blue-green-purple eyes, her hair twisted into twin buns, her bright orange overalls with little mushrooms on them that stretch to accommodate a pregnant belly. The pink birthmarks on her hands—*gods*? She is in her twenties, her smile both motherly and mischievous.

"*Bejm nova*?" I try, knowing my pronunciation must be all wrong.

"Actually, it's *bejm meedji* by now," she says, setting the breakfast tray on the bed and opening the curtains, where the warm afternoon light floods in.

Coffee in bed, I think, looking at the little bowl made of leaves. I could die of gratitude as I sip the scorching liquid, which has an aroma of gingerbread.

The window faces the outside of the stand, an endless sea of leaves. The daylight is too bright, and I feel a headache coming on.

"Big night?" Salta asks me with a roguish smile.

I don't remember much. *Did I say or do anything embarrassing?* I vaguely remember calling out Diablo's name when I was fearing for his life.

"Is Diablo okay?"

"He'll be fine. It might take him a day or two to recover, but the queen is doing what she can."

Relief is not a strong enough word. By the way my body aches and the way the cold smells different, I wouldn't be surprised if I had walked right off a map, or much farther north than I should have. Last night is mostly flashes—I remember Pink Flower and Honey, but I don't really know how I got here. Only that my detour here might have cost me the progress I made by taking the shortcut through the cave.

"It was very generous that you brought him, but you know you're free to leave at any time," says Salta.

"I want to wait for him."

"It could put you even farther behind."

"I don't mind." We may be at the back of the Race, but I can't imagine leaving here without him. I am more likely to make up for lost time if I'm with him, so being here is a risk I need to take. I remember how lost I felt the second Honey went away . . .

"You came a long way last night," Salta says. "It's no wonder you're tired. How did you know where to find us?"

"Honey brought me," I say.

"Honey?" Salta's eyes search mine.

"She's the one who told me about Pink Flower," I say. "She gave me a potion to drink, and then I could talk to plants . . ."

Salta is silent for a moment, considering what I just told her.

"The swamp is over fifty miles away."

"What? How is that possible?"

Salta nods. "Honey was always a little strange, but she had

good intentions. She was a romantic, and she made a potion for a girl she liked that ended up killing her by accident. As punishment, she was sent on pilgrimage in the wild for three years; that's what the drudas decided. She was fourteen, and that was ten years ago, apparently. I remember hearing about it when I moved here from Indiko. Honey never came back."

"How come?"

"Because she died."

My mouth opens in a little O.

Salta nods sadly. "Honey died ten years ago," she says. "Pio and the others who went to look for her found her body in the swamp, and decided to leave her there. They think she was a victim of Pink Flower."

The altar.

The crystal skeleton.

Not someone she killed . . . *her.*

But, if Honey has been dead for a decade, how did I *see* her? *Talk* to her? I remember Honey's words—

You see me, don't you? The others didn't see me.

The way she looked gray in the moonlight as she led me here, the farther from the swamp we went. Like she was fading.

"*How*?"

"Do you remember what happened right before you saw her?" Salta asks.

"I don't know . . . I went to wash up . . . Diablo was drumming back at the camp. When I got back, he was unconscious, and I put the map on him to use as a blanket."

"What map?"

"The druda map," I say.

Salta and I both realize it at the same time.

"I think the combination of the drums and the druda map might have triggered a trance," she says. "Without realizing it, you opened a gate to the shadow world, and in doing so, you allowed Honey to enter our world. Nosebleeds are a telltale sign." Salta points to the dried blood on my chest. "In your fear for Diablo's life, you managed to see Honey. But Honey didn't bring you here—*you* did. Your own abilities. The new senses you're developing.

"This is *amazing*," Salta says. "A lot of Klujns don't manage to communicate with the shadow world until well after Initiation. And convincing Pink Flower to give you her antidote is something I've rarely seen. The heart is a powerful thing," she adds. "I think Pink Flower must have appreciated your sensitivity."

It doesn't make sense—that I spent the night with a ghost. That she guided me here, or that *I did it on my own.* I drank the potion, found Pink Flower, and convinced her to give me the antidote. I stopped the flesh-eating spirit from spreading, took a leap of faith, and threw my watch away—and without it, my inner compass kicked in. I navigated and brought Diablo here. Fifty miles in a single night. And with the barrier of my thoughts and self-doubt gone, I was unstoppable.

I spoke the language of plants.

I opened a gate to the shadow world.

My mind spins—I have difficulty believing I did all that. This *body*. This *mind*. This *courage*. That I developed these senses . . . without even *trying*. It just *happened*.

"The queen has been calling Diablo for a while now," Salta tells me. "Because of his illness, he couldn't feel it. I think, that because of your connection to him, you picked up on the message instead, and that's why your instincts brought you here. Even if it meant going off course . . ."

"I'd do it again."

Salta catches me looking at her pregnant belly. "It's Pio's," she says. "The guard you saw last night. He and Diablo were childhood friends. Diablo's come here a lot over the years and is well liked."

Salta places a candle in a lantern. She spins it, and it throws shadows of running wolves on the walls.

"If you choose to wait for Diablo, then you'll be dangerously close to the back."

"I *know*. But it's a risk I need to take. Plus, my body needs the rest."

She nods. "I would have done the same for Pio." Then she adds, "If you're staying here for the next few days, then you're not going to stay in bed all day. I have some work to do this afternoon, but I'll come and get you around sundown."

I'm in a new stand—and I am free to wander around. And, by the sounds of it, this stand is unlike Circo. The next few days stretch out in front of me with endless possibilities. I can use this time to rest and plan for the following stages of my journey. With Diablo healed, we'll be that much faster. *If he doesn't choose to leave me now*, I think. *Now that I've learned the "basics."*

Staying here is a risk worth taking. A *strategy*. We can learn a lot through constant movement, but we can also learn a lot by being still.

"Take a shower," Salta tells me. "There's plenty of water, and none gets wasted, so don't worry about a time limit. You can stay in there until the water runs out. I'll bring in some new sheets, clothes for you to wear, and ointment for your cuts."

She hovers at the doorway. "Also . . . I've gotten to know Diablo well by now, and I've never seen him change his plans for anyone."

There's a twisting, coiling feeling in my stomach.

* * *

I remove my soiled clothes and step into the outdoor shower nestled between the branches of a tree. I pull a string, and hot water pours down over me. It massages my scalp and runs down my back and shoulders, loosening my knots and bringing life back to everything it touches: a scorching ecstasy.

I scrub myself with green soaps and shampoos and breathe in the comforting smells of lavender, eucalyptus, and lemon balm. I shave my legs and armpits with a crystal blade but leave the rest. There's a little fuzz between my legs, and I don't know what young Klujns do to style themselves *down there*, but it feels feminine and natural, so I decide to leave it. Then, I sit on the wood floor and let the hot water run over me, melting the frost that's stored deep inside me. Eventually, the water runs out, but not before my skin is red and blistering.

I've never felt cleaner. I comb my lengthening hair, which is thicker and curlier than it's ever been and almost reaches my breasts. I brush my teeth with a black bamboo toothbrush, then wipe the steam off a crescent-shaped mirror and stare at my reflection.

At first, I don't recognize the girl I see.

A girl-woman hybrid.

I move closer to the glass and take in the sight of me, this almost stranger. She looks seventeen or eighteen, as though a natural, accelerated puberty has taken place inside my body. My eyes are a vibrant purple, and my lips blushed with pink, like a tattoo left behind from my floral kiss. My nose and cheeks are salted with white freckles of frostnip. I should have lost weight from the constant walking and the lack of food, but I only seem to have grown in mass, petite but chunky, with a slash of ribs visible underneath my breasts, like claw marks in the sand, a thickening bum and legs. The little pockets of puppy fat around my hips have turned to muscle, and my cheekbones are more pronounced. I'm not used to seeing my nakedness like this, but for the first time in my life, I like this body.

Back in the room, Salta changed the sheets and laid some clothes on the bedspread. There's a new bralette-and-underwear set, white with green flowers. I have a white costume for tonight. It's beautiful, and I feel like a new person when I slip into it. There's a long-sleeve top, soft as clouds, with long, jewel-encrusted pants that are so flowy they look like a skirt. A pair of matching shoes with a thin sole. A moon crown with white roses, angel aura quartz, and rainbow moonstone.

My hair dries in perfect curls, and when Salta returns around sundown, she does my makeup. She dabs glimmering powder over my cheekbones, and paints my lips white. She tattoos my hands with algae ink, a watery paste that glows and that Salta tells me will last a few days like henna. I want to ask her what's going on—what this celebration is about. At Circo, we dressed like this before the challenges and fights, but something tells me tonight is different. Salta's demeanor is playful, and the atmosphere in the stand feels friendly. I remember Sherman's book talking about Klujn festivals and how winter is a constant celebration of light.

"You look beautiful," Salta says when she finishes my makeup. For once, I decide to accept the compliment.

I deserve to have fun, I tell myself.

A brief pause before I go back to the wild, into the harshest cold and the most challenging part of the Blood Race. Into that area that humans call the Snowy Mountains, but that Diablo has referred to as the *Territory of the Gods*. I have to trust my instinct, my strategy, my plan—

That staying here is a good thing.

That I *will* arrive at Circo on time.

And that, after Initiation, I will find a way to get the king's heart.

"You picked the right night to arrive," Salta beams. She drapes the moon crown on my head and sprays me with rose mist. "Come on," she says. "Yulia is about to start."

31

As Salta leads me through the stand, I am wonderstruck. Sibu is a living fairy tale of treetop Klujns and animals, a buzzing celebration of light. The air smells like pine, gingerbread, and campfire, and every surface glows with candles, lanterns, and sculptures of Moonlight Leaf. Cherry-haired Klujns dressed in white for tonight's festival walk along the wooden passageways, but there are also a lot of Klujns from other stands as well, a mix of eye colors and skin tones. Some of the Klujns look at me, but most leave me alone, as though they are used to seeing travelers. I had no idea that such a place *existed.* I mean—I knew that there were different stands in the Boreal, with Klujns who lived in various environments, but this . . . *Right above my head and I barely noticed it.*

I follow Salta up and down ladders and bridges, past hidden plazas. Sibu is like a giant split-level house with a thousand nooks. You never know what you'll find around a bend. I see children sitting at long, moss-covered tables, painting glass ornaments with their fingers. Others make flower crowns and wreaths out of balsam branches. Acrobats balance on wires suspended between trees, impervious to the heights, while others in lower plazas walk on stilts a few meters off the ground. There is more circus atmosphere here than I ever felt at Circo, and I wonder why—is it a connection to the original stand that Salta talked about, Saltimbanka? The result of a harmonious stand? One where the main form of entertainment is not violence. It is a true hidden gem—a nocturnal winter wonderland, where the only thing missing is the snow.

Salta takes me to one of the lowest plazas, where we can reach down and pet the animals at ground level. There are spotted wolves, moon bears, fuzzy lamas, and those gigantic golden-antlered reindeer. Butterflies rest on the reindeer's golden antlers, which are decorated in winter flowers and seeds. I love animals; looking into their eyes I see the truth. I see innocence. Being around them makes me feel closer than I've ever felt to knowing what my true purpose is.

I don't want to leave this plaza, but Salta tells me there is still plenty to explore. We wind back up toward the mid-levels somewhere between trunk and crown, where most of the stand seems to be situated. Everywhere I turn, there is something interesting to look at. Decorations and ornaments and lights, all beautiful and tasteful and wintry. Plazas where friends stretch out on nets or fabrics, performers dance and twist their bodies into secret languages, communal dinners, ceremonies, and games. Some plazas contain only lovers, different genders or the same, lying in each other's arms on naturally dyed cloths of dandelion or marigold, oblivious to the outside world. Nothing is too intimate for a stranger's eyes to witness, but I find my heart beating faster at these couples, their closeness and the lack of shame.

We pass small clusters of treehouses where dyed cloths hang to dry on clotheslines in a rainbow of forgotten colors—beetroot, chocolate, carrot, seaweed, lime.

I am in awe of this world and wish I had time to explore Sibu's secret corners. I imagine something is always going on, no matter the day of the week; one could never get bored here.

It would be the perfect stand, I think. *If it wasn't for the heights.*

"Don't worry, you'll get your tree legs eventually," Salta tells me as we cross a tightrope bridge with only a flimsy vine to hold onto. "It took me a while when I first moved here."

"Where are you from?" I ask. I vaguely remember her mentioning it this morning.

"Indiko," she says. "It's a coastal stand." I wonder if coastal stands are alike—maybe that's why we have gotten along so fast.

"Why did you move here?"

"*Love*," she says. "Sibu is a popular stand, mostly because of its queen. I fell in love with it on my Blood Race. Then I kept coming back year after year, as many Klujns do, and one of those years, I met Pio. We lived in Indiko for a while but decided to move back here."

"How did you meet?"

"A mating game," she says. "Pio had just finished his Race at fifteen—he's seven years younger than me. I was twenty-two. In human years, that is. And I guess in human years, it's what you would consider illegal, but he was an early bloomer and has always been much more mature than me. He's twenty-two now, and I'm twenty-nine. We're about to finish our first union in the spring."

"What does that mean?"

"That we can choose new partners," she says. "Or choose each other again."

"Do you think . . ."

"Oh, we're staying together," Salta grins. "We were made for each other. He has plans for a big family, and while I would have preferred to wait ten or twenty years," she says, patting her pregnant belly, "I have a traveler's heart, and a lot of my work involves traveling, but when I failed my druda training, we decided to try—not that we had to try very hard."

"You failed your druda training? *Why*?"

"Apparently, I'm too social," Salta grins. "I talk too much. But it might have been a blessing in disguise."

Salta and I arrive at a central plaza, where easily a couple hundred Klujns are gathered. The plaza has an immense tree at the center, branches lit up with a thousand lights.

"The mother tree," Salta explains. "Like the queen of a stand, she keeps all the knowledge of the forest."

The mother tree's trunk is surrounded by a net that some Klujns sit or lie on like a giant see-through trampoline. Around the net a wooden platform circles the entire plaza like a promenade, and there are hanging stalls around the outside suspended from the branches of the neighboring trees.

"Welcome to the hanging markets," she says.

We join the crowd and walk clockwise along the wooden platform, and I'm grateful to be on more stable footing now. Artisans peddle their wares, selling everything from drinks to food to toys to sweets—so many sweets that my mouth waters at the sight of all these delicacies. The piles of fudge and maple candies. The gingerbread wheels decorated in edible glitter and carrot cookies with creamy frosting and chocolate-coated cinnamon sticks. There are colorful fabrics shaped into stylish clothes, jewelry made from many crystals, and fragrant candles for all occasions. There are so many things to tempt the senses: a playground for adults just as much as children.

"Winter is one long celebration," Salta tells me. "Yulia lasts about two or three weeks, from the solstice until the Ice Moon. There's something going on every night in different parts of the stand. Sometimes it's overwhelming, because no matter where you are, you always feel like you're missing out."

Yulia makes sense to me now— the winter solstice, when the sun is farthest from the earth. The longest nights, the most moonlight. A time to stay up all night and absorb as much moonlight as your bones will hold. I don't know if I ever learned what the human *midwinter* celebration was, but if they did give a reason as to why it was celebrated, it made less sense than this one.

"So what's going on here?" I say, gesturing around at the plaza. There are more Klujns than before, sitting on the net, huddling under blankets, as though waiting for a performance to start.

"*You'll see.*"

We stop at a stand selling drinks and a sparkling white one catches my attention. "That's quartz water," Salta says. "I wouldn't recommend it unless you want to *dance your animal*, and I wouldn't do that unless you're at ground level," she says. She speaks to a female she knows, exchanging words in their rapid dialect, and the woman hands her two cups of steaming brown liquid with cream on it, dusted in gold leaf.

"Try this instead," Salta says, placing the warm drink in my hand. I take a sip, and it might just be the best thing I've ever tasted. It's sweet, but not overly sweet in that human way that will make me sick and send my blood sugar into a frenzy. "Hot gingerbread milk," Salta says, and I've just found my next favorite drink.

We continue to walk around, sipping our beverages. Despite the vendors selling things, no money exchanges hands. Salta didn't pay for our drinks, and everything here appears to be . . . *free.*

"How does it *work*?" I ask Salta. If there are a few hundred Klujns here, maybe four or five hundred—and they don't use currency.

"Everyone is required to work in the gardens for a few hours a day," she says. "Or a few days a week, depending on the time of the cycle and what needs planting or harvesting." I wonder where these gardens are, but Salta points toward the canopy. "Then, each Klujn has their individual gifts and talents. Some are costume makers, crystal workers, or guards. Some work with the children, while others care for the animals. We usually live with our families and friends in clusters of houses and take care of our own food and chores communally. But on occasions like these we like to get together and share everything."

"What if a Klujn doesn't want to contribute?" I ask. Surely, out of these hundreds of Klujns, they don't all share the same work ethic.

"We're like bees," Salta says. "It's in our nature to work, serve, and help the queen. That's what makes a healthy, balanced stand. *Purpose* is what makes us happy. We have performers who are also cleaners and mystics who are also chefs. Sure, some Klujns are lazier than others, but there's no place in a stand for a Klujn that doesn't pull their weight. A lot of those are weeded out in the Blood Race.

"And usually," Salta says. "The communal work we do doesn't surpass four or five hours a day, which gives structure to our day but also leaves a lot of time for other things."

"Like?"

"Like this," she says, patting her pregnant belly with a wink. "But other things as well. We weave, forage, practice magic, learn languages, host rituals, and dance. We cook, eat, fire-gaze, see friends, play music, and forest-bathe. There are warm rivers and cold plunges and saunas. There's no such thing as an average night here, and we can't do our work if our bodies are not aligned. You'd have to be here for a year, or seven, before a night would repeat itself.

"Me, I like to travel. And I make ornaments as well."

"Ornaments?"

Salta nods. "But, most of all, I am a gardener like you will be and just like everyone else."

I finish my drink and look around for a garbage can.

"Just drop it," Salta says.

"What?"

"Drop it."

"Isn't that . . ." *Littering*, I want to say. It was a big problem back home, where kids would throw wrappers into the river and treat it as a garbage can. I tried it once and quickly regretted it when faced with Diana's fury. Waste had become a problem in the world, with too much of it and nowhere to put it. What was thrown into the ocean eventually found its way into our bodies.

"They're made of dried autumn leaves," Salta says. "Like most of the paper we use here. It'll decompose in a few days." I look at the cream-colored paper that has maple leaf markings I hadn't noticed before, in faded red, yellow, and golden hues. It makes so much sense, and I don't know why humans don't do it—to use something that's already dead. I move over to the net, drop my cup through one of the gaps, and watch as my cup soars down to the forest floor—which must be a few hundred feet below. My stomach drops when I realize again how high we are.

"Humans won't find it strange if they come across a forest of discarded cups?"

"Humans don't come through here," Salta answers. "And even if they did, our camouflage surrounds the entire border of the stand, so all they would see is nothing before walking in the wrong direction."

I watch Salta, who is so cool, likable, and at ease in this world. I want to ask her more about her relationship with Pio and their marriage—or *union*—but the lights in the trees dim, and conversations fade to whispers. I hear the sound of an instrument, like a haunting cello sound, and Salta says, "Come. I know the best seat in the house. It's one of the guards' posts, but it's not being used tonight."

Salta leads me to a tree and climbs up a ladder of pegs. She is surprisingly agile for someone so pregnant. I follow her up, until we reach a little wooden platform just large enough for the two of us to sit on—I'm suddenly glad that I didn't drink the quartz water. Salta takes an olive-green blanket off a hook and drapes it over our laps. From here, we have a view of the markets below. The crowd's chatter dies, and haunting music fills the night. Listening to it, I think of Salta and Pio's story. Neither of them is from Sibu, although I imagine Pio has lived here since the Estrella raid, which is probably most of his life. I think of how Salta was accepted here and built a life. And that how, once you complete your Blood Race, you can choose any stand to call your home. Any queen to call your own.

Circo is not my final destination, but a landmark.

After Circo, and after Grouse, I can go anywhere . . .

"What about you?" Salta whispers over the music.

"What about me, what?"

She shrugs. "Have you ever been in love?"

"No."

"You answered that without even thinking."

I look at Salta's curious eyes. I feel like I can confide in her, but I'm not sure how to put words to my feelings, like trying to name the colors here.

"I think . . ." I start. "I've maybe had a crush."

"Had or have?"

"Have," I say because there's no getting past her eyes.

"Okay," she says, "that's a start."

"But it's stupid," I tell her, cringing at myself for saying it aloud.

"Why is it stupid?"

"Because it's impossible."

"Why is it impossible? Have you told the person?"

"I couldn't. I would die."

"You wouldn't die. At worst, you'd be a little embarrassed. But what if the feeling was mutual?"

"It isn't."

"How do you know if you haven't told the person?"

My cheeks flush and I don't answer.

"I think I know who you're talking about," says Salta. "Nothing makes or breaks a couple like the wild."

"We're not a couple." Then, after a thoughtful pause, "Is it supposed to hurt this much?"

"Only when it's not right." Her words are a punch to the gut, even though I know she's right. "What I mean is—something can be *not right* because the person doesn't know, or because they know and they're not ready."

"Like I said—it's stupid." I want this conversation to go away. All the years I aged in the wild disappear, and I'm a teen schoolgirl again, with stupid fantasies of a romance that will never see the light of day. But, deep down, despite my embarrassment, it feels good to have told someone. *It's quite fun to talk about.* At Circo, all we would talk about was survival.

"Look," Salta says, like a friend or an older sister, "Diablo is an amazing person. He's been through a lot in his life, and since . . . well, since some personal things happened, he's become more focused on his goals. He's become very guarded. But just because his heart is closed now, doesn't mean it will be forever."

"So what should I do about it?" I ask. "Forget it?"

"Not before telling him how you feel."

"I can't do that."

"Why not? One day we will all be bones."

"That's depressing."

"But it's true, isn't it? When I wake up, I always ask myself—*what's the bravest thing I could do today?* Sometimes, *the bravest thing* means working in the cold—we coastal Klujns love our warm weather. And one day, almost seven years ago, that *bravest thing* was telling Pio that I liked him—a conversation that changed everything because he had no idea. He was in his own world, as most males are."

"You made the first move?"

Salta nods proudly. "I did."

"Even if I told Diablo . . . he'd never be interested."

"You can't know what you don't know," Salta answers. "And even if he isn't, it's not about his reaction. You'll free yourself by saying it." She pats my knee with sympathy. "We've all been there. But just because two paths are separate, doesn't mean they will be for life. You can't force someone to walk on your path, and you shouldn't leave your path to walk on theirs. But if it's right, those paths will intersect in the end," she says. "Whoever is meant to be in your life will be there. That is the forest way."

I want what she and Pio have, but I'm afraid of it. Of love or a relationship. I don't know what scares me more—being abandoned or feeling trapped. Because on the other side of the fence, you marry someone and then you stay with them until you die. Love has little to do with it.

The cello music is joined by other instruments. I look up at the mother tree and see seven performers dressed in white hanging from the tree, each dangling on a gold silk. The performers start to spin and dance around the tree, like a majestic winter carousel, crisscrossing fabrics and creating shapes with their bodies. That's when I realize that they all have white eyes. *Drudas.*

"What are they doing?" I ask Salta, emotion in my throat

now, but whether from the dancers, the music, or our recent conversation, I'm not sure.

"They're working with the other stands," she says. "Moving the weather."

"What does that mean?"

"They're helping trees do their work," she says. "This is the real reason Yulia exists. Hundreds of stands are working together to regulate the weather and move moisture from the coast inland."

"Why?"

"Because when forests are cut down, moisture can't travel anymore, and normal weather systems break down."

Floods in one place, droughts in another, José, the orphanage chef, once told me, when we were talking about the Amazon, which used to be a rainforest before it was cut down for meat production; because cattle needed grass to graze and crops to eat. A lot of these climate catastrophes were related to trees, or the felling of them.

I'm completely hypnotized by the acrobats and their moving bodies. The sky whitens, and I wrap my arms around my body, chilled by a sudden breeze. "How does *circus* come into it?" I ask Salta, still whispering to respect the music and the work the drudas are doing.

"The origin of *circus* comes from our round arenas," she says. "Our arenas are portals; places where the veil thins and we can access hidden worlds, or our gods can visit us. They often take the shape of animals—and we think that depictions of these circuses are what inspired European humans to start animal circuses in the first place. Only they didn't understand the nature of the work we're doing. Circuses are a place for creation. For moving our bodies and dancing with our gods," she says. "Because we are water, and water was not meant to be stagnant."

I remember the glowing drawings in the cave—arenas are places of creation, not places of slaughter and bloodshed. Humans stole circus from Klujns; they took Klujn stories and gave them new meanings, and those new meanings changed the world.

Places of creation, not stages for violence.

I watch the drudas, completely rapt, as they continue to dance around the mother tree at the end of their long silks. Their white eyes are in a trance, connected to some other frequency, and I wonder what it feels like to be up there, soaring from those heights, seeing what they're seeing . . .

And the crowd below, the children and the young and the adults and the elderly, all mesmerized as they sit in a religious silence. They've probably seen this ritual yearly, but it still means something to them.

My neck hurts from looking up, but I can't stop staring . . .

Moved to tears and absolute silence.

As the sky grows whiter, pregnant with a winter smell.

It's magic, I think.

And yet, it's what trees do every day.

Who would've thought? That I would end up here, deep in a strange forest, in a stand I didn't know existed until last night. Undergoing my Blood Race, and still far from a finish line. Yet, having one of the best nights I've ever had.

But I don't care about Circo, the past, or the future. Right now, there are only these performers, tracing runes with their bodies, casting spells in the sky, diving into hidden worlds, shadow ones, or opening the gates to the gods. Until, all of a sudden, the music reaches its crescendo and—

A million perfect snowflakes fall from the sky.

It's magic, and it isn't; right on cue, winter has arrived.

32

The next afternoon, I draw open the curtains and find a winter wonderland outside my window. All the branches have white shadows. After a breakfast of chocolate-peppermint oats and my new favorite gingerbread milk, Salta announces that she's taking me to see the queen. Most of the stand is still asleep after last night's festivities, and I enjoy the early afternoon quiet. Salta and I climb a series of tree staircases until we reach the canopy. Amid the lush, vertical gardens is an animal sanctuary. There are white sloths cradling the branches, mystical birds, and even monkeys. Salta leads me across a wooden walkway, at the end of which is a massive dead tree, its dark entrance split like a V. Hundreds of glass ornaments of all sizes dangle outside it; some colorful and some clear.

"What are those?"

"This one catches bad spirits," Salta says, gesturing to a large, clear ornament with thin glass filaments inside. She points to another one filled with black smoke. "That is the aftermath." She points to others one by one. "This one wards off curses, this one attracts good dreams, and this one acts as a talisman—for a safe journey."

"What about this one?" I ask, touching a tiny ornament the size of a cherry tomato. Inside is a miniature ecosystem—an infinitesimal world of soil, sand, water, moss, air, and tiny crystal seeds that are as fine as salt.

"They're the little worlds I make," she says. "They contain the right amount of everything they need for their ecosystem to stay balanced. Water, air. I bring them with me on my travels, and bury them in hard-to-reach places. This glass will take a million years to decompose," she says. "And when it does, it'll give birth to new worlds. Our birds and animals will help spread these little seeds, which will grow into forests, jungles, and reefs once again. Think of it as a miniature seed library so that if humans bring us to extinction, our life forms will start again."

"In a million years?"

Salta nods as though she's talking about next year, but her colorful eyes are bittersweet. I don't know how Klujns can be so patient.

A windchime clangs, bringing us back to the present. Salta breaks eye contact and enters the queen's place without knocking.

We enter a round workspace filled with gentle sunlight. Hundreds of crystals hang at different heights and cast their broken rainbows onto the walls of the dead tree. *What a fascinating place to live.* A small auditorium of wood and magic. The queen is barefoot with red frizzy hair and green robes. She stands with her back to us, at a table against the wall.

"It's nice to meet you, Ava," she says with the English of a frequent traveler, although her voice bears no human accent. Her tone isn't dulcet like Salta's but smoky. "We met before, briefly, but I didn't introduce myself."

The queen turns around, and my heart skips a beat—

The bearded woman from my dreams.

Now she's here, standing in front of me . . .

Her eyes have been burned into two charred peaches. I'm shocked by the grotesque sight of them but try not to show it. Despite the queen's blindness, she appears to be looking right at me. I imagine they used to be green before whatever happened *happened*. Her skin is pale with a hundred brown birthmarks—*god* marks. A wispy red goatee on her chin makes her look grotesque and slightly unsettling; the kind of creature you would find on the posters advertising freakshows, which usually accompany a circus.

"My name is Celestinja," she says. "Most call me *Cee*."

"How . . . ?" I stammer. "I mean—it's nice to meet you, but—"

"How did I get in your dreams?"

Celestinja smiles. I don't feel comfortable calling her by her nickname. It would be like calling Daciana *Daci*, which feels all wrong—not how you should address a Klujn queen. But Celestinja doesn't feel like a queen. She feels like someone who could be your aunt—*or your uncle*—but more importantly, your friend.

"I've been calling Diablo for a while now so I could talk to him," she explains.

"Like . . . telepathy?" I ask.

"Queens and drudas have special relationships," she says. "We can communicate through the soil's algae networks, through animal messengers, with the wind, or in dreams. Sometimes, thinking about a person is enough, if they are thinking about us too. The stronger the link, the clearer the message. As long as the weather is clear, and both parties are open to receiving it. Otherwise—like human telephones—the call does not go through, and we do not have answering machines.

"And even though Diablo is not a druda yet, he is only months away from training and has always been important to Sibu."

"How come I could see you?"

"Because of Diablo's injuries, his natural gifts were not working as they should be. I imagine that, because of your connection to him and your openness to the unseen and disbelieved, you answered the call instead."

"The night I arrived . . ." I stammer. "Was that a dream too?"

"I'm afraid not. I had to draw a bit of your vitality. I apologize for the intrusion, but Diablo didn't have much time."

"My *vitality*?"

"He needed a transfusion, and vitality—like blood types—is hard to match. As the only other Estrellan here, Pio tried to help his friend, but his didn't work. I tried to wake you, but after your long night, you were dead to the world. Your vitality saved his life," she says. "Diablo didn't tell you what the Hunters did?"

I shake my head; he didn't, but I didn't ask.

"Humans like to use our kind and our animals for many purposes," she says. "The young and healthy, of course, because they have more vitality than the old. Some drink it, some bathe in it, but some take a transfer directly into their veins. In the case of Diablo, Hunters almost bled him dry. My guess is that they used his vitality to restore the general's health. After that, with Diablo impaired, he was in a weakened state. Vitality can replenish on its own, but it takes days. This is how a simple forest spirit that he could have easily repelled under normal circumstances managed to enter his body and wreak so much havoc; it is much like having a weakened immune system and catching a virus. And, whether consciously or not, you brought him here, even if that meant going off course from your own journey. You are the reason he's alive."

"He should have told me," I mutter. "I could have helped him."

I should have known, when I saw that catheter in his arm. Humans didn't *give* him anything, they *took* from him; took until they could no longer take. Because of Diablo's vitality, Santos could be healed by now. Why else would they let Diablo leave? It was mission accomplished.

Maybe my vitality is the reason he kept me around, I think. Perhaps he knew that I could restore him to health, but he didn't want to ask. *Or maybe he didn't want it because it's tainted.* He hates anything to do with humans.

"He's prideful," says the queen. "And fiercely independent. He wasn't always like that, but the years have worn him down."

"But do I have vitality—if I'm half human?" I ask. "Couldn't that hurt him somehow?" It's strange to imagine that a part of me is inside him. He must *hate* that. Celestinja shakes her head with all the patience in the world. "But my father is a Hunter . . . a *human* . . ."

"Father, maybe, but not necessarily in the *traditional* sense."

"What do you mean?" I hate feeling out of my depth, but most of the things I know about Klujn reproduction are things I've learned from humans. When I heard *half*, I assumed . . .

Well, the obvious.

"It's not what you think," George had said.

"You are more Klujn than you realize."

"How?"

"I have a feeling about you; one that could only be confirmed with a trip inside your mind."

I'm dead silent. I don't understand what's going on. "This Race has started to open you up, slowly," says Celestinja. "First, at Circo, and now, here. Being open is what allowed you to see me in the first place. And, in exchange for saving Diablo's life, I'd like to help you now."

"Help me how?"

"I want to help you heal the parts of you that are still broken," she says. "To help you understand your past so you can put it behind you and live the life you deserve. I can see that your growth is hindered by certain traumas and weights you've been carrying around. Like soil packed too tightly, it's been keeping you from growing to your full potential. Where your physical growth is astounding—your strength, stamina, instincts, and the way you spoke to Pink Flower—your emotional development is lacking. Socially, emotionally, and even *romantically*," she says. "Especially when it comes to communicating your true feelings. You have blockages, and I'd like to help you remove them—if you let me—so that you can finish the Race as you were meant to, and this detour won't hinder your progress."

Celestinja gestures to a staircase carved into the wall, descending to lower levels. I'm scared at the idea of going down there. There are some things that I'm in no hurry to relive. But I know that what the queen has offered me is a great privilege. One that I imagine doesn't come around often.

I glance at Salta, who has been quiet this whole time, and she smiles in encouragement. "I can come with you."

"I'd like that."

"Great," says Celestinja, the strange bearded queen. Her smile reveals a split tongue. "Salta—I can always use an extra pair of hands for the drum."

33

We wind down until we reach an earthen floor. Celestinja instructs me to take my shoes off, and I do. In the center of the room is an ominous circle. I remember Salta saying that their circles are portals—places where the veil thins— and suddenly I'm not so sure I have the grit to do this. But, the voice of strategy chimes in. *If this can help me make up for lost time, isn't it worthwhile?*

"Is it . . . *dangerous*?" I ask Celestinja, who is already preparing some herbs and crystals for my journey.

"No more than a walk in the jungle," she answers, and somehow, there's a twinkle in the dark pits of her eyes. She is so comfortable in blindness that I wonder if she was like this since birth or if she chose this fate for herself somehow.

"Humans shy away from the darkness, but the only way through is by leaning into it, speaking to it, seeing what it wants. The darkness has a lot to teach us."

Salta nods encouragingly. "I'll be here," she says, taking a seat off to the side, and the queen places a small drum on her lap. Celestinja guides me to the center of the circle. Then she places a chunk of flower quartz in my hand, dabs my forehead in something wet and herbal, and places a blindfold over my eyes. Sight dissolves into sounds. The queen tells me to lie down in a fetal position, on the side of my choosing, and I choose the left because it feels more comfortable. Then, she drapes a blanket over me and steps outside the circle.

"Today," the queen says, in a quiet voice designed for an audience of three, "you experience one of the greatest traumas that humans and Klujns face—birth. Or, in this case, rebirth."

I feel anxious. Like I'm going on a dark ride into the basements of my mind, although this is no Swampland Safari Log Ride. The queen is right, though, about the pieces of memories stuck inside me like giant splinters—the shame and despair that infects so many of my waking moments. That make it impossible to just be *happy*. Because I am haunted by ghosts without faces, and what the queen is offering me is a chance at normalcy and lightness.

I hear Celestinja as she begins to walk around me, the scratch of her robes against the ground. She lights a smudge stick, and I smell black sage, juniper, and rose. The queen fans thick clouds of smoke over my head as she chants in a language I've never heard. The deep, ethereal lament fills my chest, making my throat vibrate. Salta plays the drum steadily, and I feel it in my bones. There's the occasional rattle, an instrument that sounds like the rain.

I grip the cold crystal in my hand like an anchor to this world. A candle blows out—the only candle in the room—because the world behind my blindfold goes from deep red to absolute black. And then Celestinja kneels by my side, two hands on me, but I feel like there are many more—hundreds of invisible hands pinning me down. Suddenly, I get the feeling that we're not in a tree anymore but in a forest clearing, surrounded by the sounds of a busy woodland night.

I lie there on the earth, curled like a seed before life, paralyzed. I try to settle my nerves by breathing in for three counts and out for six, because my lungs are the only body part I can control. Then, the queen places a hand on my forehead and another on my right hand, where the scar of Wolf's bite is. I feel a surge through my body, and I see the river, the swirl of bubbles, as he pulled me from the water, dragging my two-week-old body onto the shore of the orphanage before he brought me back to life. It's like that memory was lodged in my hand that whole time, and with one touch, she frees it.

"You have stories inside you that need to be told," says the queen. The drums and the forest sounds continue. The sound of rain and a crackling fire. Nothing more peaceful, nothing more organic.

But I'm scared, I'm shaking.

Celestinja continues to touch different parts of my body. She presses a hand against the crescent moon scar on my forearm, and I see the moment it was branded on my skin at Circo; I see myself straddling Elizabeth and punching her face from side to side in my delirious rage; I see my baby claws sprouting from my fingers in front of a rapt audience; I see the betrayal in Wendy's eyes.

"Good, good," says Celestinja, but I don't know how any of this is good. It's horrifying. The things I've done, the shame I feel.

I don't want to meet my own darkness, I want it to stay safely buried underground.

Even though I'm blindfolded, the images I see are as sharp and vivid as reality. The queen touches the scars of my mother's runes, the spiral one, and I see a slithering snake with gold eyes.

"Let it come," says the queen. "Let it out."

Celestinja touches my belly, right under my belly button,

and I'm sitting in home studies, eleven or twelve years old, as Mrs. Verity hands out tampons. A few weeks later, when I get home, I pull my undies down to see a red-brown mud on them. I find the tampon, take it out of the packaging, and try to push it inside my body. It doesn't want to go in at first, but then it does and stays at the edge where it hurts. Diana comes in and startles me; I feel embarrassed. She leaves and comes back a few minutes later with a cloth pad. Diana tells me in a kind voice that there are chemicals in the tampons. Things that will make us bleed more than we should, and make us weak. They are designed for that. In the process, they will make many women infertile.

The memory forms a hard pit in my womb.

But as Celestinja touches it, it goes away.

The queen's hand glides up to my belly button, and there I feel the violent *thwack* of an axe running through me.

Then the queen touches my new white freckles, and I'm back in the woods with Diablo, looking at him across the fire. Feeling things I'm not supposed to feel.

There are other fragments, too, that aren't memories—

Diablo and I lie in a tent underneath a red sheet, skin to skin.

I look into his violet eyes, which are turning white.

A red union takes place, where he and another Klujn are bonded. I can't see the female's face, can't know if it's me.

Then, I am standing on a moonlit beach. Looking at my own dead body.

I am drifting, floating over an entire Territory, the Boreal a smoking wasteland below me.

Finally, Celestinja places her whole hand over my heart and presses down. My heart releases a fireworks finale—

George.

Wolf.

Daciana.

Glory.

Diablo.

To feel love is to hurt; to be abandoned by those I needed, time and time again. How can I open my heart, in a world that will only hurt me? This is why I have always hidden behind walls. Because, behind these walls, no hurt gets in. *But no love gets in, either.*

Then the drums and rattle resumes—unless it never ended—and I am sinking into the earth. The faster the rhythm goes, the faster I sink until I am drowning in soil, sucked down by some terrestrial maelstrom. And then, I am a planted seed, awaiting birth.

I am in my mother's body. I hear the echo of a lullaby she sings through the walls of her skin. In her body, I am safe.

The wind rustles, and there's a key scraping in a lock and a voice I think is George's. "It's almost time," he says. There is a long pause, and then my mother says—

"*Wait.*" She hesitates, wondering if she should tell him. But inside her body, I feel what she feels, the amount of love she has for me, the kind that can't be reasoned with. "If you want Ava to survive, untie my hands and take me outside. If you can't get me out there in three minutes, she'll die."

"Why are you telling me this?"

"So that you'll get what you need, and you'll let us go."

"You shouldn't have named her," George says. "It'll only hurt more."

I hear him hovering in the doorway. "I'll need to bury her," says my mom. "And when I do, let me pull her from the soil. And if it can't be me, let it be you, but no one else, please."

"Why?"

"Do as I say, and you'll see," she answers. "But please, don't let it be any of those men."

Then, my comfortable home begins to rock like a train carriage. I am being forced from my home, even though I don't want to leave. My mother screams, and her fear is inside my every cell.

I am born under the glaring lights of the Loudhouse lab, but I am not breathing. Even though I can't see, I can feel the faceless men all around me. George yells—

"*Outsiiiiiide*!"

There's movement and yells and a stampede of feet. There's running and rain and a hazy full moon, and then there's soil, as my mother buries me. I am still not breathing; not alive, but not dead, either. And here, in my nest of soil, I feel the earth charging my little bones. A feeling of being *home*.

I am a crystal seed.

One that can grow into anything.

And then, my left hand pierces through the soil. A hand closes around mine and pulls me into the world. I feel George's skin, his hand, and a spark runs from his body into mine or from my body to his.

I see his heart, and I love him.

Then—*thwacckkkk*! A Hunter brings an axe down and severs my umbilical cord, and I feel a shudder run through me. Something that tells me that I have now entered a world where I will never be safe. A feeling of loss, of separation, of grief. Of being disconnected from what I need. My mom, who gave up the secrets of her kind so that I would survive.

A baby, born in an arena of faceless men and rifles.

Wrapped in a blue blanket.

I am taken back inside and placed in a small glass cage, where I am poked and prodded and connected to wires. I am given medicine that will kill all the vibrant cells of my microbiome and make me lose my animal instincts.

For those two weeks, I become a little circus exhibit. The first of my kind to survive. In my cage, crying and crying and crying, but no one comforts me. I am a curiosity. I am science. I am connected to all these wires, when the only wires I have ever needed are the earth, the rain, and my mother's arms.

34

The drums stop, and Celestinja takes off my blindfold. I sit up, tired, blinking the room back into existence. Salta is still seated in the corner, watching like a concerned friend, and Celestinja is on the ground beside me, looking as tired as I feel. "You did well," she says. "You were very brave."

"George . . ." I start, expecting my throat to be blocked but it's oddly clear, like a little frog was blocking it and now it has hopped away.

My gut, my womb, all feel clearer too, like a tumor there has dissipated.

"Like I said, he isn't your father in the *traditional* sense," says Celestinja. "Some of the Hunters resort to sexual violence. We don't talk about what was done to the Bessi-Maso women and some of the Estrellans. But your mother was lucky in her misfortune—your father is different. He made her feel as comfortable as he could in that environment."

"So, my mother wasn't . . ."

Inseminated. Raped. Forced into a pregnancy she didn't want.

Even though I can't imagine George doing any of those

things, I can imagine him following orders. *How else would she have gotten pregnant with me?*

"What do you know about self-reproducing Klujns?" says Celestinja. My jaw almost detaches from my face.

"I heard that . . . I don't . . ."

"Most female Klujns can develop this mechanism," she says. "Especially ones who are hunted. It happens in captivity more than in the wild, but it is still possible in both cases. It can be triggered when there aren't any available mates or as a survival mechanism, which we sometimes see in aging Klujns."

"But what about my eyes?" I ask.

"A Klujn baby's first parent is their mother. Their second parent—whether male or female—is the first to bond with it after birth."

"Bond with it how?"

"The first to touch its hand," she says. "Just like the soil imprints on the baby, the second parent's DNA does as well. A mistake that humans made once, that I'm sure they never made again on purpose, because it is quite spooky to witness."

"So my blood is . . ."

"Mostly Klujn," says the queen. "With a few of your father's traits. But not enough to be considered a *hybrid*. You are your mother's daughter. She made you by herself."

I don't know if this is a shock or a relief—that George didn't hurt my mother. That she self-reproduced. That she trusted him more than the others. The good I saw in him, she saw as well. Maybe his love for me wasn't a lie. Maybe he really *was* a puppet, caught in a lifelong mime.

"Your eyes are unique," says Celestinja. "The way they change from one color to another, depending on how you feel or what environment you're in. It shows your adaptability, or the two worlds inside you competing for attention. Eye color usually changes slowly, over time, as I'm sure you saw with your new friend Salta and many other Sibunites. The eyes simply cannot lie—they show a Klujn's true allegiance. And you are loyal to both sides.

"I imagine the more time you spend in the wild, the longer they'll stay violet. And, who knows, if you one day choose to make Sibu your home, where you are more than welcome, they may even be green. You have the makes of a really special Klujn," she says. "When I was cleaning your energy field, I already saw a few gods vying for your interest." The thought gives me a chill.

It's all too much to take in at once. This rebirth experience was frightening but healing, too, I imagine, with time. For now, my clothes smell like a fortune teller's tent and I feel like I could sleep for a hundred years.

"Tonight, you sleep," says Celestina. Are all queens mind readers? "Tomorrow, Diablo and you will leave. He will walk with you until the Territory of the Gods, until your stores of vitality are replenished. I only took a small amount.

"Over the next few days and weeks, a purge will happen. Some more memories may continue to rise to the surface. You may experience a *chrysalis* as you shed your old life and make room for your new one. But do not be afraid—sometimes we need to slow down in order to speed up.

"Forgive yourself, Ava," she says. "For the things that aren't your fault, and even the ones that are. Forgive others, too—in a world that wants you to be hateful, kindness is the greatest act of rebellion. Just because your mother's story was tragic, doesn't mean that yours has to be. The world is not ugly or beautiful; it depends on where we place our focus. There comes a pivotal time in a young Klujn's life where we must let our trauma go and no longer let it define our lives. Where we must decide if we are victim or victor, predator or prey.

"Of course, by predator, I don't mean someone who maims and kills senselessly, who controls and manipulates and torments, but someone who is intrepid and authentic, who understands their worth and is willing to fight for it. Who has alpha energy."

Celestinja looks at me, and despite her blindness, I feel like she can *see* me. Then, she tells me that at the end of my journey, I should find a body of water to swim in. Alone and naked, where my purge would be complete. I should conduct a ritual to honor my past, let it go, and begin this new relationship with myself.

"How will I know that it's the end?" I ask.

"You'll know when the moment is right. But the end of a journey is just the beginning of another. It's the same with death—a cycle that keeps going. A bug that feeds a flower. A river that feeds an ocean. A body that feeds a tree."

* * *

After a hot shower, a nap, and dinner, Salta makes me change into black overalls with embroidered butterflies and a thick cream sweater underneath. Aside from our different hair colors and her bulging belly, we could look like sisters. She tells me I'm not spending my last night at Sibu in my room, then takes me to a small, secret plaza, where Pio and some of his musician friends are playing for a crowd of a dozen Klujns. As I listen to the musicians, my tired eyes play tricks on me, and the music notes travel through the air like wisps of colorful smoke. The music is not just for the ears; it is a visual feast.

Around midnight, Diablo arrives. The musicians stop to greet him, and I realize how popular he is at Sibu. He looks healthy and strong, and there's a spark in his eyes I've never seen before. My heart beats rapidly, and I suddenly feel nervous.

When Diablo's eyes find me, there's a small half smile on his lips that puts me at ease.

Salta watches me with a look that cuts through lies and false appearances. "*What?*" I say self-consciously.

"Nothing," she hums, and then the musicians start again, playing strange instruments made of twisted plants with a breath-percussionist that makes music with his lungs, an impressive capacity for breath that could rival Diablo in an underwater contest. Pio takes a break and comes to sit on Salta's other side, and Diablo sits next to him, two bodies away from me.

Klujns may be hunted, I think, *but living on the knife's edge of life and death makes everything feel more visceral. It makes every moment precious. Humans do anything to try to prolong their lives—chasing fertility, long marriages, or immortality in a bottle of vitality or corpse medicine—but in how many of those moments are they genuinely present and happy?*

A Klujn union lasts seven years.

Then it expires or is renewed.

There is something beautiful about not needing to own someone forever.

To appreciate the beauty of a moment.

Pio wraps his arm around Salta, and I watch them out of the corner of my eye, finding myself wishing for what they have. It's something I never knew existed before—a relationship that isn't a prison. A love that doesn't restrict you, where you're free to grow toward your own wild suns.

Looking around at the plaza, I see that love is different among Klujns. It's everywhere. It's not about longevity but *moments*. It's not about ownership but freedom. It means the real possibility of loss, but that loss doesn't stop Klujns from *loving*. There is the love of friends, of family, of music, of ritual, of the night, of community and service. Love is like water; it takes all forms.

I watch the side of Diablo's face as he watches the musicians, wondering what he's thinking, wishing he was thinking of me. If I could bottle a moment, place it in a glass ornament that would last for a million years, I would bottle this one.

At the end of the night, Salta walks me back to my room. It was a perfect night, although my feelings are no longer innocent. My new friendship with Salta, my love of Sibu, which has begun to feel like home in two short days, and my growing feelings for Diablo. Sibu has shown me that even the friendliest, most balanced stands believe in the Blood Race, and that hardship makes us grow. This motivates me to find my finish line once and for all.

"Any advice?" I ask Salta when we stop outside my little nursery treehouse. The next time I see her, if I ever see her again, she'll be a mom.

"For the Blood Race, or everything else?" There is no getting past those blue-green-purple eyes.

"*Both*."

"Live in the arena, Ava. Be the star performer of your own life. It takes courage to expose yourself, but it's the only way to live."

"That's it?"

Salta smiles, then she hugs me like a sister. "Finish your Race and then come back to visit me. *Bejm nini*, sister."

"*Bejm nova*," I grin, because the sun is already rising.

This time, my pronunciation is spot on.

35

I leave Sibu with a heavy heart. As Diablo and I head southeast into the Snowy Mountains, the cold pierces deeper than ever. We follow trails made by the hooves and paws of wild animals, walking through a landscape of glittering snow and cracking ice. The fire crystal in my bag has never been more vital, as I retrieve it every hour or so to raise my body temperature back up. The sun is like a white hole in the gray sky, and with insufficient daylight, I feel more tired than ever. It's crazy to think that we are slowly inching toward the three-quarter mark. Going forward, I know things will only get more difficult—and they will undoubtedly get *colder*.

Diablo and I don't talk much. I don't know why our silence feels different from our previous treks. Maybe it's me, filling the air between us with my strange new feelings and overthinking. Diablo might not sense that anything is different. It might all be in my head.

We cross pine-dusted valleys, and I'm hungrier than ever. Salta packed me a few meals for the road and some sweets from Yulia. I devour them all to replenish my depleted stores of energy. I blame the weather for my hunger because my cycle is still a week away. When my next blood comes, that will mark the official five-day countdown to the Ice Moon. I can sense that the spotted wolves aren't far behind.

The cave shortcut saved us about a week, minus the detour to Sibu and the lost days there. According to Diablo's calculations, we are near the middle-back but don't have too much time to play with. Now, my upcoming proof of passage is starting to feel real . . . and daunting.

"Tonight, you eat," Diablo says a few days in, nearing the inevitable end of our trekking partnership. He throws a judgmental look at the sweets I can't get enough of—the gingerbread wheels I've been trying to bite discreetly. "Tomorrow, you start fasting."

He's right—I need to fast for three days before my proof of passage, and I can no longer delay it. I'd be lying if I said I wasn't nervous about a god visiting me in my sleep. The last thing I want to do is summon something I'm not ready to meet. As much as I dread the encounter, I know the days left in the Blood Race are counted. Every day, I need to dig deeper.

Diablo and I walk up and down mountains, listening to the sounds of winter. Winter in the air, winter in my bones, winter freezing the hair in my nostrils. Diablo is back to full health now, with his superhuman stamina, and doesn't need things like rest or sleep. His bare feet—not frostbitten, but a standard brown—are impervious to the cold. Even though he doesn't say it, I know I'm slowing him down. That he is bringing me back on track out of politeness, to make up for the detour I took to save his life. Soon, we'll go our separate ways, and I have to prepare myself mentally for that. Diablo doesn't need to say it—I know it in my gut. That by tomorrow, he'll be gone.

The thought makes me emotional.

"Don't cry," he says without turning around.

"Sorry." Then, I change course with my reply. "I thought you said a person should cry freely in the wild. Something about the preservation of energy."

"Yes," he answers. "But if you cry now, in this weather, you'll get frostbite on your cheeks."

My sad mood dissolves at once.

Star-performer energy, I think.

"And Ava?" he says. "The next time you cry, don't say sorry."

An hour before sundown, we take refuge in a cove. A turquoise alpine lake stretches out to a glacier's base. It is probably one of the most beautiful places I've ever spent the night. Never mind the fact that an avalanche could easily take us out. I pray to the gods of the Snowy Mountains—if such specific gods exist—that they let us stay here without incident.

On the beach is a campsite, already erect and with good infrastructure. A large black sleeping tent with a dozen mattresses on the ground, blankets, and warm, waterproof sleeping bags stuffed with the shed fur of spotted wolves. There's a fire pit outside, where a few embers still glow from a recent visitor, and a smaller tent that Diablo tells me is a sauna. Karavaning Klujns must have stopped here on their travels, or young ones competing in their Blood Race. Here, at the edge of the Territory of the Gods, where the night skies are rumored to be some of the darkest in the Boreal, and the icy breeze is not benign.

"That's the path you'll take tomorrow," Diablo says, pointing to a narrow trail that weaves between mountains. "The base camp is about an hour's walk up that way."

It feels like a luxury to have a roof over our heads. We'll be sharing a tent tonight, never mind that it's the size of a small house. Still, the night ahead stretches with possibility, and I wonder how the sauna works. My fantasies begin to take me down a honeyed road until my survival brain kicks in and tells me that there's less than an hour until dark, and it's my turn to get a fire going. The light of day will disappear faster here behind the tall glaciers.

I don't need to use my fire crystal, and this fire is the easiest one I've ever made. I add two logs and blow, and the embers do the rest, resurrecting into flames. As I stare at the flames, I think I hear a lone wolf's howl coming from the path Diablo pointed out, but that wouldn't be right. The wolves are due to come from the other side. The silence of Nature can make you start to imagine things sometimes.

Diablo goes for a plunge in the lagoon's glacial waters, and I'm cold just thinking about it. He comes out, torso naked, his tattoos glimmering in the dusky light. A patchwork of animals, plants, eyes, and maps that look like rivers. Then, as he dries himself and begins to collect food for my last meal, I go in search of more firewood, which is a challenge here where everything is moist or frozen. I take a little path into a forest behind the beach, and it's the safest I've felt wandering away from camp. There are no snares here. The blue sky turns pastel, clouds pretty enough to put on a stick, dip in sugar, and eat. My mouth waters, and I realize I'm still hungry even after everything I ate today. I'm a little skeptical about how this whole *fasting* thing will go down.

Along the path, I come across an airplane. A small, crashed thing I've seen in the likes of historical documentaries, but it doesn't have any Military or Hunter insignia on the side, no triangle or diamond emblems. The plane is riddled with bullet holes. It was shot from the sky and crashed to the ground where it caught fire. The only part of the plane that's still intact is the tail, where there is a symbol that looks familiar. It reminds me of the pin José—the orphanage chef—wore on his bloodied apron.

The plane must have belonged to foreign Territories trying to get in or rebels attempting to get out.

I step carefully into the wreckage, which is tilted like the tunnel of a funhouse. There are skeletons in the front seats, but near the back I glimpse an unclipped seatbelt, which gives me hope that someone managed to escape. A newspaper is tucked in a seat cushion, and I see the headline:

THE WORLD MOURNS THE ASSASSINATION OF LAURIER MÉLIE:

A Dark Day for Nature, Humankind, and Democracy.

Underneath the headline is a large black-and-white photo of a middle-aged Black man with kind, wrinkled eyes holding a curly-haired girl in his arms. She has a plush toy of a white sloth. I go to pick up the newspaper, but the old thing disintegrates in my hands, falling like confetti. A little breeze takes the rest of it away. The newspaper is gone, but I remember the curious headline. *The World Mourns*—like one unified place that has nothing to do with this Territory. A world we never hear anything about because everything is about our maps and our borders and our history. *A Dark Day for Nature, Humankind, and Democracy.*

I don't know much about democracy, but I think it has something to do with voting, everyone deciding on the greater good of the whole. Our world only has one leader who decides everything for us, which makes it an *autocracy*, not that that word ever gets passed around. And Grouse took over from his father. This means that before Grouse and Pepito Silver, this Territory—or continent—was democratic. This so-called *world* also cared enough about Nature to list it in the headline, *before* humankind. But where are they? These kind and well-intentioned humans who care about the greater good? Who can publish things like this in their papers without retribution? Are there Klujns in their Territories, and are they treated like Klujns here?

Something tells me not.

"You should have told me you were going exploring," Diablo says, and I jump, startled, as I turn to see him standing in the doorway of the plane. "Most Klujns I know are too afraid to come in here."

"How much do you know about human history?" I ask Diablo, gesturing to the crumbled paper at my feet.

"Bits and pieces." I know he acts disinterested, but he's the kind to be informed. Whatever Grouse and his father have done to the Territory affects Klujns, after all.

"Who is—*was*—Laurier Mélie?"

"You ask so many questions, Ava."

"I'll stop asking stupid questions, then."

"Not stupid, just many." Diablo sighs, and I decide not to push it. Is that how he sees me—as a nag, always wanting something? Information? But information has been my means of survival out here.

"He was the last leader of Quebec—back when it was a province in a country. He was a good man, as good as humans can be." Diablo complimenting a human—this man must have been a *saint* or something.

"He fought for the protection of the environment and wanted to join the One World Treaty. But Silver didn't like that—and so he killed him. Then he moved north and claimed Canada, which was the most habitable land left, rich with resources, and with the least amount of natural disasters. But there was nothing amicable about the acquisition."

"So Silver is responsible for all of this?"

"Silver started it, and Grouse continued it. But there is

another family name that is just as bad—Santos. Silver and Grouse come from wealth and privilege, with their money and Military connections. But the Santoses are the true Hunters. They are descendants of those who destroyed the Amazon.

"When those two families came together—the power and the field experience—this country didn't stand a chance."

But why destroy the Territory? Take away people's freedom and brainwash them? What was there to gain? We are one Territory, but we are also a world, a single atmosphere surrounding a rock that's hurtling through space, and whatever *one side* does has repercussions everywhere. Silver, Grouse, and the Santoses must know their actions would only hurt themselves.

Unless they know, I think, *and they don't care.*

Because they will be long gone by the time that happens. When there are no forests left and no more breathable air. The survival of one species, at the expense of all others.

But extinction will visit us all in the end.

Klujns know this, because they are preparing for the worst.

As the sun begins to set around us, Diablo's words haunt the air. I feel sad for Mélie, this man with kind eyes, and the little girl in his arms. I find myself wondering what could drive a person to do that—to kill someone who was trying to do good in the world.

"How could the world let this happen?"

"They tried to intervene. But Silver's Military was unmatched, and they had enough weapons and bombs to destroy the world at the touch of a button."

"If Klujns know this, why don't they fight back?"

"It's not in our nature to fight. We cannot fight against their weapons. The only way we can fight is by continuing to create. To travel to places that have been destroyed and try to restore them."

"He's going to destroy it all," I say.

"I know."

"And Klujns are going to let it?"

"If they burn us, they will end up dying from the smoke of their own forest fires."

"But Klujns could go extinct. Spotted wolves and . . ." all of Klujnkind's beautiful animals.

"That is why our work matters. Some time in the future, life will flourish again on a planet with or without Sapiens."

A million years from now. Just like Salta said.

"How can you be so fucking *patient*?"

Emotion swirls inside me—at the genuine threat of extinction, of losing all that is beautiful and strange, but also at Diablo's own acceptance of it.

"Humans are impatient, they want immediate gratification, and that will be their downfall. Whereas we derive pleasure from patience. From giving back—to our descendants, and to a future world."

The plane doesn't exist anymore, and I'm lost in the whirlpools of his eyes. The way he says *pleasure*, and the images that flood my brain.

Skin to skin in a red tent.

I want Diablo to take me in his arms, but I know he won't.

It makes me sad—the idea of *extinction*. All the Klujns I met, the creatures I saw, and the forests I walked through could be gone a few years from now. And the good humans, too. Even if new life emerges, it will never be the same. I will be gone, and everyone I love will be as well. Bones in the earth.

Maybe it's my humanity that makes me impatient and want everything *now*. Still, I can't help but wonder if there's a balance—thinking about the future while still enjoying your life. Being able to have a bit of *pleasure* now.

I feel sad for this Territory and its doomed fate.

But it *is* reassuring to know that a world out there once cared.

If only Grouse and Santos and even Warwick were dead.

If only the Military was weakened.

If only civilians woke up to their sweetened poisons . . .

After the destruction of the Amazon, the Boreal is the earth's largest remaining forest. If Grouse goes for it, as he is planning, we will reach a point of no return.

The heart inside my chest wants to believe that it can be saved. That Klujns and humans can learn to work together. Just like the prophecy at Circo said—the sun, the moon, and the seed.

Humans, Klujns, and rebirth.

After I complete my Blood Race, I have to see bigger than me.

I have been looking too small.

But for a Territory to experience rebirth, every individual has to, as well. If only they could drink a magic potion and awaken at the same time. Feel a sense of urgency, a desperate need to protect all that is worth protecting. But people won't change until they have a personal, meaningful experience with the forest and its animals. Safe in their houses, it's so easy to close their curtains and ignore the horrors going on outside. They claim to love their children, but they are leaving them a dead world. They would rather continue on in ignorance then awaken.

Diablo hovers there, watching my sadness. "I have an idea," he says, almost like he wants to cheer me up and shake the ghosts out of my eyes. "There's something I want to show you."

I'm still grieving the confetti promises of a world that was on the precipice of change but went the other way. A world that has forgotten how to read omens in the sky and listen to the voices inside their gut ecosystems. A connection I felt as a baby that was taken away from me, until I learned to be wild again.

I am not perfect. I am still learning, but I have come a long way.

I wish the same for everyone else.

Diablo signals for me to follow him, and we leave the carcass of the airplane. I look back at the unclipped seatbelt.

A *survivor*.

Hope is a small flame.

36

Diablo and I stand waist-deep in the frigid lake, the coldest water I've ever felt. I've stripped down to my undies and bralette, which I only realize are sheer when it's too late. "Is the lesson on how to freeze to death?" I ask him, my arms wrapped tightly around myself, my molars clenched so hard I'm scared they'll disintegrate. We've only been in the water for fifteen seconds, and I already feel as though my bottom half is being skinned alive.

"Learning to be uncomfortable is a skill that will put you above others," he says, and I try not to look at the canvas of his tattooed chest. The waterline is far below his navel, and it looks like he's wearing nothing else. He's thick, and I imagine squeezing his flesh with my hands. "Keep breathing," he says. "No matter what you're going through. It'll trick your nervous system into thinking that you're okay."

But I'm not okay. I'm far from okay.

"If you panic in deep water, you'll drown," Diablo says.

"Deep water?!"

I feel comfortable in *shallow* water. Deep water is terrifying, especially when it's dark.

"Is that what proof of passage is?" I ask him. "Are you giving me a clue?"

"I don't know, but proof of passage usually involves water."

"How deep are we talking about?"

"You should never go deeper than thirty meters," he says. "Or a hundred strides. Never past the dark line."

The dark line. I don't like the sound of that.

"How long has it been?" I ask, wondering how he's keeping time, but I imagine he doesn't need a timer to do that.

"Forty-five seconds."

"*Only*?"

"Go lower," he tells me.

"I . . . *c-can't*," I stammer, but that's not entirely true—*can't* and *won't* are so often intertwined. When it comes to survival, and you're on your own, there's no one to make excuses to.

"Lower," Diablo says, and I listen to him this time. We both sink lower into the water, the surface line like a knife that skins my torso now, all the way up to my neck, strangling it like a loop of barbed wire.

I don't know how a lesson on *freezing* is important when we should be staying as warm and dry as possible, but I know there must be a method in his madness.

"When you put your head under, you'll experience the feeling of fight or flight," he says. "You stay. You fight."

We balance on our toes with bent legs, the waterline at our throats. My bralette has gone entirely see-through, which incentivizes me to stay. I steady my breaths, and we breathe together a few times. It's true that facing something so painful and powerful forces you to be fully in your body because the chatter in my head dies down, and I become completely present in this cove, with Diablo across from me.

"Now go under," Diablo says, and we both take a breath

and submerge our heads at the same time. I keep my eyes closed because I have no desire to see what creatures live in this lake or if the slippery stones I stand on are really that. After we resurface, I want to run away—but Diablo grabs my wrist and looks at me with stern eyes.

"Fight it," he says.

I squirm. It takes every atom of my being not to run out of the water screaming. But after a few moments of deep breathing, the cold doesn't feel as bad as before. Diablo and I drift above the surface, facing each other, breathing in and out in unison.

"How long has it been?"

"One minute."

The longest minute of my life.

"We'll do one more," Diablo says. "We shouldn't do more than two minutes for your first time."

"Couldn't we get hypothermia?" I say *we*, but I mean *me* because Diablo is immune to the cold.

"Generally, the longest you can stay is about one minute per degree Celsius, and this water is around three."

"I think I'm already hypothermic."

"Are you confused? Forgetting things?"

"I've forgotten why I agreed to do this," I say.

It's the first banter we've had, and it feels good.

"The more you expose yourself to the cold, the more your body will get used to it," he says. "When you learn to do hard things, doing hard things becomes easier. Also, the cold is anti-inflammatory and an antidepressant."

"I wasn't depressed."

"When I found you in that plane, you were crying enough to get frostbite to your toes." Diablo smiles, and I smile back. He tried his hand at humor, and I want to encourage him. It feels good to not only be talking about the road.

"Now, for the last thirty seconds, I'm going to ask you a question, something to focus on, and I want you to tell me the answer when we reach the shore. If you remember it, you've passed this test."

"What's the question?"

"What's the only thing more powerful than thinking you can't?" he says. *Some kind of riddle.*

"I don't know."

"Don't answer it now," he says. "Think about it. *Don't forget it.*"

Like my last night at Sibu, I want to seal this moment in a little glass jar or an ornament. How miserable I felt in that plane and how present and alive I feel now. The unadulterated joy and euphoria that's beginning to flow through me.

Alone in this cove.

Just Diablo, the moon, and me.

Then, the future catches up with us too quickly. Without looking at a watch or a candle clock, Diablo declares that our two minutes are over. I rise out of the water too quickly and slip on a rock, splashing backward and drifting toward the glacier. Diablo reaches out, grabs my ankle, and pulls me back toward him. He pulls a little too hard, and our bodies collide, my arms around his shoulders and my legs around his waist. Instead of pushing me away as a reflex, I feel his strong hands catch the flesh of my bum as we stay there, pressed together for a second that feels much longer than that. A chill erupts in my body, which has nothing to do with the cold. *Chill* is not the right word to describe it, because the feeling is warm. Something that pulses and aches to be filled, a hunger of a different kind. For a brief eclipse of time, infinity in a second, I feel what it's like to be touched, to be half naked in the arms of a boy I like. The mass of his body between my legs and his smell, which is even better wet. Those strong arms and the slight squeeze of his hands that speak a language he doesn't speak with words.

But then, after a second, we both pull away. Diablo looks embarrassed or self-conscious, eyes downcast. "I'm sorry."

"An accident," I answer. In the brief silence that follows, I wonder if it *was* a moment or just all in my head. Maybe all of this—this chemistry or crush—is entirely one-sided. After all, I am a young human-Klujn who still has her "stamp." The look in Diablo's eyes neither confirms nor denies if there was meaning behind what just happened.

A cool, icy wind blows, and I squeeze my arms over my chest. Diablo's eyes look down at my transparent white bralette and then instantly look away. "We should go and warm up," he says. "You've been in this water for too long." I smile, because the night is far from over, and there is still the matter of that sauna. The pleasure of heat after cold.

This is my first night in the wild—aside from Sibu—where I feel like we aren't merely surviving but *thriving.*

Then, I hear a sound. A wolf howl.

I feel watched by an unfriendly presence. There's another howl and snickering voices.

We are not alone in our cove.

Diablo and I turn to look at the beach—

Where the young Klujns are.

37

Of all the coves in the Snowy Mountains, why did they have to choose this one? I should have known they had been here based on the embers in the fire pit, but I had never imagined they'd be this far behind. There are five of them, all Circo Klujns with red eyes—four females and one male, standing shoulder to shoulder on the beach like it belongs to them. Seeing them after so many days spent obsessing about them feels surreal. Especially the one in the middle—*Warwick's daughter*—the fierce, feminine one who seemed interested in Diablo. She has been hardened and made even more beautiful by the wild. And, if she didn't know I existed, she does now. I wish I could rewind the clock to a minute ago, to all the hope I felt before they arrived.

We've been in the water too long and need to get out. I can't feel my legs anymore. Diablo issues a quick warning. "Be careful. Klujns that have grown up together can develop a pack mentality. You can't trust them. Especially not *her*," he says, pointing to Warwick's daughter. She is the only one who draws my attention for all the mean power in her eyes. Similar to her dad, but without his sense of humor and jovial charm. "*Ariana*."

As we leave the water, I do my best to hide my body with my hands. I feel the wash of Ariana's eyes on me the entire way, a hard stare that makes me feel even more naked than I am. Ariana is even more beautiful from up close, too beautiful to believe, with her cascades of thick brown hair braided down her scalp in five thick snakes. She smiles insincerely, revealing a set of crystal beads stuck to her white teeth, some Blood Race fashion I didn't know about. The claws that protrude from her fingers are large *adult* ones—she is a true alpha female, and she knows it. She looks like she could pounce on me or challenge me to a fight. I'm grateful that Diablo is here because, without him, I don't think she would be exercising so much self-control.

Still, the look in her eyes says, *Sleep with your eyes open.*

I stop in the ankle-deep water, about fifteen feet away from her, and I'm unsure how to proceed. Thankfully, Diablo takes control of the situation and addresses them in their Klujn dialect. She answers but keeps her eyes on me the entire time. "They've just returned from their proof of passage," Diablo explains. "The weather in the mountains was bad, so they came back here to have fire."

Ariana looks down at my baby claws, which I didn't even realize were out. She asks Diablo something, and even though I don't understand his reply, I hear the mention of *Daciana.* I keep my posture straight and my eyes on hers because that's half of what confidence is about, but the other half—the half you're supposed to *have*—is nonexistent right now.

"I'm going to go change," I say, making up a quick excuse to get out of her eyesight.

As soon as I disappear into the sleeping tent, I realize my hands are shaking badly. I make a beeline for my mattress in the corner and the makeshift clothesline where I strung my clothes up to dry. I change into my nighttime garments, taking as much time as possible because I dread going back out there and seeing her. I didn't even notice the others—that's how focused I was on her. I sit on my bed and clutch the fire crystal, watching the eternal flame caught in the clear quartz. Its warmth spreads into my hand and around my body until I eventually stop shaking.

Outside, I hear their voices. Part of me wants to stay in here all night and hide, but the longer I stay here, the harder it will be to resurface. I pause at the canvas doorway, trying to hear their conversation—a strange mix of Klujn interspersed with English. I hear the purr of her feminine voice and her laughter, and I hope Diablo isn't falling for her charm. What are they even talking about?

Finally, I gather my courage and join them outside by the fire, where the six of them are sitting. Diablo to the left, then Ariana, and then the rest of her posse, whom Diablo briefly introduces—

To Ariana's right is Nora, who sits on the same bench very close to her. Closer than a friend. Nora is athletic, wearing fashionable clothes she must have made herself, her head shaved into circus stripes. Next is Ferta, a tall, large, imposing girl who holds a weapon. She seems like the designated guard. Next is Taro, the only boy, thin as a leaf and vibrating like one. His eyes are quick and nervous. Then, lastly, to my immediate right is Nini, with black curly hair and algae-ink tattoos of eyes on her hands. I like her style, and her energy feels kind, but she stays quiet. One thing is clear: by choice or submission, Ariana is their leader. They've been on a long adventure together, but the dynamic isn't as amicable as I thought it would be. Like her father, Ariana leads through fear. But what I burn to know is—if Ariana's an alpha, how are she and her group so far behind?

"Where did you get that?" she asks in English, and I realize she's looking down at my fire crystal. I feel nervous about my every word, like I'm talking to a popular girl, one who wants to kill me, and her energy makes me lose all the confidence I thought I'd gained.

"In a cave."

"What cave?"

"It doesn't matter where, just that she found it," Diablo says. "So where are the others now?" Diablo told me they had just returned from their proof of passage, but no one tells me what it is. Judging by their wet hair, Diablo was right about it involving water. But Ariana isn't about to make my life any easier.

"We all left together at the start," she tells Diablo. The strange mix of languages continues, but she uses English to say the things she doesn't want me to miss—the worst things.

They left as one group of sixteen, but they quickly broke into smaller ones. A girl—Milia—died trying to summon an astra on the second night. Another died in a landslide. This is how Ariana's group became separated from the group in front. Four are ahead of them, probably already at Circo, and four are still behind, not likely to make it there on time. And one died today while retrieving his proof of passage.

"He drowned," Ariana says, looking right at me now.

"Who's in front?" Diablo asks.

"Kalab, Oumi, Oso, and Fina," she says. "Although Fina doesn't belong there—she's been dead weight from the start. But because Kalab is so . . . *good-natured*, he's been helping her. If you ask me, she deserves to be in last place or not finish at all."

Ariana goes on to list all of the trials they had to face out there—storms, impasses, avalanches, and mud-like quicksand. Flooded rivers that were too dangerous to cross. Other rivers that they *did* cross, where they got swarmed by freshwater jellyfish. Then there were the haunted crystals, which they mistook as fire crystals, and touching them made them hostage to dark, disturbing visions for weeks.

Nature hindered their progress at every turn.

"It was one nightmare after another," she says, glaring at my fire crystal like I'm responsible for her struggles. By the sounds of it, they had a harder time than we did. Nora lost three toes to frostbite, Ferta lost a finger, and some of their injuries lie deeper.

I do the math—if four of them have arrived, and five are still here, that means that only nine will make it out of sixteen. Ten, including me. *So this is the middle group*, I realize; the one that got held back because the winter was particularly harsh. *I can't believe we caught up.* Even with our detour, Diablo and I managed to make good time—and maybe that's what Ariana is most upset about. Having Diablo is a greater asset than I realized—I underestimated the value of walking with him and the sanctuary that Sibu provided. In all our misfortunes, we were lucky. These young Klujns were together, but they didn't have much fun. Maybe George was right about the fact that when young Klujns have too much time, they waste a lot of it. Or maybe their Blood Race has been more brutal than previous years, and by taking another route from Red River I avoided most of it.

Ariana's eyes continue to search mine, wondering what I know that she doesn't, and if I'm a threat to her alpha status. Her big claws look ready to tear me apart. "We're going to leave for Cirço tomorrow," she tells Diablo. Her eyes are sharp with me but soft with him, full of glittering rubies. "We should be able to get there in a day, before the storms hit. That way, we'll have plenty of time to prepare for Initiation."

Circo is a *day* away from here?

That seems impossible.

It's crazy to think that we're sitting around the same fire, but they're at least three or four days ahead of me because they've already collected their proof of passage. Without that crystal, I cannot cross the final distance.

Diablo cooks and offers them food, which they accept and eat with hungry hands. He offers me some, and Ariana watches keenly to see if I'll accept it, but I don't. My stomach is now a hard knot, tied too many times to be loosened, and I decide that if I start fasting early, I could make up some time. Being in Ariana's presence brings out a competitive edge that I didn't know I had.

"Are you sure?" Diablo asks. "This might be your last meal in a while." I nod; sadness is a good appetite suppressant, and I'm still grieving this wasted night.

As they eat, Ariana continues to get in my head, talking about the blinding whiteouts that are coming, the freezing rain, and the dangerous sastrugi mountains ahead, her large adult claws glittering in the firelight. After dinner, a jar of something strong gets passed around, and I'm surprised to see Diablo take a swig. Ariana looks directly at me: "I think it's time the children went to bed."

I want to think of something clever but words fail me, and the *last* thing I want is to cry in front of her. I mutter a quick "I was going to go to bed, anyway," before I disappear into the sleeping tent, feeling pathetic. One thing is clear: Ariana is a predator, and I am the prey.

Humiliated and defeated, I crawl into my sleeping bag. A hundred good comebacks drift into my head, but it's too late to use them now; she won the battle, and all I can do is clutch my fire crystal and take comfort in the knowledge that her Blood Race was rough. I can hear Ariana as she continues to joke around, probably at my expense, and even Diablo laughs. The sound of his laughter is a rare, foreign thing. It's like he's different around them, just like he was with his friends at Sibu. *Maybe I'm the only one he's serious around.*

Curled up in my sleeping bag, I experience my first hunger pain. *It's starting,* I think. *Three days of fasting ahead, minus a few hours.* But nothing could make me go out there, eat some food, and begin the timer again at zero.

I feel a pang of sadness thinking about that sauna.

When the fire crystal gets too hot, I tuck it under my pillow for safekeeping. I don't want Ariana anywhere near it. With the young Klujns outside, my fear of avalanches or frostbite goes away. It's not Nature I'm afraid of, but *them.* In this frozen wilderness, these mountains feel like my only friends. I drift off to the sounds of their laughter, their drinking, and their howling at the moon, celebrating the completion of their proof of passage and this final stage of their Blood Race.

I dream of nothing, and when I wake up in the morning, the camp is quiet, and my body is frozen stiff. I am alone in the tent, and the other beds look untouched. *Strange.* They didn't sleep here.

Outside, the fire is only embers now, and water has been poured over it so that it cannot be revived. In the snow, I see six pairs of footsteps leading east. The young Klujns have gone, and Diablo has gone with them, without so much as a goodbye. A moment that I tried to prepare for, but one that still hurts. *Diablo is gone.* I can almost hear the sound of Ariana's laughter carrying through the mountains.

I go back into the tent and crawl back into my sleeping bag in an attempt to shut out the early morning cold and the feeling of being so alone. My tears wet the pillow. I slide my hand under it, desperate for warmth, and that's when I realize—

As a parting gift, Ariana has stolen my fire crystal.

38

Alone again, with only the mountains and the sky. Now, survival is not a matter of alliances, influences, or strategies. Survival is about me and Nature, and the dangers of Nature are ones that I can stand. As tempting as it is to follow their tracks to Circo, I know I can't do that without my mandatory proof of passage. I decide to leave this camp and head for base camp. I'd rather walk when I still have energy, and the hungrier I get, the more exhausted I will feel. So, I pack up my limited belongings, grateful that I still have Glory's compass, the rune book, and the map—not that I've had any breakthroughs on how to use it, except my brief run-in with Honey, that unexpected visitor from the shadow world.

Then I start the one-hour climb to base camp. I know the routine of walking by now, of survival, of keeping my fingers from freezing, but today, with the wind blowing the wrong way, I struggle to lift my feet and trudge through the deep snow. The hour walk turns into a few hours, and a surprise predator arrives: my mind. I second-guess every crossroads and decision I have to make. The cold is even harsher on an empty stomach, but I know I can't give in—not that there is much to eat here anyway. The path is narrow, with a vertical drop to my side at least five hundred feet deep. After a near-slip, my intrusive thoughts have a field day, imagining falling to my death, cracking my skull open on the ice below, and no one finding me, *ever*, or caring that I was dead. Maybe one day, a hundred years from now, an expedition would find my mummified corpse and pause for a moment to ponder who I was and what god I pissed off to end up at the bottom of this ravine. *No one cares if I live or die*, I think, a deeply unsettling thought. But then I realize it's up to me to *make them care*, to show up at Circo alive, which powers me to keep walking.

My feet ache beyond belief, but to stop is to freeze, so I keep going. I reach base camp just before sundown and realize it was a good idea to come early. I may not have survived the trek had I left a day later because of my hunger, my mind, and the wind—which only howls louder now. *Ariana wasn't lying about bad weather.* I find myself hoping that they get caught in it, although that isn't a very nice thing to think. She has Diablo with her now.

The infrastructures at base camp are a bit more rustic than they were at the cove, but at least there *are* infrastructures. A few small black sleeping tents and little black flags with runes that glow in the dark.

I scavenge the tents for bedding and choose one to make a nest in. There's a fire pit outside that's more of a snow tub, and I don't have anything to make a fire with. In one of the tents, I find a bit of plant jerky that I could imagine Ariana leaving to tempt a stranger with and slow their progress so, as difficult as it is, I throw it on the ground and use my dirty sandal-shoes to stamp it into oblivion. I can't afford the possibility of a sleep-eating session in my famished delirium.

From base camp, a dozen trails spread upward in all directions, like ski slopes, each entrance marked by an altar and a flag with a glowing rune. It screams: *Do not enter until you are ready.* I walk up to the start of each trail but never cross that invisible line.

I have well and truly arrived in the Territory of the Gods.

It's the kind of place where your eyes see things in the shadows, and no shadow is innocent. Where your ears hear ghost symphonies in the silence.

And now that I'm here, all I have to do is wait.

And wait.

And wait some more.

I find a surviving shrub of Moonlight Leaf and put a bunch of leaves in the snow tub, like Diablo did in the Carniflora. A white glowing orb fills the pit. In my fatigue, I can almost trick my brain into the illusion of heat. But after the first stars appear and the wind speaks of a nearby blizzard, I realize that sleeping may be the best way to pass the time.

I feel safe in my little tent cocoon, wrapped in a dozen sleeping bags and blankets, although I am never safe from my dreams. I try to steer them to a good place as I fall asleep, to fantasies that involve Diablo and me in a tent under a sheet. However, very quickly, my subconscious takes over, and the peaceful visions turn into nightmares.

That night, I hear a crying baby. Crying and crying and crying. But no one comes to comfort it.

In the morning, I'm grateful for the sun, however distant, and the break in bad weather. In the absence of food, other sensations become more heightened. Watching a butterfly land on a winter flower. An ice-blue river cutting between glaciers, filled with speckled otters. The other animals that visit base camp. And before long, I start talking to them.

"Hey, Mr. Arctic Fox."

"Hey, Moon Bear."

"Hey . . . what *are* you?"

I spend time sitting on rocks, practicing my breathing techniques and breath holds and finding pleasure in a good stretch. I collect things I can use as offerings, like crystals, painted beads, and bunches of herbs. I get to know the base camp like the back of my hand, walking as close to those slopes as I can, translating the runes until I know them all by heart. I try to find a translation for the most prominent scar on my arm, that snake-spiral, but I can't find it anywhere in my book. But I do manage to find the symbol I saw on the tail of the plane—the same one José wore. A rune taken from Klujns.

It means *journey home.*

But home—to what?

When I run out of things to do, I read stories in the clouds, trying to imagine what they were before they were clouds and what they'll next become. I hug trees, feeling their pulse of soothing energy, and realize that I may be losing my mind. But it feels good, and the trees I hug are grateful. *Maybe humans are crazy for not hugging trees enough*, I think. *Or not hugging them at all.* It feels weird to be in a Race but also sitting still.

I imagine Ariana and her posse arriving to a joyful welcome and lots of applause. What it must feel like to arrive and be told that you belong. They must be taking warm baths, stuffing their faces, and sleeping on comfortable mattresses with their wolves at their sides. Preparing for Initiation. It makes me sad and lonely, but sadness is an excellent motivator. I wonder if this is what chrysalis feels like—being stuck between two worlds but belonging to neither. Not a caterpillar anymore, but not yet a butterfly. Not a maggot, but not a moth, either.

At night, I invent rituals for the moon and trace new

constellations in the sky. I watch the constant spectacle of space until I grow too tired or cold. In my sleeping bag, I continue to build on the fantasies from the night before, but I always fall asleep before anything *interesting* happens. My dreams get stranger and more twisted.

The crying baby is back.

I feel a darkness entering my tent, reaching and reaching and reaching. I try to move, but I'm frozen still.

By the third day, my hunger pains are gone and I feel a new energy begin to spread inside my body; like I don't need food after all.

And, by the third night, it happens.

I've just drifted off to sleep when I feel that familiar sleep paralysis begin to take hold.

The baby cries and cries.

I open my eyes, but the rest of me can't move.

I am on a mattress island in the middle of a circus tent, surrounded by black water. The tent is a miniature jungle. Around the outskirts are animals of every kind, all black with gold eyes.

Gods.

Then, a black ripple moves toward me, inching closer and closer . . .

It springs from the water and pins me down to the mattress, entering through my mouth, filling me with images.

A rune of a circle with a little squiggle inside.

An altar of blue crystals.

A large, round, frozen lake with a black hole in the center that looks like a retina.

The moon and sun on either side of the sky.

The sky is a lavender color, with a single cloud, shaped like a wolf.

When I wake up, I'm relieved to find that my tent is no longer a jungle filled with menacing gods. The only animals around are a family of gigantic blue snails gliding up the tent flap, leaving glistening trails like the jet streams of Military planes.

I feel a lump under my pillow, pull it out and see—a dark blue lapis lazuli. Blue like the altar from my dream.

I know exactly where I need to go.

The god of the Lake has visited me in my sleep.

It's finally time for my *proof of passage*.

39

Ponytail, fishtail braids, or rose buns? I know it's pointless to care about my appearance when I'm not performing for an audience, but I can't decide how to style my hair. I decide on a curly ponytail, more volume than I'm used to working with. I don't have any makeup, but I pinch my cheeks and tuck the lapis lazuli into a round pocket in the front of my outfit, against my heart. I leave my belongings in my tent because I know I'll be returning here, and I get going, using a bit of Moonlight Leaf to light my way in the early morning darkness. In my vision it wasn't clear if the dusky light meant the start or end of day. I reach one of the paths I've been studying for three days and finally cross the invisible barrier, armed with my empty stomach, a clear mind, and surprising energy.

I begin the steep climb toward an arena of ice and snow. The trek is arduous on the thighs, especially after a few days without much exercise, but I feel good, all things considered. I see glowing runes screaming their warnings the entire way.

Are you sure you're ready?

But are you really sure?

Base camp becomes just a speck in the distance, and when I get to the top after an hour's climb, I see it—a round, frozen lake dusted with snow. In the center, a perfect black opening, three strides across, staring upward like the retina from my dream.

The arena for this challenge.

Behind it, a mean glacier.

By now, the day is brightly burning and the sky above my head is cloudless. I drop a sleeping bag on the ground, then sit inside it and wait for clouds to gather in the sky. Without Diablo or anyone else to discuss it with, I suddenly begin to second-guess myself. Was I *really* fasting for three days? Has it been three days or *two*? How can I be sure of anything when I was talking to the moon one minute, and the next I was hugging a tree? Am I actually ready to meet this god and complete this challenge? But this is do or die. When that wolf appears in the sky, my timer will start.

I reassure myself that if I *had* broken my fast, the Lake god wouldn't have visited me in my sleep; the crystal wouldn't have appeared. My mind is on my side today, and for that I'm glad.

I need to trust myself.

I need to keep breathing.

I need to find a place of calm.

The day is short and passes quickly. When clouds finally appear, I walk to an altar on the shore, where I place a small flower wreath as an offering to the gods for my safe passage. Then, I step onto the lake and cross that frozen desert. I've watched countless Nature movies where the thin ice cracks and the Explorer gets trapped underneath it and immediately dies. Luckily, that doesn't happen. It's midwinter—it must be getting close to Day Zero, not that that means much out here, other than the fact that the ice under my feet must be a couple of inches deep, at least. More than enough to support me.

I reach the small, black arena in the middle. From here, I can see that the water is a dark turquoise, and who knows how deep it is? There is a buoy in the middle, the dried husk of some plant, with a rope that travels down to infinite depths. I remember Ariana saying that one of their friends—or *comrades*—drowned here, and I hate to imagine what happened to his body. *This is why Diablo gave me the lesson*, I realize. *So I wouldn't panic.* If I panic, I could pass out, and there is no one here to fish me out. I don't need to touch the water to know it's cold—as close to freezing as water can get, and probably the coldest water I've ever felt. But, no matter what happens today, one thing is sure—

I'm getting wet.

The clouds above my head are thickening, and a shape starts to form. I slip out of my shoes and step on them because the snow burns my soles. Then, I take off my warm layers, down to my "costume," which is a beige jumpsuit Salta wore during her own proof of passage retrieval, embroidered with jewels.

Three degrees, three minutes. Any more would put me at risk of hypothermia, lowering my body temperature to dangerous levels. Even three minutes is pushing it without a fire crystal to return to. But the water here could easily be colder than that . . .

Whatever I do, I need to do it fast, then rush back to camp, which is still an hour down. There is no room for panic. Once I dive in and grab that rope, there's no turning back.

I watch the sky as the white clouds continue to build.

I see a body now, legs, a tail.

I am moments away from my starting gun.

I don't want to do this, but I have no other choice.

The sun is already dipping toward the west, and the moon is rising above the mountains to the right, both in the sky at the same time.

My spectators have arrived.

I keep breathing despite the growing chaos in my body. Trying to bend the limits of my biology. *I can do this*, I think, pushing Ariana out of my mind. The way her words reached inside me like hands, pulling up the confidence that I thought had deeper roots.

And yet here I am, still Racing, still fighting.

And I realize that maybe resilience is its own kind of courage.

To show up.

To endure.

To survive.

The star performer is allowed to be scared as she steps into the arena. What matters is that she does. Because courage isn't about being fearless. It's about being scared out of your mind but doing it anyway.

I push the rest from my mind, everything that will happen after. I focus only on my breathing and this moment, as the white clouds begin to form a head . . .

Then, when the wolf is fully formed, I step off my shoes and lower my body into the freezing water. I was right about it being colder than the other day, but I keep breathing so I don't lose consciousness.

I grip the edge of the ice, and then reach for the buoy. The slick, slimy rope that is my lifeline. *Three minutes. One chance.* The clock is already ticking. With no more time to waste, I take a deep breath.

And I go under.

40

The cold is an exorcism, a bed of nails that presses at me from all sides. Liquid torture. But that is not the worst of it; underwater now, I see the rope sinking into those turquoise depths, with knots at every ten-foot interval, some of them with a glinting crystal inside. The rope disappears past the edge of light—*the dark line*—a hundred feet below, and beneath it, a harrowing darkness that makes my insides squirm, and I panic and reach for the surface.

I emerge from the water, coughing, spluttering, and gripping the buoy. *I can't do this.* The water beneath me is deep enough to drown a thousand times. That darkness is the scariest thing I've ever seen. *I don't know what lives down there!* I keep my breaths steady and my brain oxygenated. *Calm.* Without Diablo or even Honey, I am the performer and the coach. I must retrieve a crystal—without *panicking*—and pull myself out. No one is coming to save me here. There is just me. Mind over matter.

The wolf cloud over my head is already shifting, and I realize that even though I've just started, I'm already running out of time. I silence the screaming voice inside my head that tells me I can't. *I've got this,* I think. *Focus on the rope and nothing else.* I've only got one more chance to get this right.

I take a few deep gulps of air, followed by the most enormous breath I've ever taken, saturating my every cell and molecule. Then, when I'm ready—as ready as I'll ever be to free dive into a bottomless lake toward terrifying darkness—I go under.

The water is so cold it stings my eyeballs, but I have no choice but to keep them open. I grip the rope with my hands and begin to pull myself down, one slow gesture at a time, using the other hand to squeeze my nose and equalize my stinging ears.

After the panic fades, and I decide to not let my mind hurt me with its knives, I find that peace and stillness again, the same one I felt in the cave. My heart slows to impossible as I pull myself down, deeper and deeper into the buzzing silence. I reach the first knot, where the crystal has already been taken. After that, I easily make it to the second, where I see a crystal. *Proof of passage.* I reach for it, but then a voice inside me says—*no.* Not that this was easy by any means, but it wasn't hard enough.

At Circo, in the cave, when we retrieved our hourglasses, they were all different sizes, and the bigger ones held an advantage. I look down the length of the long rope, which has no end in sight, and wonder if the same logic applies—if there is an advantage to going deeper. I imagine there must be because why would the second crystal be here, but the third and fourth be gone? The others dove deeper because it was important.

My body was made for water. I need to push my limits. In this Race where I am so far behind, where I could arrive at Circo and be seen as an impostor, I want to prove to them that I belong more than ever. In the worst-case scenario, I can still pass the second knot on the way out.

So with my lungs still nice and full, I decide to keep going down. Past the third and fourth knots, where the crystals have been taken. The fifth and sixth ones as well. The deeper I go, the more the pressure builds inside me. The lapis lazuli sits against my chest like an anchor, making it easier to sink. As the water gets darker and the opening above my head gets smaller, the rays of sunlight dwindle. Down and down I go, and that's when I realize that all these lower crystals have been taken. Doing the math, I realize, if I am the tenth—or eleventh—person to attempt this challenge, and each knot is ten feet apart, then the crystal I want sits just below the dark line.

Now, I face a difficult choice—swim deeper, or take the easy way out? But it's only been a minute or a bit more, so I decide to continue.

I reach the last knot above the dark line where, sure enough, the crystal has been taken, and I imagine that Ariana—with her mean, competitive edge—was the one to grab it. Beneath it, another ten feet down, I see another glimmering crystal, and I realize my math was right. Diablo warned me not to go down there, but I've come all this way. It's so close I can almost touch it.

And there, on the edge of darkness, the first contraction starts.

One minute and a half, I think. *Halfway.*

And so, despite the warnings, I pull myself down into the dark zone. I feel an immediate shift in temperature; the cold gets colder, and the remaining sunlight disappears. The pressure in my ears and chest is so intense now that through the vibrating silence, I can no longer hear my heart. I reach for the crystal—

And a large, black shadow swims toward me.

A sinister riptide, its form nebulous and ever-shifting, like a jellyfish made of black ink.

It comes toward me, and I freeze.

The shadow knocks violently into me, and I lose my grip

on the rope. My lifeline. With the heavy stone against my chest, I am free-falling, sinking through a black sky toward those bottomless depths. I lose my bearings.

I finally manage to free the lapis lazuli from my costume and drop it, watching it disappear into the darkness, but it's too late—I've been dragged too far down, and I've wasted too much air. The water pressure is so strong that my lungs are now the size of bread buns. I'm dizzy and disoriented, and I feel the black shadow moving around me, closing in, as I fight another contraction and then a third.

And that's when I hear a voice.

Come here, it says. One voice at first, then many.

Stay with us.

This can be your home.

I look around, trying to see faces in the dark, but I find none.

You belong here, Ava, the darkness says.

Then a warm, tempting current surrounds me.

It's bliss.

Doesn't that feel good? the voices say. *I know how to make your suffering end. Up there, you'll always be fighting. Up there, you'll always feel pain. Sorrow. Loneliness. But there's none of that here.*

Then, in this dark, silent underworld, I see objects. A floating galaxy of mementos from my life. My favorite plush toys as a child. Pages from Catrina Sherman's books. That blanket with every breed of dog imaginable. A few crayons, paints, and paintbrushes. And, in the middle of this suspended universe, a pale body drifts; a corpse that looks almost angelic. She turns toward me, slowly, with closed eyes, and that's when I realize—

It's *me*.

I am the drifting corpse.

Queen of this dead, suspended universe.

The darkness continues to speak to me in gentle voices, tempting me with a thousand promises, the peace it knows I crave. And, lured by that warm current, I start to listen, and it is the most loving, nurturing voice I have ever heard.

No one sees you in that world. You are invisible to them. But here, you matter. I see you, Ava. You deserve to be free.

I don't know why, but I think of Diablo then—the night in the cove, the moon, his touch.

You imagined it, the darkness says. *It was all in your head. He'll never love you. He'll never love anyone!*

She knows exactly what to say to make it hurt, but I listen to her mad choir, I listen, because she's right, everything she says is right . . .

You will always be alone.

No one will ever love you.

You will never belong.

The darkness is right. The surface world is too far away, too cold and lonely. I don't want to fight my way out of this lake, fight my way to Circo, fight to be accepted, and then keep fighting, always fighting, with so little peace in between. I just want to stay here in this warm current.

A few more contractions pass, but I've lost track of time. How long has it been? Two minutes . . . two minutes and a half? It doesn't matter anymore. Time doesn't matter where I'm going.

Come to me, she says.

I start to drift toward my own corpse's arms, toward a place called Peace. A few bubbles escape my mouth.

I'm sorry, I think, to the mother who gave up so much for my life. *I can't do this.*

As I think the words, I'm reminded of Diablo's riddle, that I forgot as soon as we got out of the lake.

What's more powerful than thinking you can't?

As I keep drifting toward my own dead body, the answer comes to me: *knowing you can.*

More bubbles—which snap me back to the present.

Break the spell that these underwater spirits have placed on me.

The water around me is cold again, and the corpse in front of me is not mine but the drowned boy's.

A violent contraction shakes my lungs, reminding me that I'm alive.

I look up toward that faraway circle of light, my only way out, which looks like a moon in a black sky. A large black bird flies over it, the same one I've seen before although I can't remember where.

An omen.

Telling me I'm *right.*

That I should *fight.*

And when I decide that I *want* to live and I *want* to be here— a powerful shift takes place inside my body, my little cells picking up their weapons, ready for the mother of all fights.

I kick up toward the light, the pressure so thick that it feels like I'm swimming against a current. I finally find the end of the rope, and grab it. The shimmering crystal is there, the deepest one, way deeper than the dark line. I grab it, tucking it into my costume where the lapis lazuli was. Then, I begin to pull myself upward; nothing measured or oxygen-saving about my movements now. I reach and pull and reach and pull, fighting against the water pressure, and, bit by bit, the circle of light grows bigger. As I continue to pull myself up, the darkness gets angry that I've rejected it, vicious now.

I hear the shrieking baby, the howling wind.

My mother's lullaby turning into shrieks.

I know what it's trying to do, this darkness; it's trying to make me go back down to the peace and stillness and the warm water.

But I won't, I can't—*not today.*

The baby's cry reaches a glass-breaking frequency, but still, I push through those horrible sounds, the pressure, and my desperate lungs. In the last thirty feet, my movements slow down. I can barely move. Twenty feet, ten feet . . .

More bubbles pour out of my mouth.

Five feet, then three . . .

I am moving in slow motion, running on empty.

Finally, I break the surface, pulling myself up onto the ice.

The shrieking baby continues to fill my ears, the loudest and most horrifying sound I've ever heard, filling these mountain ranges.

I suck in a few deep breaths and then I roar—

"Shut *up*!!!" I see the darkness swirling underneath the ice beneath me. I start to punch at it, left and right, side to side, trying to chase away the darkness in my mind, the darkness in my heart, the fear that it *is* me and I *am* it, and we are the same thing, that everything she said was right. I scream as loudly as I've ever screamed before, as my fists continue to pound the ice, just like they smashed Elizabeth's skull from side to side, but it's my knuckles that split open, my blood that coats the ground.

"I don't want to be a victim anymore!" I scream, like an angry, mournful wolf, trying to kill that darkness below the ice. To banish the intrusive thoughts that make me feel like I don't deserve to be alive. The limiting beliefs that have always held me back. The voices that know exactly where to slice their little knives.

"I deserve to be here!" I yell, my bleeding fists still wild. I punctuate my cries with more punches of the ice.

"I deserve to be loved."

"I want . . . I want . . ." I trail off, my energy spent.

And then I say in the smallest voice,

"*I want to love myself.*"

My fists stop moving, covered in blood and cuts. I've barely made a chip in the ice, but the darkness has retreated, replaced by my own corpse's face, her violet eyes open, her skin and lips blue, gazing up at me.

I see her as a stranger would, as my mother would, and it makes me sad, the way I've been treating her. Hurting her, when all she wants is to be nurtured. It makes me angry—that I've been so unkind. I don't want to hurt her anymore. I want to take her in my arms. I want to say sorry for all the times I mistreated her with my thoughts and with my words. I should have treated her like a friend, a best friend, a partner, but I can't get those moments back. This girl, who deserves everything.

I stroke her face, but the bloody ice separates us.

That's when I realize there is no corpse beneath the ice—

The ice is a mirror.

I'm staring at myself.

"I'm sorry," I tell her. Me. "Please forgive me."

"It's okay," my reflection says. "I forgive you."

Then I roll onto my back with my proof of passage against my chest.

41

The next adversary is the cold. By the time I make it back to base camp, I have large red welts on my legs from running and sliding down the steep path. I change out of my costume, put on all the dry clothes I have, and crawl under a small mound of sleeping bags. Sometimes, the cold is a story that speaks to my skin, but now, it speaks to my bones. My shivering is earth deep, and as my frozen blood thaws, the throbbing is agony, like there are a thousand fire ants inside my body. I stay there, shivering and cradling myself, until the worst of the cold and the pain eventually disappear.

As afternoon turns into night, the nightmares start.

The purge that Celestinja talked about.

I see George, watched by Santos as he's forced to drown my mother's wolf five times while my pregnant mother watches. The spots on Mahta's back vanish with each drowning. *No pressure, no crystals.*

I see my distraught mother in her cell, with Mahta's corpse next to her. And then, inside the dead wolf's belly, there's movement.

My mom, distraught from grief, takes notice.

Her claws slice out of her hands, and she makes an incision in her wolf's belly, reaches in . . .

And pulls out a tiny wolf cub.

My Wolf.

Mahta was *pregnant*.

Wolf is born with only four spots on his back, but miraculously, he is alive.

Then, I am a large black bird flying over a burning forest. It's summer, the sky is filled with ash, and I am lured by the sound of a lullaby.

I see my mother in the woods, running with me in her arms and Wolf at her feet, having escaped the Loudhouse. The moon is now waning, almost a new moon. The forest is burning, and the Hunters are closing in.

And then, she is cornered.

George is there, talking to her, and right before Santos arrives with his glaring flashlight—

He shoots her.

He kills her.

Not Santos.

George.

The images continue to rush through me like a fast-moving river. And when the river runs clear, the debris swept away, I am back in that circus jungle tent of black animals with gold eyes. A two-week-old baby cries and cries on a mattress island. I walk toward her, treading through the black water, pick her up, and look down at myself.

"*Shhh*," I say, rocking her gently. She stops crying, and eventually, she falls asleep. I stroke her tiny pink lips, and she suckles on my finger in her sleep. I feel my mother's love for the little creature in my arms. The patience and kindness I need to learn to harbor for myself. A strange, new thing is born.

"We're going to be okay," I tell her.

I mean it.

I will protect her with my life.

* * *

My fever lasts all day. A long, constant wave of agony overcomes me as my baby claws fall out, one after the other. Replaying Mahta's drownings, Wolf's bloody birth, and my mother's death over and over in my head, and the knowledge that George shot her.

I don't know what triggered my baby claws to fall out—was it the icy challenge or something else, something emotional? Either way, it's like my body said, *You are ready. It's time.*

My hands are on fire, throbbing with a supernatural pain, but I have nothing to soothe them. No anesthetic. When my crystals are on the verge of falling out, I help them, squeezing the claw bed like I'm popping a large pimple. It hurts like hell, but when the first claw falls out, I feel immense relief. I look into the dark fleshy hole of my right index finger, where I see pink flesh, bone, and the glistening crystal tip of my adult claw, sitting there, waiting to come. Once all my baby claws have fallen out, the real pain starts as my adult claws start grinding against the bone, moving up my fingertips, searching for the way out.

Ahhhhhohhhhhhhowwwww!

I scream, I moan, I howl.

I sound like a rabid animal, but there is no one here to hear me. I'm deliriously tired, but I can't sleep with this pain. It is so intense that I feel dizzy, shaky, nauseous, my body covered in a cold sweat. And, unlike the swift arrival of my baby claws, my adult claws take their time.

It is a long labor.

And then, between bouts of sleep or delirium, I see them,

these crystals that look too big for my hands. The thick, sharp viață moves through my narrow cuticle-opening, stretching and breaking it, before sprouting from my fingertips like crystal mountains.

I lift my new claws up to the light drifting in through the tent door. They are too heavy for my hands. There's a beautiful shimmer inside them like a trapped rainbow. The bedding is soiled in blood and fluids, and my little baby claws are scattered around, like the beads of a necklace broken in bed.

No wonder I felt so much pressure in my hands when I was growing up. So much energy, pulsating and reckless.

The pain is just a memory now, but the exhaustion remains.

Exhaustion like I've never felt.

Like I could sleep for days.

I drift in and out of time. The sun rises, and an hour later, it sets. It rises, and it sets. Birdsong trills, and then the moon rises. I don't know how long I stay in this strange chrysalis, but when I finally wake up, I feel incredibly nauseous. I barely open the tent and lean out in time before the vomit comes. In a heaving, violent motion that pinches my heart, I empty out my insides, and all these dark memories come rushing out in a stream of black vomit. It pours and pours and pours, and when I've finished throwing up, a voice inside me says—

The worst has gone.

After purging, I feel oddly awake and clearheaded. Still, it takes me a second to get my bearings. The nausea has passed, the pain as well, and I feel thirstier than ever. My mouth is dry, my lips cracked. I shovel a few handfuls of clean snow into my mouth. It's not as satisfying as water or snowmelt, but it does the job. The snow is fluffy and white, and there's about a foot of it that wasn't there when I finished the challenge. The first speck of a glowing moon begins to rise behind the mountains.

I feel something damp in my sleeping bag. I pull myself back into the tent and see something even more concerning—*blood.* Between my legs, like I've had my period for a few days now. But it isn't due to start again until the waxing moon . . .

In the distance, I hear a howl. I dismiss it, because I've been hearing so many things in the silence, but then I hear another, closer this time. I look outside again and do a double take, confused. A waxing moon stares back at me, fat and round and only a day away from being full, with a pale blue shimmer to it. *The Ice Moon.* It can't be.

How long did my chrysalis last?

Not hours, but *days.*

There's a third howl, this one closer, and I recognize it—*Wolf.*

I turn to look at the path.

The wolves are here.

42

They howl like a macabre twilight choir. Five of them, including Wolf; not as many as I expected, but it makes sense, if sixteen Klujns left Circo and about a quarter of the population is considered royal. Wolf is the only white one; the others are brown, red, blue, and gray. Cresting the nearest mountain to my left and slowly making their way down toward base camp, only a thousand feet away.

There's no time to lose. I scramble around my tent for the essentials. *I lost a week.* My mind reels. I was in the middle of the pack, and now I'm at the very back, with only one day and a couple of hours left until the Ice Moon rises.

Exile.

I grab my most important belongings. Then, I feel something warm lost in the laundry heap of my bedding. I frantically search for it, hoping that a fire crystal may have magically appeared under my pillow like the lapis lazuli, but it's Glory's pendant. It warms for the first time since leaving Circo. I squeeze it, and see—

A mountain ridge, a large frozen lake covered in sastrugi, and a forest of evergreens on the other side.

And, somewhere behind that green wall is a finish line.

I know where to find Circo.

I throw Glory's compass around my neck and grab my bag. Then, I leave the safety of my cocoon only to see that the wolves are halfway down the hillside. I turn my back on them and sprint the other way, east, toward the mountains and the rising moon. *One last mountain range. A frozen lake. A forest.* The moon guides me like a compass point, and I don't need a map to know where I'm going. I know, I know, I know.

As I run into the mountains, I feel an energy activate in my bones, a power and clarity I've never felt before. Unlike my run to Sibu, where I felt slightly drunk and altered, I now feel like a battery inside me has finally come to life. My body is light, my legs fast, and the landscapes blur as they travel by. I'm going too quickly for my brain to give the orders or fully comprehend what's happening. I am an athlete, a long-distance runner, and the cold doesn't bother me anymore. The wind lifts me from behind, allowing me to run faster than I ever have.

And, sometime during those first few miles or hours—because time and distance mean nothing anymore—I realize that my bones are *glowing.*

My crystal skeleton must have absorbed moonlight, and now it's using it for the first time. An energy that feels clean and pure and euphoric, like what I imagine riding a wave to be like. Or *flying.*

Lunasynthesizing.

The realization that I'm not broken—that I possess some intrinsic, magical chemistry—gives me a wave of adrenaline that I ride across that last mountain range. My breathing is neither slow nor fast, and my heart keeps a steady rhythm. I am a human-shaped fire crystal, an eternal flame trapped in clear quartz skin, and when I decide that the wind, snow, and cold can't hurt me, they finally leave me alone.

I run all night, watching the moon's arc as she travels across the sky. The moving constellations in their milky blue light. I feel connected not only to my mother but to her ancestors, who each ran their Races in different stands across different periods of time. I am alone, but not alone. Never alone, I realize. I am plugged into the heavens, connected to everything. I feel a sense of synchronicity I've never felt before.

I am not Ava, I am all of Klujnkind, all of Nature, all of time.

I run through the night, the dawn, the day, and then it's afternoon again in the blink of an eye. The last mountain range is behind me, and the path descends onto an immense frozen lake covered in sinister mountains of meringue. *Sastrugi.* Here, the wind is wicked. I cannot run in a straight line. I have to run up and down and around these slippery mountains, avoiding deep, ugly crevices. But Glory's pendant continues to warm against my chest, a very promising sign.

I lose sight of the wolves for a while, trying not to make a habit of looking over my shoulder, but when my Race is slowed down by these relentless mountains, they catch up again, always a few hundred feet behind. As dusk returns and the colors change, the Ice Moon pierces the horizon, as blue as a cornflower. *Only a few hours left.* The landscape is flooded in a dreamy blue light, and the abundant moonlight gives my bones a second charge. I climb up a steep, snowy mountain face. using my claws as ice picks. They are still sensitive, but they do the trick. When I reach the top, I see a narrow ridge that I can follow all the way down to the end of the lake.

I start walking along the ridgeline, a sheer drop on each side, but then, all too quickly, a new wind comes, turning the sky white. It's stronger than any wind I've ever felt, and I have to stay close to the ground so it doesn't knock me over. *A whiteout.* The storm steals my visibility, and I can only see a few feet in front of me. All I can do is cling to the ridgeline and continue, one cautious step at a time.

With the moon out of sight, my energy level drops quickly, and I feel tired for the first time.

Then I see a figure about twenty feet away, a flash of magenta that looks out of place in this white ocean. A color I last saw in the swamp. But it's not Pink Flower—it's a *boy.*

I stop when I reach him, and after a day of running, the sudden lack of movement feels unnatural. He looks as surprised to see me as I am to see him. The boy has red eyes, only these red eyes seem kind. Filled with worry and urgency. His light brown hair is styled in a hundred tiny twists with dancing crystals at their ends, his eyelashes frosted. But is he coming from the front—or from the back?

"Where did you . . ." I mutter.

"I'm Kalab," he says, like introductions are important right now. He gestures to the side of our giant sastrugi mountain, and I look over to see a girl crumpled on the ice about fifty feet below in a dark crevice. Not moving. I recognize her from the cove—*Nini.* The one with eye tattoos on her hands.

"Where did you come from?" I ask him.

"From the front," he says. "I was with the group who arrived first. Ariana and the others got back a few hours ago. They got caught in a storm and had to wait it out underground. I overheard them talking about what happened. That they lost Nini. I was praying for someone to show up."

"I think you need a bit more than prayers."

"It worked, didn't it?" Kalab smiles despite the circumstances, his red eyes kinder than any Circo Klujn I've met. "Can you help me?"

"What do you need me to do?"

"I need someone to help me bring her up," he answers. That's when I see that Kalab holds a coil of rope in his hands. "I can't go down there on my own. I don't even know if she's alive."

I look back down at Nini's immobile body. There's no telling if she's dead or just unconscious, but if she's still alive, then she won't have long left in this weather. I know I need to keep running, that I don't owe this Klujn anything, but Kalab is desperate. Nini won't survive if I don't help him. His energy is kind, and despite previous betrayals, I feel I can trust him.

"Okay," I say, "but we have to be quick."

I look over my shoulder, where visibility is still low. I can't see the wolves, but they could be anywhere by now. I can't see the moon, either, but I know she's rising fast.

"Up or down," Kalab says. "You decide."

He offers me the rope, and I wonder if it's a trap. But I remember Ariana talking about his kindness, the way he helped the girl called Fina.

"Down," I say because I don't have the strength to pull them both up. Kalab tosses the rope over the edge. He twists it around a rock, then wraps it around his wrist. I grab the loose end and start to rappel down, praying it won't break as I lower my body down into the crevice. I reach Nini after a few minutes and see that she's still breathing. There's a big, bloody gash on the back of her head that doesn't make much sense with the angle at which she fell.

"She's alive!" I call up to Kalab, my voice barely louder than the wind, and he lets out a whoop of relief. I twist the rope into a harness around my waist, then pick up Nini's body and grip the rope on the other side of her. Kalab starts to pull us up. If he drops us, or if my harness breaks, then Nini and I will plummet and fall, shattering like porcelain dolls. But the boy is strong and determined, and before I know it, we're tipping over the edge, back to the relative safety of our ridge.

"Thank you," Kalab says, but there's no time for celebration. I look behind me and begin to see colors forming in the white.

Brown, red, blue, gray, white.

It's the wolves.

Thirty feet behind.

"*Go!*" I yell. Kalab grabs Nini, and I follow as we race down the ridgeline, along the last stretch of lake before we enter the forest. Here, the wind finally ceases, and the whiteout clears. I can see the moon again, rising and rising above the pines, but the battery in my bones is almost depleted.

"Run!!!" I scream, my voice feral, but I don't know if I'm talking to Kalab or to myself. I'm not running from the past or the fear of exile anymore, but running toward the future I want, and all the good it can hold.

I start to see glowing runes on the trees, which gives me hope that we're getting closer. Like road signs leading home, but I see no finish line.

Kalab and I sprint through the woods, as the moon rises higher and higher. Glory's pendant continues to warm. I'm in so much pain, but I can't stop. I have no idea where the wolves are, but it's not about them anymore; it's about me giving everything I have.

"This way," Kalab says, and we reach a wider path. I see a small clearing in the distance. Circo must be on the other side of that. I need to keep going, but even with the moon in sight, my battery is dying. Glory's pendant burns now, but I don't know how much more I can take.

We burst into the clearing. Kalab trips on a log, and I crash into him. We both collapse, and I can't pick myself back up. My glowing bones are now invisible, my battery officially dead, but I don't know if we made it—there was no finish line.

No invisible wall.

No sparks.

All of this distance, and all of this time . . .

All to fall short?

Suddenly, the wolves are there, surrounding us, framing the blue Ice Moon as she reaches her zenith. Wolf is there, his paws on my chest, and I don't understand what's happening. *Is he rejecting me? Attacking me?* Kalab mutters something, but I don't hear him. He repeats it, and this time, I understand.

"We're *here.*"

That's when I realize—the wolves are around us, which means they're no longer walking. The Race is over. In this little clearing, which must be an entrance hall of some kind. Wolf isn't rejecting me—he's making sure that I'm all right.

"*Zuh nini,*" Kalab says, looking at the sky. I gather that *nini* means *midnight.*

And *zuh* means *blue.*

Above our heads, the sky is flooded with cyan light.

We made it, I think.

Just in time for Blue Midnight.

43

The blue moonlight ripples across the sky in infinite halos, like a pebble dropped in a lake. *We're here. Circo.* I barely have time to wrap my head around what *arriving* means, the immensity of what I've achieved. The Race is already behind me, and being here presents new problems that I hadn't allowed myself to entertain before now. I am a stranger to this stand, and if the king is back—and has any sense of intuition—he will know that my intentions are not pure. A new clock is ticking now, and there are only two weeks before Darkest Day. Not only do I need to kill Warwick and get his heart, I also have to find a way back across all that distance I crossed. *But one thing at a time.*

We have barely been in the clearing a minute when the wolves leave without goodbye. I hear voices—hoarse and gruff, followed by the pad of little feet. "There's more, there's more," a male voice singsongs, an all-too-familiar one. "I smell two or three."

And then I see them—Oak and Poppet. The little yellow-eyed Klujns that hosted the fights at Circo. They come from Raynn, a long-ago-raided stand, but the splash of red in their irises suggests they are well and truly on Warwick's side. They peer down at me, Oak smoking from his pipe of Klandestine, Poppet holding her menacing wooden scythe.

"Two and a half," she says. I must be the *half*.

"Made it by the skin of her teeth," Oak says.

"Or the bones of her feet."

I follow Poppet's eyes down the length of my body to my battered legs, which look like a pin cushion of pine needles and twigs, all the way to my feet. Or should I say—my *foot*. Because there is one missing. My left foot has simply vanished, like half of a magician's assistant after being placed in a box and sawn in half. At first, I wonder if I lost it to frostbite, but there is no wound, no squirting blood, no bone or ligaments, just a straight line separating flesh from invisibility. I squint, and that's when I realize—

My left foot has fallen right at the invisible boundary of the stand in a no-man's-land. I pull my leg toward me, and what was gone suddenly appears.

"Not so fast," Poppet says. She walks over to my foot and places the blade of her scythe along my ankle like a particularly sharp anklet. "What are the rules again?"

"Whoever falls short is exiled," Oak recites.

"She didn't fall short," Kalab says, coming to my defense.

"But her foot did," Poppet replies, as she places more weight on the scythe. The blade starts to carve a line. "The impostor has to make a choice: If she wants to stay, her foot's not welcome."

"There's no violence allowed between the time the first of us arrived and the day after Initiation," Kalab says. "Those are the rules. If you need to be reminded, I can call the king."

So Warwick is here.

"That won't be necessary," Oak interjects, looking genuinely afraid. "Best not to bother him. He's busy writing his speeches for Initiation and he doesn't want to be interrupted." Then he looks at Poppet. "Let her impostor-foot stay for now."

Poppet presses her scythe a little deeper into my foot, and then I feel the weight release. A thin line of blood on my ankle curves like a sneer.

"Well, who will look after her?" she asks. "It sure as shade ain't me. Can't have her running around freely, not on the northern side, at least."

"Don't look at me!" Oak replies. "I have a new costume to make, since *someone* spilled elderberry jam all over my old one."

As Oak and Poppet squabble back and forth like a married couple, another Klujn enters the clearing. I see a slim, red-eyed guard of average height with short brown hair and a stoic expression. I've seen him before.

"*Palo*," Kalab says with relief. And that's when I remember—Palo was one of our main Blood Race guards, in charge of looking after the human girls. I didn't get to know him, but he was never mean or more forceful than he had to be.

"I've been instructed to bring her to the southern camp before Initiation," says Palo. "To avoid any . . . *disturbance*."

"Well, it's too late for that," Oak huffs. "We've already been disturbed. And my costume isn't going to finish its—"

"Oh, shut up and smoke your pipe," says Poppet. "I'm going to my tent."

After the small Klujns leave, Palo looks at Kalab. "Will you two be all right from here?" Meaning him and Nini. Kalab nods, picks up Nini's still-unconscious body, and gives me a look that says I'm in safe hands before he disappears.

"I'm sorry about that," Palo says as he helps me up. "I'm surprised to see you again."

"I'm surprised you remember me."

"In all the time that I've been in charge of human performers for the Blood Race," Palo says, "not one has turned out to be Klujn." There's a glint in his eyes, a trace of violet in the red. He could be Diablo's younger brother, albeit with skin a few shades paler.

"I imagine that Warwick will want to talk to me," I say, and my insides twist at the thought of that future conversation. What lie can I give to mask the real reason I'm here?

"He does. But Oak and Poppet weren't lying—the king wants to focus on Initiation. He takes his public appearances very seriously."

Palo takes me through the stand. Circo's in a forest now, not a mountain, tents huddled in anxious clusters. Skull lanterns cast spooky shapes onto the branches as we wind through the camps and plazas. There is no feeling of *play* here like there was at Sibu, only bare-bones survival. It feels like a place that is still rebuilding itself after the horrors of the raid it lived; a stand on the cusp of chaos or entropy.

"What did you mean by *southern* camp?" I ask Palo, anything to stop my thoughts from spiraling.

"Since our journey here, things have been divided. When some of the original Circo Klujns began to support Daciana, Warwick's guard Bruto—in the king's absence—tried to keep us in line. Now, the king is back, but in poor health, and the stand is as fractured as it has ever been. These have been difficult times."

"Then why stay here?" I ask. "The ones who don't support Warwick?"

"Winter is a dangerous time to go our separate ways. Each side has things the other needs."

"Can't Daciana challenge Warwick?" I'm not entirely sure how the Queen Trials work, but I think one leader can challenge another, if I'm remembering correctly.

"Even though Warwick is ill, Daciana is in no place to challenge him at the moment," he says, and I find his words concerning. "But such decisions won't be made until . . ." Palo trails off, and I dread to imagine the end of that sentence. "Let's just say that Circo is not a normal stand anymore. It hasn't been since Warwick killed the previous queen. It hasn't had drudas in a long time or contributed to the work of our species. Now, we're at a division—the coastal Klujns want to continue east, and Circo Klujns are turning toward a leader who becomes more vengeful by the minute."

We reach a bridge over a vast, frozen river. Here, a body has been impaled. The body is still upright, like the one in the corn maze, a spear traveling all the way up its body and out its open mouth. The dead Klujn has green robes and white eyes. A *druda*. From *Sibu*. I don't know all that much about drudas, but killing someone who is so valuable to the stand and who can live over a hundred years, as Diablo said, feels like a crime.

"What happened?" I ask Palo, transfixed by those milky white dead eyes.

"The druda came to give us a message, but Warwick didn't want to hear it. This was a way of telling the other stands not to interfere. And for those in the southern camp to stay in their place."

We cross the bridge, and Palo takes me into the southern camp, where the streets are heavily guarded by red-eyed Klujns. *The equivalent of lower Circo*, I realize. The *slums*. The forest clearings are populated by Klujns with different-colored eyes: I see violet, indigo, cerulean blue, and jungle green. Despite the watching guards, the place feels more convivial than the north, like a gypsy encampment. We pass plazas with glowing blue-green fires, music, and games. Snowy gardens and sculptures of Moonlight Leaf. Children tell stories to their parents, groups of friends cook meals, and lovers hide between hanging fabrics colored in raspberry, blueberry, and sage. Even in times of tension, there is still a sense of play. I feel safer around these Klujns who know what it feels like to be *other*, to be unwelcome somewhere.

Palo and I weave between the tents and plazas, and I offer the Klujns we pass a timid smile, not knowing how my presence here will be received. They treat me much like the Klujns at Sibu did—curious but mostly indifferent, like they've seen travelers before because they're travelers too.

Palo leads me into a tent, which I'm surprised to see is a family tent, where two mothers and their two sons sit at a low table having dinner—or breakfast. They have pale olive skin, the adult women with god marks on their arms. One of the women wears a veil over her face, and the other's eyes are a deep ocean blue.

Bessi-Maso Klujns, I think.

"We don't talk about what was done to the Bessi-Maso women," Celestinja said.

Palo nods in polite greeting and then walks to the back of the room.

"This way," he says, taking me through a hidden door, down a few steps, and into a place I instantly recognize.

Daciana's tent.

The tent where we were allocated our crystals, and where we got ready before the fights. Only now, instead of thirteen vanities, there is only one. The rest of the room is being used as a lounge, with a central fire, a bathtub in the ground, and a daybed to the side. Newly dyed fabrics hang to dry from makeshift clotheslines. It is like stepping out of the present and into the past, like I could walk outside and find myself at the original Circo, and not here, in the middle of a snowy forest, somewhere on the northeastern reaches of the map George showed us in class.

At the back, a curtain of crystals leads toward a tunnel and what I imagine to be Daciana's sleeping quarters and the medicine tent. A hooded Klujn stands to the left of it, hanging up another piece of richly colored fabric. "Daciana?" I say, feeling scared all of a sudden—after all this time, I still don't know if she really wants me here or if she meant what she said about me going *home* to humans. I *did* go home, only to realize that Red River was not my home anymore. That I didn't have a home, but maybe I could find the answers I needed in the wild.

The Klujn turns around—it's not Daciana, but *Glory*.

Her claw compass sears against my chest, burning my skin.

"Ava . . . it's so good to see you." She lunges at me and gives me the first real hug I've had in a long time; the kind you can really get lost in. And in this strange, familiar tent in a strange, unfamiliar forest in a divided stand, I am reunited with this almost stranger who suddenly feels like family.

"You made it," she says. "I knew you would."

When we break apart, Glory looks over my shoulder at Palo.

"I'll come back later," he says, and Glory smiles in gratitude. Then she and I are alone, taking each other in. Glory looks older than I remember, more mature and womanly, like her stunted body has finally begun to develop. Her hands are wrapped in bandages.

"What happened?" I ask.

"Oh—it's nothing you need to concern yourself with." Glory looks me up and down, a smile lighting up her kooky features. "Looks like we have a few birthdays to celebrate." Her face, which I first found grotesque, is beautiful. She wears less makeup than before, and her hair is wild. She no longer wears her pendant of baby claws, a cruel reminder of the raid and what was taken from her.

"What happened to your necklace?"

"I lost it somewhere along the way," she says. "I think it was a blessing in disguise. Losing things. It tends to make room for new ones."

Like Morgan's watch.

And everything else I left behind.

I'm relieved that Glory survived the woods and the snares. That she made it here despite Bruto's violence and Warwick's reign of terror. That someone as gentle and sweet and beautifully weird as her could endure a world where death exists around every bend. Maybe she's stronger than I gave her credit for. If I ever thought she was fragile, Glory no longer looks it. The wild has changed her in all the right ways—it's almost as though she has taken Daciana's place.

"*Ava.*" Glory studies my eyes in a way that feels like she's reading them, catching herself up on my adventures. I wonder if Diablo has told her anything. "It looks like you have stories to tell."

I don't know if by *stories* she means anything else—like the fact that I spent most of my time in the wild with her older brother. But Glory doesn't seem to be in tune with her romantic side, unlike Salta, and by *stories*, she probably just means the tales of my travels. I want to know where Diablo is, and why he didn't come to greet me, but I'm also worried about—

"Daciana's in the next tent, resting," Glory says, and the news is a relief.

"Can I see her?"

"We need to get you cleaned up."

"*Please* let me just see her first." It's not that I don't trust

Glory, but I need to make sure that Daciana is really *here*. Alive and breathing. She *is* my grandmother, after all, even though I tend to forget that. She's the only link I have left to my mother.

"Okay," Glory says. "But you have to be quiet. She's either sleeping or traveling—and, either way, she won't want to be disturbed."

I nod, and Glory leads me through the beaded curtain and down the tunnel until we reach the doorway to her room. I peer inside but can't see much from where we're standing. A mattress on the ground, a fire, vases of black marigolds. Daciana's wolf, Rhea, lies at the foot of the bed, black with one white spot left on her back. She is skinny, and her belly is swollen. I take a light, quiet step into the room and see that Daciana's eyes are half-open, somewhere else, lost in some sort of trance.

"Where is she?" I ask Glory in a whisper. The idea of *traveling* in your mind is still foreign to me.

"Meeting with the other queens, I imagine. Exchanging information. Making plans."

Then, I see a grotesque sight—Daciana's legs are covered in coral mushrooms, just like the ones in the forest.

"*What—*" I start, repulsed. I remember that, like Carnifloras, coral mushrooms break down dead matter and turn it into something the forest can use again. It's like Nature has already begun to claim her, even though the queen is still alive.

My eyes travel up to Daciana's midriff, where her stomach bulges like she's carrying a full moon inside her body. And it makes sense, then, why she's *resting*, why Warwick hasn't killed her yet, and why the entire stand feels like it's waiting for something to happen.

"She's due anytime now," Glory says, "and even Warwick wouldn't kill a baby."

And that's when I realize—her body is beginning to decompose because her remaining vitality is being used to cultivate the new world inside her, life and death warring inside the same flesh.

Daciana is *pregnant.*

44

Glory runs me a bath and sprinkles in hemp milk and flowers, surrounding the tub with flickering candles. When I slip into the hot water, all the weeks of cold are quickly forgotten. Glory massages my scalp and untangles my hair. She trims my split ends and rubs scented oils in to enrich the dryness. I feel bad accepting her generosity, but being pampered is the best feeling in the world.

Afterward, Glory gives me a warm, soft robe to wear. Then, we sit on the ground by the central fire, on a handwoven rug of forgotten colors, and she gives me the first manicure I've ever gotten—although this is no traditional one. Glory trims the extra cuticle skin around my claws and opens a little jar of black paste. She works well despite the bandages on her hands.

"It's an ointment that will help the skin around your new claws heal and prevent infection," she explains. "I still can't believe you birthed them without any kind of anesthetic." She sounds impressed.

I watch Glory as she works, dipping my fingers one by one in the jar of black paste, then uses a little brush to sculpt them into a pointed tip. She adds gold leaf to the still-wet paste, "*for decoration*," and I enjoy this strange Klujn manicure. I dry my hands by the fire, and once the paste has hardened, Glory massages my hands with rose oil.

"There," says Glory, when she has finished.

"Thank you." I look down at my long, sharp, beautiful claws, which are almost two inches long with the black paste on. "How am I meant to do anything with them?" Glory lets out a small laugh.

"Don't worry, you'll get used to it. The only thing you might have trouble with is buttoning a shirt, so maybe stay away from buttons for the next few days."

My eyes return to the beaded curtain that leads to Daciana's sleeping tent.

"How is it possible?" I ask the question that's been on my mind since I saw her.

Glory tells me that the pregnancy wasn't planned, of course. The only baby Daciana had was my mom when she was in her forties, which was also unplanned. She hasn't had any lovers since her seventies—a detail I could have gone without. Her self-reproducing mechanism was provoked by the raid, and the news of Diablo's capture, a sort of *swan song* by her body before death, the way the leaves of deciduous trees are brightest right before they fall.

"That's why Warwick's been keeping her around," says Glory. "Otherwise, he would have killed her as soon as he got here, but he's waiting for the baby to be born."

"Can't she escape? Can't all Estrellans leave?"

"She's much too tired for that, and her Klujns won't abandon her as long as she's alive."

Glory tells me about their journey in the wild: The road from Circo was incredibly tough, and Daciana's belly started growing almost immediately. As she grew more tired, Glory had to take over, and Palo helped tremendously. When I ask her why the two groups didn't separate, Glory says that despite their differences, traveling in winter is dangerous for any Klujn, and they were stronger as a unit. The "foreign" Klujns—she uses that word sardonically—needed the Circo Klujns' winter knowledge, whereas the Circo Klujns needed the "foreigners" shelter-building skills, food, clothes, and medicine. Both groups decided to stick it out, but now they're here, on the cusp of a decision.

"It all hangs in the balance," Glory says. "There's been a tense feeling in the air. And I've been seeing omens. Warnings."

Rhea the wolf comes in while Glory is talking and sidles up next to me. I pet her swollen belly, and Glory tells me that it's a sort of ghost pregnancy out of empathy for her master. Rhea places her large head on my lap, an impossible and comforting weight, and I'm touched by the loving gesture. Her personality is so different from Wolf's. Rhea falls asleep and starts to snore, a single fang poking out from her big black lips. I stroke the tangled fur behind her ears and she moans. She is a bit smaller than Wolf in the way old things shrink, but still larger than any dog that has ever walked the planet, cyborg dogs excluded.

"So, what's going to happen now?"

Glory doesn't answer. Like Diablo, her hands are constantly moving, always making. With my manicure over, she spreads a piece of dyed cloth in front of her, drawing a pattern on it with chalk. She's making a costume.

I feel like I could melt into this rug and sleep for a decade, but I force myself to stay awake because I don't know how much time we have.

"Now, you're going to sleep, and then I'm going to help you get ready for Initiation," she says.

"And after?"

"One thing at a time."

"Where's Diablo?" I work up the courage to finally ask. My cheeks flush, but Glory doesn't notice.

"On the northern side. Warwick is keeping him away from us. He has his suspicions that Diablo helped Daciana orchestrate the escape, so he doesn't want us to be able to communicate."

Although I'm sure they still have their ways.

Glory finishes tracing shapes in the fabric and begins to cut it.

"Sorry," she says. "I was hoping to have your Initiation costume finished before you arrived."

"You're making *me* a costume?" I ask, stunned, looking at the fabric. An indigo that feels as rich as a peacock's tail and as melancholy as outer space. Next to it is a rich pink that looks like mixed berries and spring love.

"We have a superstition," Glory says, "that if you make a costume, the Klujn is more likely to return from their Blood Race in time. I was worried because I didn't have time to finish it, with everything going on . . ."

"It *worked*." I feel touched by the gesture and her confidence in me.

Diana refused to buy government-approved clothes and always made them herself. I spent my whole life wearing hemp overalls, patchworked pants, corduroy skirts, and hand-me-downs sewn from something she had worn in a past life. The only government clothes I wore were my school and gym uniforms because those couldn't be duplicated, but they always left me with rashes. Diana had told me that, much like the ingredients in our food, our clothes could also harm us. The skin is the body's largest organ, and what we put *on* is as important as what we put *inside*. *Polyester* and *nylon* were just other words for *petroleum.* Diana said that the only uniforms made from non-toxic fabrics were Hunter and Military. Coincidentally.

I watch as Glory makes me a costume from scratch, tailor-made to fit my new, changing body. Glory asks me what shape I want the neckline, how short I want the crop top, and which crystals I want embroidered in the pink fabric. I never really liked pink before but I have a new appreciation for it now, after meeting a certain flower. She stitches pockets into the flowy purple plants, and then I try it on. Glory adds a pin here and a needle there, telling me that she'll make some adjustments.

Next, I choose accessories. Every Klujn will wear a crown. I get to pick what three featured crystals I want on the top, in the center, pointing up toward the sky. Some use this as an opportunity to tempt a god they have their sights on, but others just choose stones they like the look of. Then Glory starts working on the shoes—"*a thin sole that still lets you feel the ground.*"

"Are you allowed to tell me about it?" I ask. "Initiation?"

"I don't know what it is," Glory says. "It's different every year."

"But . . . what normally goes on?"

"It's like the Blood Race is an audition," she says. "During Initiation, the gods determine how you performed out there, and one of them chooses you. A first tool in your toolbox, a first mark."

"Like—depending on who arrived first?"

"Order of arrival isn't the only thing that matters. The first, second, and third females aren't always the ones who cross the finish line in that order, but the ones who are the most impressive."

"Impressive how?"

"What path you took, what strategies you used, how much you learned, and how much you pushed yourself. Anyone can run fast, but not everyone can be alone with themselves and open up to the experience. That is what makes a true alpha and a valuable asset to the stand.

"After, the gods will reveal the first three females. Although, that title doesn't mean much until the spring when the mating ceremonies start, and who knows where we'll be by then. There'll be a Homecoming celebration after Initiation until sunrise, when the birth is scheduled." She nods over to Daciana. "And after that, the no-violence ban will be lifted."

I feel scared all of a sudden. *Have I done enough to pass Initiation? And what will happen after sunrise? Is Warwick planning on killing Daciana?*

I know the Sibu queen said that I had gods vying for my interest, but if there's one thing I've learned, it's that expectations often lead to deceit.

"What's the survival rate?" I ask Glory.

"It depends on the group," she says. "Last year's group was pretty weak and had an easy winter. Four or five didn't make it through Initiation. This year's group is better overall, and the winter was hard, with more chances to impress the gods, so I imagine that only two or three will die." *Only two or three.* Out of ten. I don't like those odds.

Initiation is not a finish line.

Neither is Homecoming.

After Initiation—granted I survive—I will only have a few hours left before the birth is scheduled and less than a night to get Warwick's heart.

It's all happening so fast.

"How was your Blood Race?" I ask Glory. "And your Initiation?"

"It was . . . *different*," she says. "Because my claws had been taken, I couldn't compete in the traditional sense. Actually, before me, in this stand any Klujn who couldn't physically complete their Blood Race in the wild was automatically exiled. But Daciana convinced Warwick to change the rules like they do in other stands, and in that sense, he was fair because he agreed to it."

"Then how did you complete it?"

"I underwent a different journey—one inside a tent. A journey in my *mind.* Some of the able-bodied Klujns will say it's easier and that we're cheating, but if you saw half the things I did, you would never close your eyes. Diablo says that physical trials are easier; a mental Blood Race is more advanced, according to him, like some of the challenges Klujns face during the Queen Trials."

I imagine that not going into the wild with the other Klujns didn't help Glory's status as an outcast, but doing it in that way must have helped her in new ways—because Glory is far from an average Klujn. She has gifts that I can only guess at.

"I'm glad that Daciana fought for me and the others," she says. "If I'd been forced to do it the old way, the Circo Klujns would have killed me or left me to die." *Poor Glory.* She has been through so much in her short life and remains cheerful and sweet. Endlessly generous and giving. I wonder what a mental Blood Race looks like, but I can't imagine it's fun.

And these Queen Trials.

"And Diablo?"

"He did his in the wild, of course, but entirely on his own."

That's hardly a surprise.

"That's when he discovered Sibu," she says. "And, year after year, he kept going back. He always liked it there, and then he met Vivija."

"Vivija?"

"Forget it," Glory says. "One thing I need to tell you about

Initiation that's crucial: Whatever you do, *never* turn your back on a god. I mean it in the literal sense. Whatever you see . . . whatever happens . . . don't turn around. Keep going straight, but never, ever turn around. Keep your proof of passage in your dominant magic hand—that's your left one. If a god chooses you, and you accept, it will enter into your crystal. You'll bring the crystal back to the arena and show the crowd your first marking." Glory is uncharacteristically serious. She gestures to a raised pink birthmark on her brown skin, shaped like a fern.

"Is that . . ."

"The god of Lightning," she says. "One of the most solar—and *violent* gods—aside from the god of the Sun and the god of Creatures. I didn't choose him—he chose me."

But Glory's birthmark doesn't look like the one Diablo was touching when he beckoned that god and killed the poachers.

It's not a spiral.

"Can you turn a god down?"

"You can, but it's risky. If you say no, and no other god is interested in you, then you'll fail Initiation."

"And by fail, you mean . . . ?"

"Die. And it's not pretty." Glory sighs. "If I were you, I would accept whatever god chooses me and learn to work with them. Whatever happens, don't panic. To be chosen by a god is a privilege, and not all are picked."

"How do I know what animal corresponds to which god?"

"It's better that you don't," Glory answers. "You should go in with an open mind."

There's so much more I want to ask Glory about Initiation and Homecoming and the birth, and what will happen after sunrise when the no-violence ban is lifted, but right now, all I want is my bed.

"I think that's enough for now," Glory says. "You need to

rest. I'll wake you up at dusk." *Dusk.* I have no idea what time it is now, although I imagine it must be early morning.

"I can make you a special tea to help you sleep," she says, "but I don't think you need it."

"Can you make me something so I don't dream?"

"Dreams are useful," she says. "They show us things we need to see."

"I know, but I've been seeing so much lately."

Glory smiles and boils some water. Mixes it with herbs and leaves. Then she hands me a steaming ceramic bowl.

I thank her and take a sip.

After that, a dreamless sleep comes quickly.

* * *

I wake up sweating under one too many blankets, the fire still flickering next to me. The costume is finished now, hanging next to the vanity. It's the most beautiful thing I've ever seen, tailor-made for me in priceless, quality fabrics. Rhea is still there, curled up next to me. Maybe she senses that I'm related to Daciana, and that's why she has adopted me.

The veiled woman from next door brings in a platter of fruit, nuts, figs, and coffee and lays it on the ground before me. In her broken dialect she tells me to eat food, not too much, mostly plants. Then, she disappears back into her tent. I taste the coffee first, which has a butterscotch flavor to it. I'm not as hungry as I thought I would be after a week without food, but it feels good to eat.

The coffee wakes my mind up, and I feel energized again. Then Glory comes, and it's time to get ready. I do a simple makeup on myself, while Glory does my hair. Then, I slip into my costume.

When I'm finally ready, Glory stands behind me as we both look into the mirror. She tells me I look beautiful. And even though tonight is about me, a part of me wishes Diablo could see me like this. My eyes are a fierce violet—I don't remember the last time they were brown.

With an hour to spare, Glory teaches me a game that reminds me a bit of Snakes and Ladders. It's a strange, funny moment; a break from reality. I am here, at Circo, with Glory, who is trying her best to distract me so that I don't feel my growing nerves. I am a performer, about to walk on stage and jump through my final hoop. But for now, I am playing a game.

Glory doesn't let me win as I had imagined. In fact, she is incredibly ruthless when it comes to competition.

"Unlucky in cards, lucky in love," she says with a wink.

Then, midnight comes with a resounding horn, and Palo arrives. He looks at Glory with poorly disguised longing, and I wonder if something happened between them in the wild, or if his desires exist only in the world of the invisible and the unsaid, like mine and Diablo's story.

Then, Palo looks at me and smiles somberly.

"It's time," he says. "Initiation is about to start."

45

Pink opal, flower quartz, and moonstone. Those are the three crystals that I chose to place at the top of my moon crown. I don't know the properties of the first two, but moonstone has become familiar to me. For the others, I decided to go with *feeling*. I clutch my proof of passage in my left hand, that glimmering viaţă seed. Tonight, I must earn the first tool in my celestial toolbox and hope to be chosen by a god. Any god. *Which one will it be?*

Palo takes me northeast along a new trail. I wear a long black cloak over my costume, with the hood pulled up to hide my costume, as is custom. The crown's weight anchors me to the present and stops my thoughts from wandering too much, but it's hard not to spiral. The rest of my life—and the many decisions I have to make after—are all waiting for me on the other side of this final test. The other young Klujns had more time to settle in, recover, and prepare . . . I wonder how Kalab is doing and if Nini has been nursed back to health.

Occasionally I glimpse the moon, still as fat and blue as when I arrived. Palo leads me across a small bridge to an island nestled between the camps. We arrive at a clearing with a pointed big top tent drenched in blue light. A thousand tiny lights are strung from the top to the masts, emitting a fantasy glow. A crowd of red-eyed Klujns are pushing into the tent's main entrance; this is a Circo affair. The tent is striped in black and charcoal gray and resembles an ancient black carousel. I feel like I can see the swirling silhouettes of animals in the darkness, but maybe that's just my eyes playing tricks on me.

"This way," Palo says, taking me around to a performer's entrance on the side. We enter and walk past a few rows of gradient seating to a dugout in the first row, the same level as the stage. I am the first one to arrive, which I'm grateful for because I'm not mentally prepared to make small talk with Ariana. Palo tells me that the others will be brought in in reverse order of arrival, and then he leaves.

I look at the stage, thirteen strides across like most Klujn arenas, filled with a pool of sinister black water. A balance beam dissects the stage, stretching from one platform to another. There are three standing hoops along the beam with a meshlike cloth between them that forms a black tunnel. Basically, you start at one end, walk through the tunnel, and exit on the other side. Whatever happens inside that tunnel happens out of sight.

What could be so bad?

The inside of the tent is dimly lit with suspended lanterns. There are easily a hundred Klujns here already, creating a dark festival vibe. I notice Oak and Poppet sitting in their little booth to my right, just behind the second platform. Poppet has on a large, red clownlike collar, and Oak has a matching one in white. It's funny to see Oak's costume and know the backstory behind it; the jam he spilled and the stain he had to remove. It makes it feel a little less serious somehow.

"What are you smiling at?" I look up to see Kalab, escorted by another guard.

"Nothing," I mutter, as he slips into the seat beside me. "Just those little clowns." Kalab wears an exquisite lime-green costume beneath his cloak and has kohl around his eyes. His shoulder touches mine, even though the bench is long enough for personal space.

"How's Nini?"

"Recovering," he says. "The healer put her in an induced coma while he operates on her. He said she was lucky to survive."

"Because of the cold—or the fall?"

"Neither." Kalab looks angry for the first time. "She didn't fall. She was clubbed in the head, and I think I know who did it." *Ariana.* Maybe she saw Nini as a threat, and wanted to get rid of her. "Thankfully, Nini will be able to complete her Initiation when she's fully recovered. It won't be the same, but she'll still get to earn her place."

As the Klujns continue to fill their seats, I see bets exchange hands and feel too many eyes on me. I'm grateful to have the hooded cloak as a shield. Another guard arrives, and Taro shuffles past us with anxious eyes. To my surprise, Ferta comes next, even though I feel like she could have easily beaten Ariana. Then Nora comes in.

"My twin," Kalab says. "Although we're not as close as we used to be since she's been with Ariana. But, at the rate that Ariana goes through mates, it probably won't be long until I get my sister back."

After Nora comes Ariana, who, by no coincidence, was the first in her group to arrive. She looks striking in her regal black robe, with three mean-looking crystals on her crown. Ariana stops in front of me as she passes.

"I'm surprised you made it, after losing your fire crystal," she says. "I told Diablo it was harsh to take it, but there was no swaying him."

I try to think of a clever comeback, but I don't have to.

Ariana's gaze lingers down to my new adult claws dipped in black and gold. Something in her eyes shifts when she sees the size of them, rivaling her own. Instead of hiding them, I keep them on display. Let her look. Let her *see*.

Ariana takes her seat, and my neck prickles with something new: a swirl of victory. Still, her words pierce me.

Diablo took my fire crystal?

I know Ariana'd do anything to psyche me out like she did in the cove, and I can't let her. Most of the things that come out of her mouth are probably lies, but I sense that she's telling the truth about this. But *why* would Diablo take away my lifeline?

"She's playing with fire," Kalab says. He points to the crown on her head. "Black Diamond. Three of them. She's trying to summon the god of Creatures." *The darkest, most violent god.* It makes sense that Ariana is trying to tempt him.

"Of all the gods, that's the last one you want to work with," says Kalab. "Sure, it's the most powerful, but that power has a price. Like the astra she made Milia summon in the first week—that's the real reason the group broke up."

"What do you mean? What astra?"

"They're moving tunnels of energy," says Kalab, "that can help you travel places faster. You could say they're 'operated' by the god of Creatures. Ariana wanted to find one so she could take a shortcut, but she made Milia do her dirty work for her. Milia wasn't ready, of course, and she . . . well, she died, and it wasn't pretty. There is little that Ariana wouldn't do for control. Her only loyalty is to herself, and whomever she thinks can help her be more powerful. Just like her father."

Warwick probably gave her human bones to play with when she was a toddler. Now, Ariana sits with her posture straight and those black diamonds at the center of her crown, convinced she can seduce the most dangerous god. I wouldn't mind being thrown in a ring with her. Maybe I would die, but it would be worth it just to get a couple of punches in.

Nora tries to hold her hand but Ariana pulls away.

"Hey, it's okay," Kalab says, placing a large, calm hand on my leg. "Don't let her affect you. That's what she wants." His hand is just an ordinary hand, not one that fills my belly with fireworks. I nod, but I can't bring myself to speak. I'm shaking with anger and confusion about Ariana and the fire crystal and Diablo—who is still nowhere to be seen.

Next to arrive is the rest of Kalab's group—Fina, who has a broken arm in a sling of fabric, followed by Oso and Oumi. It feels surreal to be sitting on this bench together now, ten performers who have been on such different journeys, about to be assessed by some unknown powers. An *audition.* I thought about these Klujns so many times, and now we're here, and one of them has even become my friend.

"It's starting," Kalab says.

I look at the entrance on the left, where a guard enters. The tall, long-faced, big-chinned male I saw at Circo who holds a menacing spear. *Bruto.*

And then the king arrives in crimson robes, his dreadlocks knotted with grizzly mementos, his outfit androgynous, a mix of suspenders and corset. Behind his entertainer's smile he looks feverishly weak and pale.

There's total silence now, as Warwick begins to move around the room in a clockwise motion. It's funny to think that he takes his speech writing seriously; maybe the "cannibal-king" has a fear of public speaking!

"Welcome, welcome," Warwick says, walking along the narrow walkway that connects the bleachers and the liquid stage. "What a delight it is to be gathered here after a brutal winter. I can't say the Loudhouse food was to my liking." Warwick grins, twirling one of his bone-festooned dreadlocks, and the crowd laughs with the sound of tongues smacking against palettes. He loves to be merry, and he is a good host, I'll give him that. There is an air of sentimentality—or finality—to his mood. As though things are not beginning, but ending. "Luckily, my stay there was short, and my departure *explosive*.

"Tonight, on the edge of Black River, we come together to celebrate our young Klujns and their remarkable effort in the wild. A warm welcome is due to our brave young—the ones that made it here, of course. Out of sixteen who ventured out before the last Blood Moon, only nine prevailed. Well—nine and a *half*—for we have a surprise visitor."

And precisely what I wanted to avoid happens.

Every pair of eyes in the room is now on me, including Warwick's evil guard.

"Our final, surprise guest made it here by the skin of her teeth. Or the hair of her toes," he says.

Warwick looks happy that his scripted joke was well-received. *He must have added that one in at the last minute.*

The crowd continues to laugh at my expense, and I can't tell if Ariana looks pleased or upset that I'm getting all the attention—even if it *is* negative.

Warwick stops directly in front of me, and I try to keep my expression as blank as possible. "Now, let us not be too harsh on our guest," he says. "For she has family here." Warwick moves on, continuing his loop around the stage, projecting his voice into the stands, the host of his underground cabaret. It's hard to tell what he *really* thinks about my being here beyond the fun and games. I realize that Diablo must have warned him I was coming, so the surprise was on Warwick's terms.

"The challenge will be completed in order of arrival," the

king says matter-of-factly. *Let's get down to business.* "On the horn, the first performer will walk up to the platform," he says, making a walking gesture with his fingers. "Where a guard will place an hourglass around their neck. On the second horn, they will climb the stairs to the platform. Then, on the third, they will walk along the balance beam and enter the tunnel. As soon as they have entered the tunnel, the three-minute timer will start. They must be in the tunnel for at *least* three minutes before they emerge. Remember to hold your proof of passage in your magic-dominant hand," he tells us. "As a reminder for our guest—that is not the hand you use to wipe yourself, but the opposite."

I try to ignore the laughing crowd; a cacophony.

That's it? I think. *Three minutes in a tunnel?*

There has to be a catch.

Warwick is an entertainer, after all, and he doesn't reveal all his cards at once.

Right on cue, he says, "Oh, I forgot one little detail."

Warwick gestures toward the stage like a conductor, swishing his arm in a dramatic gesture, and suddenly, the black-mesh tunnel erupts in black flames. The entire structure is engulfed, from the first hoop to the third. I can feel the heat from here, and I'm sitting fifteen feet away.

And then, Warwick delivers the final words of his speech, well-rehearsed for maximum emphasis: "In the wild, you dove into the reaches of a frozen lake," he bellows. "Tonight, you walk through *fire*."

Fire.

We walk through *fire*.

For three minutes.

Suddenly, I can't hear the roaring crowd for the galloping of my heart.

46

Once, I passed my finger through a flame and accidentally touched the blue part. The burn hurt for three days. Another time, I went to take a tray of apple muffins out of the oven with a tea towel and the pad of my hand touched the rack. The burn blistered and then formed a scar that took a year to heal. The takeaway: Fire is not to be messed with. The last person who did—consciously or not—was Reesa, and I watched her burn alive, watched the layers of her flesh melt away, one after the next . . .

Burning alive has to be the most horrible way to die. I always felt so sorry for those who ended up at the gallows; Diana wouldn't let me watch the executions on television, but sometimes we did at school. Decapitation was the fastest, albeit a little gruesome. Hanging was the most humane, unless the Executioner hung the rebel or Klujn an inch above the ground so that they could reach with their tippy-toes and it would take them a few days to die. But burning . . .

Burning has to be the most violent, the most excruciating.

And in no way am I ready for that.

No wonder Glory told me to take it *one day at a time* when I started jumping ahead. How can you take a *fire walk* for granted? This isn't a walk across hot coals, either—it is a whole other level of immersion. I'm surprised that the survival rate is not lower, all things considered, and I don't think I'm ready for a leap of faith of this magnitude. *But what choice do I have?* If I don't believe I can walk through fire and survive, I will burn. Magic or not, I need to walk through that tunnel.

"Let's see if you did enough to please the gods," Warwick hums, taking his seat on a front-row bench across from us. The flames grow hotter, and there are little swamps in my palms. I don't remember ever being this nervous at Circo. I don't know if it's because of the fire, the crowd, or these waiting gods. Or the fact that I have to *audition*.

I've always struggled with that word, *god*. A mysterious, masculine force we thank for our successes and blame for our defeats, keeping the onus of responsibility off ourselves. If there *is* a god, I don't think it would be singular. I think a little piece of that god would be inside each and every one of us. Like drops of water in an ocean.

God, Nature, universe, spirit, love . . . *Aren't they all words for the same thing?*

I realize now why Diana didn't send me a tent, a sleeping bag, or a box of matches. Why Diablo was sometimes harsh. Because I had to learn to do things on my own. I *needed* Nature's tough love. The Blood Race wasn't about cruising to a finish line. It was about learning and growing, because the best way to learn how to make a fire is by making one.

This challenge isn't as simple as a fight, where I can look my opponent in the eye and determine what their strengths and weaknesses are. Three minutes in a burning tunnel is not something the human body can survive. In order to survive it,

I have to believe in something I've never seen; trust the safety net is there before I take the leap.

I look down the line, where each Klujn holds their proof of passage out of sight, wondering if they are as nervous as I am. Then, the first horn sounds, and Oumi kisses Oso goodbye. She takes off her cloak, revealing a striking caramel costume. She looks nervous but prepared, a concentration that makes me wonder if I missed another lesson somewhere.

Oumi walks out from the other side of the dugout and to the base of the platform on the left. Her guard places a tiny hourglass around her neck, and on the second horn, Oumi walks up the five platform steps. She squeezes her proof of passage crystal in her hand—the hand used for magic; the one that sprouts from the soil at birth and not the one used for everything else. Her crystal is the same size as mine, but not as clear. I wonder if the depth impacts the clarity of the crystal somehow, like diamonds and carats.

The third horn sounds, and Oumi is deathly focused. She takes a few determined strides then pauses, measuring the fire. Despite the roaring flames and the fresh sweat on her brow, she doesn't falter. She breathes in and out, in and out.

And then, Oumi enters the tunnel.

I wait for a shriek, but I don't hear it.

Oak and Poppet turn over a giant hourglass with black sand inside. *Three minutes.* This is not a race of speed but of taking one's time, being immersed in that black inferno for *long enough.* The audience can't see what goes on inside that tunnel; maybe it's for the best.

Then, the black sand runs out, and the three minutes are over.

Oumi finally emerges, balances on the last stretch of the beam, and lands on the second platform. Miraculously, not a single inch of her is scorched, not even a strand of hair. She still has her crystal, and there's a new pink birthmark on her arm, her first one.

"The god of *Rivers*," says Kalab. "That's the one she wanted."

I don't know where it stands on the spectrum of good versus bad, lunar versus solar, but judging by the look on Oumi's face, she's relieved. The crowd applauds with their usual tongue-tapping, and then Oumi's guard joins her on the other side, taking the hourglass from her and giving her cloak back. Then she comes back to our dugout, the same but also completely changed, her *stamp* lifted, the official finish line, which also marks the start of her new life. Going first must be hard, but going last is horrible. Now, I have to watch everyone go before me as my nerves continue growing inside me. Soon, I won't be able to walk.

I scan the crowd for Diablo, but he's nowhere to be seen.

With barely enough time between acts for the audience to settle down, it's Oso's turn. The first-arriving male.

"I spent most of my Race with them," Kalab says. "He and Oumi both deserve their place."

As Oso, in his storm-gray costume, disappears into the flames, I realize that this challenge is exactly like Klujn magic. Whatever exists inside that tunnel only appears when you believe in it first, like creation's leap of faith. This is perhaps why a Klujn could walk into a burning tunnel and come out unscathed, while a human would burn. You *have* to believe in it for it to work. Whether you think you can or think you can't, either way, you'll be right. So my options are believe . . . or burn.

Three minutes go by in a flash, and Oso emerges onto the second platform untorched. He reveals his birthmark, the god of Mountains.

Again, that doesn't sound so dark.

Third is Fina. She wears a shade of red that looks too bold for her, and the makeup under her eyes has already smudged. I remember Ariana saying that she was basically *carried* by her teammates, and I wonder if Fina thinks she did enough to impress the gods or if that's the source of her worry. Her crystal is so murky that I imagine she took it from the first knot, only ten feet down. Whatever happened or didn't happen in the wild, the gods already know. And everything else that she kept private, the gods are about to find out.

On the platform, Fina's eyes dart around too quickly, looking for her friends' faces in the crowd, but they can't help her now. I feel very worried for her. She isn't focused, and her fear shows. It's palpable. Like she didn't face enough adversity.

Then, the third horn sounds, and Fina steps out onto the balance beam. She wobbles and almost loses balance—the crowd reacts with a hiss, the Klujn equivalent of booing. Fina catches herself but looks shaken by the near fall and the audience's reaction.

Fina stumbles again, and she pauses a foot or two away from the entrance of the tunnel. Her hands look slippery as she readjusts the grip on her crystal. As Oak turns over the giant hourglass, Fina closes her eyes, grimaces, and goes to take her first step inside . . .

But then she opens her eyes and her face twists into an expression of sheer terror. She turns her back on the tunnel to run back to the safety of the platform, but she's stopped in her tracks by invisible hands. Then—*crack*. Her sling-arm snaps backward at an impossible angle, bone piercing skin. Then, her other arm snaps, followed by her kneecaps, snapping backward like bird legs.

Crack, crack.

Fina's neck is pulled violently around, facing the tunnel she turned her back on, shattering her spine.

Crunch.

Black smoke hands reach out of the tunnel and pull her in, and the fire intensifies. More cracking sounds, like a hundred wishbones being snapped at the same time . . .

And then, after a horrifying symphony of *cracks*, Fina's body is expulsed from the tunnel and tumbles into the black water, where her form looks more like a bone soup than anything human.

It takes everything inside me not to throw up. But the mass of Fina's body stays drifting there like a particularly gruesome cautionary tale, a disturbing reminder of what could happen if you don't *believe* you can—or if you turn your back. Eventually, it sinks . . . or it is swallowed.

It brings me a strange sort of comfort to know that they—Warwick or the gods—are being just as cruel with these young Klujns as they were with us humans in our Blood Race. It wasn't a discrimination of species but Nature's brutal apprenticeship. Not that Warwick's violence was necessary, but there was more to it than just fighting for the sake of fighting. Maybe the gods were in those arenas, watching us as we grew and shone, rocks becoming diamonds. Maybe they even chose favorites, and Wendy, Ying Yue, and I made it to the end because of it.

If it wasn't for the Blood Race, I wouldn't be sitting here right now.

I don't know if Initiation in other stands is similar, or if Warwick somehow fed these gods with violence, but they are sending a firm message: *We shall not be disrespected.*

I imagine that Fina knew what she was up against—after all, she must have grown up watching trials like these. But then, if she knew, why didn't she prepare? Maybe she thought she could trick them, just like humans thought they could trick Nature, but they were wrong.

When man goes to war against Mother Nature, he seldom wins—I remember George saying that. For so long, men tried to dominate Nature, to own her, control her, rape her, cage her, and force her to produce more than she was capable of. But, in the end, she escaped man's grasp and unleashed her fury on the world.

***

Ariana is next. She looks stunning and lethal in her black costume. She greets her guard and walks up on the platform like a gymnast, poised to compete and win. She doesn't even look nervous. I try to control the rise of rage inside my body, the jealousy, and the feeling of inadequacy. Her stupid big-claw energy. Although, if we were to pull out rulers, mine might give hers a run for their tokens.

Behind Ariana's lethal beauty, there is something I don't find beautiful at all.

The final horn sounds and Ariana steps off her platform. She quickly strides across the beam and disappears like the tunnel isn't on fire. Part of me wants to hear a scream, but then I tell myself that I shouldn't wish ill on anyone. Still, a few burns would be nice.

After three minutes, Ariana emerges from the last hoop with her new birthmark. There's a startled, slightly ruffled look about her that she masks behind her well-rehearsed performer smile. Ariana quickly shows the crowd her mark to mild applause. It's unclear if people like her or just tolerate her because she's the king's daughter.

"The god of Fire," Kalab says with a half smile. "She didn't get the god she wanted."

Ariana throws on her cloak, then returns to the dugout. She

is not someone who can tolerate embarrassment or loss, and makes it seem as though Fire was what she wanted. Perhaps, for the first time in her life, she was denied what she thought was her god-given right, and the thought gives me a smile.

After Ariana, her posse goes one by one. I have nothing against them, except that they let Ariana get away with everything she did in the wild, and inaction in the face of cruelty is a crime in its own right. In the following challenges, there are a few surprises. Nora, in striking forest green, gets the god of Crystals, which I didn't even know existed. Kalab tells me that it's not part of the most popular fourteen, but there are a hundred others. Then Ferta goes, in aubergine, and she gets the god of Minerals—another unusual one.

After Ferta is Taro, wearing matte orange. I expect things to go smoothly for him because of the caliber of his group and the way he enters the tunnel with determination—a little *too* confident and lacking in humility, like he's been coached. A minute goes by, and then two, according to the hourglass. I relax a little, thinking that he's going to be fine, but then I hear a scream coming from a distant place. There's the echo of footsteps growing closer and closer, like he was far away.

Then, right as it sounds like he's about to emerge from the tunnel, I hear a burst of exploding flesh. Something ripped apart by the same hands that broke Fina's bones. It sounds a hundred times worse than decapitation, hanging, and burning combined. The crowd behind each platform is splashed with blood, including Oak and Poppet. The *wet seats*. I shield myself but luckily manage to avoid the worst of it. Then, just like Fina, Taro's rejected corpse is thrown out of the tunnel, like a mutilated doll that a child got sick of playing with. His body floats for a few seconds, like a tumor with a foot here and an eye there, and then it's slurped into a foreign mouth.

"What did he do wrong?"

"I think he got picky," Kalab says.

"*Picky?*"

Kalab nods. "I think he was offered a god, but he turned it down, thinking they were lining up for him." This confirms it: *No one is safe until they reach the second platform.*

Taro was too confident or, at least, acting that way. He'd still be alive if he had accepted his first—and only—offer. And with Taro's death, the gods have sent another message: *Don't bite the hand that feeds you, or the hand will bite back.*

I feel bad for Taro's family, wherever they are. Glory said two or three might die, and there are two dead already; the survival rate is looking grimmer by the minute.

It's Kalab's turn, and he squeezes my hand gently before he leaves. I admire the composure he has under pressure. I'm not worried about his chances. If I were a god, I would choose him. Kalab is good-natured, selfless, and strong. He arrived first, but he gave up his ranking and risked his life to go back and save Nini.

"Break a leg," I tell him, although that comment feels wrong after Fina's performance.

"Here we say, 'Lose an eye,'" he answers.

"Lose an eye," I echo, reminded of the words Mr. Wilder said to me at Scouts. That night feels like a lifetime ago. I can't imagine what it must have been like to spend the last two months in a cold, dirty cell at the DSO. It is an unexpected reminder of the world I left behind and the one I need to find my way back to somehow, when all of this is over.

"See you on the other side, Ava." Kalab gives me a deep look, his brow creasing with two little vertical lines, and then he marches to the platform. His costume is a striking lime green, the color of tropical fruit, of a carefree summer. And his claws—his *adult* ones—are huge. Not long after the sand in the hourglass runs out, Kalab emerges on the other platform with a pink birthmark on his biceps. He's been chosen by the god of Trees, which, thinking of the Carniflora, seems like a pretty nice and wise god to be selected by.

Then he comes back, and with his stamp lifted, something about him feels different, but there's no time to think about that now.

It's my turn. The first horn sounds, and I stand up on my shaky legs. *It's just another challenge*, I tell myself. *Another game.*

As I walk to the platform, there's no one to tell me to breathe, to whisper for me to calm down. I have to be my own rock. The audience is the quietest it's been tonight, and I don't know if that's a good sign. Palo greets me, taking my cloak, and there's an audible gasp when the audience sees my eye-catching costume, my manicured claws and the clarity of my crystal. I catch Ariana's look of envy and snicker; it's a small win.

Palo places the hourglass around my neck, the look in his eyes steady and kind. *Maybe it's a good thing Diablo's not here*—I need to focus like never before. At least my breathing is a well-rehearsed thing, my brain getting plenty of oxygen despite my pounding heart.

The second horn sounds, and I climb the steps up to the platform, careful not to trip and fall into that black water. I feel every pair of eyes in the room following me, including Warwick's. The king's brow is raised in genuine amusement like he's curious and excited to see how I will fare. Ariana's is the most piercing gaze of all. I feel beautiful in my costume, and feeling like the best version of *me* is its own kind of armor.

Perched on my platform in those final few seconds, I try to tune out the crowd. I zero in on that tunnel, the heat already making my eyes water. *Focus on the path and not the trees. Success over failure.* Only thirteen strides—and three minutes—separate me from the rest of my life. From having that stamp lifted forever. From belonging *anywhere* among Klujn kind.

The seconds drag out like when Diablo and I were submerged in the frozen water. I tune out my thoughts—the insecurities, doubts, and voices in my head. There is just that hoop of black flames and me—armed with my steady breaths and all the things I hope I learned in the wild.

Calm, Ava. You can do this, a little voice says from her mossy microbiome in my gut. *I'm so proud of who you've become. You were yourself every step of the way. You played with integrity and authenticity. You cried a lot, but you were so very brave. You continued on even though you were afraid. You opened your heart, and there's nothing more heroic in the world.*

I take a deep breath, comforted by the voice and the things she tells me. And by the time the final horn sounds, my mind is a still place.

I take a first step out onto that balance beam, syncing my breathing to my steps.

And then, with my proof of passage gripped tightly in my left hand, I step into the flames.

47

The heat is unbearable at first, distorting the air like a mirage, but once I step inside the tunnel, I can't feel it anymore. At the end of the tunnel, a path slopes down into a different place. I don't dare to look over my shoulder, so I keep going straight.

I take a few more steps and feel warm water lapping at my ankles. Salty. *It's the ocean.* I've always dreamed of submerging myself in the ocean, but this water is black and rancid.

I exit the tunnel to find that I'm standing in the shallows of a beach. My hourglass pendant hangs against my chest, a reminder of the arena I only moments ago left behind.

That's when I see the thousands of skeletons on the beach.

Washed-up whales, dolphins, and other animals.

The entire island is an eerie, ghostly cemetery.

But what am I looking for? Where are these so-called gods hiding?

I adjust my grip on my proof of passage, careful not to drop it.

I walk up the shore, drawn toward the scorched jungle by a woman's singing—the same lullaby I heard my mother sing.

I walk through the black, tangled vegetation, looking out for animals of any kind. I feel watched from the branches, but when I turn, whatever animal was looking at me vanishes. Nothing but shadows and illusions, and panic begins to set in—*What if no god chooses me?*

Then, I see a mottled black toad leaping off a rock. Gold eyes. I take it as a promising sign. I see a lizard, too—a giant iguana with a spiky beard. I really hope that my chosen god is not either of those—then again, I can't afford to be choosy. Maybe Taro's was a creature he didn't like, and we all saw what happened when he turned it down.

Against my chest, my miniature hourglass is still pouring; it's been about a minute and a half. It shouldn't surprise me that time feels slower here than on the other side of that tunnel. I am not in reality. I am somewhere else. Although what is reality but a radio channel—and who's to say that only one is true?

Then, the lullaby grows louder; I am getting closer. I reach a clearing at the center of the island. There is a large nest in the middle, and in the center of the nest, I see them.

Enormous, black, glimmering eggs, just like the ones at the bonfire, only much bigger.

Avarice eggs.

And then I hear it—the batting of giant wings.

The immense black bird lands on the nest and looks at me with piercing gold eyes. It is beautiful and terrifying to look at. *A god.* She adjusts her wings, and I see a gorgeous flush of multicolored feathers hidden underneath. I don't know if she's friendly, but all I can do is stay precisely where I am and maintain polite eye contact.

The god my mother worked with, I think.

I've always felt an inexplicable connection to birds, and I realize this may have *everything* to do with it.

I wait for something to happen, but it doesn't. The sand in my little hourglass runs out, and it's been over three minutes since I entered the tunnel. *How do I even get back? Where is the tunnel now?*

But I continue to concentrate on the bird because in her large, gold eyes, I see the answers I'm looking for.

I am in Red River, lost in the corn maze, looking up at the stained glass windows of the church.

She is there, watching me.

I am in the Darker Woods, after seeing the slain family of reindeer, and a shadow sweeps across the ground.

She is there, watching me.

I am at the bottom of a frozen lake, lost beneath the dark line, on the cusp of surrender, of death, and she flies across the sky.

She has always been there, all along.

My mother's bird . . . and now mine.

But what is she? *Lightning*? *Moon*? It doesn't matter—she wants me.

Instinct does the rest—I stretch out my hand and offer her the crystal on my palm. I keep staring into her golden eyes as she moves toward me. We are the same height. Then, she bats her wings again and turns into black smoke, a spiraling mass that twists into my crystal. A chill fills my body as she does—a feeling that something is wrong.

Images storm across my mind.

I hear my mother's lullaby.

She looks out the window of her cell, tracing a spiral rune on her arm. Summoning her god. I feel my mother's vengeful heart.

And then, from the sky, the avarice descends. She swoops down on the Loudhouse grounds, destroying everything she touches. She rips the limbs off men like a child plucking up grass.

A key scrapes in a lock. George is there, frantic, begging my mother to stop the destruction she is causing. She locks him in the cell—for protection, maybe, or so that he won't be in her way. In her grief, she is a woman possessed.

"Stop," I try to say, but my voice is trapped in my voice box. The images keep pouring in.

A flash flood.

My mother runs outside under an overcast sky. There are a dozen corpses on the ground and a few more in the making as the avarice pulls men apart by the eyes, the throat, the groin. A dance of torture, of cruelty, making them suffer like she has.

"Adria, no!" I hear George cry from his new prison cell, but in her anger, my mother cannot be reasoned with. She conducts her killing bird like a symphony, spreading slaughter.

My mother looks around, trying to sense me. Then, she does, and she runs through the battlefield of dying men.

There are Hunters everywhere, moaning in horror and pain. They claw their eyes out from whatever nightmare they are experiencing inside their heads, chewing their tongues and scratching themselves to death. They run in maddened circles and blow their heads off with their own rifles. They are just as mad and just as desperate as those animals in the storehouse; and maybe that is precisely what the avarice intends.

An alarm blasts from somewhere overhead, but it's no use.

No one can win against my mother and that bird, a bird roused from the shadow world.

There is only the sound of her breath as she runs through the field of destruction, oddly calm. My perfect mother, not so perfect after all.

"Ava," she says, "I'm *coming*."

* * *

I make it out of the tunnel and land on the second platform. The audience comes back into view, the stage. *What just happened?*

I want no part of the darkness I just witnessed, but it's too late. The new birthmark is already raised on my left hand, the spiral. Not a snake, but a bird. A snake that turns into a bird.

The crowd sees it, and so does Ariana. There's pandemonium.

I've been tricked, I think.

I can't believe it. And neither can the crowd.

The girl with a pink-and-indigo costume, purple eyes, and flowers in her hair, chosen by the most powerful god. The meanest god. The darkest one, not feminine or gentle, but solar as the sun. The one that Ariana wanted. The thing my mother named me after, like I am her revenge against humans.

Avarice.

Ava.

I've been chosen by the god of *Creatures*.

48

The young female Klujns are gathered around the black pond stage, like numbers on a clock that has only five hours. To my left is Oumi, then Ariana, then Ferta, and finally Nora. Ariana stares at me with fire in her eyes like I stole her god from her. The giant moon is visible through a hole in the top of the canvas, bathing us in quintuplet spotlights.

A ripple of whispers spreads throughout the crowd, and I feel the weight of their eyes. It is impossibly hard to sit still when there is so much racing through my mind; a mental to-do list that never seems to get any shorter.

"It's time for the gods to reveal to us who they have chosen as the first three females," Warwick announces. I look down at the rippling black water, wondering if the gods are in there too. Something in there feels . . . *lively*.

"This ranking will be used in the spring when they choose their profession and their mates. Now, they will each reach into the water with their crystals in hand. Black is first, gold is second, and red is third.

"Ready?" Warwick asks. The other Klujn girls nod feverishly

and throw anxious looks around. Ariana cracks her knuckles and slides her tongue over her crystal teeth. She looks ready to be crowned victorious.

"And . . . *begin*!"

The ceremony is on.

I watch the girls slip their crystals into the water and I follow suit. The water is not as cold as I expected, as though warmed by bodies. Something swishes past my hand like a fish. I grimace, clenching my abs in a constant brace against whatever it might be. The thrashing continues, but thankfully, no more violent visions enter me. Whatever entity is down there seems more focused on the crystal in my hand, as though downloading the information of my story in the wild and everything I experienced.

And then, almost as quickly as it started, it stops.

The water is still.

"And now . . . let us see!" announces Warwick.

Oumi pulls her crystal first, which is now filled with a new, powdery gold smoke. *Second female.* This only angers Ariana more, and her eyes lock into mine as though the stakes have doubled now. I am her personal enemy. Although, both of us hesitate—as though delaying the reveal because we're scared to see who the gods have picked and for their verdict to be final.

Ferta and Nora pull their crystals out at the same time—there is nothing inside them.

Which leaves Ariana and me.

First and third females.

We both withdraw our hands from the water, and it takes me a second to realize that the smoke inside my crystal is black.

First female.

Which means that Ariana is third.

"This is *bullshit*!" she screams, or the Klujn equivalent of cussing, but it's easy enough to translate her frustration by the tantrum she's throwing. For the second time tonight, she has been embarrassed. "I would have gotten at *least* second if she wasn't here." Ariana stares at me across the black pond, and the target on my back has never been so large. I hate to imagine what she will do once the no-violence ban is lifted.

Watch your back, her eyes say, as she leaves the arena, accompanied by Ferta and Nora. Only Oumi offers me a small "Congratulations" on her way out.

Warwick issues me a strange smile before slipping off into the crowd.

Then, before I understand what's happening, Circo Klujns surround me on all sides, reaching for me. They're not attacking, but smothering me in heavy necklaces of fresh flowers.

There's no time to feel victorious—I'm still shaken from my trip to that scorched island, and the god that tricked me. Smelling the flowers around my neck, I'm reminded of another kind of smell. My claws prickle beneath their manicure and that's when I realize—my stamp has finally lifted.

For life.

I can belong anywhere.

Right on cue, I see him standing by the entrance. Diablo is little more than a silhouette, but I know he's looking right at me. At my adult claws. Being crowned first female. For all the moments for him to see me, this one isn't bad. There is a look in his eyes—longing, or pride? A moment of clarity, as though finally seeing me for the first time.

Then, all too quickly, the crowd sweeps me out of the arena and Diablo disappears from my sight.

"Wait," I say, but there's no breaking away from their violent celebration.

* * *

Homecoming takes place in a snowy plaza filled with blue lanterns, winter flowers, and impressive sculptures of Moonlight Leaf. It must be two or three in the morning, and I only have a few hours left before sunrise. All I want is to find a quiet place to think and strategize, but I've somehow gone from possible exile to being the most celebrated person at this party—which feels ironic. I don't even know what *first female* means, and this party is the last place I want to be right now.

I would've taken rivers, I would've taken wind. I would have even taken the god of *Lightning* because Glory turned out fine, didn't she? But *Creatures*? An *avarice*? That horrific snake-monster-bird that gutted all those Hunters? I don't know what it made the Hunters see, but whatever it was, it wasn't pretty. I know they got what they deserved, in a way, but my mother's attack wasn't fueled by survival; it was motivated by *revenge*. The darkness I thought I had finally managed to conquer in that lake is back. I have been branded by it.

My mother's killer pet, following me from the start.

Kalab fights his way through the crowd and saves me from the onslaught of Klujns, who all seem to be trying to get a piece of me. It is an assault on the senses, and personal space is a thing of the past. He takes me to the edge of the party where there's an elaborate spread of food and drink. "Here," Kalab says, placing a blue drink in my hand with a little twig of rosemary inside. "You look like you need this."

"What is it?"

"Sparkling cornflower wine." I take a sip—it's strong and sweet, but I don't know if I should be drinking alcohol when I have so much to do before dawn.

Like find Warwick.

And kill him somehow.

But the drink makes me relax, and I take a few more sips,

chasing a pleasant numbness that begins to course throughout my body.

"That was something," Kalab says. "Do you want to talk about it?"

"It's the last thing I want to talk about right now."

"Fair enough."

I want to leave this party; I want to leave this stand. I want to disappear, but go where? Back to Grouse without a heart?

I look around at the crowd, and then I see Warwick walking down a forest path, Bruto behind him. I need to see where he's going. There will never be a right moment—the moment is now.

"I have to go," I tell Kalab.

"But this is your party. You can't leave."

"It's not my party, and I don't care about being first of anything," I say, taking off the flower wreaths I'm drowning in.

"You should care—it's quite the achievement. You must have seen some things out there," he says, looking at me like I'm an onion he wants to peel.

I take a few steps toward the path I saw Warwick wander down. Kalab follows me, a shadow I could really do without.

"*Please*," I say, raising my voice. I don't mean to be impatient with Kalab, but I need to be alone. "Where are your friends, anyway?" I don't mean for it to sound mean, but it comes out that way. *See*—the darkness is already at work inside me.

"Well," Kalab answers, "one of them is waking from an induced coma, another died tonight, and the last two are madly in love and celebrating." He nods toward Oumi and Oso, sprawled in each other's arms.

"I'm sorry, I didn't mean . . ."

"It's okay," Kalab says. "I'll give you space. Have a good night, Ava. And *congratulations*." And then he disappears into the crowd, and I watch him go. His reaction is so mature it makes me feel even worse. Kalab is not a pushover. He probably wanted to hang around me because he liked my company—until I ruined it. But how can I think about making friends when there's so many more impossible hoops to jump through? The weight of the future is as crushing as the remaining flowers around my neck.

I follow Warwick, although he is already out of sight. Shedding the remainder of my necklaces as I go like a trail of breadcrumbs, until I am down to just my costume. The night is cold and I'm not dressed adequately; I pick up my pace.

The woods are dark and there's no one around. Rounding a corner, I see a large, secluded tent. Even though the original one burned down, I recognize the duplicate.

Warwick's tent.

Bigger and more grandiose than all the others in the stand.

Bruto stands outside, keeping guard, holding a long spear. I edge silently around toward the other side of the tent and peer through a little window in the canvas. Inside, I see the same setup as before: the fireplace, the round table, the chandelier—only this one is wintry. Warwick sits alone at the table, his back to me, a feast of bread, vegera, and roasted vegetables in front of him. He is surrounded by his menagerie of rescued animals who sleep on the floor at his feet, by the hearth, and on the plush couches.

Alone and away from the crowd, the king seems vulnerable. His back is an open target. By the movements of his shoulders and head, he looks as though he's talking to himself, or perhaps he's talking to his animals. All I would need is to slice into the canvas and make a sneak attack behind him. I look around for a weapon I could use, but the only thing I find is a wooden tent peg. I pull it from the ground—it's sharp. Sharp *enough*. I keep forgetting the weapons in my hands—ten of them.

I'm about to test the peg against the canvas when I peer through the window once more. The king looks almost pitiful, feeding a three-legged miniature cow a spiral of plant from the table. *Yes*, he is deranged, but he also has a fair side—if one can learn to navigate his quickly-changing moods and sit through his elaborate and impassioned discourses. I believe that, in his twisted heart, he really *did* want us girls to learn from the Blood Race. I have trouble believing that anyone is just *bad*.

My fingers tighten around the peg, but my resolve feels shaky now. I hesitate—*Can I really do this? Take another life with my bare hands?*

I shift my weight and a branch cracks beneath me.

Soon after, I feel a cold shadow sweep over me. For a second, I fear it's a god. But, when I turn around, it's worse than that. It's *Bruto*.

His face long, his eyes hollow. He sneers, his pale fingers tightening around his spear, which makes my tent peg look like a squeaky toy in comparison.

I may be first female, I think, *but I am also awfully good at getting caught in dangerous places.*

49

The air inside Warwick's tent is thick with cedar and pine, as well as the lingering musk of his pet animals. As Bruto escorts me inside, the king turns to look at me without the least bit of surprise.

"If you want to take a swing at the king, you don't want to miss," he says, breaking into one of his trademark smiles. When I don't respond, he adds, "Well, aren't you going to sit down?"

It is the sort of question that only has one answer.

I take a tentative step forward, then look over my shoulder. With Bruto blocking the door, there's nowhere to go. I join Warwick at the table and lower myself down into a high-backed chair directly across from him. The last time I sat in this chair was at the old Circo, where we spun a wheel to see what disgusting dish we would eat. Now, there are no other girls here . . . it's just the king and me.

A bowl of floating candles on the table casts wicked shadows on his face. His dreadlocks are weighed down by grizzly mementos and there are burns on his arms that weren't there before—maybe a remnant of his trip to the Loudhouse, or his attack on Santos.

"Show me what you have in your hand," says Warwick, more with curiosity than anger, although his curiosity can quickly turn wrathful. I place the muddy tent peg on the table, and Warwick grins.

"Cute," he says. "Very cute. Let's hope my tent won't blow away come morning."

Bruto steps up next to me, clasping his spear with an eager hand.

"That won't be necessary, Bruto," Warwick says, and the guard takes a small step back. His spear is still visible in my periphery. Just like the one used to kill the druda, another unwanted visitor. "At least not yet. Let us hear what the curious traveler has to say."

My heart is beating in my throat. My hands. My toes. I've been given the stage but I don't want to be here. In fact, *here* is the last place on earth I want to be. For all his deranged humor, Warwick is still a mad, vengeful king. The one who started capturing human girls for the Blood Race, fueling humans' cycle of revenge. Who survived a decade performing at a tortuous circus, and has beaten every opponent he was ever put up against.

And now I am a prisoner in his tent.

I walked myself there.

"Wolf's got your tongue?" Warwick says, and he laughs at his own joke. Then, his eyes go from bright to dark, like an eclipse, and the temperature in the tent chills.

"I could squash you like a bug. You're inconsequential." Warwick signals to Bruto, who raises his spear with intent.

"Hold on." I need to find a way to continue through the whiteout of my fear. I need to convince Warwick of *why* he should let me live, just like I had to convince Grouse at the Loudhouse. But, unlike Grouse, the thing I need is sitting in Warwick's chest right now.

"I'm not inconsequential." I clear my throat and go on. "I broke into the most dangerous place on earth and convinced Grouse to let Diablo and I go . . . without violence. I survived the Blood Race—twice. Even though I left two months behind the others. I opened the gates to the shadow world and persuaded Pink Flower to give me her antidote. I found Sibu without a map, and completed my proof of passage on my own, retrieving the deepest, clearest crystal. I was chosen by the god of Creatures. And even though I don't know what my gifts are yet, I know they're valuable."

Listing my résumé, I feel like I'm talking about someone else: I can't believe how much I've achieved in such a short amount of time.

If Warwick looks impressed, he doesn't say it, but he doesn't kill me either, and that's progress.

"Why did you come here?" Warwick asks. "And don't say to reconnect with your long-lost *grandmother*."

After my elaborate speech, suddenly I freeze. My mind doesn't work fast enough to come up with an alternative that Warwick might believe.

"I know something that will help," says the king. He gestures to Bruto, who moves over to a little apothecary cabinet and hands Warwick a vial of bright green liquid. Warwick takes the crystal stopper out and pours half the jar's contents into a little green glass, then slides it across the table to me. I catch it.

"Wh-what is it?" I ask.

"Truth by poison."

"How does it work?"

"It is pretty self-explanatory. After you drink the potion, you must tell the truth. If you lie, the potion will know, and release its poison."

"What kind of poison is it?" I need to understand what I'm facing.

"I don't know what variety this is," says Warwick, scrunching-up his face to read the label and its tiny, cursive, handwritten scroll. "But I've never met a poison that was friendly or mild."

Of all the tests I've endured, why does this feel so much worse? Maybe because the arena is a table, and our weapons are our words.

I look down at the glass of potion in my hand. *The truth.* There is no other way. I drink the potion down, which tastes innocent enough.

"Oh, I just remembered," Warwick exclaims. "Death by quartering: The poison will make you feel as though you're being cut in fours, the way I like to eat my favorite earth-cherry cake. An agony that can last hours, or days."

I gulp, feeling the liquid rolling down my esophagus like a sinister green waterfall. It wraps around my tongue, warming and tingling.

"But don't worry," Warwick adds. "I am a good host, and I won't let you drink alone." Then, he surprises me by pouring the rest of the potion into a matching glass and drinking it in one go.

We are both condemned to tell the truth.

"Why didn't you kill me when I first arrived?" I ask, wanting to test the potion: Does it really work? Will Warwick be honest?

"I have always had a soft spot for strays," he answers. "And, after your long journey, I was intrigued by what you'd have to say."

Warwick takes control of the conversation. "But let's start with the most important question before I get carried away: *Why did you come here*?"

I feel the potion coating my tongue, and I don't need to test it to know that it probably works. The truth is the only way out.

"I came to finish my Blood Race. Remove my stamp. To have the chance to belong somewhere—wherever that is. And to get your heart," I say.

Warwick splutters and coughs in surprise. "Well, there's nothing as refreshing as the truth."

"What did they do to you? In the circuses? And what did Grouse do to you in the Loudhouse?"

"We are not here to discuss my woeful life. Let's go back to the little detail of my heart."

My hands are shaking, but my steady breaths keep my head clear.

"I went to the Loudhouse to rescue Diablo. I got caught, and promising Grouse your heart was the only way that he would let us out."

"Like this potion, my heart is poison to anyone who eats it," Warwick says.

"But the Hunters don't know that." Silence. "What's going to happen after the birth? Are you going to kill Daciana?"

"Yes."

"You don't have to kill her," I respond.

"So what do *you* suggest I do?"

"Set her free. Set them all free. Everyone who wants to leave. Let Daciana die in the wild with dignity."

"And why would I do that?"

"Because you *can*. What will you get by killing her yourself?"

"Pleasure? Satisfaction? She's been a splinter in my foot for many years."

"A splinter that can remove itself."

"Is that so?"

A tense pause. Looking across the table and the flickering candles into the king's eyes is like looking at other planets. I don't know who he is, deep down, and the tragedy of his life. But despite our differences, I need to find a way to get through to him.

"I think you've suffered a lot at the hands of humans. You

were abused and humiliated and tortured in those circuses, and I can only imagine what that would do to a Klujn."

"There were survivors," Warwick answers. "But no one survived."

I nod; I'll never understand what he endured, but I can sympathize.

"Humans are responsible for your pain," I say. "Not Daciana. If you want revenge, then she's not the person you should be going after."

"Then who?"

The wind picks up outside, and a few drops of rain fall on the tent canvas. Emboldened by the potion, I continue.

"The ones who want your heart."

For a moment, Warwick looks genuinely fascinated by where I'm taking this conversation, like he's sitting on a little boat sailing down a picturesque river, birdwatching binoculars around his neck. I keep speaking.

"You're sick, even though you don't want your stand to see it. You never had control over your life, but you have control over your death. Grouse wants your heart more than anything—he wants to eat it, inherit its power. Santos too."

"But my heart contains none of that, and even I know it."

"No. But you said it yourself: It's *poisoned*."

Warwick understands it then. I am asking him to give his life, his heart, to undergo this final act of revenge. Not on human girls who walked wayward in the woods. Not on me or Daciana or Diablo. But on those who deserve it most.

"You're clever," says Warwick. "And you're brave. I see why the god of Creatures chose you."

A chill inside my body; I don't take it as a compliment.

"You've given me a lot to think about," says Warwick. He signals to Bruto, who brings me to the door. I hope I haven't planted a seed in Warwick's mind for him to do something much worse to Daciana; I couldn't live with that on my conscience.

"If only all disputes could be sorted around a table. There may be less wars in the world."

"I don't know if anything has been sorted," I say.

"No. But neither of us killed each other, so that's always a good start."

I smile despite myself and in that moment, I see the king's duality: the terrifying, brutal Klujn who spreads suffering and terror, and the lonely Klujn still plagued by his own demons.

A victim.

Continuing the cycle of violence he knows so well.

Is he capable of mercy . . . of *change*?

"I'll see you at the birth," says Warwick. "Let us see on which side the coin will land."

As I'm about to leave, Warwick issues me a final warning: "The truth is strong medicine," he says. "But be careful—this potion is known to stay in the blood for days or weeks. If I was you, I would continue to choose honesty . . . as a precaution."

Then I leave his tent, my mind spinning.

Vengeance, mercy.

Let us see on which side the coin will land.

50

I am standing on a different trail, an unfamiliar one, my memories of Warwick's tent already fading like a dream upon waking. I take a few more steps forward and stop. I'm lost. My tongue prickles in my mouth, a reminder that I need to watch what I say until the poison leaves my bloodstream—however long that may take. I hear footsteps, turn around, and that's when I see him.

Diablo.

"Are you trying to get killed on your first night?" he asks. "What are you doing near Warwick's tent?"

I consider not answering, but the potion doesn't like that. The truth comes out before I can put a crystal stopper on it.

"Taking matters into my own hands."

"You shouldn't have done that. It's dangerous."

"Says the one who left me in the Snowy Mountains without fire."

"I should get you home," Diablo says.

"So you're not denying it?"

I stare daggers at Diablo, not rubies like Ariana's but angry amethysts. I don't know if I convey the look well or just have the appearance of a growling puppy.

"We shouldn't stay here," Diablo says. "It's not safe." He looks around, looking exhausted and weighed down, and even though I'm supposed to be angry at him, it's hard.

"Come on," he says. "There isn't much time left before sunrise. I know a place where we can go." Despite my anger, I listen. His arm is on my back, leading me away from the path, and inside my stomach is a jar stuffed with fluttering butterflies. I've missed him more than I realized.

* * *

Diablo takes me along a dark trail and to a steaming waterfall. He leads me behind the falling water, and I follow him into a small cave of fire crystals. *Fitting*, I think, considering that's why I'm angry at him in the first place. The water creates a pocket of hot, trapped air, a naturally occurring sauna. Coupled with the fire crystals, the temperature here must be at least a hundred and ten degrees.

"I don't think anyone has discovered this place yet," he says. I sit with my back against the wall, legs stretched out, and he does the same across from me. The cave is so small that only a few inches of space keep our big toes from touching.

This is all I wanted at the cove, I think. Just us, alone. Before the young Klujns came. I got what I wanted, at last, but now the air feels heavy with my anger, sadness, torment, and all the things he isn't telling me . . . and that I'm not telling him, either.

"You're angry," Diablo says.

"Yes. And confused." As much as I want to play it cool, the truth is inevitable. "You took my fire." It's a statement, but also a question.

"I did. For your survival."

So he isn't even going to deny it? I look up at Diablo, confused.

"It was my *lifeline.*"

"Yes, and you had become too dependent on it."

"I could have died."

"And if you had kept it, you would have."

I stare at him, not understanding.

"I've seen Klujns make it all the way to the home stretch," he says, "but falter a day or two before the end. The weather is notorious in the Snowy Mountains, and bad weather can keep a Klujn inside their tent. Comfort becomes a risk. It can trick you into staying put. Without your source of heat, you had no choice but to face the cold. The same with the embers at the cove."

"You put the fire out?"

"So you would be forced to move on."

"And then you left with *her,*" I say, and I don't like how jealous I sound, how petty, but the potion won't let me skirt detours around the truth.

"I left with Ariana for a few reasons," he answers. "We needed to talk strategy. Also, because she's unpredictable. By being with her, I could make sure she didn't try to kill you in your sleep."

It makes sense. It does.

But I hate the idea of them in a cave together, waiting out a storm, talking *strategy.*

And so, sweating in this cave with Diablo, separated from reality by the simple elements of earth and water, my anger at him evaporates. My flushed pink cheeks break into a smile, even though a trace of jealousy remains.

"Why are you smiling?" he asks, genuinely curious.

"Because I knew you didn't do it out of malice, but I didn't understand."

"Now you do. And it worked. You made it. And you didn't lose any fingers."

"I almost lost a foot."

"Because you stayed back to help that *boy*," he says, as though he is the jealous one now and disapproves of my budding friendship with Kalab. "You care so much about people you've just met."

"It's a curse."

"It's not a curse to care."

"It is when it hurts."

There's silence as Diablo watches me. The cave of fire crystals melts away, and it's just me and him. Reality and fantasy are separated by an invisible curtain, thin as silk. The things we say and the things we don't dare to say. What I would do to cross that line and tell him everything. But he's never given me any indication that my feelings for him are anywhere near reciprocated. They are at opposite polar regions.

"Why did you go to Warwick's tent?" he asks.

"I went to see if I was able to kill him—turns out I'm not. Then I tried to negotiate with him."

"Negotiate how?"

"I asked him to set Daciana free after the birth." I pause, my eyes avoiding Diablo's, wondering if he will be angry at me for meddling. "Then I made him a proposition: that he gives me his heart, and I use it to poison those who tortured him all those years. The ghosts that still torture him now."

"That was foolish—or brave—of you to do that."

"What did you and Ariana talk about?"

"I can't tell you that."

"Of course not," I scoff. He didn't take the truth potion; he owes me nothing. "You expect me to sit back while you and her come up with a plan, but you won't tell me what it is. It's my life, my future, and still, you're excluding me, because you think I'm not worthy of the truth. That I can't handle it! How do you expect me to just wait and see how things unfold?"

"I was actually on my way to tell you," he says. "Because you are worthy of the truth, Ava. But I smell the poison on your tongue, and I know which one it is." Diablo smiles at my expense, which only makes my blood boil. How can a simple smile get under my skin? "You deserve the truth, but not under the influence of a poison where you could easily repeat our plan to the king himself. All I can tell you for now is that you will get what you came here for."

I stare into his purple eyes, no longer afraid of them. "But you won't tell me how."

Diablo shakes his head.

"You're sad," he says. His hand reaches out and finds my ankle; it fits the curve of my leg perfectly. His energy courses through my body, comforting and warm. I try to ignore it, but it grows inside me, spreading like that flesh-eating virus in the woods . . . *consuming* me.

"I'm not sad," I answer. "There's . . . a lot on my mind. The future is coming fast, and I don't know if I'm ready to face it yet. And I'm sick of being left out. I've been excluded from things my whole life."

It's hard to believe that this conversation is really happening. That it isn't a dream, or a late-night tent fantasy. Diablo and I are here, in this cave, our bodies close, weaving an intimate web with our words. But if it's not a friendship, and it's not a romance, then what is it? What are we?

The truth is, I don't care about his plan. The one he hatched up with Ariana. I have confidence in mine, and the fact that my words may have been able to resonate with Warwick. What hurts more is that after all our time in the wild, Diablo is off having secret conversations with Ariana who wields her beauty like a black crystal machete. *Would he fall for it?* But if gestures could speak, Diablo's hand on my leg tells me everything: He cares. More than he could ever admit with words. He would give me the truth if it wasn't for the poison on my lips, and the danger that makes me.

I think about Salta's words, about telling him how I feel. That the truth wouldn't kill me, and that the worst I would face is embarrassment. Diablo and I might never get another chance like this.

"It hurts," I say.

"What does?"

"Caring."

"Why does caring hurt?" Diablo's eyes dig into mine, like there's something he hopes to hear. He moves his body closer and his hands now rest on the skin above my knee.

My makeup is smudged, my hair wild, but I don't care what I look like. I will no longer sit on the sidelines of my own life, watching others take the stage. I will be the star of my own story, even if it's hard and I face rejection or humiliation. Today, the most terrifying thing was not Initiation, or playing a game of Truth by Poison. The most terrifying thing is to be sitting here with him, trying to give a voice to my feelings.

One day we will all be bones.

And none of this will matter.

So as an earthquake courses through my body, I say, "Because I don't know if the person I care about cares for me." And then, after the longest pause of my life, the biggest leap—Diablo exhales heavily, his sigh as weighted as the pressure in my chest, more intense than at the bottom of that lake.

"*Ava*." He says my name in a way that people do before delivering bad news, before shattering your dreams. The way a parent tells a child that magic isn't real or fairies only belong in stories. *It was all in my head. In my stupid, childish head.* If I ever see Salta again, I will murder her with my adult claws.

"Forget it," I say. "It's stupid." But then, Diablo's hands slide up to my thighs and he gives them a slight squeeze just like he did in that alpine lake. Energy continues to run from his hands into my body, although this energy is not merely soothing. It is foreign, electric, and enthralling. A language of protection, and passion.

"I want to tell you something."

This is so unlike the Diablo I know or think I know. The fact that he sought me out and brought me here when he could have just escorted me to the young Klujn camp. It's like my honesty is making him honest. My vulnerability giving way to his vulnerability. Or perhaps it has something to do with the preservation of energy, but I doubt it. We're not in the wild anymore. I've never seen him like this, so stripped down and open. A black curtain pulled apart to reveal a curiosity for one night only. This is not the Diablo I know. Or perhaps it *is* him, the real him, the person he is behind those walls . . .

The hurt in my heart goes away as I listen, but it also doubles.

"After the Estrella raid, your mother took me and Glory into the swamplands. We stayed there for a few weeks. And when the Hunters came, searching the swamplands for runaways, your mother spent the last of her energy making sure that Glory and I were safe. She had no energy left to protect herself. After she was abducted, we were alone, a hundred miles from the nearest stand. I was six, and Glory was only three at the time. No six-year-old without his claws can survive that environment," Diablo says. I knew the story, but Glory never told me how they had managed to find Circo.

Diablo tells me he found a rune wheel my mother had

prepared. And, by accident, he summoned the god of Creatures. I'm so rapt by the story that I listen but don't ask questions as Diablo keeps weaving his story with dark threads. "The god of Creatures came, and I didn't even really understand what he was because I was so young. We had ceremonies at Estrella, but the children don't drink the potions until they're a little bit older. The god told me he could bring me and Glory to Circo, where Daciana was, by using an astra."

I'm reminded of George's lecture and what Kalab said at Initiation.

"Just like the wind can move the weather or create tornadoes, and the ocean can create whirlpools or riptides, the god of Creatures can form astras. They appear when you call them and can take you from one place to another, but there is always a price."

"So they're actually *real*?" I ask Diablo, stunned, and he nods.

"The god of Creatures likes revenge, but he likes innocence more. He took advantage of mine. We made a deal, although I didn't realize what I was agreeing to at the time. He brought us to Circo, using an astra, and said he would take three things from me, but not what."

And there, at six years old, Diablo began working with the darkest god.

"The first thing he took was my mother," Diablo says. "She had already been captured by the Hunters, but after that, I started having nightmares—I saw the way they treated her in captivity, the way they bred her into infertility. When she couldn't produce anymore, she was sold to a Coliséa. I saw her on stage, performing night after night. Getting injured, but not enough to die. I always hoped that the nightmares would stop, that her suffering would end, but it didn't.

"The second thing he took was Vivija."

I remember Glory mentioning the name, and I'm grateful

he's opening up. Still, it hurts to discover this side of him he's kept hidden from me all along. At the mention of Vivija, his hands leave me, like touching me is a betrayal to her memory, but I press them back against my skin.

Diablo met Vivija at Sibu, and she's the reason he kept coming back.

"Warwick and I had an agreement. I could travel more than others. Vivija and I were bonded, and in the summer, we went on our *lunah mijela* in the wild." Their *honeymoon*. "After my Blood Race, I started doing underwater training. Holding my breath. Exploring the depths. Staying underwater for a long time. It made me feel connected to Estrella. Every day, when we arrived at a new place, I went off on my own and found a body of water to swim in. Water helped me heal from the nightmares of my mom.

"One day, I went away for longer than usual. I found a beautiful, deep lake. It was so peaceful and so quiet. But when I got back to camp . . ." Diablo trails off, and I see the pain in his eyes as though it happened yesterday. "She had been . . ."

"You don't have to—"

"No, I want you to know." Diablo takes a heavy breath. "She had been discovered by a gang of savages. Poachers or Hunters or logging men. She was hung from a tree and mutilated just for the fun of it. I scared them away, but the damage was done. She died in my arms. I never forgave myself."

The thought is horrifying.

"So when the poachers came . . ." I started.

"It reminded me of that day."

"And you killed them?"

"Not directly. I summoned the god of Creatures . . ."

"And he did the rest."

Diablo nods, although he doesn't look proud of it. "The god

of Creatures is the most powerful because he is like a chameleon—he can take any shape. And, although I work with other gods, he is the one who visited me in that moment, because he felt my pain. And when there is pain, he is always there, the way water always moves to the lowest place."

"Is that why you agreed to stay with me?" I ask delicately.

"It would have been cruel to leave you on your own. Not that you weren't capable. But you were right. We were stronger as a pair."

I think about how quickly Diablo changed his mind. How surprised I was. But what happened to Vivija couldn't happen again.

"The god said he would take three things," I say cautiously.

"That's why I've always been so protective of Glory. He hasn't come for her yet, but I always feared he would. He's making me wait, and because of that, I have been forced to isolate myself from people. When I met you, I realized I didn't know who to protect anymore, because I couldn't be in two places at once. So, in answer to what you said before," he finishes. "I won't allow myself to care about anyone else as long as Glory is alive and my bargain with Creatures expires." His hands slide up my legs; they grip the bone of my hips. I feel like my entire skeleton is vibrating. A warm ache between my legs, wanting more, more, more of him.

I'm shaken by his revelations. I feel sad for Diablo, who has suffered so much from a young age.

Our faces are close now, close enough to kiss.

How badly I want to kiss him, but I know he won't kiss me.

"Is that why you want to be a druda?" I ask. "To punish yourself?"

"The wild helped me heal, and I want to give back to it. Alone, out there, I can only hurt myself." I hate to see him isolating himself, punishing himself for things that weren't his fault. One thing we have in common: We are possessed by the same darkness.

Diablo looks even deeper into my eyes. The empty space between our faces is not empty at all; it's charged like the air before an electric storm. His smell is so delicious I could eat it, his arms somewhere I could fit perfectly. His big hands still on my hips, pulsing with energy . . .

I imagine us in a tent, lying under a blanket, skin to skin.

My hands exploring his body and his hands exploring mine.

Proximity, heat, pleasure.

And what could those claws do, beyond magic?

Now that my stamp has been lifted, I feel eager to remove another "stamp." My virginity. My innocence.

I want to explore it all with him.

But Diablo's expression is hard to read and I don't know if he feels the same, if he will ever allow himself to feel anything after what happened to Vivija.

Diablo's touch leaves me, and my insides are suddenly cold despite the warmth of the cave. He pulls something out from his pocket and hands it to me. It's a bracelet of black marigolds, like the ones that grow in Daciana's tent.

"Take this," he says. "And wear it at the birth. It'll protect you."

"From what?"

Diablo doesn't tell me. He leans in and ties it around my left wrist.

"Everything will work out," he whispers. "Trust me. You'll get what you want, and you'll be able to go home."

Of course I trust him—trust isn't the problem.

"Is that what you want?"

"It's not about what I want," Diablo answers. "We are on separate journeys. You are now welcome among Klujns, but I know the human in you will not be able to turn her back on those she left behind."

It's the first time he's said the word *human* as a compliment.

"Where are you going after?"

"The coast," he answers, and my heart flutters like new wings, testing flight.

He is going to the place I have always dreamed of going: the coast, the ocean, the beach. I think a part of me knew deep down, but hearing it is crushing.

Because I made a promise to Grouse, and now Warwick, and that promise leads me in the opposite direction.

I am shattered, I am torn.

I have never faced a choice like this.

"After Daciana dies, we will take refuge in another stand that will host us before the Queen Trials start," Diablo says.

And in our cave of earth and water, a desire in me is born: to follow him to the coast, to the place where I belong.

For many more nights like this, more beauty, without the heaviness.

A sound shatters the little world we created, crashing us back into reality. Diablo pulls away and looks out the sheet of falling water.

"Come on," he says, taking my hand and leading me out. "Your chaperone is here."

Just like that, our moment becomes a memory.

Outside, Wolf tilts his head, as though surprised to have caught us in a moment. His face has been painted in algae ink like he's been to his own festival.

"It's a long story," I tell him, right after Diablo leaves, although his wise eyes are knowing.

And then, in the distance, across the forest stand and the blue hour, a siren sounds.

51

Wolf and I join a crowd of Klujns pushing east toward Black River. There are so many uncertainties ahead, so many moving parts. Only now, the decision is mine to make. And, just like my last day in Red River, I realize that I'm not ready. I'm not ready at all.

The entire stand gathers at an open-air arena on the shores of Black River. If it weren't for that thin strip of land on the other side, I could be fooled into thinking the river was the ocean. The snow has been cleared to form a sandy, lantern-lit path leading to an arena on the beach, and something stirs inside me when my shoes touch the sand for the first time. A deep, familiar longing. The faint salt smell speaks of stories I haven't lived yet, like nostalgia for the future. My innate tropical, water nature. I can almost hear the ocean's lullaby from here, calling me east, across this river and toward the Gaspésia Peninsula. Making me forget why I came here, a convincing hypnosis.

Come to me, Ava, it says.

Go where Diablo is going.

Forget the heart, forget the humans, and move on.

I have never faced a decision this difficult.

Wolf and I follow the Klujns as they walk into the arena. Only three rows of seats made out of packed sand, and the stage is dark, sandy soil. I choose the lowest bench so Wolf can sit at my feet, closest to the stage and facing north. The Circo Klujns sit to my left, on the side closest to the forest, and the others, the "foreign" ones, sit on the right side closer to the water, many with black marigold bracelets, necklaces, or flowers. I'm surprised to see some Circo Klujns wearing the same flower, but none more surprising than Ariana. *Did Diablo give it to her?*

That familiar prickle of jealousy returns.

I wonder if Klujns usually give birth in front of a crowd. But this ceremony isn't Daciana's doing, and I imagine Warwick couldn't have let such an important event go on behind closed doors.

A birth, or an execution?

A coin toss; the king has always loved games.

Around me, there are no bets or fanfare, just a somber gallows air. Glory enters and sits among the Estrellans, with Daciana's wolf, Rhea, by her side and the Bessi-Maso family. I regret the fact that Daciana and I didn't get to have a final conversation, and I feel envious of Glory for having gotten so many years with her as a mentor, for being the object of Diablo's love and protection. Poor Glory, who has done nothing to receive my envy, but I can't help the way I feel. The night and the emotions it brought up have warped my heart into an ugly, twisted thing.

The tense feeling in the air makes me anxious, and all I can do is stay present, grounded, and focused. Then, a respectful quiet spreads as Diablo brings Daciana onto the stage, helping her like an old woman crossing the street. My mouth drops—I don't recognize my grandmother at first because the sight is grotesque, shocking, morbid. She is not the beautiful old woman she was before, but a monster covered from head to toe in coral mushrooms. A freakshow oddity. Even her eyelids are weighed down by fungi, her bright purple irises barely visible beneath the infestation. What's worse is the pungent odor of decomposing flesh. She is far closer to death than I imagined.

Daciana kneels at the center of the stage, her spine bent from the weight of the ecosystem growing on her body, facing south, facing *me*. I want her to look at me and acknowledge me, but she doesn't. I still don't even know if she intended for me to come here or stay home. I want to know that she's proud; there's only so much validation I can give myself. To hear it from her would be to make it real. Diablo goes to stand guard on the right, near Glory. Then, Warwick enters and sits to the left. His face gives nothing away. Whatever he has planned, he will keep it a secret until the very last minute.

Two Estrellan musicians sit on the sand at the edge of the stage. A man sings while a woman plays an instrument. They weave a story with their words, a tale of dark nostalgia, of birth, death, and everything in between. The song is deeply haunting and moves me to tears, but I'm not the only one. Around the crowd, many other Klujns are crying, as though saying goodbye to the queen who has gotten them through hard times, who has always been a pillar for them to lean on, wise beyond worlds.

It is a funeral, with the deceased person present.

Tears pour from my eyes as I succumb to the emotions swirling inside me: sadness at the thought of losing the only family I have, and confusion at the future, my heart torn between worlds, places, people, things. But despite my pain, the ceremony is beautiful. I find it gracious of Warwick to have allowed Daciana a certain dignity in death, but knowing his volatility it could all be a ruse; everything could shift quickly. He always saves bloody surprises for the end.

Rhea watches her master, and I can't imagine that kind of bond, all the things they've been through in their eighty-plus years together, or over one thousand cycles. What it must feel like to have that connection to someone, and the pain my mother must have felt when she saw Mahta drowned in front of her, then was forced to live inside a cell next to her wolf's dead body.

For torture, pressure, *crystals*.

Maybe my mother was justified in slaying those men after all . . . But is there any justification for revenge, or does it just perpetuate more violence? Can Warwick end the cycle despite everything he's endured? By letting Daciana go and letting her die free? Can his black heart find the pink spirit it was born with?

The music continues, and Daciana squeezes the sand in her fists and stands. As she does, the sand pours from her hands like an hourglass with no end. Her eyes are glazed and violet, somewhere between two worlds, and her old woman bones start to dance. A sort of *possession dance*, like she's moving with the gods. As she does, I can almost see the silhouettes of animals moving around her in the arena like a dark carousel of horses, lions, bears, and birds. I realize that here, away from the Loudhouse, labor is induced through dancing. Under the moonlight, with her feet in the sand. Something in the melody calling the baby into the world, while a circus of gods watch and dance.

Daciana's movements intensify as her contractions build, her hands pushing against her belly, guiding the baby down. She gets down on the ground and starts to dig. She digs and digs, and when she's ready, she gives birth into the ground. No metal and concrete, no glaring hospital lights, just the caress of a setting moon. No pointed rifles, only Warwick's gaze, which looks unusually sad. If I didn't know any better, I would say that he was moved.

Then, with a superhuman effort, Daciana pushes her baby into the ground. Her bones shake from the effort, and her eyes leave trance and return to this world. Whatever swirling gods I may or may not have seen, whatever otherworldly carousel or circus, is now gone. Now that the baby is out, there's a look on Daciana's face similar to the woman in the Loudhouse's—a flicker of apprehension. But she has a rebel heart, and her courage is larger than the world. She does not fear anything, not even death.

Daciana moves back from the hole and fills it slowly, one handful at a time. Like she did at the start of the dance, she lets each handful of sand fall slowly down, letting the wind spread the grains apart. A feeling that she's not saying hello but *goodbye.*

The sky is lightening, blue hour fading.

The sun is moments away from rising.

When Daciana has finished, she flattens the sandy soil with her hands and traces a rune on the surface. A rune I recognize—

The journey *home.*

Finally, she looks up, *directly* at me, in a look that makes up for the distance, the doubt, and the silence. A moment that lasts only a few seconds but feels much longer, like when my mother was facing George on that cliff edge. The look in Daciana's eyes says, *I'm proud of who you've become. And I know you'll make the right decision.*

Something that makes me believe, in my core, that she *did* intend for me to come here after all, to find my way home. That she was testing me all along to see how badly I wanted it. That maybe I needed to go home, to realize that I didn't belong in Red River anymore. I needed to come back to Circo to know that it was just another stop, another landmark, on a much bigger journey . . .

But what now?

My heart is drawing me toward the coast, but my conscience is pulling me home.

It's okay, her eyes say, just like my mother's right before she died. But it's not. Not at all.

Tears blur my vision.

After a minute of waiting, a tiny hand springs from the soil.

Daciana takes the baby's hand and I see that delicate exchange of sparks, of information.

Then Warwick walks toward her, towering over Daciana. There's no weapon in his hands but his claws are immense, weapons in themselves. He holds a hand up, as though about to unleash the force of the Sun onto her, to finally kill her after all these years, but then his hand falls to his side. He can't. I understand in that moment: He is setting her free.

The rest happens in a flash. Daciana pulls her baby from the soil, then Diablo rushes forward to help them. Palo, Glory, and the other "foreign" Klujns take off, running down the beach toward the forest. The Circo Klujns look confused and agitated, including Bruto, but Warwick signals for them to stop. Warwick turns to look at me, and in his eyes, beyond his torment, I see it.

I see mercy.

Then, the sun pierces the horizon. And right as it does, it all goes horribly wrong . . .

A shadow sweeps up behind Warwick. The king's eyes are still on me, and he doesn't have the time to register what's happening, and for that, I feel complicit. When he turns around, he has only a moment of surprise before his daughter strikes him between the eyes with the base of her machete. Warwick falls to the ground, temporarily stunned—or paralyzed. Still conscious, but unable to move.

Ariana.

And it makes sense then, why Diablo stayed with her to talk strategy after the cove. To convince her to leave a sinking ship and go where the power goes. To turn on her own father, like the spies back home, turning on their own family. If Warwick has mercy, Ariana has none.

I sit there, just as immobile as the king, as Ariana climbs on top of her father, her adult claws long and sharp and menacing. The king's eyes are still open, still conscious, so that the poor Klujn can see and feel everything. A few tears leak from the corners of his eyes. It's hard to believe he's the same Klujn I met at Circo three months ago. The wild "cannibal" king. The look in his eyes is not that of a monster, but someone wounded. He's not just a mad king but someone who lost his way and suffered at the hands of humans. The king who likes to rescue stray animals and who is afraid of public speaking. Who has been lying to himself this whole time about his lack of powers, leading his stand farther and farther astray from their true nature, isolating them from the rest of Klujn kind.

Ariana thrusts her claws into the open target of Warwick's chest, and I see and hear everything.

There's a *crack* and a *crunch* as Ariana's hand moves past bone and muscle. And then, she closes her hand around the organ and rips it out with a spray of blood. *Warwick's heart.* It is massive, the size of a horse's heart, and a gray-black color. Still beating.

"I'm sorry," I whisper under my breath as the king dies.

I *do* feel sorry to see him die like that.

Then, Ariana throws the heart at me. "It's all yours," she says with contempt, and then she takes off running down the beach.

I catch the heart between my hands, which is impossibly heavy. Still warm and with a fading pulse to it. Warwick has a deep cavity in his chest, and his open eyes are vacant, tears drying in their creases.

"Run!" a voice yells, Kalab's voice, and then I understand why.

All the Circo Klujns, the ones not wearing black marigolds, are swarming toward me, possessed and blood-maddened.

I dive out of the way—

Just as they lunge on Warwick's body. I hear the sound of tearing flesh and chewing. The sick crunch of bones being ripped out of cartilage. Now that the king is dead, the Circo Klujns seem to be possessed by a cannibalistic force that makes them want to eat every piece of Warwick's body, as though by consuming their leader they will inherit his strength and powers. They fight over the organs that hold the most strength or knowledge—the brain, the muscles, the eyes, the tongue, the liver. Even the genitals. Oak and Poppet are there, like two wild and hungry dogs.

I glimpse the black marigold bracelet on my wrist—a sort of talisman or protection charm, keeping me sober, lucid, from something that must be innate in me, in all Klujns.

Wolf growls, and I see why.

Bruto stares at me across the carnage, his eyes fixed on the heart. And then, he comes toward me.

"Run!" Kalab screams again, pulling me away from the fray.

We take off sprinting down the beach where the others went.

And we run.

We run for our lives.

52

I am running with Warwick's heart in my arms, warm and cradled like a newborn baby. As my shoes pound the sand and then the snow, my heart beats like a drum. *Boom, boom, boom.* Wolf leads the way back into the forest like a glowing white beacon, then Kalab. I run wildly through the trees, following them, my bones with a faint glow to them, something automatic. My inner compass drives me forward, twisting left and right.

Warwick is dead.

Ariana killed him.

I have his heart.

We run for minutes, or hours. Finally, we reach a clearing where the group has settled behind a protective barrier, for there are children and elderly. The snow has melted here, and there is only rich, brown earth. A large Carniflora blocks the night sky from view, her branches scarce of roses.

Everyone watches as Kalab, Wolf, and I enter the clearing, the last to arrive. Diablo, Glory, and Palo are there, seemingly the unofficial leaders of this somber expedition, while Daciana lies on a blanket on the ground, surrounded by her stand, barely alive, cradling her newborn baby. There are fifty or so Klujns here, mostly Estrellans and ones from other raided stands but also, surprisingly, a few from Circo: Ariana, Oumi, Oso, Nora, Ferta, and a pale-looking Nini.

Still panting from the run, I look down at the heart in my hands.

It's grotesque.

I feel dizzy, nauseous, swept up by a reeling vertigo.

I stumble and fall, hitting my head hard against the ground.

The dawn sky turns midnight black.

* * *

I am in my mother's arms, and we are moving through a burning forest, as Wolf runs at her feet. He is tiny, but he is fast. I am wrapped up in my blue blanket. Santos, who was in the wild with the logging men when the attack at the Loudhouse happened, returned to find two dozen of his men brutally slain and George locked in a cell looking disheveled. This is personal now—Santos wants to catch my mother, to make her suffer. If she is caught, he will torture her until her last breath. With my two-week birthday tomorrow, I will have the tiny crystal seeds taken from my ovaries, and will likely spend the rest of my short life being poked and prodded until I end up in a jar filled with pink liquid.

My mother stops to catch her breath, exhausted. The new moon is hidden behind the thick, smoky sky, and she cannot absorb moonlight. She used most of her energy to summon the avarice, find me, and escape. Now, she spends the last bit of energy she has binding me to Wolf so he will keep me safe, so I will have someone to look over me in her absence.

My mother lies me down on the forest floor, bunching the edges of my blue blanket until they form a circle, like a miniature arena or an Ice Moon. Wolf lies beside me on the blanket, and my mother uses a murky, ailing claw to prick my finger and his paw. She binds our hands with a black ribbon and chants as she casts her spell into the night, in a hurry but focused, always focused. And then the black ribbon dissolves, and it's gone, absorbed by our flesh.

There are flashlights—and angry voices.

The Hunters are coming.

My mother wraps me up and looks around. She picks a path, only to end up where she started. She is lost, confused, and begins to panic like I did in the corn maze. I feel her fear, and I start crying.

"Shhh," she tells me, as her frantic heart beats like a drum against my ear. Then, my mother takes another wrong turn and finds herself at the edge of a cliff. Down below, a river rages. She is trapped, a prey animal worn down after a long Hunt. She turns around to find George standing there, holding his rifle.

And then, a scene I have seen so many times before plays out, only now, it is not at all like I remember.

"Let us go," she pleads.

"You know I can't do that." The look on George's face is not sinister but forthright.

"You killed my wolf five times," she says. "Five." Like she expected more from him.

"I know. I'm sorry. Santos made me do it. I didn't have a choice."

"You had a choice. You always have a choice. Some things are worth more than your life."

There's the beam of a flashlight through the trees. The general isn't far. A hundred feet, at most.

"I can't let you go, Adria," George says. "They know you're here, and you're surrounded on all sides. I did what I could, but . . ."

It wasn't enough.

My mother nods in fear and understanding. She looks down at the bundle in her arms, at me, and whispers something final, then kisses me. And then, she wraps me up tightly and tosses me into the river, and as I soar, and Wolf prepares to jump in after me, the next few seconds elapse almost in slow motion—

The brief exchange between my parents.

"If you can't let me go," she says. "Then, please, let me go."

I realize what she means, and George does, too. He has the same look in his eyes that he had when he first saw her at Estrella. Like he has just seen the most beautiful creature in the world, the most exotic bird, and wonders if he should capture her or set her free. There are tears in his bright green eyes. He doesn't want to do this. But this is about her.

"Okay," he says.

Santos's flashlight beam gets closer, and George raises his rifle and says, in a stern voice for the nearby Hunters—

"Give me Ava."

"No."

"She's mine, too."

"She'll never be yours."

And then, with a final look of respect between them, and a silent apology, George shoots my mother in the heart. A quick, merciful kill to spare her from a life of brutality. My mother's body crumbles. George walks toward Wolf and holds out his leg.

"Please," he says. When Wolf doesn't react, George shakes his leg in Wolf's face. Finally, Wolf bites down on George's ankle, severing his Achilles tendon. George yells in pain, and Wolf jumps off the cliff after me.

Santos arrives and sees his version of the truth—that George was attacked and shot my mother because he had to. But the general will always stay suspicious of my father, because the bullet came before the scream.

Santos didn't kill my mom—George did.

But he didn't kill her out of malice, but mercy.

George, who seemed to love my mother in his own tortured way, but who was stuck in a system he couldn't escape.

At least I now know the truth: Her final moment was peaceful. She died on her own terms. And despite George's mistakes, in the end, he opened her birdcage and set her free.

Peace is a current, and I let it take me.

53

Daciana's death is beautiful, as far as deaths go. All her supporters line up to say their goodbyes, one at a time, and I stay at the back of the line, not ready for that final moment. When it's finally my turn, words fail me. The queen touches my hand, and despite the ugliness of the mushrooms covering every inch of her, her touch is soothing.

"I know we didn't get much time, Ava, but time is a funny thing, and I have found that a moment can be worth a lifetime."

Tears stream down my face. I nod, even though I don't understand what she means. "Diablo told me that you had something to do with Warwick setting us free, and for that I'm so very grateful."

"I don't want you to die," I manage.

"Death is not the end. It is just another stop. Our relationship will be different now, but different doesn't have to mean *bad.* There are places where we can still meet."

"Where?"

"You already know."

The shadow world.

My time with her is over, even though it just started. I feel a warm hand on my shoulder, and look up to see Diablo. His eyes are the saddest I've ever seen in all my life. Behind him, Glory nurses the baby.

Diablo is the last to talk to Daci.

Then, when she is ready, she looks up at the sky with resolve.

Animal gods descend in a spiral and take her away.

It is that easy—as though it was rehearsed.

As though she has died a thousand times before, and has complete faith that it's not over . . . that there is something on the other side.

A light leaves her eyes, and only her flesh remains.

A vessel, but not *her*.

"She's gone," Diablo announces, and I let out a strangled cry. Because, despite these promises of a *shadow world*, there is nothing more irreversible than death. Because I can't bring her back from the dead.

She's gone.

My grandmother.

And her baby—my *aunt*—will grow up with as many questions as I did.

Glory is there, wrapping me in her arms and crying, while Diablo holds the infant. Wolf never leaves my side. The entire stand is crying, including Rhea the wolf, who walks up and lays down next to her master, head resting next to Daciana's. Rhea's breathing slows, and more time stretches between each breath. Then, her lungs deflate like a pierced balloon and don't rise again.

The wolves howl.

A queen is gone.

And Rhea has accompanied her master in death.

I wasn't prepared for so much death, but I know that's the

way it goes with Klujns and spotted wolves—one cannot live without the other. It is the way of Nature, but that doesn't make it any less sad. The Estrellans sing, and some of the other Klujns join in.

How I loved Rhea in the short time I knew her. Her easy affection. Her love of belly rubs.

Diablo watches on, emotive but practical. He passes the baby to a nursing mother and begins to prepare Daciana's body for whatever comes next. He removes Daciana's heart, as gently as one can, like a careful surgery, then wraps it in cloth. Her heart is pink as a newborn's, with a purple hue to it. The contrast between hers and Warwick's is obvious: one healthy and one not.

We form a circle around the two bodies and sing, coming forward one by one to deposit our black marigolds on the queen and her wolf. Diablo and Palo then carry Daciana's body to the roots of the Carniflora, where there is a small opening in the earth, like a dark mouth. They place her inside, head first, and the tree slowly eats her in a gentle reverse birth.

Diablo and Palo bring Rhea's body to the Carniflora next, and I can no longer control the tears that pour from my eyes, but everyone seems to be weeping just as much as me. Palo has an arm around Glory, and Diablo stands still, like a solitary tree. I wish I could console him, or that he would console me.

The grandmother I got to meet but didn't know enough.

And her wolf who loved so easily.

And now her stand is going to head toward the coast and join another, and I want to follow them more than anything . . . but there are human lives that depend on me. I can't forget Warwick's final act of mercy . . . and even though it is a strange feeling, a part of me wants to avenge him.

Because if it wasn't for Warwick and the Blood Race, I might have never found my way to Circo, to the wild, and learned that I was Klujn. I would have spent my life feeling other and out of place, never knowing what I had missed.

I can't help but think this is precisely what Daciana would have wanted—to die surrounded by her stand, who is finally free. Heading toward the coast and the possibility of new leadership. And those Circo Klujns who decided to change sides before the stand fell were given a second chance. That is so like Daciana—to forgive the past, and look toward the future. Even though she wouldn't be a part of that future.

And then the Carniflora finishes her meal, and the wolves each bring an offering to lay at her roots. A seed, a stick, a bone. Even the forest joins in with offerings of its own, the swaying trees and the singing birds, all coming to pay their respects.

I stare at the Carniflora, a magnificent but gentle beast, remembering what the Sibu queen said, almost like she *knew* what was going to happen—that life and death are a cycle that keeps going.

A bug that feeds a flower. A river that feeds an ocean. A body that feeds a *tree*.

* * *

Without a queen, Diablo is in charge, and he doesn't take the responsibility lightly. If anything, he looks uncomfortable at the idea of being in charge, but he will do anything to protect the heart and its infinite knowledge. Right now, keeping it safe until a new queen is named is his priority. However, his approach to leadership is quite democratic.

After a brief meeting, the group decides to camp here for the day and set out in the afternoon. The scouting wolves have been busy these past months digging Katacombes under the river that will allow the group to cross to the peninsula without having to swim miles in frigid waters—or risk detection.

After their travel plans are sorted, Diablo leads me down to a stream where he shows me how to clean and preserve the heart. It is a workshop of a sinister kind as we both stand knee-deep in the icy water, washing our respective hearts. Then he shows me how to wrap it in herbs, crystals, and cloth, and bind it with ribbon. This way it can stay preserved for months without decomposing.

I feel angry at him. Angry that he allowed Ariana to kill Warwick in that gruesome way. I know Warwick created his fair share of suffering during his lifetime, but he didn't deserve to be blindsided. Killed by his own flesh and blood.

"Warwick had to die," Diablo says, reading my mood, my mind, as always. I nod, although the image is still there . . . the moment Ariana pulled his heart out; the spray of blood. The tears leaking from the king's eyes.

Perhaps, like Daciana, he is finally at peace now.

"I would have done things differently."

"I know."

The silence between us is tense, but also deeply comfortable: our trip in the wild was its own sort of honeymoon, and we have shared things that so few Klujns have. Then there is last night's conversation in the cave behind the waterfall, and Diablo's hands on me. That is something that no one—not even Ariana—can take away from me.

When Diablo and I have finished, we sit on the riverbank, the hearts between us: Daciana's bound in violet thread and Warwick's bound in crimson.

"You're sad," he says.

"I am."

"Because you've made a decision."

"I have."

"You're leaving."

I nod.

"Are you going to be okay?"

"I don't know."

My voice breaks. Tears pour down my cheeks and I let them. The silence between us is pregnant. It is not at all like our previous silences. Something between us is different.

Diablo doesn't know what to say. "I wanted to give you something before we leave." He reaches into his coat and pulls out a little jar of algae ink. "It's . . . permanent. Is that okay?"

I nod again.

"Give me your hand."

I look at him curiously, eyes still watery, then place my left hand palm-up on his leg and he shifts slightly, and I wonder if my touch affects him the way his affects me.

Diablo takes out a little needle, like a long toothpick, dips it into the algae ink and begins to tattoo the inside of my wrist. It hurts, but it is a superficial pain, no more painful than an ant bite. He paints a symbol I recognize: the same one the rebels used, that José bore, and that Daciana traced in the sand when she was saying goodbye to the world.

An infinite line, looped back on itself, the loops creating four points.

Like the elements.

With the fifth element—*aether,* or *spirit*—at the center.

A cycle with no start or end.

"For now it's gray, but it will glow when wet," he says.

"The journey home."

Diablo looks surprised that I know what it is. His violet eyes look directly into mine, his smell flooding my senses.

"Coming home to your body," he says. "Coming home to Nature. To your purpose. Your stand. To *love.* And then, the ultimate journey home, to *death*. Because life is just a brief passage. A dream that goes by too quickly. We will all end up *home*, but what we do before that hour comes is what matters.

"I wish you a safe journey," he says, tracing his finger over my new tattoo, now a permanent part of me. "Until we meet again."

My body wants to be touched, and my soul wants to be loved. But touch is not enough. A finger on a wrist. A hand on a leg. A deep gaze. He has opened a gorge inside me; I want to be ravaged.

"Two paths," I say, and Diablo looks at me curiously, waiting for me to go on. I clear my throat, but the truth gets easier to say, the more practice you have.

"Just because two paths are separate, doesn't mean they will always be. If they're meant to, those paths will cross again. Because whoever is meant to be in your life will be there. That is the forest way."

It's Diablo's turn for tears.

"Sorry," he says—a humanism from having spent so much time with me.

"Do me a favor," I answer, with a wry smile, throwing his line back at him. "The next time you cry, don't say sorry."

* * *

The karavan leaves at dusk. I haven't slept. I watch them leave, still torn inside like I'm being quartered by the poison. I could still catch up to them . . .

But my feet stay rooted, my decision made.

I feel too tired to build a proper shelter, so I decide to go without one. Plus, the winter's day is warm by the crackling fire. After a brief meeting with myself—both autocracy *and* democracy—I have decided to stay here one more night, before heading out the following morning with Warwick's bundled heart. Taking a day to rest and plan can be valuable, as I discovered at Sibu, and even though I will no longer have Diablo to guide me, I'm confident I can make it back in time—if I can tap in to my body's lunar sources, the language of my bones, and slip into an altered state just like I did on the final day of my Blood Race.

Wolf and I cuddle for a while, dozing in and out of sleep. I wake up in the dark of the early morning, feeling rested. I make myself a breakfast of mushroom coffee, wild green salad, and skewers of vegera that the Carniflora kindly offers. As I eat, I stare at the druda map stretched out on the ground, thinking it's about time I figured it out.

"Looks like it's just you and me," I tell Wolf, and to my surprise, he doesn't seem disappointed. I wonder how much he understands of all this. I want to be a good master to him, for us to have a good life and be a team. I want him to trust and respect me as an alpha. He has a playful air to him this morning, and I even catch him rolling in the snow as happy wolves should.

I change out of my costume, into new clothes that Glory had thought to bring. As I take off my shoes and step onto the cold forest floor, barefoot for the first time in a long time, I feel a pulse of energy I couldn't feel before. I remember Diablo saying that you can't know a forest until you walk barefoot in it, and he's right, because now, looking around, I feel like I just drank another one of Honey's potions. The trees have gentle auras, and the flowers whisper. Everything buzzes, vibrant and alive and *connected.*

I look at the druda map, which vibrates with new energy, like something that wants to be discovered. It is round and black, like an arena or a portal. And there's something about it this time—something that speaks to me. Maybe it's my bare feet, the colossal act of telling the truth and letting the karavan go, or the new arrival of my adult claws.

How can you measure growth? How do you know when you are ready to develop new senses? I'm not sure. But now, I feel something I couldn't feel before.

I look at the black cloth.

And think about black *absorbing* colors.

Holding all the colors inside it, like Black Victorias do.

Colors . . . or *worlds*?

I think about Klujn magic and belief and how *faith* in these other worlds is what makes them real. That you can't find them if you don't believe in them first.

The earth pulses in my toes, like I'm getting close to something.

I remember when I arrived at Sibu, and think about not looking *at* but *through*. My heart beats steadily, my eyes blur slightly, and something strange begins to happen. I am somewhere between consciousness and trance, and on the map the gold runes begin to form a spiral. The amber rivers swirl.

I lift my foot and place it on the map, and when I do, a gilded staircase appears. A spiral one, leading down into the earth's center. Two dimensions become three, or three dimensions become four. My peripheral vision is now a blur, but I see Wolf watching me, and I know he will keep the heart safe in my absence.

Then, my bare feet still buzzing and my new claws prickling under their manicure, I place my second foot inside the map.

To humans, it may always remain a bit of cloth, but to me,

it is something else, something far more valuable. Belief makes the difference.

Confused, frightened, but also terribly excited, I descend into another world.

54

The spiral staircase leads me down into a dark, damp chamber, with twelve golden doors all around. Each one is marked by the same runes as on the map, too complicated to decipher. I approach a door and try the handle, but it remains closed. I try the next ten, and none of them open, until I begin to lose faith . . .

But finally, the last one does.

Beyond the door, I enter a forest at night. An enchanted place, albeit a little macabre. There are giant skull altars, sockets filled with marigold flowers. Candles of all colors hang from the branches. A cold, unearthly mist coats the ground. The smell of dead things, like the scorched jungle beach where I met the avarice.

I have entered the shadow world.

I come upon a clearing, where clusters of people—although they look mostly like shadows, their skin graying like Honey's in the end—are seated around small round tables on the ground.

As I weave between the tables, the first one I pass startles me. Seated here are the girls who died in the Blood Race: Reesa,

Bindu, Jade, Mabry, Zoe, Rory, Willa, the Brave Night girls, and even Elizabeth. Some smile and wave at me in recognition, others just stare, but even Elizabeth's stare isn't fiery or mean like I remember it. As though in this world, there are no grudges; grudges are a thing of the surface world.

"Ava!" Willa smiles brightly. She runs up to give me a hug that feels as solid as flesh. She holds no grudges for being dead. Willa wants me to sit with her, but there are still plenty of tables to explore and my time in this world feels like a measured thing . . .

Wendy isn't here, I think.

At the next table I see Circo Klujns, the ones who died in the raid, including that little boy and his wolf pup.

There are humans too—young Hunters, old Hunters.

And creatures everywhere.

The family of slain reindeer are there, watching me from the perimeter of the clearing. The mother and her babies.

And that's when I see them—sitting around one of the tables near the back—Daciana and my mother, among their ancestors. Other Klujns and queens and drudas whose faces are unfamiliar but who all seem to know who I am.

"Ava," Daciana says. "Take a seat."

I do, but I feel anxious. My mother is on her other side, and for all the dreams I've had, I've never met her, spoken to her, looked her in the eyes. She looks at me with love, a tough kind of love, and I try to overcome the fear I feel at meeting her; she was not only her darkness. That darkness was but one small part.

"It's nice to finally meet you," she says. "I've waited a long time for this moment."

But what are you supposed to say to the mother who has been dead your whole life?

"You have grown into a beautiful, strong, resilient woman."

“Thank you.”

My mother asks me what’s next on my journey, and when I tell her about the humans I need to save, she disapproves; she thinks going back is too dangerous, that I should follow the karavan to the coast. I tell her it’s too late, they’ve already gone, but we both know I can easily catch up. It feels strange to be scolded by a parent. It is the first time in my life that I have felt like a defiant teenager going against her mother’s wishes.

“You have gifts . . . important ones,” my mother says. “They shouldn’t be wasted. You should go and participate in the Queen Trials; you have the heart of a leader, and a queen’s heart shouldn’t be given to just anyone.”

“I don’t want to lead,” I tell her. Aside from Daciana, all the examples of leadership I’ve had have not been good. “I don’t need control.”

“Leading does not have to be about control,” my mother answers. “A matriarchal stand leads with its heart, with emotion and empathy. Become the leader you needed. You have already started your beautiful journey of healing, and only a healed person should lead others.”

Her words only add to my confusion and inner torment.

She reaches across Daciana and takes my hand, and I see our matching god marks.

“You’ll learn to work with the god of Creatures, and see that darkness doesn’t have to be a bad thing—if you can learn to control it. You have the language of animals in your claws, and the ability to create new life, which is what the world needs more of. Don’t throw it away by thinking about a few humans who are probably already dead.”

I pull my hand away.

“Only Ava knows what is best,” says Daciana, and I am grateful for her interruption. “Journeys are not always straight roads; sometimes they bend backward and curve around, before continuing on. Life is just a series of landmarks, and there's no such thing as ending up or settling down, only continuing on. Right now, Ava needs to decide where she must continue on to, but that is in no way permanent or definite."

Music plays, a ghostly cabaret. Looking around at the forest feast, I notice Warwick, sitting among other kings—there aren't many.

He looks at me, offering me a kind, deranged smile, and I remember the things that were said in the tent; not just a plan to save my skin, but words I meant.

That Grouse and Santos need to die in order for the world to change.

That this plan is bigger than myself and what my heart craves.

Wendy, Diana, Mr. Wilder, and the Scouts aren't here—which hopefully means they're still alive.

Still in the land of the living.

Forget the karavan for now, forget the coast. This is what you must do, the voice of instinct says.

My decision is made.

* * *

I wake up curled on the map, which is cloth again, no longer a staircase. My nose is bleeding. Wolf is by my side, keeping watch, keeping me warm, just like the night we were bonded only bigger, much bigger. More time has passed then I planned—it's afternoon again.

Are you okay? His glacial eyes seem to ask, and I nod, still trying to make sense of the scene I just saw, the strange conversation with my mom.

"I saw them," I tell him. "My mom, Daciana, and the Blood Race girls. They were all there. They all seemed to be at peace."

Wolf licks my tears away like he would when I was little, and the gesture is comforting. I wish he would tell me what to do, but he trusts me to make the right decision.

I realize that despite my mother's warnings, I need to listen to myself, trust myself, as I have on every step of this journey. Because as much love as I have for her, and as much love as she has for me, this is not her life—it is mine. Being true to myself, and following my heart is the only way forward. And, like Daciana said, journeys are not straight roads.

There is one final detour I must make before finding my one true home.

55

I spend the afternoon preparing for my journey: I collect edible plants and crystals I can work with. I recite Maple's list of *ten essential items*, and gather what I can find, what I can make, what I can carve. The Carniflora becomes a friend, one I talk to like a person, although she doesn't speak in return. Still, our communication goes beyond words, much like mine and Diablo's, and she offers me some of her bark to make a shelter with. I make a fire and watch the crackling flames and the changing sky; I feel that more snow is coming a few days from now based on the cold, humid smell in the air. Here, in my little circle of forest, I do nothing, and I do everything, like a gardener does.

Two weeks until Darkest Day, I think.

Two weeks to get back.

I can do it. I can save George, Diana, Mr. Wilder, and the others.

I can poison Grouse and Santos.

What would the Territory look like without them? Infinitely different, that's for sure. Infinitely better.

Just before dusk, I wander away from the safety of my camp.

I come across a little waterfall flowing into a pond, the banks dusted with snow and moonflowers beginning to sprout from the ground. The water isn't warm, but it's wild and untouched and that makes it so beautiful.

I remember what Celestinja said, the wise Sibu queen. That at the end of my journey, when my purge was complete, I should find a body of water to swim in—*naked*—and then conduct a ritual for myself.

So, despite the winter chill, I strip completely naked, with only the birds and the trees to judge my curves and edges. Then I sink my body into the cold water. Even though I've had some practice now, nothing ever prepares you for the shock. Fight or flight races through my body. But today, I stay. I fight.

And after doing so many hard things, the hard things are easier.

Being submerged in cold water makes me feel connected to Diablo.

I float on my back, looking up at the golden sky. The clouds are rainbow and iridescent. There, in the magical light, a perfect sunbow forms—a round rainbow, like a portal in the sky. And I smile to myself, because nothing is random out here. Despite my pain and my heartbreak and uncertainty, I am exactly where I need to be. Just because something is right, doesn't make it easy.

The tattoo on my hand glows; Diablo is on my flesh, now a permanent part of me.

After the swim, I bundle myself in warm clothes and join Wolf by the fire. I make floral tea and savor every mouthful. As I look down at my leaf cup, those little mouthfuls are like steps on my journey.

Rivers crossed.

Mountains climbed.

And all the years I've grown in such a short amount of time.

Before I know it, the cup is empty, my adventure almost over, and one day, life will be as well.

I gaze into the flames, thinking about the trials I faced. From the Loudhouse to the poachers, the caves to Pink Flower. Sibu, the Territory of the Gods, and my fire walk. It all feels like a dream now. I can't believe how much I went through in such a short time. And even though I'm sitting here now, still me, and it feels like nothing's changed, I know that, deep down, everything has. I can no longer deny what I want. But I can also no longer deny what the world needs, and that change is possible if I'm willing to fight for it.

Perhaps that desire to fight is the human in me.

While the Klujn in me wants to learn the languages in her claws, build a new happy stand, and put a stop to cruelty.

Wolf paws at me, breaking me out of my thoughts, wanting a chest rub. He is perhaps the biggest surprise of this whole journey, beginning to show signs of affection—in his own independent way. We are still getting to know each other, and I imagine our relationship will take time to build, but all good things require effort.

As the sun sets, the stars and planets come out. Little galaxies of traveling circuses in the sky, here for one night, then gone the next, off to some other galactic town. I know that my relationship with Daciana and my mom will be different from now on—one of omens, like birds and black flowers—but different doesn't have to mean *bad*. It requires a leap of faith, faith that I now have.

Wolf and I fall asleep, curled by the flames.

I wake up a few hours before dawn, and decide on my final ritual: I will make a moon crown.

I use thin vines and Black Victoria thread, weaving in crystals and flowers. As I do, I think about what's to come. My fear at that future encounter with Grouse. My sadness at letting Diablo go. But sometimes, we have to leave a coast in order to find new land. Maybe I need to let Diablo go, *truly* let him go, in order to see him again.

In the crown, I weave labradorite for change and transformation, obsidian for protection, a tiger's eye for warding off curses and taking action, a rainbow moonstone for healing and caring for myself the way a mother would, a black diamond in homage to my first god.

A rose quartz for self-love.

I find three moonflowers growing at the base of the Carniflora, where the wolves brought their offerings. They have already grown eight or nine feet overnight, their black petals opening, showing glowing blue centers. They are the most striking flowers I've ever seen and too beautiful to pick, but they give me permission. So, I cut the moonflowers with my new crystal knife and add them to my moon crown. One for Daciana, one for my mom, and one for me. A reminder that I'm never alone, because I walk with my ancestors. I may not be able to see them with human eyes, but I can feel them with my Klujn heart.

Then, I place the glowing moon crown on my head, which fits comfortably.

I peel off the manicure Glory gave me, and my adult claws glow in their full splendor. Inside them, a black-gold shimmer. I remind myself that this darkness is not me but something I can control and learn to work with.

With my morning ritual finished, I am now ready to leave. I pack up my essential items and a few non-essential ones, put out the fire, and restore the camp.

In the blue hour, the moonflowers are a spectacular sight. A reminder that light can be forged in the darkness. That just because my mother's story was tragic, it doesn't mean that mine has to be. I am writing my own story now, and I will no longer be defined by my trauma. These moonflowers are not thinking about the years they spent buried underground—they are too busy enjoying their brief lives, kissing the night.

Even though I have no idea what the future holds, that's okay. A journey starts with a step and, once I take it, the remainder of the path will continue to reveal itself to me.

Wolf is by my side, wearing a little sling I made for him to carry Warwick's heart. We look at one another.

Ready? I ask, and he understands even though I didn't speak. Something innate and *symbiotic*.

Above my head, an avarice flies, but I try to ignore it.

Cling to the pinkness of my heart.

And so, with a moonflower crown on my head, a glowing tattoo on my wrist, and my adult claws glinting in the dawn light, I take my first step on this new path.

Alive and awake and at home in my body.

Finally *wild*.

ACKNOWLEDGMENTS

I wrote *Ice Moon* during a particularly difficult time. *Blood Circus* had just released, and I was grappling with severe chronic health issues.

I had a year to write the first draft, but spent the first five months unable to even look at a screen. This book was written in small sprints and stolen moments. My journey of healing became Ava's, and hers became mine. I like to think *Ice Moon* wouldn't have been the same without it.

Thank you to everyone who has been a part of this journey.

To Blackstone, my amazing publisher, who was so patient with the constantly pushed deadlines and who always put the human before the contract.

To Dan—my editor, I am *your* fan. Your enthusiasm for this book and story has been nothing short of amazing.

Josie, Courtney, Tatiana, Sean, Josh, Francie, Adrienne, Amy, and everyone else at Blackstone—thank you for being such an incredible team. You've given *Blood Circus* a home, and I can only hope for many more books together.

To Kyla, for doing an incredible job narrating the audiobook.

To Alenka and Katy, for the beautiful cover.

To my wonderful editor, Diana, who made revisions fun (and we all know revisions are never fun).

To my family—Muck, Paps, Midi, Flora, Pooky—the best family in the world. <3

To my friends, and what a spectacular group you are—Audrey, Areli, Vanessa, Qaseem, Lindsay, Sam, and the new friends who've entered my life in recent years—Zelda, Bri, Rebecca, Steph, and many others.

To Ms. P, my high school English teacher. Thank you for bringing *Blood Circus* across the ocean to my alma mater in Brisbane, Australia.

To my wonderful new author friends, especially Zoe Eisenberg and Angela Montoya, for your beautiful blurbs. And to all the other authors who want more author friends—reach out!

To my team—my managers, Trent and Midi; my agents, Abby and Mollie; my lawyer, Cary. And Ruby, always.

Lastly, and most importantly, I want to thank you, my readers.

Publishing a book is exciting but also incredibly taxing. You pour years of your life and your entire heart into something that people will read quickly and critique. It can be overwhelming, especially when you feel like you haven't found your true audience.

But your kind words are what kept me going . . . knowing that if just one of you loved it, that it became your favorite book, then I had done my job.

So thank you to the ones who read and reached out. Who begged for a sequel. Artists get less praise than you realize, so when you enjoy something, tell them, it will never go unappreciated!

Finally, we face so much uncertainty in our modern world. Nature is at risk, and so many of us are sick, depressed, and struggling to find our way. How do we heal? By coming together.

Returning to nature. Fostering community, ritual, and unconditional love.

Together, we have the power to create a better world—not only for humans, but for all of the world's creatures.

That is our purpose as humans. In service—that's where the magic lies.

Author photograph by George Dimitrov

Camila Victoire is a French Canadian / Australian novelist, screenwriter, and producer currently based in Montreal. The author of *Blood Circus*, she was hired to write two standalone episodes for the FX/Hulu Anthology series *American Horror Stories* and developed her novella *Pandora* as part of the Fellowship for Amy Aniobi's SuperSpecial. The daughter of two performing artists, she toured for four years with a circus before going to study Writing for Film and TV at the Vancouver Film School. Her stories are nourished by her travels, from exploring the haunted forests of Transylvania to venturing deep into the jungles of Peru. For more on Cami's adventures (including but not limited to dogs, flowers, witchcraft, wanderings, and more), visit her at Instagram.com/CamiVictoire.